THRE[illegible] ORIES

HORSE IN A MILLION
THE MAGIC PONY
RIDE LIKE THE WIND

PATRICIA LEITCH

ARMADA

This Armada *Jinny Three-in-One* was
first published in the UK in Armada in 1989
by William Collins Sons & Co. Ltd

Armada is an imprint of
the Children's Division, part of
the Collins Publishing Group,
8 Grafton Street, London W1X 3LA

Printed and bound in Great Britain by
William Collins Sons & Co. Ltd, Glasgow

PATRICIA LEITCH

Horse in a Million

Horse in a Million was first published
in a single volume in Armada in 1980

CHAPTER ONE

Like leaves after an October gale, pages torn from Jinny Manders' sketch pad littered her bedroom floor. Jinny knelt in the middle of the room, her long red hair tenting her sharp-featured face as she drew, considered, and then, with a swift movement, tore off the page and sent it flying through the air to join its fellows on the floor.

On each page, ponies and horses galloped and jumped, their riders in hard hats and smart jodhpurs. Each drawing was different—in some the ponies were fat, shaggy Thelwells; on some, elegant hacks and muscled hunters. Some of the ponies scuttled between bending poles, or resisted at the length of their reins while their riders tried to grab an apple from a bucket with their teeth. The wise eyes of a hunter looked out from a cluster of rosettes, and a show pony with thoroughbred head and plaited mane was ridden round a ring at an extended trot. In one of the drawings, the horse was a chesnut Arab, leaping a spread jump of red and white poles. The girl sitting, neat and tight, on its back had long red hair flowing from beneath her hard hat.

Although all the drawings were different, the lettering on each page never changed. Each page announced FINMORY GYMKHANA in flaunting capitals.

Jinny tore the last page from her pad, stood up stretching and stared down at her drawings.

"The pony ones are the best," she thought. "Then people will know it isn't going to be a posh affair, just for fun." And she picked out the best pony drawings and carried them across to her bedroom window that looked out over Finmory's garden, across fields, down to the sea.

Shantih and Bramble were grazing in the field at the foot of the garden. Shantih belonged to Jinny. She was a pure-bred, chestnut Arab, fleet and beautiful. Every line of her body, every silken hair of her mane and tail, her delicate ears, her dark lustrous eyes and her glistening white stockings, all sang of her breeding, of her quality, her perfection. Once she had been Yasmin, a circus killer horse, but Jinny had rescued her; fought for her life when she had been starving with an injured leg on the snow-covered Finmory moors, and gradually schooled her, until last autumn when Miss Tuke's Trekking Club had held a cross-country event and Jinny on Shantih had won a red rosette.

Bramble belonged to Miss Tuke. He was a black Highland with a heavy mane and long, thick tail. He regarded the world through his dense forelock, wise and considering —a fully paid-up member of the Highland ponies' trekking union. He knew his rights.

Shantih was the stars and the moon to Jinny, but Bramble was like a pair of old, comfortable slippers. Jinny thought of him as her own.

Two years ago, the Manders family had left the city suffocation of Stopton to come and live in grey stone Finmory House that stood in its own grounds between the sea and a wilderness of moorland.

In Stopton, Mr. Manders had been a probation officer, but since he had come to live in Scotland he had become a potter and had written a book about the appalling conditions in the Stopton slums. It had been published in January, linked with a T.V. programme, and now it was to come out in America and be translated into several languages. Her eyes watching Shantih, Jinny thought about the success of her father's book, how they had not had to worry about money since it had been published, how it meant that they might live at Finmory for ever.

Jinny switched back her mane of hair, spun round and grabbed her alarm clock. "It can't be right," she thought. "It can't be only ten past two." She shook it, but since its ticking made it unlikely that it had stopped, she could only hope that it had suddenly gone slow. The clock hands denied the possibility. It had never gone slow in its life. It was only, and exactly, ten past two.

"A whole half-hour before Sue can possibly get here," Jinny thought. Until Sue arrived she couldn't be certain that the Finmory gymkhana would actually happen. On the phone, Sue had been enthusiastic, but there was so much to arrange and maybe when Sue realised that it wasn't going to be the kind of organised gymkhana that her Pony Club ran she would lose interest, might even want to go home.

Last summer, Sue Horton, who was thirteen—the same age as Jinny—had spent the holidays camping with her parents in Finmory Bay. Sue had brought Pippen, her skewbald pony, and for the whole summer Jinny had had a friend to share her rides.

"If only Sue were back," Jinny had moaned, a week before her school broke up for the Easter holidays. "It's not nearly so much fun riding by myself."

"I thought this was to be the Easter of the Inverburgh Show?" Mike had asked. "Thought you'd be doing nothing but schooling Shantih, so you'd be brilliant to make up for last year's disaster."

"It is and I am," said Jinny severely. "But it would be more fun if Sue was here."

She ignored her brother's remark about last year's Inverburgh Show. He was right. It had been a disaster, an absolute disaster. "But it was all Clare Burnley's fault," Jinny thought. "Really I knew that Shantih wasn't ready for a show."

The Burnleys owned Craigvaar, a large detached house a few miles from Finmory. They didn't live there, but came up from England to spend their holidays in Scotland. At Easter, Clare brought two of her horses to Craigvaar. She took them both to the Inverburgh Show and always won all the cups.

"But of course it means absolutely nothing to me," she had told Jinny once. "I won my first cup in a Leading Rein class when I was three, and really I've just gone on from there. To tell you the truth, one has quite a shock when one doesn't win. One really takes it for granted, doesn't one?"

Hearing the sound of Clare Burnley's loud, self-confident voice in her ears made Jinny screw up her face with disgust. She had spent last Easter seeing Clare and her horses through a golden haze, until the haze was swept suddenly away and Jinny had realised what a fool she had been.

"If Sue were here," Jinny had said hurriedly to Mike, switching off from anything to do with the Burnleys, "we could have a gymkhana of our own. Sort of trial run for Inverburgh."

"Have it whether Sue is here or not," said Mike.

"You'd help me organise?"

Mike had grinned, pushing his fingers through his short, curly hair.

"Well, not really," he said. "There's the football team, and Mr. MacKenzie says I can drive his tractor."

"There you are," said Jinny. "That's why I need Sue."

"What's she doing?" asked Mrs. Manders.

"Don't know," said Jinny. "I'd a letter from her at Christmas and it's still my turn to write back."

"Perhaps she would like to come up for the holidays," Mrs. Manders had suggested. "Petra will be away on her music course most of the time. Be no problem."

"Oh yes," said Jinny, who had forgotten that her sister would be away. Petra was nearly sixteen years old, and, as far as Jinny could see, did nothing but bath herself and play the piano.

"Phone her," said Jinny's mother. "No harm in asking."

Jinny hesitated. "I wouldn't want to leave Shantih," she had said, "so I don't expect Sue would want to leave Pippen, and it would be far too expensive to bring him with her."

"She did last summer," said Mike.

"Behind their car."

"Galloping?"

Jinny had ignored him.

"Go on, phone," encouraged her mother. "For all you know, Sue may be longing to come back to Finmory. Do it now, then you'll know."

"Right," said Jinny. "Action this day."

She found Sue's phone number from one of her letters, looked up the correct dialling code and dialled. Holding the phone to her ear, she waited, listening to it ringing out, wondering who would answer. The phone rang on and on. Jinny's breathless expectancy changed to a dull certainty that there was no one at home.

"Count ten rings and then I'll put it down," she thought.

She had reached eight when someone lifted the receiver, and a breathless voice said, "Hullo," and added, "Sue Horton here."

"Nearly put it down," said Jinny, "I'd reached eight."

"What?" said Sue. "Pardon."

"I was counting to ten . . ."

"Jinny!" yelled Sue. "It is, isn't it? Jinny Manders!"

"Yes."

"You never wrote back. Not since Christmas."

"I meant to," said Jinny. "How are you?"

"Rotten," said Sue. "Pippen had a warble."

"A what?"

"Ghastly sort of maggot thing," explained Sue. "The fly lays its egg on the pony's leg. The pony licks its leg and swallows the egg. It hatches out and works its way right through to the pony's skin. A lump comes up on the pony's back, and once it's ripe, out pops the grub."

"Disgusting," said Jinny. "Poor old Pippen."

"Worse to follow," said Sue. "I didn't know about warbles, did I? So when I saw the lump on his back I thought it was only an insect bite, plonked his saddle on, and rode him at a rally. Killed the grub stone dead. It went rotten, and the vet has just been here gouging it out."

"Yuch."

"I know. Poultices for the next week and not to be ridden for three or four weeks. Just when the holidays are here. I could scream."

"Do," said Jinny. "You'll feel better."

Sue screamed.

"Well, in a way . . ." Jinny began, and was going to say it was a good thing that Pippen had been struck down, then changed her mind, realising that Sue couldn't be expected to see it quite like that.

"I'm phoning you to find out if you'd like to come and spend Easter with us. I said you wouldn't because of Pippen, but if your mother would look after him it would be a chance to come here." Jinny paused, half afraid that Sue would consider her heartless and yell that she couldn't possibly abandon Pippen in his warbled state.

"You could ride Bramble," offered Jinny, when Sue didn't speak.

"I'm struck dumb," said Sue. "It would be super. I'd love to come. I'd need to ask first, but I'm sure Mum would keep an eye on Pippen. She's quite keen on him now."

"I thought we might have a Finmory gymkhana," said Jinny.

"Yes! Oh yes!" enthused Sue.

Mrs. Manders came out to the phone, tapping her watch and mouthing, "What are you gossiping about?"

"Need to go," Jinny said to Sue. "Poverty-stricken parent grabbing phone."

"I'll ask," said Sue. "Whenever they get home."

"Phone me back."

"Will do, but I'm sure it will be O.K."

"Good," said Jinny. "Love to Pippen. Bye."

Sue had phoned back later in the evening to say that she could come, but her mother wanted to speak to Jinny's mother to make sure she was really wanted.

"I'll write. Tell you about the gymkhana," said Jinny, giving the phone to her mother who made "but of course we'd love to have her" noises to Mrs. Horton.

Jinny's school had broken up on the Wednesday and Sue was to arrive on the Friday. Jinny had been expecting to go with her father into Inverburgh to meet the train, but, to her dismay, the car had been full of a load of pots bound for Nell Storr's shop, where he sold his pottery.

"Sue will think it very odd if I don't come," Jinny had stated indignantly. "Asking her here, and only you to meet her."

"I'll explain," said Mr. Manders. "Can't be helped. Full load of goodies for the Easter tourists."

"Couldn't I hold them on my knee?"

"Sorry, the car's packed. I'll have Sue back here at the double."

Mr. Manders—balding, red-bearded, and wearing his potter's image of black jeans and pink smock—had driven off, leaving Jinny standing at the back door.

"Bit mean," she said aloud, feeling herself on the edge of umbrage. "Bet I could have fitted in somewhere."

"Don't sulk," Jinny told herself. "Don't spoil it. In two and a half hours Sue will be here." And the thought of the gymkhana blew up inside Jinny, filling her with excitement.

Dashing through the stone-floored kitchen, she leapt up the broad flight of stairs, ran along the long corridor and up the almost vertical stairs that led to her own room.

Jinny's bedroom was one large room, divided into two by an archway. One window looked out over Shantih's field to the sea. Jinny's bed was in this half, so she could sit up in bed and see Shantih first thing in the morning.

The window in the other half of her room looked out in the opposite direction, over the stretching moorland to the far mountains. One of the walls in this room was covered with Jinny's drawings and paintings. On the opposite side was the mysterious wall painting of the Red Horse. It had been there when the Manders had come to Finmory. Yellow-eyed, it charged from the wall, hooves plunging through a growth of white flowers.

Jinny had found some felt-tipped pens and, kneeling on the floor, started to draw posters for the gymkhana. She seemed to have been drawing for hours and yet, if the clock was right there was still over half an hour to wait until Sue arrived.

Jinny sat watching Shantih and Bramble nibbling each other's necks, and thought about mounted games. "Definitely bending," she decided. "And possibly musical poles."

A lean figure walked across the garden, towards the path that led to the sea. Shadowing his heels was Kelly, a grey shaggy dog. It was Ken Dawson who lived with the Manders. He had followed them to Finmory from Stopton, where he had been on probation for an offence that he had had nothing to do with. Ken was eighteen, tall and lanky, with fair, shoulder-length hair. His rich parents sent him a cheque through their bank every month but refused to see him.

Last autumn, Ken had gone to Holland to work for a master potter, and Finmory had been lost without him. Jinny remembered the emptiness and the fear of the months when Ken had been away and she had thought that he would never come back. She shivered, perched on the sunlit windowsill. But it was over now. Past. Ken had come home to stay.

"Cross-country or show jumping?" Jinny wondered, scribbling the words on the back of a poster sketch. It would depend on Mr. MacKenzie—which field he let them use.

"Need to be one sort of showing class. Perhaps Best Turned Out Horse and Rider . . ."

Jinny heard the sound of the car. Sheets of paper flying from her, she sprang for the door. Tearing through the house, she was just in time to reach the front door as the car drew up. Sue flung the car door open and came running towards Jinny.

"Wait till you see what I've got," she cried.

"What?"

"Can't tell you. Must show you," said Sue. Her wide, generous mouth was set in a huge grin; her hazel eyes twinkled with laughter as she teased Jinny.

"Lovely to see you," said Mrs. Manders, coming out to greet Sue. "What kind of journey did you have?"

"Boring," said Sue. "Couldn't get here quickly enough. It is very, very kind of you to invite me," she added, being polite but all the time laughing at Jinny.

"We're so glad you could come," said Petra, shaking hands. "Jinny's got this idea about holding a gymkhana. Be warned."

"I know," said Sue. "I think it's a smashing idea, and

wait till you see what I've got for it. Dad sent it. I think he's so pleased not to have me groaning around the house, going on about Pippen's warble. Even the thought makes him sick."

Mr. Manders brought Sue's case into the hall.

"It's in there," Sue said. "Do you mind if I open it here? Mum would, but she'll never know and I must let Jinny see it at once."

Jinny watched as Sue crouched down and unlocked her case. "Something for the gymkhana," she thought. "Something that Mr. Horton has given us." Jinny held her breath. Stopped herself imagining that it could possibly be . . .

"A cup," cried Sue, holding aloft a silver cup. "For Finmory's gymkhana."

Jinny let out her breath in a long gasp of total admiration. She stared, spellbound, at the cup. It wasn't a mean, goose-eggcup size, but satisfyingly big, with silver handles on either side so that when you cantered your winning round you could hold it up above your head.

"Actually, it's not new," Sue admitted. "Dad won it years ago. But you'd never know. There's nothing on it, only the place where he was meant to have it engraved but never got round to it. It's to be for the best horse or pony. The one who wins the most points. Games, showing and jumping. Well, say something. Don't just stand there."

"She can't," laughed Mrs. Manders.

"How did you know?" demanded Petra. "Only last night she was going on at us all, about how we must be the only family in the world who had never won a cup. How all other families had rows of silver cups."

Jinny hardly heard her mother or her sister. Beneath her she felt the smooth beat of Shantih's galloping hooves, in front of her reached Shantih's arched neck and delicate head. The applause echoed in Jinny's ears as she rode. In one hand she held Shantih's reins, and in the other she held Sue's cup above her head.

"A cup!" she said at last. "A real cup for Finmory's gymkhana!"

CHAPTER TWO

"I thought we'd ask Miss Tuke to be the judge," said Jinny to Sue.

"Won't she be trekking?"

"Saturday should be O.K. for her. That's the day the trekkers change over. I phoned her up about the gymkhana and she more or less agreed. I thought we could ride over tomorrow and ask her properly."

Sue was sleeping on the camp bed in Jinny's room. Mrs. Manders had said it was ridiculous when there were so many empty bedrooms in Finmory, but Sue had insisted that she would much rather share with Jinny so they could chat. They had gone to bed at about ten, now it was half-past twelve and they were still chatting.

"And on our way there, we'll make sure that Mr. MacKenzie hasn't changed his mind about letting us have his field," said Jinny.

Mr. MacKenzie's farm was the only other building close to Finmory, and Jinny knew the old farmer well.

"Imagine them all turning up, and Mr. MacKenzie barring the way with a pitchfork in his hand."

"We'd have to hold it on the shore," said Jinny, and saw, for a moment, ponies racing across the sands or a cross-country course set out between the boulders. "But he won't. He likes Miss Tuke."

Jinny heard her parents' bedroom door open, her father's footsteps marching down the landing.

"Get to sleep," he shouted up at them from the foot of Jinny's stairs. "It's long past midnight."

"We are asleep," Jinny yelled back.

"Good," said her father, and pounded back to bed.

Next day was blue sky and high, wind-blown clouds, flying light and shade chasing over the moors.

Immediately after breakfast, Sue and Jinny caught Shantih and Bramble and gave them a thorough grooming, so they would pass Miss Tuke's eagle scrutiny.

When they had saddled up and were ready to go, Jinny went back into the house to let her mother know that they were away. Ken was standing by the window, drinking his own brew of herb tea. He never ate or drank anything that came from an animal.

"Going to pot?" Jinny asked him.

"I am," said Ken.

"We're riding to Miss Tuke's."

"And what a morning for it," said Ken. "Use your ears. Smell it in. Feel how your eyes carry it all into your head. Hear the silence. Hear the roar of constant re-creation. The lion's roar. The NOW."

"To ask her," continued Jinny, "if she'll come and judge at our gymkhana."

Ken groaned. "What a nonsense," he said mildly. "Judging! Phawgh, I spit it from my mouth."

"I expect," said Jinny, "Miss Tuke will present the cup."

She didn't add "to me", but she knew Ken knew that was what she was thinking.

"Why ever do you want to tie tin cups on to yourself?"

"It means you're a winner," said Jinny, knowing she was wasting her time arguing with Ken.

"Winner?" mocked Ken. "There's nothing to win. We all have everything."

"It means you are the BEST and everyone else knows you are the BEST."

"Listen to how you weave yourself into a web of wanting," said Ken, looking straight at Jinny.

"Right," said Jinny. "I want to win that cup. I do. I don't care what you say. I think it's dreadful the way this family have never won anything. All other families have cups they've won, and I'm going to win it. Sue has won lots of cups."

Ken shrugged, rinsed out his cup at the sink, holding it under the running tap water and drying it with care before he hung it from its hook.

"Do what you must do," he said to Jinny.

"Smug," said Jinny, as he went off to the pottery, but the word wouldn't stick because he wasn't.

"Take care," said her mother, when Jinny found her.

"As always," said Jinny.

"And the milk can," reminded her mother.

"As always," said Jinny.

Bramble trotted beside Shantih as the two girls rode down the path to Mr. MacKenzie's farm.

"It is super being back," said Sue, gazing about her as she rode. "We don't exactly live in town, some people call it the country, but it's not like this. All this space and freedom."

Glancing at the moorland stretching to the mauve-blue mountains, and down to where the cliffs of Finmory Bay were jet against the sea dazzle, Jinny knew exactly what Sue meant, but this morning her mind was on other things.

"I'll bet your family have won lots of cups," she asked, checking up in case she was wrong.

"A few," admitted Sue. "Pippen has won some at Pony Club things."

"How many?" demanded Jinny, wanting facts.

"Five. Of course, I only kept them for a year, but they give you a little one with your name and the date on it and that is yours to keep. Dad has several he's won for his bowling, and Mummy has two that she won years ago for dog training."

"I knew I was right. Proper families all have cups."

"All they are is a nuisance to dust."

"Because you've won them," said Jinny. "It is quite utterly different when you've never won one."

Mr. MacKenzie, hearing the sound of hooves in his yard, came out of the byre.

"It's yourself returned," he said to Sue.

"It is."

"And wise you were to go south for the winter. Only those with the screws a wee bit loose would be staying here for the snows to catch them."

"My screws must be rattling," declared Sue. "I'd stay here all the time if I could."

"You'd think, to be looking at you, that you'd have more sense. Now you'll be here for the milk," he said to Jinny, taking the milk can from her, clattering its lid and making Shantih dance sideways in a flurry of mane and tail.

"Mike will collect it," said Jinny. "We're riding over to Miss Tuke's to see if she'll judge at our gymkhana next Saturday. In your field?"

"I was not forgetting it. You can be having the flat field for the day. It's dry enough now. You'll not be doing much damage to it."

"Good," said Jinny thankfully. "Are you coming to spectate?"

"If you give me your word on it that Miss Tuke will be for the jumping, I'll be there."

"She might be," said Jinny, thinking that she couldn't imagine Miss Tuke show jumping.

"I saw her once, and the old horse she was on went as neat as sixpence right to the jump. To the very jump he went, put his front feet together and stopped to say his prayers. But Miss Tuke was not for the stopping, on she went and took the jump by herself and to hell with the horse."

The old farmer paused, and spat reflectively into the midden.

"And when she got herself up, was there not a hole in the ground as if a bomb had hit it. Oh, I'll be there if you can promise me the likes of that again."

"I'll ask Miss Tuke," promised Jinny.

"She'll be remembering it fine. They'd to move the jump away from the crater before the show could go on. Be asking her yourself," said Mr. MacKenzie.

"Don't worry, we will," Jinny assured him. "And it is all right about the field?" she called after him as he turned into the byre.

"Aye, but mind now, I'm expecting to see Miss Tuke in action."

"Do my best, but I think she'll be judging," Jinny promised, as she and Sue rode out of the yard.

"He is in a good mood," said Sue, remembering Mr. MacKenzie from the summer.

"I think it's the new grandson. He was only three months old when I saw him, but if you'd put a pipe in his mouth and a cap on his head you'd have sworn it was Mr. MacKenzie."

They trotted on until they came to the first of the forestry roads that led to Miss Tuke's. Shantih, feeling the softer ground beneath her hooves, clinked her bit and with a half-rear suggested they gallop.

"O.K.?" Jinny called back over her shoulder, but already Shantih was away.

For minutes, Jinny was lost in a blur of speed. Shantih's effortless stride was so smooth that Jinny hardly moved in the saddle as Shantih stretched low to the ground, her ears laid back, her nostrils blood-red pits. Bramble's heavy hoofbeats drummed behind them.

Jinny waited until Shantih's first burst of speed had worn itself out, then she sat down in the saddle and, playing with the bit, speaking gently to her horse, gradually settled her into a collected canter. Sue drew level with them, tugging valiantly at Bramble's mouth.

"He's like a train," Sue yelled, as Bramble carried her past Jinny.

"Once you're in front he'll stop pulling," Jinny told her, as Bramble surged ahead, and his storming speed steadied into a bustling but controllable gallop.

"I haven't galloped like this since I was here," Sue gasped, when at last a closed forestry gate made them stop. "Miss Morris would have heart failure. Only the Orange Ride is allowed to canter. We're in it, but the minute Pippen begins cantering she's squeaking at us to steady up."

"Can't you gallop when you're riding by yourself?"

"There really isn't anywhere," stated Sue. "You don't know how lucky you are."

"I do. I used to live in Stopton. You couldn't even keep a pony in Stopton."

"I do think Shantih has improved," Sue said, as they rode on. "Or you have."

"Bit of both," Jinny said, clapping Shantih's hard shoulder.

"She just took off with you before, but she was cantering beautifully for you there."

"I've been schooling her like anything," admitted Jinny. "I've entered her for the Inverburgh Show. Not that I expect to win anything. I only want her to behave herself. It's the Saturday after our gymkhana."

"Can I take Bramble?"

" 'Course," said Jinny. "You can enter on the field. Actually, it's mostly agriculture, sheep and cows and tractors, but there are a few horsy things. Open Jumping classes, open to anyone on anything. There was a boy last year on a Fell pony. He only had one refusal, but Clare Burnley won it on her fancy showjumper." Jinny snorted with disgust at the thought.

As they drew closer to Miss Tuke's, Bramble's head went up, he whinnied with excitement and made sudden, excited dashes forward.

"He always knows," said Jinny. "Wait till you get nearer—you won't be able to hear yourself think."

When Bramble reached the hoof-rutted path that led to Miss Tuke's trekking centre, he threw up his head, almost banging Sue on the nose, and gave vent to a clarion whinny. Again and again, completely ignoring Sue's correct aids, he stopped and screamed to his fellow Highlands.

Miss Tuke was standing in the yard, a muddle of rope halters in her hands.

"Jolly glad to see you," she cried, which Jinny took to be an excellent omen. "Was going to have to do the whole job myself. Taken me three trips at least. Been the whole blooming day at it, but now that you've turned up we'll do it in a oner."

"Do what?" Jinny asked suspiciously. "We've come to

see you about our gymkhana." But Miss Tuke wasn't paying any attention to her.

"You're the Horton girl, aren't you?" she was saying to Sue. "Don't tell me. Never forget a name. Sue. Sue Horton. Your old man took rather a header. Never forget a trekker. How is he? Recovered?"

"Totally. Back to his bowling."

"Best thing," said Miss Tuke. "Hadn't got the makings. No stamina. Now, take a couple of halters each. Leaves three for me. Should manage. I'll ride Donald—solid as a rock."

"What are we going to do?" Jinny almost shouted.

"Bring them down from the hill. Don't need them for the trekking yet, but with the tinks arriving I'm taking no chances. The meat men are paying a fortune for horse flesh. Putting temptation in the tinkers' way, leaving them up there. Get the little blighters down where I can keep an eye on them." And giving Jinny and Sue two rope halters each, Miss Tuke marched off to the stables.

"The winter's been too much for her," Jinny whispered. "Gone bonkers!"

"Dangerous," giggled Sue. "Better play it her way."

Miss Tuke came back from the stables, leading a miniature carthorse. She had a bucket of pony nuts hanging over her arm and three halters tied round her like climbers' ropes. Clanking the bucket against the bay pony's side, she heaved herself into the saddle.

"Trek forward," she called, rousing Sue and Jinny to follow her.

"We've been press trekked," said Sue, forcing the reluctant Bramble out of the yard.

"But what are we going to do?" demanded Jinny, trotting Shantih alongside Miss Tuke.

The bay Highland swished his tail and snapped at Shantih.

"Donald!" roared Miss Tuke in thunderous tones. "Of course, he's used to being in front," she added to Jinny. "Not accustomed to being charged from behind."

"Where are we going?"

"Subnormal?" asked Miss Tuke. "All the brain bashing you've had, falling off that mad mare."

"Where . . .?"

"Up the hill, to bring the rest of my ponies down to the paddock. Be heels and teeth, but we'll manage."

"How far?"

Miss Tuke gestured vaguely towards the skyline and the mountains. Jinny groaned. Since they had come to ask Miss Tuke to judge for them, they couldn't very well refuse to help her.

First they followed the track of trekking ponies' hoofprints between high avenues of pine trees, then they went through a forestry gate which they left open.

"Less hassle on our way back," Miss Tuke said. "I'll pop back and shut it this evening."

They rode on along the forestry track until Miss Tuke opened a gate that led on to the steep hillside.

"Nearly there." Miss Tuke pointed to a wire fence about halfway up the hillside. "Look out for them there."

"Won't they be difficult to catch?" Sue asked.

"Not a bit of it. They see me as meals on hooves."

There was a shrill neighing, a stampede of hooves, and a mob of Highlands came careering down the hill. At the wire fence they broke to left and right, squealing and kicking as they plunged and bucked.

"I bet they haven't had a halter near them since the trekking finished last year," Jinny said, low-voiced, to Sue.

"Whoa the ponies! Steady the little horses! Whoa now," Miss Tuke called in calming tones as they climbed towards the fence, but her voice only seemed to make the ponies more excited.

"They know the bucket," she said. "Be fun and games when they realise what's what."

They rode alongside the fence, the Highlands racing beside them, until they came to a gate.

"Now I'll go in," announced Miss Tuke, in the manner of a lion tamer about to enter a lion's cage. "Off you get and I'll hand them out to you one by one."

Grasping the bucket in one hand and shouting threats

and curses at the top of her voice, Miss Tuke thrust her way into the mass of Highlands.

"Sunk without trace," said Jinny, as she vanished from sight.

"We should have asked her about being the judge first," said Sue.

"No point now she's trampled to death."

In minutes Miss Tuke had re-emerged, towing a dun Highland behind her.

Jinny gave Shantih to Sue, who was already holding Donald, and went to take the pony from Miss Tuke.

"Tie a knot in the halters," she told Jinny. "Don't want them strangling themselves," and Miss Tuke dived back into the mass of ponies, who were all fighting to grab their share from the bucket.

In no time the bucket was empty, and all seven Highlands were haltered and on the other side of the gate.

"Bingo," exclaimed Miss Tuke, when she rejoined them. "Now, let's sort them out."

With a threat here and a yank on a halter rope there, Miss Tuke divided up the Highlands.

"Get back on your ponies," Miss Tuke said to the girls, "and I'll hand the ropes up to you."

She stared disapprovingly as Jinny hopped alongside the excited Shantih, trying to control her until she could spring on to her.

"Stand at peace, you crazy woman, you," bellowed Miss Tuke, losing her patience.

Shantih sprang to attention, the tips of her ears meeting in surprise and giving Jinny the chance to spring into the saddle.

Miss Tuke, controlling the ponies with one hand, somehow managed to pass halter ropes up to Jinny and Sue. Jinny found herself in charge of two dun ponies. Sue had a grey and a bay; Miss Tuke, two bays and a steel grey.

"Keep behind me," warned Miss Tuke, as she struggled back on to Donald. "Let them know who's boss."

"But I'm not," gasped Sue, as Bramble lashed out at the

grey, and the bay pony flung itself back to the full length of the halter rope.

"Off we go," shouted Miss Tuke, ignoring Sue's plight and starting to walk on downhill, coping somehow with three Highlands, Donald and the empty bucket.

It was easier once they were moving. Copying Miss Tuke, Jinny yanked at the Highlands' ropes, keeping their heads beside Shantih's shoulder.

"Shout at them," she told Sue, whose bay Highland was going backwards in an attempt to avoid Bramble's heels.

They were halfway down the hillside, and Jinny was just beginning to think it possible that they might reach the forestry track without some of the Highlands breaking loose, when, springing from nowhere, two brindled lurchers came racing across the moor towards them.

"Hounds of the Baskervilles," said Sue in despair.

"Hang on," yelled Miss Tuke, as the dogs, snapping and growling, sprang at the ponies' heels. "I'll chuck the bucket at them."

Jinny tightened her grip on her Highlands' ropes and dug her knees into her saddle.

"Get away with you," yelled Miss Tuke, and aimed her bucket.

Jinny heard the bucket crash to the ground, and Sue scream as Bramble charged off down the hillside in terror, the two Highlands plunging about him. She caught a glimpse of one of the lurchers leaping at Shantih, felt Shantih lash out, then explode beneath her as she reared up away from the dog.

"Steady! Steady!" yelled Jinny, as she felt the halter ropes burning through her hands. Trying to hold on to the Highlands, Jinny had dropped her own reins and Shantih, feeling herself free, put in one huge, starfish buck, then took off over the moor. Jinny could do nothing but try to hang on to the Highlands and stay on top of Shantih.

"Whoa! Whoa!" she cried desperately, as she tried to fumble for her reins and turn Shantih uphill.

The grey pony that Sue had been leading galloped past

them, its long halter rope dragging about its legs. Jinny glanced back, trying to see what was happening to Sue. In that instant, something made Shantih shy violently and Jinny was pitched out of the saddle, to fall into a confused mass of legs and hooves that for a second were plunging dangerously close to her face and, in the next, were galloping over the hill away from her.

Visions of broken legs caught in ropes or reins flashed through Jinny's mind as she struggled to her feet. A piercing whistle rang out over the hillside and Jinny knew why Shantih had shied.

A scarecrow man wearing a greasy, navy-blue suit with a scarf tied at his neck and a checked cap set on the back of his head, was standing close to Jinny. He glanced down at her, his dark eyes hard and glittering in his swarthy, unshaved face. The lurchers had left the ponies and were slinking unwillingly towards him.

Miss Tuke, shouting at the pitch of her lungs, still well in control of her three Highlands, came, mighty as a battalion of horse, trotting towards them.

"Get off this hill," she was roaring. "Get off my land."

The man's gaze flickered over her. He turned without hurrying and began to make his way back up the hill. From somewhere out of the bracken, a boy of about eight or nine, smear-faced, in torn jeans and a man's jacket, joined the lurchers and ran after him.

"You're here on Alec McGowan's farm and you'll stay on his land, or I'll have the police to you. Stay off my hill!"

Neither the man nor the boy glanced back. They reached the fence, ducked between the wire strands while the lurchers cleared it in an effortless, roe-deer leap, and in minutes they had vanished from sight round the hillside.

Jinny, who had been watching, mesmerised, came back to the reality of loose ponies and Shantih grazing with her leg through her reins—her only pair of reins.

"That's it started," blazed Miss Tuke. "They'll be round the house at all hours of the day and night. Picking up anything they can find. Nothing safe until we get rid of them. Why Alec McGowan lets them camp on his land I do not know. And I suppose this means I'll need to get another bucketful of nuts."

It took them nearly three hours to catch the Highlands. The grey pony Sue had been leading refused to come near them and, in the end, they had to drive it loose into Miss Tuke's yard.

"There," exclaimed Miss Tuke, when at last all seven ponies had been turned out into the paddock that stretched up into the hills from her yard. "Can keep an eye on them there."

"Pretty long eye," said Jinny, watching the ponies high-tailing it up the hillside with the other Highlands who had already been in the field and had come down to investigate the intruders. "They'll be out of sight in a moment."

"Be down for nuts," said Miss Tuke. "I'm using some of the others for trekking. They'll all be together. Out on that mountaintop I had to make a safari to check up on them. Now, shove your gees into a box and we'll have some food ourselves."

Seated in Miss Tuke's study, over egg and chips followed by apple pie, they discussed the gymkhana. Miss Tuke had taken Jinny's phone call seriously and had been organising things from her end.

"All fixed up," she said. "Only too pleased to judge. Been in touch with the other members of the Trekking Club. Think they're all coming. Sara on Pym, Moira on Snuff and I'm providing Highlands for the others. I've two trekkers arriving today for a fortnight's trekking. Say they're experienced, which could mean Badminton or able to post. I'll bring them over with us. We'll all ride over. Grand trek! They'll love it and I'll survive."

Jinny sat listening, fascinated by Miss Tuke's organisation. Until now, the gymkhana had only really existed in Jinny's dreams, but Miss Tuke had pinned it out in reality.

"Now, let's get the classes sorted out. I thought one for Best Turned Out Horse and Rider—gives everyone a chance—and Best Suited Horse and Rider, for a giggle. Three jumping classes – Mini, Midi, Maxi," said Miss Tuke, writing the classes down as she spoke. "Mixture of walls and jumps? See what there is. Three games—don't want to drag it out. Musical poles? Bending? I've got poles. And a potato race?"

Jinny and Sue nodded in silent agreement.

"How's the publicity going?" Miss Tuke asked, as she came out into the yard with them.

"I've more or less decided on the poster," said Jinny.

"Cow's tail!" exclaimed Miss Tuke. "Get it into the village shop at once. We want a few spectators."

"Monday," promised Jinny.

"Who is in the Trekking Club?" Sue asked, as they rode home.

"Three Hay boys and three ladies who ride Miss Tuke's Highlands. And Sara and Moira, who have their own ponies."

"Eight," said Sue. "And two trekkers. You and me—that's twelve. Not bad, if they all go in for every class."

Jinny gulped and nodded, seeing Mr. MacKenzie's field overflowing with Highlands.

"Watch out," Sue mouthed. "On your right. Under the trees. The tinkers."

Catching the fear in Sue's voice, Jinny searched the dark shadows of the pines. Standing so still that they seemed to be growing out of the ground, were the two tinkers they had seen at Miss Tuke's. The two lurchers lay at the man's feet, heads on outstretched paws, ears alert.

As Sue and Jinny rode towards them, neither the man nor the boy moved. They made no sign that they had seen either the girls or their ponies.

"Nice day," said Jinny, but her voice sounded high and strained; her smile felt pinned on to her mouth.

The man's black eyes stared through her, making her almost unsure whether she had spoken or not. From his hand dangled four dead rabbits.

"Gosh," said Sue, when they were past. "I see what Miss Tuke means. I wouldn't want them prowling about my house at night."

Jinny didn't reply. She didn't really know what she felt about the tinkers. She wasn't furious with them the way

Miss Tuke was, and she wasn't afraid of them like Sue. "Least they're not plastic," she thought, and for a moment Jinny saw herself riding with them, travelling on.

"Let's trot," said Sue, kicking Bramble.

Jinny looked back. The man had turned and was watching them. His eyes in the shadow of the trees were as lustrous as Shantih's, yet they had a cruel glitter that made Jinny shiver.

"Come on," said Sue impatiently. "We want to get the poster done tonight."

"We can put in about the cup," said Jinny, touching Shantih into a trot, and instantly her head was full of nothing but gymkhana plans.

CHAPTER THREE

First thing on Monday morning, Jinny and Sue rode into Glenbost with the gymkhana poster. Sue held Shantih while Jinny took the poster into Mrs. Simpson's sell-everything shop.

"Well?" said Mrs. Simpson, regarding Jinny without enthusiasm. "It's yourself is after the worm this morning."

She was standing behind her counter, holding a long-handled feather duster which she flicked randomly over cheese and wellingtons, chocolate biscuits, vegetables and tins of paint.

"We're holding a gymkhana at Finmory," Jinny explained.

"And what sort of thing would that be?" interrupted Mrs. Simpson, stopping in mid flick, feather duster motionless.

"A gymkhana," repeated Jinny. "You know. Competitions for ponies. Jumping and racing. It's all on the poster."

Jinny ducked under the feather duster and spread the poster out on the counter.

Mrs. Simpson looked at the decoration of galloping ponies without a sign of interest. She studied the events and read the gold lettering that announced the cup, without a shade of expression showing on her face.

"The cup," said Jinny, pointing. "There's a cup for the best horse and rider."

Mrs. Simpson's duster did a quick sortie over a cluster of buckets that hung from the ceiling. "It'll be thirty pence," she said, "for the week."

"Thirty pence?"

"That's what I'm charging. You'll be wanting it in my window, I'm thinking, and thirty pence it will cost you, paid in advance."

"Well, I do. That's what we brought it for, so everyone will see it and come. It says—look—spectators welcome."

"Thirty pence," repeated Mrs. Simpson.

Jinny, who hadn't expected to pay anything, had to go out to borrow the money from Sue.

"I think I've got fifty pence in my pocket," said Sue. "Here, take your idiot until I prise it out."

Shantih, impatient at the delay, was tiptupping about, head raised, nostrils flared, tail kinked over her back. As always, Jinny could only think how beautiful she looked when she was excited like this.

"Shall we go down on to the beach afterwards and school?" Sue asked, giving Jinny the money, so that Jinny knew Sue saw Shantih as wild and untrained, not free and romantic as Jinny saw her.

But it was different now, Jinny thought. Shantih wasn't wild and uncontrollable the way she had been a year ago, and Jinny looked back with a self-satisfied, well-done-Jinny-Manders glow, over all the schooling she had done during the past weeks.

"Right," said Jinny. "I'll just pay Mrs. Scrooge, then we can go home by the shore and school on the sands."

Mrs. Simpson took the fifty pence, gave Jinny her change, tore a strip of Sellotape from the roll on her counter and, leaning across battlements of toilet rolls, sacks of sugar and a mound of butter, stuck the poster in the window.

"It's squint," said Jinny.

Mrs. Simpson snorted, feather duster at the ready.

"It is," said Jinny. "Honestly."

Grudgingly, Mrs. Simpson tore off another scrap of Sellotape and straightened the poster.

"You will come, won't you?" said Jinny.

"It's that man MacKenzie should be having his head examined, encouraging you with such goings on," she said, giving high-speed, furious flicks at the side of bacon sitting on the slicing machine.

"Bye," said Jinny.

"Looks smashing," said Sue, as they examined the poster from outside.

"Super," agreed Jinny. "You can see the bit about the cup from here."

"Do you think there is anyone else with a pony who might see it and come?"

"No," said Jinny. "Not a chance. I'd know about them if there was anyone. Still, I expect lots of children will come to watch."

They rode down to the shore, clattering over the bank of sea-smooth pebbles and then on down to the sands. The tide was out and a glimmering expanse of sand stretched before them.

Jinny trotted Shantih in wide circles at a sitting trot. She rode with long reins, feeling her horse relax. Then, gradually, she gathered Shantih together, asking her to balance herself, take more of her weight on her quarters, lift her head, lighten her forehand. They circled at a collected trot, then, when Jinny was satisfied that Shantih was really using herself, she touched her on with her leg and they were cantering. Not the mad surging burst of speed that had been so typical of Shantih a few months ago, but a smooth, easy change into a balanced canter.

"Good," Jinny whispered. "Good. Well done."

As they cantered round, Jinny felt her mouth spreading into a grin of delight. She turned Shantih to make a figure eight, and realised that Sue had stopped schooling and was watching them.

"Easy now, easy," Jinny murmured.

At the centre of the figure eight, Shantih changed legs with a perfect flying change. Jinny let out a long sigh of satisfaction. She was still teaching Shantih to change leg without breaking into a trot, and today had been the smoothest change she had managed.

"You have improved," said Sue, when Jinny slowed Shantih down and walked towards her. "Wish I had Pippen here. We could have a dressage comp."

"Go on," said Jinny, remembering how well-schooled Pippen had been. "You could have given us a demonstration ride. Shall we jump?"

"Where?"

"Mr. MacKenzie's field. It won't be cheating because we'll be changing all the jumps before the gymkhana."

"O.K.," said Sue, and they rode to Mr. MacKenzie's field, the only flattish field for miles around.

There were six jumps made from a collection of poles, old deck chairs, rusty oil cans and rotten straw bales.

"Have you been jumping those?" asked Sue suspiciously. "They're far higher than you used to jump."

"Well, Shantih is better now," said Jinny. "She understands what it's all about. Shall I jump first? And then I think we'd better put them down a bit for Bramble."

"Proceed," said Sue. "I am ready to be impressed."

"Never know," said Jinny. "Perhaps she won't jump at all today."

But she knew it wasn't likely. Already Shantih's ears were pricked and her eyes alight at the sight of the jumps.

Jinny gathered up her reins, cantered a circle, and, still moving at a collected canter, rode at the first jump. Shantih approached it steadily, calmly judging her take-off, and soared over it in a perfect arc. Hardly increasing her speed, she cantered on to the next jump and leapt sweetly over it, her forelegs tucked close to her body.

Jinny turned her and they cantered up the other side of the field, taking the jumps with the same effortless ease. Down the centre of the field they went, Jinny easing her fingers on the reins and allowing Shantih to increase her speed so that they were galloping towards the spread jump in the middle of the field. With a gay whisk of her tail, Shantih cleared it and went galloping on until Jinny asked her to canter.

"Stun," announced Sue, as Jinny walked Shantih calmly back towards her. "I'm into stun."

"She has improved," agreed Jinny, trying to keep her grin under control as she clapped Shantih's sleek neck.

"Improved! She's not the same horse. That's what it is. You've sold that mad crazy horse you had in the summer and bought this one from Caroline Bradley."

"Huh," said Jinny. "I might have known you'd spot the difference."

"How did you do it?" demanded Sue.

"Worked," stated Jinny. "Well, I thought hard about it. I knew she could jump because of jumping Mr. MacKenzie's gate and an enormous jump over a waterfall, so really all I had to do was calm her down between jumps. I made the jumps tiny and schooled her in a circle over them till she was hardly noticing them. It was just like trotting in a circle. Then I made the circle bigger and sort of sneaked up the height on her."

"Child's play," said Sue, mocking. "Anyone could have done it."

"There were moments," admitted Jinny. "She went bonkers one night. Crashed through them all without jumping at all and took off with me. We finished up on the shore going straight for the sea, and when we reached the water she tipped me off and galloped back to Finmory without me. Didn't you?"

Shantih ignored her, pawing the ground with an elegant foreleg. Such things were in her past, if they had happened at all.

"Let me have a go," said Sue.

"I'd better take the bars off the spread," said Jinny, jumping to the ground. "And I'll squash down some of the others."

When Jinny had made the jumps into more Bramble-sized obstacles, Sue took him round. They had four refusals at the first jump and then Bramble realised that Sue really meant what she said. Head down, he charged round the jumps, getting right in under them before he shot vertically into the air. At the spread in the middle of the field he stopped dead, slipped his shoulder and deposited Sue, head first, into the jump.

"If he does that on Saturday, Mr. MacKenzie won't need Miss Tuke—I'll do instead," said Sue, as she remounted.

"Now get on with you," she shouted, and rode at the jump again.

Her heels kicking tightly into Bramble's hairy sides, Sue drove the pony over the jump.

"You should see his expression," said Jinny. "He is not happy."

"Happy!" exclaimed Sue. "I'll happy him. He's like a flying bedstead compared to Pippen."

"Don't," cried Jinny in horror. "Don't let him hear you saying things like that about him."

"That is nothing to what I shall be saying about him before Saturday," threatened Sue.

They rode back to Finmory, reins loose, feet free from their stirrups, the spring air warm about them.

"Will you have it engraved now?" Sue asked.

"Engraved?" asked Jinny, puzzled. Then she knew what Sue meant. "Don't be daft. Anyone might win it."

"Handful of trekking ponies and me on Bramble? You're bound to win the cup."

"I'm not," denied Jinny, feeling herself blush. "Sara's pretty good—and Moira."

"Not as good as Shantih," teased Sue.

"Well, nearly," said Jinny. "Better at games, I should think. Much better."

"You don't really think that."

"Let's canter," yelled Jinny, and before Sue had time to collect herself, Shantih and Jinny were galloping up the path to Finmory.

Giggling, Jinny looked back over her shoulder at Sue bumping up and down on Bramble. "That'll teach her to think I'm sure I'll win the cup," thought Jinny, as she urged Shantih on. "But you do," said the voice inside her head. "You're sure you'll win it."

"Rubbish," replied Jinny, forcing Shantih to go faster.

They spent the rest of the week preparing for Saturday. Mrs. Manders agreed to sell lemonade, biscuits and rolls on the field. Petra had left for her music course, but Mr. Manders, Mike and Ken all agreed to be stewards.

"You see, we won't be free to help," Jinny explained to them. "Sue and I are riding. But we'll make out score sheets for you and it will all be quite easy."

"As long as Miss Tuke is in charge," said Mr. Manders, "we will manage."

Miss Tuke arrived on Thursday evening with her van full of things for the gymkhana—bending poles, professionally painted red and white poles for the jumps, numbers for the competitors and stakes and rope to mark off the ring.

"Climb in," she said to Sue and Jinny. "We'll drive this lot down to the field."

"Actually," said Jinny, "we have more or less built the course."

"Good show," said Miss Tuke. "That's what I like, getting things done. Still, always room for improvement."

They improved for most of the evening, and by ten o'clock the jumps that Sue and Jinny had built were completely changed.

"Start the way they are for the Mini. One pole up for the Midi, and for the Maxi we'll add straw bales and change the centre jump into an in and out," Miss Tuke stated, hands on hips, when they had finished. "Showing classes first, round the outside of the jumps. Jumping next. Lunch break. Then games last of all. How are we for rosettes?"

"We made them," said Jinny, "out of plaited straw. Ken showed us how to plait it. I've drawn horses heads in different colours to stick in the middle of them so we'll know which is which."

"They're better than bought ones," said Sue.

"Great," said Miss Tuke. "And what about this cup?"

"Points for each class. Three for first, two for second and

one for third. Then all the points are added up and most points wins the cup," said Jinny.

"Make a scoreboard," warned Miss Tuke. "Stick it up where they can all see it, or we'll be here till next week squabbling about who's won. Justice must not only be done, it must be seen to be done."

"Will you present the cup?" Jinny asked.

"Lord, no! I'm the judge. Ask Mr. MacKenzie."

"Oh yes," agreed Sue. "He'd love to. He is coming. He was telling us about . . ."

Jinny kicked her hard on the ankle and quickly asked Miss Tuke when she thought her trek would reach Finmory.

"Should make it for eleven. Leave sharpish. Now, let's get these bending poles stacked away. Take them down to the yard. That should be nearest for you on Saturday morning."

Mr. MacKenzie, hearing them in his yard, came out in shirt sleeves and braces to see who it was.

"You'll be performing on Saturday?" he asked Miss Tuke.

"Judging," replied Miss Tuke sharply.

"Och, och," said Mr. MacKenzie, fixing Miss Tuke with his pale blue eyes. "It's surprised I am to hear you've the time for that, and the tinkers camping on your very doorstep."

"Scoundrels," snorted Miss Tuke. "If I set eyes on them I phone the police."

"Wise you are," said Mr. MacKenzie. "But what else would you be doing, a helpless wee waif like yourself."

"The girls would tell you the trouble we had with them."

"Not a word," lied Mr. MacKenzie.

"We did," exclaimed Jinny.

"Not a word did I hear of it," insisted Mr. MacKenzie. "So, come you in for a wee dram and be telling me yourself."

Jinny and Sue walked back to Finmory through an evening that was pastel shades of grey and mauve.

"Not tomorrow but the next day," said Sue.

"Rosettes to finish. Scoreboard for the points. I thought we could pin it on to the table where Mum's getting the food. Hammer to knock in the bending poles. Petra's trannie, which she won't know about because she's not here, for Musical Poles, and potatoes from the farm for the Potato Race."

"Biscuits to buy," added Sue, "and rolls."

"I'm worn out," said Jinny. "No wonder they need all those Brigadiers and Majors and troops to organise Wembley."

"And they have longer than a week to do it in," agreed Sue.

"But they don't have Miss Tuke," said Jinny.

By three o'clock on Friday afternoon they had done everything, except for buying biscuits and collecting the rolls which Mrs. Manders had ordered from Mrs. Simpson.

"We're riding in for them," Jinny said, when her mother reminded her about them.

"Don't leave it any later."

"Going now," said Jinny. "Sue's bringing in the horses."

They had almost reached Glenbost when Jinny was sure she could hear the sound of hooves.

"Listen," she said, interrupting Sue's account of a mounted paperchase during which she and Pippen had got totally lost. "Isn't that a horse?" Jinny stopped Shantih so that she could hear better.

They could both hear the sound of hooves coming towards them.

"Definitely," said Sue. "Who can it be?"

"Don't know," said Jinny, as Shantih goggled in the direction of the hoofbeats. "Can't be Miss Tuke. Anyway, it doesn't sound like ponies."

Bramble whinnied and a high-pitched neigh answered him. Then round the corner came two horses.

A heavy grey with a hogged mane and Roman nose was being ridden by a large girl who looked about eighteen or nineteen. Her blonde hair curled round a solid face. She was wearing an immaculately-cut riding jacket, breeches and boots. In one strong hand she held the grey's reins, with the other she gripped the reins of a black thoroughbred whose gleaming coat was slickered with white light as he danced and cavorted alongside the grey.

"Glory be!" the girl cried, in a rich, plum-pudding voice. "If it isn't Jinny. But how super to see you again. We were all in the Bahamas for the summer, and it was such a flying visit at New Year that I just didn't have a tiny minute to drop in. Of course, I didn't have the nags up with me so I knew you wouldn't really mind. But I must say, it is rather super to meet you like this."

Sue looked in surprise from the girl's smiling face to Jinny's scowling, clenched expression.

"Shantih has come on. Why, she looks quite presentable now. You have done her well. I'm utterly amazed."

Staring straight ahead, Jinny rode past the two horses and their rider.

"Well, er . . . good-bye," said Sue awkwardly, and trotted after Jinny.

The girl shouted something that Jinny couldn't quite make out. It sounded like, "See you," but she couldn't be sure.

"Not if I see you first," thought Jinny darkly.

"Who was that?" demanded Sue, catching up. "Why didn't you speak to her?"

"That was Clare Burnley and you could say that I hate her."

"She seemed to like you O.K."

"I can tell you now," said Jinny, "because I don't suppose it matters, not now. Last Easter, a pair of ospreys nested on the moors. You know how rare they are in Scotland. Well, I was supposed to be guarding their nest when Clare lured me away. While I was away with her, her rotten brother came and stole the eggs."

Sue gasped with satisfactory disgust.

"She knows I know and she'd the cheek to talk to me again."

"They're super horses," said Sue.

"The grey's called Huston and the black is her show horse called Jasper. She brings them both up from Sussex so she can win the cups at Inverburgh Show. It was Clare Burnley that presuaded me to take Shantih to the show last year, long before she was anything like ready for a show. And she's got the nerve to say she'll see me!"

"She said," Sue repeated accurately, "see you tomorrow."

"Well she won't. It's the gymkhana."

"I think that's what she meant," said Sue.

CHAPTER FOUR

Jinny woke to the sound of pouring rain. She lay perfectly still, hearing it drumming against the window, storming over the rooftop and lashing through the trees. A wind moaned in from the sea, gusted over Finmory and howled over the moors.

"I don't believe it," Jinny thought. "There hasn't been a really wet day for weeks. It can't be. Not today."

She shut her eyes again and lay still.

"When I wake, the sun will be shining," she told herself. "When I open my eyes, it will be a blue day."

Jinny counted to ten, sat up, opened her eyes and the gale was still there. She jumped out of bed and stared down the garden.

Shantih, her coat stained rust-red with the downpour, was standing with her quarters turned against the wind. Her mane was soaked to strands of hair against her neck, her forelock plastered against her rain-carven face. Bramble's head was down, his lower lip touching the grass, his eyes screwed shut. He stood against the fury of wind and rain as his ancestors had stood against the ice age.

"Blooming, blasted weather!" said Jinny aloud, waking Sue. "Blasted rain!"

"What a day," said Sue. "What will you do? Phone Miss Tuke and cancel the whole thing?"

"No!" exclaimed Jinny. "We can't do that. It's to be a practice for the Inverburgh Show next Saturday. And there's the cup. Of course we can't cancel it. They don't cancel Badminton or the Grand National just because it's raining."

"Will Miss Tuke come?"

"If it was a weekday she would be trekking in it, so I don't see why she shouldn't. It's not all that heavy."

"Looks heavy enough to me," Sue said, and Mrs. Manders agreed with her.

"You're not going ahead with it?" she said in shocked tones when Jinny and Sue joined her in the kitchen.

"Of course," said Jinny. "We've all got wellies and oilskins. When you've organised a thing, you can't back down because of a little rain."

The phone rang and Jinny dashed to answer it.

"What's it doing with you?" demanded Miss Tuke's voice.

"Bit wet," admitted Jinny grudgingly.

"Pouring down with us. I've had Moira on the phone. She's still game. What do you think? I'll need to let them know if you want to call it off."

"Oh no! It's not nearly wet enough for that."

"Right you are," said Miss Tuke. "We'll be over. Trek forward."

"Was it Miss Tuke?" asked Mrs. Manders.

Jinny nodded. "Just checking that everything was O.K. here. They'll be over about eleven."

"Incredible," said Mrs. Manders.

"We'd better bring ours in before breakfast," said Jinny, wanting to escape from her mother. "Not that it will make any difference. Five minutes out in this and they'll be soaked again."

Sue and Jinny put on oilskins, sou'westers and wellingtons and launched themselves into the rain-swamped garden.

"Not so bad when you're out in it," said Jinny, running to the tackroom for halters.

Hearing them coming, Shantih and Bramble stampeded

to the gate where, nipping and kicking, they fought to get through first.

"Stand up with you," Jinny growled, struggling to get the halter over Shantih's ears as she reared her way through the gate. Running at her side, Jinny took her into the stable and shut her in her loosebox.

Glowering, ears pinned back, Bramble crashed his way into his stall.

"I'm drowned already," moaned Sue. "Gallons of rain pouring down my back."

"Banned," said Jinny. "Forbidden. For the rest of the day we must not mention the rain, on pain of excommunication."

Sue grinned. "O.K.," she said.

"No point in grooming just now," said Jinny. "Might as well go in and eat and then go down to the field."

Mrs. Manders fed them a breakfast of fried potato scone, bacon and egg.

"You'll need to dish out the lemonade from the car," suggested Jinny, hoping her mother was still willing.

"Thought hot soup from Thermoses as well."

"Yes. Even better."

"And I'll steward from the car," said Mike.

"You will not," said Jinny. "I've got plastic sheets to cover the scoreboards. You write underneath the plastic. But you'll need to bring the cup in the car. Put it behind the windscreen where people can see it. And they can collect their numbers from the car. You will all be there by eleven, won't you, so we can start whenever Miss Tuke arrives?"

"Sir! Yes, sir!" exclaimed Mike.

After breakfast, Jinny and Sue walked down to the field.

"At least the jumps are still standing," said Sue, as they went through the gate and began walking round the course. "By the time we reach the Maxi jumping, it will be really poached up."

"I know," agreed Jinny despondently. "Miss Tuke's Highlands could turn the Sahara into a quagmire, never mind this."

They brought the bending poles and the hammer from the farm, then, deciding there was nothing else they could do, they went back to Finmory to groom their horses.

"Useless," cried Jinny, after half an hour's dandying. "Sodden she is and sodden she will remain."

"They'll all be the same."

"Reckon so."

At a quarter to eleven, Jinny, holding a restless Shantih, and Sue on a sullen Bramble, were standing in Mr. MacKenzie's hay shed waiting for Miss Tuke and her trekkers, while the rain poured down as heavily as ever.

"Here they come," said Jinny, as Shantih, hearing the approaching ponies, began to paw at the floor of the shed.

"Be watching my good ground, now," warned Mr. MacKenzie, sack over his shoulders against the rain. "Keep that varmit under control."

Miss Tuke, in brilliant yellow oilskins, led the trek. Behind her came two bearded men in their early twenties riding dun Highlands.

"First two the trekkers," Jinny informed Sue. "The next two ladies are in the Trekking Club. Then Peter, Jim and George Hay. Peter's the oldest, on the black pony. He's quite good. Rode round the cross-country at Miss Tuke's. That's Moira Wilson on Snuff. He belongs to Moira. Very fast. And Sara Murdoch on Pym. He's her own Highland, but stubborn."

"Some day," Sara shouted, greeting Jinny. "What rain!"

"Rain?" said Jinny, staring about her. "I see no rain."

"We're drenched. Don't forget we've been riding for miles."

"I'll leave this fellow in one of your boxes," Miss Tuke said to Mr. MacKenzie. "Can't judge and ride. Jinny, lead on to the field. I'll be with you in a min."

Jinny swung herself up on to Shantih.

"This way," she shouted. "The gymkhana is down this way," and, making sure they were all following her, Jinny rode on.

Suddenly there was a rattling, crashing, engine noise behind them and lurching into the farmyard came a horsebox being driven by Clare Burnley.

"Oh, no!" cried Jinny. "Not her. She can't come. Not her."

"You can't send her home," said Sue. "She'll need to stay now she's here."

"Oh death," swore Jinny, and, turning her back on the horsebox, she led the trekkers into the field. The horsebox came lumbering after them.

There was a confused half-hour while the trekkers collected their numbers from the Manders' car, discovered the hot soup and decided to have it now instead of lunch time, and then had to nip round Mr. MacKenzie's yard trying to find suitable places to spend a penny.

"The first class," roared Miss Tuke, against the wind. "Best Turned Out Horse and Rider."

Clare Burnley led the grey, Huston, down the ramp of her box, tightened his girths, pulled down her stirrups and, mounting, rode into the ring.

Walking round the ring on Shantih, Jinny gazed despondently at the rest of the competitors—riding macs, anoraks and plastic raincoats were soaked, hard hats spouted waterfalls, tack was spongy, while Clare Burnley's white riding mac was just starting to darken, her tack glistened, and Huston gleamed as he stepped out with a sure stride.

"Beyond me," said Jinny, to no one in particular. "It is beyond me how she has the nerve to come here after last year. If I were judging, I would disqualify her."

Miss Tuke, after doing her best to inspect the tack and riders' turn-out, placed Clare Burnley first, Moira Wilson second and George Hay third.

Ken presented the plaited straw rosettes.

"Oh, how sweet," exclaimed Clare, taking hers. "I've never known a gymkhana where they couldn't afford to buy rosettes."

"No entry fees," snapped Miss Tuke. "All free."

"Forget that you won it," advised Ken. "Look on it as a thing of beauty, a light-bringer. That's what they used to be. To carry the light from one harvest to the next."

"Really?" said Clare. "But how sweet."

"Class two," announced Miss Tuke. "Horse and Rider Best Suited To Each Other. I've had a good look at you all, so trot on round until I make up my mind."

Shantih, fretting against the rain, struggled to canter. Grimly, Jinny held her back. Twice the bay Highland in front of them had lashed out, narrowly missing Shantih's leg.

"Steady, steady," muttered Jinny through clenched teeth, as Shantih fought to get her head down and buck.

"Walk," called Miss Tuke, and to Jinny's disgust she again gave the first prize to Clare. The second went to a nervous Trekking Club lady on a nursemaid Highland, and third to Sara Murdoch.

"Thought she might have given it to you, Shantih being the same colour as your hair," said Sue.

"No chance," said Jinny. "Miss Tuke thinks Shantih is THE most unsuitable horse of the year."

"Jumping classes next," organised Miss Tuke, and Jinny thought that the jumping was what really mattered—she had to show them all how Shantih had improved. She had to beat Clare Burnley.

"You may enter for either Mini, Midi or Maxi. Up to your honesty to choose the highest jumps you can manage. Sara, you are Maxi."

"Oh, but Miss Tuke I can't . . ."

"Maxi," decreed Miss Tuke. "Now Paul, you're first for the Mini."

One of the bearded trekkers trotted into the ring and bowed to Miss Tuke.

"Never before have I left the ground whilst balancing on a horse," he announced. "Feel privileged to be present."

As the non-jumpers did their best to make their ponies walk over the Mini jumps, Jinny sat on Shantih, staring crossly about her. Already Clare Burnley had six points. "And I've not got one," thought Jinny furiously.

A small figure was crouching against the wall. Jinny rode Shantih closer to it, and saw that it was the tinker boy who they had seen when they were catching Miss Tuke's ponies.

He was wearing the same ragged jacket and jeans. His black hair was sleeked down on to his head, and his face was shiny with rain. At his side was one of the brindled lurchers. It was sitting upright with the boy's arm round its shoulder. The boy's eyes were fixed on the pony in the ring, his expression one of rapt delight.

"Hi," said Jinny, riding up to him. "Isn't it wet?"

The boy flinched, his arm automatically swinging up to protect his head while the lurcher bared its teeth, snarling at Jinny.

"Not welcome," thought Jinny, and rode on.

Peter Hay was the first of the Maxi jumpers. He had two refusals and a bar down at the double. Moira on Snuff charged round the course and had four down. Mike and Ken rebuilt the jumps. Sara was next and had a refusal at every jump.

"Me next," said Sue. "Right now I'd give anything to be sitting on Pippen, warbled or not."

Bramble crabbed into the ring, his neck bent against the rain, and cat-jumped, tossing Sue on to his neck at every jump. At the fourth jump of bales and red poles, he slipped his shoulder and deposited Sue neatly into the mud, then stood gazing down at her with an innocent expression on his face.

"Mr. MacKenzie does not know what he's missing," moaned Sue, riding out of the ring after three refusals at the double.

"Don't worry," said Jinny. "He'll hear about it."

"Jinny Manders," shouted Miss Tuke, managing to boom and sound irritated at the same time. "We're waiting."

Jinny flurried into the ring at a sudden, ragged trot. In front of each of the jumps was a sea of poached mud. "Whatever will Mr. MacKenzie say," Jinny thought, feeling her reins slimy between her fingers, her hat biting into the back of her neck.

Miss Tuke blew her whistle and Shantih bounded forward of her own accord. Blinded by the rain, Jinny felt her soar skywards over the jump and, as soon as she touched down on the other side, she bucked. With a half-rear she tore down the field to the next jump, cleared it effortlessly and raced on, totally out of control.

Round the foot of the field they went, and up the other side of the ring, Shantih taking the jumps like a steeplechaser. At the top of the ring Jinny fought to turn her, but her reins were far too long and Shantih charged on out of the ring.

Tears of rage and frustration mixed with the rain streamed down Jinny's cheeks. She had been so sure that Shantih had stopped her uncontrollable galloping, that she had learnt how to jump calmly and sensibly. And now, to behave like that in front of Miss Tuke, the pony trekkers, and worst of all, Clare Burnley . . . Jinny groaned with despair as she at last managed to bring Shantih to a trot and then to a walk.

"Idiot horse," Jinny told her. "They are all right. You are mad."

Shantih turned her head, drifting sideways against the rain. Her ears were flattened to her head and her eyes goggling with nervous excitement.

"Disaster," said Sue, riding up on Bramble.

"But you saw her. You saw how she had improved—and now back to her stupid nonsense," and, staring through the sheeting rain, Jinny watched Clare Burnley jump a clear round, her showjumper treating the Maxi course with contempt.

"She's won," said Sue. "No doubt about it, she's the best."

"She shouldn't be here," exclaimed Jinny. "Nine points! Shes got nine points for the cup. No one else has had a chance."

When the rosettes for the jumping had been presented, Miss Tuke announced an hour for lunch and added that the soup flasks had been replenished.

The trekkers crowded round the car, grateful for the hot soup, and suddenly Jinny remembered the tinker boy. She looked round for him and saw that he was still crouching against the wall, with his arm round the dog. She gave Shantih to Sue, and filling a cup with soup and taking a cheese roll, walked across to him.

"Here," she said, keeping a wary eye on the lurcher. "I've brought you some soup."

"Don't want it," said the boy. "I've not got no money."

"It's free," said Jinny. "My father paid for all the food. Go on, take it."

Without looking up at Jinny, the boy stretched up his hand and took the cup and the roll from Jinny. He drained the hot soup in one gulp, tore the roll into two pieces, cramming one half into his own mouth and giving the other bit to his dog.

"Do you like ponies?" Jinny asked him.

The boy nodded, wiping his mouth on his jacket sleeve.

"Can you ride?" Jinny asked, when he didn't speak.

"Aye. We have the ponies sometimes and we ride them."

"And dogs?" said Jinny.

"Zed's mine," said the boy, clutching the snarling dog closer to his side. "He works best for me."

Suddenly Miss Tuke's heavy hand descended on Jinny's shoulder.

"Get out of here," she shouted at the boy. "Get back to your camp and stay there."

Cringing, the boy scrambled to his feet. The lurcher leapt at Miss Tuke, snarling, lips rolled back, but the boy kept a tight hold on its collar.

"He's not doing any harm," exclaimed Jinny indignantly. "He's 'spectators welcome'. The only one who has come. He can stay if he wants to."

"Leave him here and the next thing he'll be crawling about the farm, picking up what he can find. Now be off with you."

"No," said Jinny. "He's got as much right to be here as anyone else." But already the tinker boy had swarmed over the wall and was running across the fields, down to the sea.

"What a beastly thing to do," stated Jinny, scowling at Miss Tuke. "What a foul, rotten thing to do."

"Nonsense. Go back to Finmory and find your tack gone. You'll sing a different song then, my girl."

"He was only enjoying himself. Sitting watching the ponies."

"Are you running this gymkhana or are you not? If you are, it's about time you came and gave us a hand in the ring."

Silently, Jimmy supposed that Miss Tuke might be right. She followed her across the field to help her father and Mike to knock in the poles for Musical Poles.

"At least they all seem to be enjoying themselves," said Mr. Manders, taking the hammer from Jinny and knocking the poles in himself. "Clare Burnley has star quality."

Ponies and riders were grouped around the lowered ramp of Clare's box. She stood inside the box, regaling her audience with tales from her horsy past. Jinny could hear her loud, arrogant voice and the trekkers' admiring chatter.

"She's telling them about all the cups she's won," said Jinny grimly. "And when she gets back to England she'll tell them about how she won this cup, bringing her posh horse to a gymkhana like this."

"It is a bit your own fault," said her father. "Didn't you think of putting some sort of limit on who could enter?"

"Only allowed to enter if you're totally hopeless," suggested Mike.

"Shut up," warned Jinny. "I am not in the mood to be teased. I am totally and utterly low."

Clare wasn't placed in Musical Poles. The lady from the Trekking Club, who had been second in the Suitable Horse class, won it. Her pony trotted round, obviously listening to Petra's transistor with both ears. The second Mr. Manders switched the music off, the pony bolted for a pole and stood stock still beside it. All its rider had to do was to put her hat on the pole. Moira was second and Peter third. Jinny was first out, since Shantih refused to go near the circle of poles.

But Clare won the bending and the potato race.

"Of course, he's not what one would choose for games but, let's face it, there's not much competition here today," said Clare, to one of the bearded trekkers.

"I really think you're wonderful the way you ride. Make it look so easy. Still, I expect you've been at it since you were a kid."

"You might say I was more or less born in the saddle," confided Clare.

"Puke, double puke," thought Jinny, overhearing the conversation.

Mr. MacKenzie, sourly surveying his churned-up field, presented the cup to Clare.

"Thanks frightfully," said Clare.

To Jinny's disgust, she held it above her head with both hands while everyone clapped.

For a second, Jinny saw herself taking it from Mr. MacKenzie. A real cup. The first her family had ever won. The first Shantih had ever won.

"It should have been mine. I should have won it. Not her. Not that Clare Burnley," thought Jinny sullenly, not clapping.

"You didn't even win one point," said the voice in Jinny's head. "Shantih was just as wild as ever."

"It was the weather," protested Jinny. "She was upset by the rain. It was that Clare Burnley."

"You wouldn't have won it anyway."

"If she hadn't come, everything would have been different."

Clare Burnley rode out of the ring and came straight up to Jinny.

"I really have enjoyed myself," she said. "When one is used to big shows one really does so enjoy a little do like this. Utterly fascinating. Thank you so much for organising it." Clare held out her hand to Jinny.

"I can't," thought Jinny. "I cannot shake her hand. I cannot."

"Oh," said Clare. "Having a tiny sulk, are we?"

"It wasn't fair," said Jinny, the words bursting out of her. "It wasn't fair, bringing a horse like Huston here. It's not fair taking them to Inverburgh Show, but to bring him here and carry off the cup . . ."

"Dearie me," laughed Clare. "That's what's wrong, is it? The cup? Goodness, I'd give the wretched thing to you. Means absolutely nothing to me. I've got dozens of the things."

"Clare," called the bearded trekker, whom Jinny had heard talking to Clare earlier in the day. "We're going back now. Do give me your phone number and we'll see if we can fix something up."

"In the book," Clare replied, turning to ride over to him.

As she rode away, she looked back over her shoulder at Jinny. He face, half-turned, seemed to Jinny to lose its smooth mask of monied security, was suddenly naked, her eyes coldly calculating, her mouth tight and grasping.

"But, of course, if you want to win a cup for yourself there's always Inverburgh Show."

CHAPTER FIVE

Sunday, after Saturday's rain, was a grey day, as if the gale had washed the colour out of the world. As Sue and Jinny wandered down to the field to clear up the remains of the gymkhana, the moors stretched in greyness to the mist-shrouded mountains. The fields reaching down to the sea were grey-green, even the jet shards of the cliffs were toned to dark grey shades, standing out from a sea of liquid-grey metal.

"Miss Tuke's coming for them tonight," Jinny said, pulling the bending poles out of the ground. "We'd better take them down to the farm and stack them in the hay shed."

"Couldn't we just leave them here?" asked Sue.

"Leave them another night and hordes of tinkers will descend from the hills to steal them."

"Right enough," said Sue.

"I don't mean it," said Jinny. "I don't mean it at all. Tinkers aren't crawling about waiting to pounce on things. That's all in Miss Tuke's head."

"You don't believe they ever steal things, do you?" said

Sue, as they carried the bending poles, the red and white posts and the rope and stakes down to Mr. MacKenzie's. "You just imagine them raggle-taggle-gypsy-oing. They're not really like that. They do steal. That's why people don't like them, don't want them camping near them."

"Not steal," insisted Jinny, as they went back and forward between the field and the yard. "Maybe poach or lift an old bucket that's lying about a back door, but that's not stealing. I think Miss Tuke bringing her ponies down from the hill because there are tinkers camping at the next farm, is plain silly. Fancy thinking they would steal them for meat!"

"Do you know, in England some native pony breeders have nearly stopped breeding ponies because the meat men will pay more for a pure-bred pony than the people who are wanting to show them. It's not a few pounds, it's hundreds."

Jinny felt her stomach clench tight with a sudden spasm of fear. The fact of horses being sold for slaughter was so terrible that Jinny couldn't even allow herself to think about it.

"I don't believe you," she told Sue.

"Choose how," said Sue. "It's the truth. No one near us would dream of sending their pony to a sale, just in case."

Jinny clanked down the milk can she was carrying at the byre door, and from the door of the farmhouse Mr. MacKenzie appeared in his Sabbath suit.

"I'll be filling it for you after church," he said.

"We'll fetch it this afternoon," said Jinny. "Miss Tuke is coming over tonight to collect her poles. O.K. if we leave them there?"

"I'll have the eye open for her," said Mr. MacKenzie. "It was the disaster of a day you had yesterday."

"A wash out," said Sue.

"Now it wasn't exactly the rain I was thinking of, although you'd plenty of that right enough. It was more the little matter of the cup."

Jinny scowled across at him. She had known he would have something to say about it.

"The likes of yourselves setting up the wee gymkhana so that her ladyship can add another cup to her collection!"

"How was I to know she'd be here?" asked Jinny indignantly.

"Och now, the halfwit would have known that a cup would have drawn Clare Burnley to it. Like a moth to a candle that one is for the cups."

"I never even thought of her being back at Craigvaar," Jinny said, as Ewan MacKenzie, one of Mr. MacKenzie's sons, drove into the yard to take his parents to church.

When Jinny and Sue had finished stacking the poles in the hay shed, they gathered up the litter that had been left behind in the field and did their best to stamp down the ploughed earth around the jumps.

"He won't be very keen to let you hold another gymkhana," said Sue, surveying their efforts.

"Indeed no," said Jinny, being Mr. MacKenzie. "I just hope he'll let me go on jumping here this week. We've got to practise for Inverburgh. I've got to practise every day."

"Not today," Sue said. "You never jump your horse the day after a gymkhana."

"We'll go for a ride then," said Jinny. "Though I don't think it would make any difference to Shantih. Maybe she was too fresh yesterday."

"Maybe," said Sue.

Privately, Sue thought that Shantih would always be too impetuous to make a showjumper. She didn't think that anything Jinny did would make her completely reliable, but she knew Jinny too well to mention it.

As they walked up the drive to Finmory, a sports car scorched past them and stopped at the front door. A young woman in a patchwork tweed coat got out.

"It's Nell Storr. She buys our pottery," said Jinny, waving.

"So it is," said Sue, remembering Nell from last summer.

"I'm not coming in," stated Nell. "We're late as it is. Root out Ken. Tell him I'm here."

The front door opened and Ken, with Kelly at his heels, walked out.

"Bundle in," said Nell.

"Where are you going?" Jinny demanded, instantly alert to think that Ken was going somewhere that she didn't know about.

"Over to Melden," said Nell, as Kelly jumped into the back of the car and Ken folded himself into the seat beside her. "Fabulous woman there. Paints pebbles. Out of this world."

"Take peace," said Ken. "I'll be back tomorrow or Tuesday. Yesterday was too much. The screams of those wretched horses."

"What does he mean, screaming horses?" asked Sue, as they drove away.

"At the gymkhana," explained Jinny. "Ken thinks that horses with bits in their mouths are screaming all the time, only our ears can't hear them."

"Oh," said Sue politely.

After lunch they caught Shantih and Bramble and rode to Glenbost.

"Will the moors be much too wet?" Sue asked hopefully.

"Much," said Jimmy, "but we can go on along the road for a bit further."

"O.K.," said Sue, and they trotted on, following the road to Ardtallon.

Since it was Sunday, the road was quieter than usual and they were able to ride side by side, discussing ways in which Shantih could be turned into a steady showjumper before Saturday.

"She can jump higher than Clare's horse, honestly she can," Jinny was saying, when they heard the roar of a heavy vehicle coming up behind them.

Sue pulled Bramble back, tucking him in behind Shantih, and Jinny glanced round to see a crashing, rattling mass of cattle float bearing down on them.

"Going far too fast," Jinny thought. "Don't know who it belongs to. No one round here."

The float careered past, being driven by a man in a tweed jacket and cap to match. As he passed Jinny he turned his head to stare at Shantih.

"He'll know us again," Jinny thought, steadying Shantih who had leapt forward, breaking into a sudden canter.

"Road pig," said Sue.

Suddenly a dog leapt over the dry stone wall that separated the moorland from the road.

"Look out!" Jinny screamed uselessly.

The float driver made no attempt to stop or swerve. His front wheel caught the dog and flung it into the air where, to Jinny's horrified gaze, it seemed to hang, a spread-eagled, stuffed toy, before it thwacked down into the road.

They galloped to where it lay, jumped down and crouched beside it. It was a large brindled lurcher – one of the tinker's dogs.

"Not dead," said Jinny, feeling its heart. "Unconscious. Been hit on its back leg."

There was a bleeding gash on the dog's upper thigh. It lay strangely twisted, making Jinny think that it might have damaged its spine.

"And he didn't even stop!" cried Sue.

A noise above them made them look up, as the tinker boy hurtled over the wall to land beside them.

"Zed!" he cried, kneeling down beside the dog, clutching its head into his knees. "What did it?"

"Cattle float," said Jinny. "We saw it. Your dog jumped over the wall in front of it."

"Me da will shoot him," said the boy.

"Don't talk so soft," said Jinny sharply. "Come on, we've got to get him to the vet. If it had to happen, it couldn't have happened in a better place. The vet's house is just round the next corner. Better try and do something with his leg before we try to move him. Come on, help me."

They made a thick pad out of paper handkerchiefs and Jinny pressed it against the gash in the dog's leg, while Sue took off the tee shirt she was wearing under her sweater and they wrapped it round the paper pad. But it was no sooner in place than the blood had soaked through it and was trickling down the dog's leg again.

Jinny took off her anorak, laid it on the ground, and they

lifted the dog on to it. As they moved the dog it gave a half snarl, half yelp, then lay back unconscious again.

"If you each take a side," Jinny said to Sue and the tinker boy, "you can carry him between you, and I'll ride on to the vet's and let him know we're coming."

Jinny cantered along the road, and trotted up the path, with its border of garden gnomes, to the vet's house. A man's face appeared at the window and, with a surge of relief, Jinny recognised Jim Rae, the vet. He was at the door as Jinny dismounted.

"A dog's been hit by a cattle float," Jinny gasped. "The others are bringing him in."

"Round to the surgery," said the vet, lifting a ring of keys from a hook by the door and leading the way to a surgery built on to the side of his house. "There's a loosebox round the back, put your horse in there."

Jinny led Shantih round to an old-fashioned loosebox and left her.

"I'll take your end," she said to Sue, meeting them on the path and taking the side of the anorak that Sue had been holding. "You can put Bramble in with Shantih."

Jinny and the tinker boy carried the dog into the surgery.

"Let's have him on the table," said the vet. "That's the way. Easy now." Carefully, they slid the dog off the anorak on to the table.

"Now, let's see," said the vet, beginning to examine the lurcher.

Sue joined them and they stood silently watching, staring at the vet's face for any sign of how seriously the dog had been hurt.

"Well, you're lucky," said Jim Rae at last. "Nasty tear in his leg, but apart from that, nothing broken. I'll get him stitched up before he comes round."

With sure movements the vet stitched up the dog's leg. Watching, Jinny didn't feel squeamish the way she did when she watched operations on film. It was too interesting—so interesting that she forgot about everything except the vet's skill and the need to help the injured animal.

"There," said the vet. "How's that?"

"Perfect," said Jinny.

"A-plus," said Sue.

But the tinker boy never spoke. His dark eyes were fixed unblinkingly on his dog.

"I take it the dog belongs to our friend here," said the vet. "So not much point in telling you to make sure he's kept quiet for the next day or two. He'll be off after the rabbits again as soon as he can run. Isn't that so?"

"Aye," muttered the boy. "Jake'll make him."

Suddenly the dog shuddered and scrambled to its feet. With a cry of joy the boy dashed forward and flung his arms round the dog's neck, burying his face against the dog's shoulder, whimpering against the dog with small cries of delight.

"He'll do fine," said the vet, lifting the dog down. "Keep him away from lorries in future."

The boy gave one quicksilver glance round the faces that were watching him, ducked his head to the side with a quick jerk and, holding his dog by the collar, bolted out before anyone realised what he was going to do.

"Well," said Sue in disgust. "He didn't even say thank you."

"If you'd been brought up by Jake Brodie you wouldn't be saying thank you, you'd be getting out while the going was good," said the vet, beginning to clear up.

"Do you know the tinkers?" asked Jinny.

"I've seen to their animals from time to time," said the vet. "Jake's a hard man. I wouldn't cross him if I could help it." And Jinny remembered how the boy had flung up his arm to protect his face when she had spoken to him yesterday.

"Will the dog be all right?" asked Sue.

"Good chance," said the vet. "They're as tough as the kids, the ones who survive."

"What about the stitches?" asked Sue. "Won't you need to take them out?"

The vet shook his head. "Knew there was no chance of the tinks bringing him back. The stuff I've stitched him up with will dissolve once the wound has healed."

"I'll bring the money tomorrow," said Jinny.

"Forget it," said the vet. "I daresay there'll be a couple of hares left on my doorstep before they move on."

"Yuch," said Jinny.

"Very tasty," said the vet.

That evening, Jinny, Sue and Mike went down to the farm to wait for Miss Tuke and to help her load the poles into her van.

"Half-past nine," said Mike, when they had been waiting for ages. "Did she say when she'd be here?"

"Not exactly. She only said when they'd finished trekking."

"Must be having an evening trek," said Mike.

It was almost ten before Miss Tuke drove into the yard and jerked to a stop. She jumped out of the van and came striding across the yard. They could see at once there was something wrong. Her eyes were blazing, every hair on her head seemed electric with fury and her lips worked as she ranted to herself.

"Been hanging around for me, have you?" she asked. "Sorry about that. Had one awful day. It has happened. Knew it would. Two of my ponies gone."

"Gone?" echoed Jinny. "You mean broken out?"

"I mean," said Miss Tuke, "what I say. Gone."

Mr. MacKenzie, having heard the van, had come out to join them.

"Yesterday. Last night. Don't know. They weren't there this morning when I went to feed them."

"It'll be those broken-down old hedges," suggested Mr. MacKenzie. "It's time you were after taking a darning needle to them."

"Nothing could get out of the hill paddock," stated Miss Tuke. "Wire right round and neither Polly nor Moll could jump four feet to save themselves. Of course, the first thing I thought of was that they'd got out somehow. Organised the trekkers to help and not a break in the hedge. Gate was shut."

"You'd be searching the moor for them? They're cunning

blighters, the Highlands. Could have crept through somewhere."

"Searched for miles. That's where I've been. Not a sign. Phoned the police. P.C. Hutchins has all the details in his notebook and, if it's left to him, there they'll stay until he's eaten the poor brutes in his breakfast sausages."

"You mean you think they've been stolen?" gasped Jinny. "But who would steal your ponies? Who?"

"Well you may ask. The very ones you were feeding up with soup yesterday. That's what I'd say."

"That boy wouldn't steal anything," exclaimed Jinny. "He wouldn't steal ponies."

"You think it is the tinks?" asked Mr. MacKenzie.

"No doubt," said Miss Tuke. "I've been round to Alec McGowan's. He took me over to the camp and, of course, there wasn't a sign of a horse anywhere near them. That rogue, Jake, sneering at me. I'll be back tomorrow and P.C. Hutchins will be with me."

"What else will you do? Where else will you look?" asked Jinny.

Miss Tuke flung her hands wide, shaking her head with rage and frustration.

"They could be anywhere. Never see another trace." And Miss Tuke began to load the poles into her van, crashing them in as if they were the horse thieves.

"It's absolutely terrible," said Jinny, as they walked back to Finmory. "I can't believe it, honestly I can't."

"The police will do something about it," said Mike. "They don't let anyone go about pinching other people's things."

"I'm going down to see Shantih," Jinny said when they reached Finmory, making it obvious that she wanted to go alone. Leaving the others, she sped across the garden to the horses' field.

"Shantih," she called. "Shantih."

A low whinny answered her as Shantih lifted her head from grazing and, with pricked ears and dark eyes, bright at the sound of Jinny's voice, came stepping through the grass to wait for Jinny at the gate.

At the sound of Shantih's whinny, relief flooded warm and sweet through the whole of Jinny's being. Ever since she had heard that Miss Tuke's ponies had been stolen she had been frozen with fear that Shantih would not be in her field when they got back to Finmory.

Again Shantih whinnied, calling to Jinny.

"If there were a million horses and I heard Shantih, I'd know it was her," Jinny thought, as she climbed over the gate and flung her arms round Shantih's neck.

"Shantih," she whispered against her horse's neck, and suddenly tears were running down Jinny's face. She had been so afraid that the field would be empty, that she would never see Shantih again.

"I thought they'd stolen you too," she told Shantih, as she rubbed her eyes dry against the back of her hand. "I couldn't bear it if anything happened to you."

Jinny wished desperately that Ken and Kelly hadn't gone away with Nell Storr. "Kelly would hear if anyone came near Finmory," Jinny thought, and she shuddered at the thought of the tinker they'd called Jake creeping around Finmory House at night. Jinny imagined the horse thieves as silent shapes in the darkness, coming down to the horses' field to lead Shantih and Bramble away and sell them for meat.

Someone moved on the other side of the gate. Jinny leapt back, screaming.

"Jinny," said her father's voice crossly. "I thought this was what you'd be doing, standing down here imagining all sorts of nonsense. Come on in. It's nearly eleven."

"Whee!" said Jinny, her heart thumping in her throat. "I thought you were the horse thieves."

Hurriedly she took a piece of carrot from her pocket and gave it to Shantih. Bramble came bustling across to get his share.

"Move it," said Mr. Manders.

Jinny walked back to Finmory, her arm linked through her father's arm.

"I never thought of it before," she said. "As long as they were in their field I was sure they were safe."

"Perhaps Miss Tuke is wrong," suggested Mr. Manders. "Maybe they have only strayed."

"Don't think so," said Jinny, shaking her head. "She was sure the ponies had been stolen. It's not like Miss Tuke to panic over nothing."

CHAPTER SIX

"Dry day," thought Jinny, as she opened her eyes to a bright morning. She thought, "Inverburgh Show. The cup. Clare Burnley. School Shantih over low jumps. Steady her," all in quick succession, all muddled together.

She stretched, sat up in bed, glancing across at Sue who was still asleep, then Jinny jumped out of bed and leant out of her open bedroom window.

"Shantih!" she called. "Shantih!"

For the first second, Jinny didn't believe her own eyes, for of course Bramble and Shantih must be in their field. Of course they must. They always were, always.

"Shantih," Jinny called again, her voice high-pitched with fear.

Deluging back into Jinny's memory came the recollection of the horse thieves who had stolen two of Miss Tuke's ponies.

"Shantih!" Jinny screamed.

The field gate was shut. They hadn't pushed it open and escaped that way. From her window there was only one corner of the field that Jinny couldn't see. It was possible that they might be there, but Jinny knew with a clemmed certainty that Shantih would never stay tucked into the corner, out of sight, when she was calling her. Bramble might, if he was on strike, but not Shantih. Not Shantih.

Jinny tore off her nightdress, pulled on sweater and jeans, forced her feet into sandshoes still laced from the night before, and hurtled through the house to the back door. Her hands struggled to turn the key, then she was running as she had never run before, down the garden, past the stables to the horses' field.

Jinny vaulted the gate, went on blindly until she was standing in the middle of the empty field.

"They've broken out," she told herself, and ran round the hedges looking for a place where they could have pushed their way through. But there was no gap with broken branches and tell-tale hoof prints. The hedge was as strong as it had always been.

"Shantih," screamed Jinny, "Shantih!" as if her voice could conjure her horses from the empty air. "Bramble!"

Jinny turned back, her legs suddenly too weak to carry her, her arms hanging uselessly by her sides. She reached the gate and leant against it. Out of her mouth came a sobbing groan of shock and misery.

"What's wrong?" demanded Sue's voice. "What on earth's the matter with you? Why are you going on like that?"

The sound of Sue's sharp efficient tones cut through Jinny's hysteria. She pushed her hair back from her face, gulped hard, trying to speak.

"They've gone. I knew last night. I should have brought them in. Stayed up to guard them. The meat men have got them."

"They'll only have broken out," Sue said, staring round the empty field. "Pippen does all the time. Once he was nearly on the motorway. We'll get them back."

"The gate was shut and there's nowhere in the hedge where they could have got out."

"They could have jumped out," insisted Sue.

"They never have before," said Jinny. "Why should they now? Why last night, just when Miss Tuke has had her ponies stolen?"

"Let's look down on the shore," said Sue, and began to run down the path to the sea.

Jinny followed her, not because she had any hope of finding Shantih, but because for the moment she couldn't think what else she could do, except to follow Sue and for a few more minutes cling to the hope that Shantih and Bramble might be there, might only have strayed. But Jinny was sure she hadn't strayed. Already she was sure that Shantih and Bramble had been stolen.

The shore was bright with sunlight shimmering on sea and sand. The gulls' cries ripped the early morning silence. The black cliffs were withdrawn and menacing against the glittering water.

There was no trace of Arab or Highland; no crescent hoofprints marked the sand, no chestnut shape picked fastidiously at the seaweed, no black bulk, lips drawn back, fed on the sea holly.

Jinny stood perfectly still, staring out over the deserted shore to the impersonal expanse of the sea. The horror of the first shock began to die down, to settle into a leaden weight in her chest.

"Shall we search round the cliffs?" suggested Sue.

"No point," said Jinny. "If they were here we'd see the hoofprints. We'd better get back. Phone Miss Tuke. Tell Dad. Phone the police."

Jinny ran steadily back to Finmory. She found her father standing in the pottery, still gritty with early morning, a mug of coffee in his hand.

"Shantih and Bramble have gone," Jinny said. "They didn't break out. The gate was shut. Someone's been here in the night and taken them away."

Mr. Manders looked in astonished surprise at Jinny's pale face, her eyes stretched wide and her mouth tight, holding back tears.

"The same men that stole Miss Tuke's," said Jinny. "Must be."

"Why would they want to do that, to come here?" asked her father. "It's much more likely that they've got out somehow. Probably gone down to Mr. MacKenzie's. They'll be down there now, eating his hay. That's much more probable."

"I'll phone him first," said Jinny, "just in case. Then I'll phone Miss Tuke."

Mr. MacKenzie hadn't seen Shantih or Bramble. They were not in his yard.

"Now don't you be letting that imagination of yours go galloping off with you," he said to Jinny. "It's on the moor they'll be. Gone for a wee visit to my Shetlands. It's the day for the visiting."

"There's no way they could have got out unless they'd jumped out, and if they'd been as excited as that I'd have heard them galloping about."

"Now wait you a minute," said Mr. MacKenzie, his voice suddenly serious. "It's now it's coming back into my head. I'd to be shouting at the dogs last night. Woke me with their barking, so they did."

"Didn't you go down to see what was wrong?"

"I'd the wee look out of my window and not a thing stirring, so I was thinking it would be a fox they'd heard, but now I'm thinking you should be giving the police a wee ring. It's not like Betsy to be barking for nothing."

"Then why didn't you go down and find out what she was barking at?" demanded Jinny, and slammed the phone down.

Jinny phoned Miss Tuke next.

"Blasted tinkers," she said. "It's them. I'm sure of it. Phone the police or get your father to do it. Pay more attention to him. I'm meeting P.C. Hutchins at ten and we're going over to the tinkers' camp. They'll deny everything, of course, but we may pick up some clues."

"Shall we come with you?" asked Jinny.

"No point. I'll let you know what happens. You get on the move. Scout about. Try Glenbost. Someone may have heard something strange last night."

"We will," said Jinny.

"Blasted, thieving tinks," said Miss Tuke again, before she rang off.

Mr. Manders phoned the police station at Ardtallon to report what had happened.

"They want details of the missing horses," he said, giving the phone to Jinny.

"You'll be knowing Miss Tuke at the trekking?" the

policeman asked, after he had taken down the descriptions.

"She's had ponies stolen too," said Jinny.

"We're making a visit to the tinkers' camp this morning," said the policeman. "I'll have the look about for your two while we're there."

"It might not be the tinkers," said Jinny. "It might be properly organised horse thieves."

"Indeed it might," said the policeman. "Or then again it might be yourselves are needing to take a wee walk round your hedges."

"Miss Tuke has wire round hers."

"So she was telling me, but I'm thinking you should both be taking a walk over the moors, just in case they're wandering about up there."

Jinny sat at the breakfast table crumbling the piece of toast which she knew she wasn't going to eat.

"They all believe they've strayed," she thought. "But I know they've been stolen. I know it."

It was almost as if the air round the field gate had still held some echo of the night's happenings; some turbulence left by the strangers coming in the dark, leading away the startled, unwilling horses; some message left behind that Jinny had been able to understand.

"I'll take you down to the village after breakfast," Mr. Manders said. "We'll ask around and see if anyone heard anything last night."

"And we'll talk to Mr. MacKenzie," said Jinny. "He might remember more about his dogs barking."

But when they drove past the farm there was no sign of Mr. MacKenzie.

"Stop on the way back," said Mr. Manders, driving on.

In the village they went first to Mrs. Simpson's shop. Drinking in the details to be retold to all her customers, Mrs. Simpson shook her head regretfully.

"Never a murmur did I hear," she said, and called her husband from the back shop. But he too had heard nothing unusual.

"Miss Tuke as well," moaned Mrs. Simpson, enjoying

herself. "That ordinary, decent people can't sleep in their beds without such things going on is a shame on us all!"

Sue and Jinny went to ask at the schoolhouse while Mr. Manders spoke to the men at the garage.

"Nothing," said Jinny, knowing from her father's face that the garage men hadn't been able to tell him anything either.

"We'll try some of the crofts," said Mr. Manders. "No harm in asking. If Mr. MacKenzie's dogs were disturbed there's a chance that someone else heard whatever disturbed them. But be polite," he warned.

It took ages asking at each croft. The crofters all knew Jinny and Shantih and had to be told every detail, but no one could help them.

"Poor Mrs. Simpson," said Mr. Manders, when they had been round all the crofts. "She won't be able to tell them her hot news. They'll all have heard it."

They drove back to Finmory in silence.

"If only Mr. Mackenzie had got up to find out what his dogs were barking at," said Sue, as they got out of the car in the farmyard.

"Don't start," warned Jinny. "Don't start 'if onlying'. Does no good. Too late for that."

"It's not a thing more I can be telling you," said Mr. MacKenzie. "When I heard them barking I took a look out of the window and not a thing was stirring, so I gave them a bit of a shout and back I went to bed."

"What shall we do next?" demanded Jinny. "Where shall we look next? Now, this minute, someone has Shantih. I've got to find her NOW, before . . ." but Jinny couldn't go on.

"Maybe Miss Tuke and the police force will have found them with the tinkers. She'll be more than a match for the tinkers, that one. It's Jake himself will be turning pale when he sees her coming."

"But what can we do?" repeated Jinny.

"Have you had the look over the hill?" suggested Mr. MacKenzie. "You be finding my Shetlands and I'm thinking you'll be finding that mare of yours."

"Take us ages on foot," said Jinny, but it was a last flickering hope; a useless activity to fill in the eternity of the afternoon.

"If your father would be driving you over to Ewan's, you could be taking his ponies. They're a couple of idle beggars. A jaunt over the hill would be doing them no damage."

Jinny remembered the two heavy, dun Highlands that Mr. MacKenzie and his son Ewan rode when they rounded up Mr. MacKenzie's herd of Shetlands and brought them down from the hill for the market each year.

"Could you take us over?"

"If we go now," her father said.

"Right," said Jinny.

Ewan MacKenzie's farm was about six miles away. When they drove into the yard, Ewan was waiting for them.

"Scoot out," said Mr. Manders. "I'll be here for hours if they lure me into the kitchen, and I must get some work done."

Sue and Jinny scooted out and Mr. Manders drove away.

"He's very busy," Jinny explained.

"That's the pity," said Ewan. "Maggie's got the teapot on. We'd the phone call from the old man telling us your troubles, so I've brought the two of them in for you, and it's welcome you are to have the use of them. Be keeping them at the farm while you're needing them."

"Thanks very much," said Jinny. "Mr. MacKenzie thinks that they might be on the hill with his Shetlands, so we're going to ride up and look."

"It's the terrible business altogether. Come you both in and be telling us about it."

Reluctantly, Jinny and Sue followed Ewan into the dark farm kitchen. His wife was pouring out cups of strong black tea and setting them on the table with plates of scones and cake.

It was nearly two before they escaped and went with Ewan to the hay shed, where two carthorsy Highland ponies were standing, tied to the shed posts, munching hay. They were both duns, with dense manes twisted into witch knots and tails woven with dead bracken and thorn twigs.

Ewan brought saddles and bridles. The leather was bone dry and the metal rusty. He swung the saddles on to the ponies' backs, sending up clouds of dust, and then crammed the bar snaffles into their mouths.

"Aye," he said, "they're canny beasts. No just what you're used to, but they'll carry you safe over the bogs, so they will."

He gave the reins of one of the Highlands to Jinny. "That's Jock," he said. "And this is Belle." He handed Belle's reins to Sue.

Ewan waited until Sue and Jinny had mounted.

"Aye, it's fine you'll be on those two," he said. "And be letting me know when you find your own."

"Will do," promised Jinny. "Thanks very much. Cheerio."

Belle and Jock lifted one slow, sober hoof after the other as they made their way up the hillside.

"Not fast," said Sue, her heels raising a dust storm from Belle's sides.

"But sure," said Jinny, as she allowed Jock to pick his own way over the rough ground. She knew it didn't matter. If they were on racehorses it wouldn't make any difference. Shantih and Bramble weren't on the moor. Jinny was only there because she didn't know what else to do. Didn't know where else to look for Shantih. Ken would be home in the evening. He might know.

Eventually they found the Shetlands, clustered together in a sheltered hollow. Some of the mares were stretched out on the grass, enjoying the spring sunshine, while others were grazing. One whinnied a warning as Sue and Jinny rode up.

There was no sign of Shantih or Bramble. It was obvious that they hadn't been near the Shetlands.

"Not here," said Sue.

"If Shantih had been loose up here she'd have found the Shetlands," said Jinny. "May as well get back home."

They rode back to Finmory, Jock and Belle moving at their own deliberate pace. Jinny knew from the gathering dusk that it must be quite late. Soon it would be a day and a night since Shantih and Bramble had been stolen.

Jinny gazed into the future. By the summer would she look back on yesterday as the last day she had seen Shantih? The last time she had seen Bramble—dear, comfortable, solid Bramble? This Easter be remembered all her life as the Easter when Shantih was stolen and never recovered? Jinny howled wolf-terror over the darkening moors, for it could be that way. It was only too possible that she would never see Shantih or Bramble again.

"Do you mind?" said Sue. "Going on like a raving idiot. That isn't going to help. We had to search the moors in case they were there with the Shetlands. Now we know for sure they aren't on the moors we can start and search for them in other places."

"Like what other places?" said Jinny miserably.

Sue didn't reply.

They left Belle and Jock with Mr. MacKenzie.

"I'll be keeping them in the wee paddock," Mr. MacKenzie told them. "And I'll be leaving Betsy off her chain tonight, just in case there's any sign of your friends."

"Has Miss Tuke phoned?" Jinny demanded, as soon as she got into the kitchen.

"Yes," said Mrs. Manders. "Dad spoke to her. She went with the policeman to the tinkers' camp this morning, but they found nothing. No trace of anything suspicious, and naturally all the tinkers swore they hadn't been away from the camp last night."

"What's she going to do now?" asked Jinny.

"Advertise," said her mother. "She's including Bramble and Shantih in the advertisement. The police have circulated descriptions of them all and they'll be on the lookout at any horse sales and slaughterhouses."

Diving from the kitchen, Jinny just made the bathroom before she was sick.

By half-past ten, Ken still hadn't returned.

"He said he might not be back," said Mrs. Manders. "You'll see him tomorrow. No point in staying up any later or you'll be too tired to do anything tomorrow."

Reluctantly, Jinny agreed. Sue had gone to bed at nine, saying that if she stayed up any longer her face would split with yawning. She was fast asleep when Jinny went into their bedroom.

Jinny sat down on the edge of her bed—elbows on her knees, head buried in her hands. The day's happenings unrolled like a newsreel behind her eyes, from the first moment when she had discovered the empty field, to the hopeless, leaden despair that weighed her down as she sat listening for the sound of Nell Storr's car that would bring Ken home.

It was after midnight before Jinny gave up. She undressed, crawled into bed and, pulling the bedclothes over her head, cried in silent misery. It was all too terrible, too terrible to have happened. Although Jinny's brain knew that it had happened she could not make herself believe it.

CHAPTER SEVEN

"Miss Tuke is positive the tinkers have taken them?" asked Ken.

Jinny nodded. "She's sure."

Ken had got home in the early morning. He'd read a note from Mr. Manders telling him what had happened, and woken Jinny. They were sitting in the dawn-bleak kitchen and Ken, having listened to Jinny's account of yesterday, was trying to think where they should look today.

"Do you think it was them?" Ken asked.

Jinny considered. "Might be. They're the most suspicious," she said.

"Not very likely," said Ken. "They've only just arrived, got work and a camp site. If they were going to steal horses they'd wait until they were ready to move on, wouldn't they?"

"Then who?"

"We don't know, but the tinkers will. There hasn't been

horse stealing going on more or less next door to their camp without them knowing about it."

"Why didn't they tell Miss Tuke if they knew?"

"Would you have told her if you'd been a tinker? You'd have kept your mouth shut. They wouldn't want to tell the police anything, but if you rode over you might be able to find out something. Try to blend in so they stop noticing you. See everything without staring at anything."

"We'll go this morning," agreed Jinny. She was rather vague about what Ken thought they should do, but it seemed as good an idea as any to have a look at the tinkers' camp herself.

"I'll go over to Ardtallon," said Ken. "A word here and a word there. See what's blowing."

He uncurled his long legs from under the kitchen table, stretched, then, soft footed as a cat, walked out of the kitchen. Minutes later, Jinny heard the front door closing gently behind him.

Jinny's father wasn't too keen on them visiting the tinkers' camp by themselves.

"I could drive you over in the afternoon," he offered.

"But we want to ride," Jinny said. "After all, Sue is here on holiday and we'd rather go by ourselves."

"Well, be sensible. Don't do anything crazy. If the police and Miss Tuke couldn't find anything, there's nothing there to be found."

Jock and Belle were difficult to catch. Even in Mr. MacKenzie's small paddock they managed to avoid capture until Mr. MacKenzie came out with a scoop of oats. He stayed to help them tack up the ponies, heaving up the stiff canvas girths and giving Jinny directions on how to reach Alec McGowan's farm.

"You'll find the tinks camping down by the river. Be taking a care for them now. Don't you be pushing your noses in where they're not wanted. If you see Alec McGowan, be telling him I'll be at the market next month."

"Will do," promised Jinny, her heels thwacking into Jock's sides, her riding stick battering against his hairy quarters as she tried to ride him out of the yard.

"Now they're trotting don't let them stop," Jinny warned Sue. "Keep them moving."

"My bum's numb," moaned Sue. "This saddle is made out of cast iron."

Suddenly the sound of approaching hooves made the Highlands dig in their toes in an emergency stop. Clutching handfuls of mane, Jinny just managed to wriggle back into the saddle as Clare Burnley, riding Jasper, her black horse, trotted round the corner in front of them.

"Poor darlings!" she exclaimed, looking down on Sue and Jinny from the height of her thoroughbred. "I've heard all about it and it is too ghastly for words. Daddy has had alarms fitted on all our boxes and the tack room. Was she insured?"

Jinny stared blankly at Clare. She hadn't even known that you could insure horses.

"No? Lord, how foolish. I was saying to Ma that one would have rather a job getting the insurance to cough up before the Show, and if you did get the cash out of them, where would one look for another horse up here? But, of course, if you weren't insured . . ."

"We're going to find Shantih," Jinny told her.

"Oh, one would rather fear not. These gangs are so frightfully well organised. Has one any hope at all?"

Jinny gathered up Jock's reins and, her heels battering his sides, her stick bouncing off his coconut-fibre coat, she charged him into electronic speed and forced him past Clare.

"Steady on," exclaimed Clare, as Jasper shied. "No need to get into such a state. In fact, one would think that you'd be rather glad to have her taken off your hands. She does make such an utter fool of you in public."

"Seems a nice girl," said Sue, catching up with Jinny.

"One does always find her so utterly charming," Jinny replied, too worried about Shantih to be really annoyed by someone as rude as Clare.

Jock and Belle settled into a trot as heavy and steady as their walk.

"Clockwork," said Sue. "They're computerised."

"Silicon chip," said Jinny, her mind full of nothing but the thought of Shantih—the dreadful knowledge that every minute might be the minute when Shantih was being led into a slaughterhouse.

"They wouldn't sell an Arab for meat," she said to Sue, seeking reassurance. "They'd get more money selling her, wouldn't they?"

"Dunno," said Sue. "They get so much for meat nowadays."

"Thanks very much," said Jinny.

"But probably an Arab would be different," Sue added hurriedly. "In fact, I'm sure it would be."

"Don't bother," said Jinny. "You told me the first time."

When they reached the forestry track that led to Miss Tuke's, they kicked the Highlands into a gallumphing canter.

"Left here," said Jinny, when at last they reached the turn-off that Mr. MacKenzie had told her about. "Through this gate," she added, letting Jock settle back into plod.

"What shall we say?" asked Sue, as they rode up a field and Mr. McGowan's farmhouse came into sight. "Are we going to mention the horses?"

"Not if we can help it," said Jinny, as they rode down to the river. "Ken said we were to try not to be noticed, but I don't see how we can manage that. They're bound to notice us."

"Play it by ear," said Sue, without much conviction.

"More or less what Ken meant" Jinny agreed.

The tinkers were camped in a shingly swerve of the river bank. A track led from their camp over the fields in the direction of the farm. Two battered vans were parked on the track, and the camp itself looked like a mound of ancient tarpaulins with a tin chimney stuck on top of the mound—as if someone had picked a giant black mushroom, put it on the ground and stuck its stalk on top of it.

As they approached, a young woman who had been sitting on the ground by the fire stood up, shouted something, and two teenage boys came out of the tarpaulin mound and stood staring at them. Three ragged-looking terriers, bouncing and yapping, came scrabbling towards them.

"What are we going to say?" insisted Sue, her voice squeaky with nerves.

Jinny didn't know and didn't care. The tinkers were her only link with Shantih. There must be some way she could find out what they knew.

An old woman with grey hair hanging about her face came out of one of the vans, joined the younger woman, and they both stood staring as Jinny and Sue rode up.

"Would you be wanting to buy a flower from the tinker folk?" whined the old woman, holding out a large wicker basket filled with flowers made from wood chips, and small wicker plant pots. "Buy a flower." She stretched out a claw-like hand and gripped Jinny's knee.

"They're lovely flowers," said Jinny. "Did you make them yourself?"

"I did. You'll not be knowing the work of the tinkers, grand folk like yourselves."

Five or six ragged children had come out of the vans and were staring up at Jinny and Sue with pale, closed faces.

"We don't have any money with us," Jinny said. "Or we would like to buy some. We might come back and buy some now that we've seen them."

"Be doing that," said the old woman, tightening her grip for a second before she took her hand off Jinny's knee.

"If you've not the money to buy anything you'll be riding on then," said the young woman. The menace in her voice was October ice on water.

There was a silence when Jinny couldn't think of a thing to say—a silence that grew tighter as the dark eyes of the tinkers stared up at them, devouring, without expression.

"I must ask them if they've seen Shantih," Jinny thought, but she knew it would be useless. If she asked directly, they would tell her nothing. But she had to ask. Had to find out. She couldn't ride off without asking. Then, suddenly, she knew what to say.

"Really we came to see how the dog is. We're the girls that took your dog to the vet after the float hit him."

The younger woman's face relaxed into a slow smile. She spoke in a low voice to the older woman and the boys, and the tension had gone. The old woman urged them to take their pick of her flowers, the two boys praised Jock and Belle, and the young woman said they must stay until Tam came back. He was out with his father and the dogs, but they would be back in a moment and they would see for themselves how well the dog's leg was healing.

Jinny and Sue dismounted. Their arms through their reins, they picked flowers from the woman's basket while the children hoisted each other on to the ponies' backs. The young woman piled sticks on the fire, flames leapt up round the soot-black kettle.

Jinny imagined what it would be like to live with the tinkers. Not to live in a house, but to live outside. Not to think about keeping clean, or being polite, or caring what other people thought about you. Knowing always that they were suspicious of everything you did and didn't want you near them. Jinny saw herself sitting round the fire at night; waking outdoors on a summer morning; selling wooden flowers around the villages, basket over her arm, riding bareback on Shantih.

"Shantih!" the word turned like a knife in Jinny's heart.

She looked carefully round the camp but there was no sign of halters or any other tack. No sign of horses.

"Do you have any ponies of your own?" Jinny asked one of the boys.

"Aye, times," said the boy.

Suddenly the terriers burst into a flurry of yapping. Over the track from the farm came two figures—a man and a boy. Two brindled lurchers, one with a hind leg tucked close to its body, ran in front of them.

"Tam's coming now," said the young woman. "It's Jake himself will be wanting to thank you for your kindness."

As the man and the boy came closer, Jinny saw that Jake was the same man who had been on Miss Tuke's hill, the same man who had stood silent and dark in the shadow of the pines and stared after them when they had ridden past —when she had been riding Shantih.

The boy, Tam, ran with the lurchers, and when he reached Jinny and Sue he gripped his dog by the scruff of its neck and pulled him over so that Jinny and Sue could see his injured leg.

"He's still fit for the rabbits," he said, beaming at them.

"Oh good," said Jinny.

"It does seem to be healing," said Sue, as Jake came striding up, kicking the boy and the dog out of his way.

"Get out of here," he said in a low snarl.

"Jake," said the young woman. "What's at you? That's the lassies who took the dog to be stitched. We've them to thank . . ."

"Get away from here," Jake roared, his face livid, his lips drawn back from his lower teeth, his eyes narrow slits.

"We only came to see how the dog was," exclaimed Jinny.

"It was the two of you who were on the hill with that Tuke woman, and her bringing the police to snoop around my camp. Get out with you both."

The smell of spirits reeked from the man's breath.

"Jake, man, you're wandered. It's the lassies had the dog stitched up," said the young woman.

Jake spun round on her. Jinny saw his clenched fist aimed at her head, saw her shield her face with the same movement that the boy had used to protect himself when Jinny had spoken to him at the gymkhana. Jinny shut her eyes, heard the blow hit the woman, and opened her eyes to see her fall to the ground, her mouth bleeding.

"Get off with you," roared Jake, advancing on them.

Sue and Jinny were on their ponies and up the track almost before they knew what they were doing.

"But I didn't ask him," cried Jinny. "I didn't ask about Shantih." And she pulled Jock round and forced him back to the tinkers' camp.

"I didn't come to snoop," Jinny yelled. "I came to see if you knew anything about Shantih? She's my horse, a chestnut Arab, and she's been stolen. Do you know anything about her? Tell me. You must tell me if you know. Please! Please!"

For a moment the man stood without speaking, then he gave a low whistle and the two lurchers sprang at Jinny. Jock, from a dim, wolf-haunted past, squealed a high, pig squeal, half reared and lashed at the dogs with his forelegs before he spun round and went galloping back to Sue and Belle.

Before they reached Sue, Jake had called his dogs off.

"Come on," said Sue, urging Belle on. "No more of this. Pippen needs me."

"But they must know something. They must know, or they wouldn't have been so mad at finding us there. They know where Shantih is. They know where the ponies are."

"We're not going back," stated Sue. "He'd kill us, and he'd never tell you."

"We could search for them."

"Look," said Sue. "The police and Miss Tuke were here. They had a warrant to search the place. They didn't find anything. What makes you think we would?"

Jinny didn't answer, but rode on unwillingly with Sue. They went through Mr. McGowan's farmyard and down a lane leading away from the farm.

Jock stopped—legs foursquare, head high.

"Whatever now?" growled Jinny.

There was something coming towards them, something scrabbling along the ditch at the bottom of the hawthorn hedge.

Coated with mud, dead leaves and twigs, the tinker boy, Tam, crawled out of the ditch at their side. For a moment he stood with his head cocked to one side, listening.

"Do you know where Shantih and Bramble are?" demanded Jinny. "Tell us if you know. You must tell us."

Tam paid no attention to her urgent questions. He was like a wild creature that any second would plunge away and vanish.

"They're up there," Tam said in a low whisper, and he pointed to a track that led over a hillside in the middle distance. "They took them up there."

Jinny and Sue looked where the boy was pointing.

"Where could you hide ponies up there?" asked Sue suspiciously.

"Up in the Barony," muttered the boy. "Aye."

They stared up at where the boy had pointed.

"How do we get there?" demanded Jinny. "How far is it?"

But when she looked down, the boy had gone.

CHAPTER EIGHT

"He's vanished!" exclaimed Sue, unable to believe her eyes.

"He can't have," said Jinny. "He's got to tell us more."

She stared urgently up and down the lane. Standing in her stirrups she peered over the hedge, then rode up and down the lane shouting for Tam, but there was no sign of him.

Eventually Jinny caught a fleeting glimpse of him, almost out of sight. He was running full pelt, low to the ground, heading back to the tinkers' camp.

"No point in following him," Jinny said. "We'll not get anything more out of him."

"Do you think he really knows where they are? He might be making it up."

"Of course he does. He only risked coming to tell us because we had his dog stitched up for him. Jake would murder him if he knew. He wouldn't have come to tell us unless he was really sure."

"We can't reach that track from here," said Sue, for although they could see the track stretching across the next range of hills, there seemed no way of getting to it.

"Better ask at the farm," said Jinny. "We'll give them Mr. MacKenzie's message."

The farmer's wife opened the door.

"Morning," said Jinny. "We've brought a message from Mr. MacKenzie of Finmory Farm. He told us to let you know that he would be at the market next month."

"Och now, Alec will be pleased to hear that. I'll be letting him know. That'll be Ewan's ponies you're riding?"

"They are," said Jinny. "We're having a day's trek. Mr. MacKenzie suggested we should ride to the Barony, but we seem to have gone wrong."

"Aye," said Mrs. McGowan. "You'll need to go out on to the road again, go back the way you came and watch out for a gate. You'll see it easily enough. The fine broad track it was once when they still farmed the Barony, though that will not be yesterday, more's the pity."

"Is it a farm?" asked Sue.

"Och, it's nothing but an old ruin now, but once it was a bonnie wee bit farm."

"Do we follow the track all the way?" Jinny asked impatiently.

"Aye, to the very door. I daresay it's overgrown a wee bit nowadays. If it's used once a year it would be surprising me. But you'd best be getting on with you, for it's a fair step up to the Barony."

"Thanks," said Jinny, urging Jock forward. "Thanks a lot."

At a steady trot they rode back down the lane, turned right and rode on, keeping a look-out for the gate. They saw it at last—a rickety bundle of lichen-covered timber, tied to the gatepost by wire.

Jinny jumped down, untwisted the wire and lifted back the gate.

"She was right," said Sue. "No one ever comes through here. That gate's had it."

"Yet the wire's new. You'd think it would be rusty but it's not. There's the old bit. Look, someone's chucked it in the hedge and fitted this new bit round the gate."

"And wheel marks," said Sue, pointing to the soft ground at the side of the gatepost. "Someone's driven through here and not long ago, I'd say."

Jinny struggled to drag the gate back, retwisted the wire and sprang back up on to Jock.

"Come on!" Jinny yelled, as she kicked him into a heavy, thumping canter.

As they followed the track over the hills, Jinny refused to allow herself to think that they had found Shantih and Bramble, that it was possible that they were at the ruined farm.

"Don't think it," she warned herself. "It may be other ponies Tam saw. Some farmer may be grazing his ponies up there. They may not be stolen ponies at all. It may not be Shantih." But the leaden weight that had been choking her since she had first discovered the empty field had gone.

Jock and Belle had slowed to a walk that, despite all efforts, was rapidly slowing to a plod.

"Miles," said Sue. "It must be right in the hills."

Looking back, Jinny could see McGowan's farm as a tiny, toy building, the loops of the river drawn on to the fields by a child's paintbrush and the tinkers' camp a hardly visible mound by the river bank. She shivered, thinking for the first time of what they would do if Jake was sitting waiting for them—a giant spider in his web of crumbling walls. Jinny longed for Shantih's speed. If she had been riding Shantih she would have been safe, for no one could have caught her then.

"Have you decided what we are actually going to do when we get there?" asked Sue.

"Spy out the place," said Jinny vaguely. She had only thought of seeing Shantih again, of knowing she was safe.

"Can't spy when we're riding these two," said Sue. "They'll hear us coming."

As she spoke, they rounded a corner of the track and the old farmhouse lay in a hollow in front of them.

"Quick," said Jinny, "back out of sight in case there's a lookout."

"Should we just ride up?" suggested Sue, when they were both safely round the corner again. "All we can do just now is look for the horses. Make sure they are here, then ride back and tell the police."

"No," said Jinny. "If they are here we've got to set them free. Once they're loose on the moors they'll be safe. They'll find their own way home."

"But if we set them free what will happen to us?" said Sue. "Don't think whoever has stolen them is going to stand there and say thank you."

"Don't care," said Jinny. "As long as Shantih and Bramble are O.K. They won't slaughter us."

"That's daft," said Sue.

"You'd be the same if it was Pippen."

Sue didn't reply, and for a minute they sat astride their ponies staring at each other.

"I'm going," said Jinny, jumping to the ground and tossing Jock's reins to Sue.

"But . . ." began Sue.

"Makes sense," said Jinny. "They're not so likely to see one of us, and if they do catch me you can ride for help."

"Wait, I'll go," Sue said, but Jinny was already walking quickly round the corner.

There were no windows facing the track, only the crumbling wall of a building that looked as if it had once been a byre. Jinny searched for any sign of life, but all she could see were a few black-faced sheep.

"Nothing disturbing them," Jinny thought, and began to walk on towards the farm. "I'll tell them I'm a Girl Guide," she decided. "That I'm doing my Rambler's badge, that I've got lost. Wonder if I should be wearing a uniform?"

Jinny wasn't sure, but knowing a Guide wouldn't be wearing a hard hat she left it with her stick by the side of the track.

Just on the borders of Jinny's mind was the vision of Shantih; of how she was there only a few minutes away; of how she would look up, knowing Jinny; would whinny a welcome and come cantering to meet her. The picture was so clear that it was almost real. Jinny could see Shantih's dished face, wide eyes and velvet muzzle. Almost, Jinny could feel Shantih's hard neck and her silken fringe of mane. But it was not real. It had not happened. Not yet. Jinny pushed the dream out of her head.

She crept up to the wall, stood with her ears strained, listening for any sound that might be men or horses. Placing each foot gently down on the wrack of dead nettles and weeds, Jinny made her way along the wall. She peered round the end of the wall into the skeleton of what had once been the byre. At one end, milk churns and dairy pails lay in a confused, rusting litter. Down the sides of the byre Jinny could still make out where the cattle had stood, their troughs silted under a debris of dirt.

At the far side of the byre, a door that seemed to lead into the farmhouse kitchen stood half-open.

Jinny dug her nails into the palms of her hands and, breathing slowly, climbed over the rubble of the wall and crept across the byre. She waited by the door but still there was no sound. Inching forward, Jinny peered round the door into a stone-floored kitchen.

At first glance, Jinny saw only the sagging ceiling, cobwebbed walls and old sacks stuffed into broken windowpanes. Then she took in the crushed beer cans littering the floor, a table made from milk crates and an old bench that had been brought in from outside. The fireplace of the range was full of fresh ashes and littered with cigarette ends. But the room was empty. No one was there now.

Jinny ran across the kitchen, opened the back door of the farm and stepped out into the yard. Its soft mud was scored with wheel tracks and hoofprints. The doors of a high, corrugated shed were wide open and the hoofprints seemed to come from inside the shed. Jinny dashed across. Peering into the half-dark, she saw that the floor of mud and decaying timbers was pitted with hoofprints and thick with dung. The smell of horses was heavy in the air.

Jinny stood quite still. Caught on a nail in the corrugated iron were several long chestnut hairs. They were Shantih's. Shantih had been here but they had taken her away again. Jinny was too late.

Jinny turned blindly into the yard. The weight was back in her chest, squeezing the breath out of her lungs so that she had to snatch for air. Where would she look now? Where? They had driven the horses away. If they had left last night they could be anywhere by now. Jinny imagined Shantih and Bramble crammed into a cattle float, standing terrified as they were driven through the dark. She could not imagine the men who had stolen them, men who would take a horse from its own field as if it were a pound of butter in a supermarket, who could steal a living animal as if it were an object.

"Please God," breathed Jinny. "Please God."

Sue, riding to meet Jinny, knew from her face that she hadn't found the ponies or Shantih.

"We're too late," Jinny told her. "They've been there but they've taken them away again. There's nothing we can do."

"For goodness sake," said Sue, "of course there must be something. Did you search the place? Look for clues. There must be something to tell us where they've gone."

They rode back to the farm, tied the ponies up and went into the kitchen. Sue looked round the room in disgust.

"What a filthy mess," she said, pushing the door wide open to let in more light.

"Bus tickets, cigarette packets, paper bags with the shop's address on them," said Sue, searching about. "Anything at all that might tell us where they've come from."

"Doesn't mean they'll be going back there," said Jinny despondently.

She wandered through the rest of the deserted farmhouse, but there was only dirt and decay. The staircase grinned with gap teeth where stairs had fallen in, the bannisters had been chopped down and carried off. All the other rooms except the kitchen were open to the sky.

"Not a thing," said Jinny, crossing the kitchen and going out into the yard.

She stood staring at the shed doorway, trying to picture Shantih and Bramble being led through it. Then something caught her eye. On a rotting water butt at the farm door there lay a copy of *Horse and Hound*. Someone had put it down and forgotten to lift it. Jinny picked it up. It was last week's issue. One of the horse thieves must have put it there and forgotten about it.

"This proves it wasn't the tinkers," Jinny said, showing it to Sue. "They'd never buy *Horse and Hound*."

"No name or delivery address on it?" questioned Sue.

"Not a scribble," said Jinny, examining the cover.

She flicked through the pages. Show horses and ponies stood in ribboned splendour, an Arab head tore at Jinny's heart, elegant men and women advertised expensive horsy clothing. There were advertisements at the end of the magazine—horses for sale, jobs vacant and future shows. Almost on the last page someone had doodled round one of the announcements, making a frame of heavy biro lines.

"Whareton Horse Sale," read Jinny. "Largest Horse Sale of the North. Whareton Sale Ground. Thursday, April 20th. Commences 10.00 a.m."

"Sue, listen!" Jinny screamed, and read the sale announcement out to Sue. "That's this Thursday. Not tomorrow but the next day. Look, they've marked it out specially."

Sue snatched the magazine from Jinny. "Yes!" she shouted. "Yes! That's it. That's where they're taking them."

"Must be," declared Jinny. "Must be. Look at the size of it. 'Over two hundred and eighty horses and ponies.' They'd think that no one would ever find stolen animals amongst that lot."

"Bet that's where they've taken them," said Sue.

"Come on," urged Jinny. "We've got to phone Miss Tuke."

"We've got to get there," Jinny said, as they hustled the ponies back down the track. "We must be there."

"If Miss Tuke won't go, will your dad take us?" asked Sue.

"Might," said Jinny. "If he won't, we'll go by train. I've got enough money for fares in my box."

"How will we get them home?"

"Take bridles," said Jinny. "Ride them home."

"But what about . . ." began Sue, then stopped.

Jinny didn't ask her what she had been going to say. For a second it had all seemed possible. The chance of finding the *Horse and Hound* had been so lucky that she had dismissed the necessity of getting to Whareton, the impossibility of finding Shantih and Bramble amongst so many horses.

"We will get there," she said to Sue. "We will find them. We MUST."

CHAPTER NINE

"I'll come round right away," Miss Tuke said, when Jinny phoned her. "Get all the gen." And in no time Miss Tuke's Pine Trekking Centre van was parked outside Finmory and Miss Tuke was inside, drinking coffee and listening intently to Sue and Jinny.

"First things first. Have you phoned the police?"

Mr. Manders said he had and that they were going up to Barony Farm first thing the next morning.

"Excellent," said Miss Tuke. "I'll phone when I get back home. Must link up with the police at Whareton Sale. Have our work cut out trying to track them down at that rodeo."

"You mean you'll take us? You'll go?" demanded Jinny.

Although it was still only the early evening, the one thing Jinny wanted to do was sleep. She hadn't even had enough energy left to think about how they would get to Whareton if Miss Tuke hadn't wanted to go to the sale.

"Take my horsebox," said Miss Tuke. "Bring the four of them home in that. *If* we find them. Who's coming? Jinny? Sue? How about a man? Might need some brawn. Mr. Manders?"

"Can't possibly. I've an article to write for Monday. It must be posted by Friday and I haven't even started it."

"Ken?" asked Jinny.

Ken was sitting on the floor, Kelly stretched beside him.

"Me? Go to a horse sale?" he asked incredulously. "I would go frantic!" And he waved his arms, windmill about his head, fighting off the imagined horrors of the place. "No way."

"Please," said Jinny. "To find Shantih and Bramble. Please." But Ken didn't answer.

Jinny was too weary to argue and Miss Tuke had already abandoned the idea.

"I'll be over tomorrow night about ten. Must trek tomorrow. Arranged for the trekkers to be Inverburgh shoppers on Thursday. We'll drive by night. Reach Whareton sevenish. Give us time for breakfast and be in plenty of time for the sale."

Miss Tuke stood up, slapping her hands, palm down, on to the table.

"We'll show them," she said. "Whoever they are they won't get away with this."

As Miss Tuke passed behind Jinny's chair she clapped her hand on Jinny's shoulder. "Don't forget that mad creature's bridle. Don't want you being dragged round a horse sale trying to control her in a halter."

Jinny tried to smile, knew that Miss Tuke was being optimistic to make her feel better, but her face wouldn't move. It was as if her muscles weren't strong enough, had suddenly grown too tired, as if all her energy was being used up to keep her acting in the same way as other people, to stop her running madly round the house screaming, crying out that they must find Shantih and Bramble and bring them home, that they couldn't go on being polite and ordinary when something as terrible as this had happened.

"I won't forget," said Jinny.

"Well done," said Miss Tuke. "That's the spirit. Warm clothes and flasks. Be ready."

Although Jinny had felt so tired, when she did get to bed she couldn't sleep. She lay talking to Sue until Sue's answers became more and more drowsy and eventually stopped altogether.

Still Jinny couldn't sleep. She heard her parents and Ken going to bed and then the house settling into silence. She counted to one hundred and then back to one, but still there was nothing in her mind but the misery of Shantih gone "and no more mine."

"Where is she now?" Jinny thought wretchedly. "Now, this very minute?" And because the worst was possible—that already she might have been slaughtered—the best was possible too—that Shantih might have kicked her way to freedom and found her way back to Finmory, might be standing at the field gate waiting.

Jinny jumped out of bed and looked out. There was just enough moonlight to be certain that Shantih was not there.

Jinny turned and padded through to the other half of her bedroom. She stood in front of the mural of the Red Horse. It seemed to glow in the darkness, its yellow eyes blazing as it charged from the wall through the painted blue-green branches and the heavy-petalled flowers.

Although she knew it was only a painting, there was a part of Jinny that was afraid of the Horse. The dark, secret part of Jinny that she kept battened down, knew the Horse as a magic power. Now, in the darkness, it pushed up into Jinny's consciousness and because it was night-time she held out her hands to the Horse and whispered Shantih's name.

"Shantih," she mouthed, "Shantih," over and over again as if it was a spell or an incantation.

Jinny did not know how long she stood there, but when at last she stopped repeating the name she knew that Ken must come with them to Whareton Sale. If Ken did not come, they would not find Shantih.

Miss Tuke phoned before breakfast to tell Jinny to be sure to bring her insurance certificate with her.

"I'll bring Bramble's. Proof of ownership might be necessary."

"She's not insured," said Jinny.

"Predictable," said Miss Tuke. "Then go over to the vet's this morning and get him to sign a description of Shantih, stating that he's willing to identify her if necessary."

Sue and Jinny rode over to the vet's.

"I'd know her all right," he assured them, as he signed Jinny's description. "This to prove ownership? Miss Tuke should have no trouble. Most of hers are marked. One you have, the black Highland, he's got a nick in his right ear. That'll be noted on her insurance."

"That's right, he has," said Jinny. "I just thought it was where he had cut himself at some time."

The afternoon was endless. Jinny suffocated under minutes as long as hours.

"We should be doing something NOW," she nagged at Sue, who was reading.

"Nothing we can do," said Sue, not lifting her head.

Restlessly, Jinny went to look for Ken but couldn't find him. She trailed up to her bedroom to stand in front of the Red Horse, but by day it was only a painting and could tell her nothing.

Jinny sat on her windowsill, staring out at the empty field, at the sea, shades of amethyst under the clear spring sky. Sometimes in her imagination she walked into the sale to find Shantih straight away, standing tied in a row of horses, turning to whinny as she recognised Jinny; and Bramble, glowering to himself under his forelock, furious that any self-respecting trekking pony should have been treated in this way. And sometimes they were driving back to Finmory, the horsebox empty and rattling. How would that be? Where would she look next? What would she do then?

"If Ken doesn't come, I won't find her," thought Jinny. "He must come," and she went back to searching for him.

At last she found him working in the kitchen garden.

"I've been looking for you everywhere," declared Jinny. "Where have you been?"

"Here and there," said Ken vaguely.

"You will come with us to the sale, won't you? It's to find Shantih. If you don't come, I'm sure we won't find her. Miss Tuke's O.K. but she's not like you. She'll organise things, but you'd look. If Shantih and Bramble are there, you'd find them."

Ken lent on his fork, staring into the distance.

"It will be like torture for me," he said. "Terrified animals. Men shouting, hitting them. Horses that have worked all their lives for humans, chucked out like garbage."

"It's to find Shantih and Bramble. To save them. It's for them. And some of the horses that are there will be going to good homes."

"If you cared even that for an animal," said Ken, snapping his fingers, "would you send it to a sale? They're wild, free creatures and we've taken them and nailed metal to their feet and put metal in their mouths. They are all created wind-swift and beautiful. What would it be like, a true sharing between men and horses? And look what we do to them."

"I know," said Jinny. "I do know and I want it to be like that too—riding bareback without bridles, only love. But it's not like that. Shantih's real and it's the real Shantih I love. That's why I've got to go to this sale and find her. If you come, we'll find her. I asked the Red Horse and you *must* come with us."

Never in a hundred years would Jinny have told anyone else but Ken about the Red Horse, but she knew that he would understand.

"I'll come," said Ken. "I would have come anyway. It's just that when something like this comes up, I always try to find ways round it, ways out. Really, I'm soft through and through," and he smiled in self-mockery. "We'll find them. Let us cultivate our little gardens." And Ken went on digging.

Mrs. Manders had made a special evening meal, but there was only Jinny and Sue to share it with her. Mike was at Ardtallon at a football match, Mr. Manders was writing, and Ken was eating his usual meal of brown rice and vegetables.

"Look at it this way," Mrs. Manders said, trying to cheer Jinny up a little. "If you hadn't found the *Horse and Hound* with the sale marked in it, you would be sitting here with absolutely no idea of where to look for them. At least this way you can do something positive."

"It's no use," said Jinny, pushing away the plate of her favourite chocolate peppermint ice cream. "I can't eat any more. I know you're right and that's sensible, but it's not the way I feel."

Tears were hot behind her eyes and she got up quickly and ran out of the room.

"I'd be just the same if it was Pippen," Sue said. Ever since Shantih and Bramble had been stolen she had been making nightly reverse-charge phone calls to check that Pippen was recovering satisfactorily from his warble, but really to know that he was safe. "If it was Pippen, I don't know what I'd do."

"What is Jinny going to do if she doesn't find her at this sale?" said Mrs. Manders.

Miss Tuke arrived shortly after ten. She refused coffee and bustled Sue, Jinny, Ken and Kelly into the cabin of her horsebox. Sue had a shopper with four flasks in it, two with soup and two with coffee, and several bags of Mrs. Manders' sandwiches and baking.

"Glad to see we won't starve," beamed Miss Tuke.

Jinny had two halters and Shantih's bridle. It had been almost dark when she had at last forced herself to go down to the stables to fetch them. It had felt strange, taking Shantih's bridle from its hook, as if it were an action that had once been familiar and that she hadn't done for years. Yet it was only three days since she had last ridden Shantih; four days since the gymkhana, when all that had mattered had been to win the cup. Jinny had hurried out of the stables not looking at the empty box, slamming the door behind her, shuddering as she tore up the path back to the security of the house.

"Phone us whenever you find them," Mr. Manders said, waving goodbye.

"We'll be thinking about you all the time," Mrs. Manders called. "Good luck. I'm sure you'll find them."

Spinning round in a ferocious U-turn, Miss Tuke drove the box down the drive.

"Map in the door pocket," she said. "Navigators all of you. Can't expect me to drive and map read."

The horsebox bounced along the narrow country roads, its headlights slashing swathes of silhouetted hedgerows and frantic glimpses of trees lit from beneath, that rose out of the blackness and fell away almost before Jinny's eyes could focus on them. It was an unending kaleidoscope of electric colour. Gradually the twisting leafy roads gave way to broader roads that looped over rolling hills.

"Be on the motorway soon," Miss Tuke said. "Stop for a bite of grub before that."

Squashed in the cabin they shared soup and rolls and apple pie.

"Straight on to Whareton," Miss Tuke announced, as they drove on to the motorway.

At first, Jinny tried to keep awake, gripped by the phantasmagoria of motorway signs that sprang at them from the darkness like weird electronic ghouls on a ghost-train ride. Cars and coaches zoomed past them, zombies crouched over steering wheels, whey-faced passengers staring out from their glass cages. All bound on desperation errands they hurtled through the night.

Kelly and Sue were fast asleep. Ken stared, glaze-eyed, straight ahead. Miss Tuke swore at other drivers and Jinny fought to stay awake, to experience the force and power of this unknown night world. But in spite of herself, her eyes closed, her head dropped heavily on to her chest and she slept.

"Stopping here for the loo," roused Miss Tuke. "Then coffee."

Jinny jerked awake from a dream of Shantih, fumbled out of the cabin more than half asleep.

Back in the box she clutched her mug of steaming coffee in both hands. Her teeth chattered. She was drawn tight and shivering into the clenched centre of herself, was glad of the warm crush of bodies in the cabin, glad of Miss Tuke's bouncy self-confidence. She stared out at the brilliantly-lit concrete-and-glass, science-fiction structure of the service point where they had stopped, and shivered uncontrollably. Ken put his arm, tight and strong, round her shoulders.

"It's a nightmare," he whispered. "See it for the dream it is. Be without fear."

"Four hours more and we'll be there," announced Miss Tuke, stabbing the map with her blunt forefinger. "We'll contact the police whenever we arrive. They'll know about us."

The next time Jinny woke, the motorway was bordered by rows of red-brick houses and brick-edged patches of garden. The morning sky was aflame with scarlet and sun-gold clouds.

They drove through the empty streets of Whareton and stopped for breakfast at an all-night café.

"Straight on here, right, second left at traffic lights, then on until we see the sale ground," Miss Tuke said, repeating the directions the waitress had given them.

Above the high, wrought-iron gates set in the blank, whitewashed wall, Jinny read the giant letters of WHARETON SALE GROUNDS. Somehow the night had brought her from Finmory to here. Had Shantih and Bramble travelled the same road? Or were they still on the road, swaying to the movements of the box that was bringing them to the sale?

Jinny forced all doubt from her mind. Ken had come with them. They would find Shantih.

CHAPTER TEN

Miss Tuke followed the arrows that pointed the way to where the horseboxes were to be parked. She drove into a large, gravelled parking area. Already horseboxes and floats were fringing the space. Two bay ponies were tied up outside one of the boxes. A man led a black thoroughbred out of a trailer and across the parking space. It reared up, striking out against the grey city sky. Three children with riding crops and noise tried to persuade a stubborn pony to leave its box and risk the perilous journey down the ramp. Anticipation tingled in the air.

"Sale starts at ten," said Miss Tuke. "We'll each get a sale catalogue. Jinny and I will go to see the auctioneers and the police. Ken and Sue, split up. Look around. Remember they may have changed the ponies' appearance. Bramble has a nick, halfway down the inside of his right ear. My two are mouse duns—mouse colour with darker manes and tails. They've feathers at their heels, but they may have been clipped. Moll is 13.2, Polly slightly higher. Both galled on their front legs. Farmer I bought them from used to hobble them. Shouldn't think they could disguise that."

Jinny tried to concentrate on what Miss Tuke was saying, knowing it was important, but she could hardly stand still for her eagerness to be in the sale ground. Her eyes checked on every least movement in case it should be Shantih.

"Meet back here at a quarter to ten," finished Miss Tuke. "We'll arrange a rota for watching the sale ring." And she marched into the sale ground, Jinny trotting at her side.

Most of the sale ground was divided into pens by metal bars, and, to Jinny's surprise, many of the pens already had ponies in them. Some were filled with a mass of youngsters, packed in so closely that heads rested on other pony's necks and on rumps still fluffy with their baby coats. Their eyes were staring, their nostrils wide, their ears trembling to the sights and sounds of this alien place. Numbers were pasted on their rumps.

"Scrub," said Miss Tuke. "Been here all night."

For a moment, Jinny allowed herself to see it as Ken would see it. Saw the snatches of fern and grasses in the ponies' manes and tails and knew that they must have been separated from their herd, brought from open spaces to the waiting cattle float. She felt the terror of the journey to the sale, saw the stark panic in their eyes as they waited. She knew what Ken meant when he talked about the screaming of the animals.

"Don't," said Jinny to herself. "Don't see it. Don't let it get at you. You're here to find Shantih. There's nothing you can do. Horse sales go on all the time. Slaughterhouses kill animals all the time, everyday. You're here to find Shantih and Bramble. That's what you're here for."

"Brisk up, Jennifer Manders," said Miss Tuke, as if she could read Jinny's thoughts.

Jinny pushed her long hair back from her face, squared her shoulders and shook the weariness of the night's journey out of her head.

"Right," she said. "I'm here."

They went first to the auctioneer's office where two young men were drinking tea and arranging papers.

"The police will have informed you about us," Miss Tuke told them. "We're down from Inverburgh. Chasing stolen horses. Tuke is the name. Three Highlands and one Arab. More or less certain they're here."

"You need to see Mr. Forrest, the auctioneer, ducks. He'll be here in half an hour."

"We'll be back," said Miss Tuke, and they went in search of a policeman.

The one they found was decidedly younger than the two men in the auctioneer's office. Miss Tuke regarded him with displeasure.

"Officer," she said, standing squarely in front of him. "I am Tuke. Miss Tuke . . ."

"Ah, good," said the policeman. "Stolen ponies, isn't it? Got the details here." He flicked open a notebook.

"And an Arab," said Jinny.

"Chestnut," read the policeman. "White face, four white stockings. Five/six years of age."

Jinny was speechless at such efficiency. For a moment it almost seemed as if the policeman would point to a horse-box, telling her that she would find Shantih inside it, but he only took his walkie-talkie out and called up two other policemen. When they arrived, one was comfortingly older than Miss Tuke.

"If you spot the horses, let us know. Don't do anything yourselves unless the situation is desperate, then be sure to send someone for us at once. We want you to get your horses back but we also want to catch the men who did it. Been getting away with far too much of this sort of thing.

Been a lot of it in the north, but if it's the same bunch, they've never been so far as Scotland before."

"Did you get the other horses back?" demanded Jinny. "The ones they stole before?"

"Don't you worry yourself about that," said the older policeman—adult speaking to child—"you enjoy yourself. Have a good day at the sale," so that Jinny's faith in him vanished.

"Should we find anything," continued the policeman to Miss Tuke, "we'll call you over the loudspeakers. We'll keep our eyes skinned and keep a watch on the meat men. They often buy up ponies before they get near the ring. Swop them from the box that brings them here into their own."

As the policemen left, the young man winked at Jinny, giving her the thumbs-up sign. Jinny grinned back, her eyes searching the sale ground for Ken.

They went back to the auctioneer's office and found Mr. Forrest, who was more interested in his sale than in stolen ponies.

"Shall we leave it in the hands of the police?" he said.

"Here are the details of the stolen ponies," said Miss Tuke, ignoring his suggestion.

"Two mouse-dun Highlands, one black Highland," said Mr. Forrest, reading Miss Tuke's list. "Common," he said. "Be about sixty Highlands here today. Check the catalogue for yourselves. No saying what colour yours will be by now. Chestnut Arab. Now we might notice her. Don't see them so often. A few here today."

"We'll be at the ringside," said Miss Tuke. "Might have to cause a disturbance. You'll know what's what." Then she stomped back out to the sale ground.

Everywhere that Jinny looked there were horses and ponies. Some were tied in rows to rings set in the walls, some jigsawed into the chequered pattern of pens now nearly all filled with animals.

Children climbed on the bars between the pens. Boys with sticks copied their elders, thumping and banging on unsuspecting rumps. Girls held out sweets. Men struggled to control fit horses excited by the noise and smells of the place. Women in headsquares, sheepskin jackets and boots led in native ponies. Horsy mothers walked beside children, demonstrating the patent safety qualities of the pony they had outgrown.

There were horses and ponies of every shape, size, type and temperament. Far, far more than Jinny had expected to find.

Jinny paused, staring round, wondering if any of the men who jostled about her might be the men who had stolen Shantih and Bramble, might be the dreaded meat men, for they must be there although there was nothing to distinguish them from any other person at the sale. Jinny longed to run wildly through the sale ground calling Shantih's name, searching until she found her.

"Catalogues," said Miss Tuke, looking at her watch. "Then back to the others. Don't wilt yet."

Ken and Kelly were waiting for them. Sue came running up minutes later.

"There are so many," she gasped. "Masses of Highlands, but I haven't seen any Arabs yet."

"We'll take it in turn to wait here," Miss Tuke said, leading the way to the entrance to the sale ring. "Best place. Spot them as they're waiting to come into the ring. Galls on the forelegs above the fetlock. Check every Highland in case they've been at them with a paint pot. You'll all know Bramble and Shantih. Anything remotely Brambleish, check his ear. Nick on the right ear. O.K.?"

They said it was.

"I'll take the first hour, then you lot come back here and we'll see how we're doing."

Ken's face was set into a hard mask—mouth clenched, eyes ablaze with disgust at all that he saw around him.

"I've started working my way round the pens," said Sue. "So I'll just go on. A lot of them have Highlands in them."

"I'm going to search for Arabs," said Jinny, ducking away from Ken. Having forced him to come, she felt too guilty to stay with him.

She hurried down the rows of tied horses, hope springing as she saw chestnut hocks and quarters; fading when a chestnut head with a Roman nose and piggy eyes looked round at her. Twice Jinny caught a glimpse of horses that for a rending second she thought must be Shantih, but when she got closer to them they were not anything like her.

The catalogue said there were six Arabs. Jinny found them all—one sorrel and five greys. Not one of them could possibly have been Shantih.

"Whoever stole them must have made their entries before they knew what horses they would be bringing," Jinny thought. "So probably Shantih won't be entered as an Arab. She'll be 'Lady's riding mare' or 'Well-mannered hack'."

"Will Miss Tuke come immediately to the main gates," boomed the loudspeaker. "Miss Tuke is wanted at the main gates."

Jinny froze, hardly able to believe her ears.

"It means they've found them," she cried to a complete stranger, before she ran, dodging and skipping through the crowd, towards the main gates.

"If Miss Tuke has left the ringside there's no one to watch the horses they're selling now," Jinny thought suddenly. "They may not have found them all. Shantih could be in the ring now and we'd miss her."

Jinny spun round and dashed to the sale ring. Ken was standing at the entrance.

"I'm here instead of Miss Tuke," he said.

"Shall I stay?"

Ken didn't answer, and after a minute Jinny decided that there was no point in both of them being there.

"I'll go and see what's happening," she said, not exactly speaking to Ken, rather announcing her departure.

There was only the young policeman at the gates.

"I heard you calling Miss Tuke," Jinny told him.

"We've got two of your horses," he said. "They're over by one of the pens." He pointed to where Jinny could just make out policemen's uniforms among the crowds.

"Only two," thought Jinny, as she raced across. "Oh, please God, let it be Shantih and Bramble. Let one of them be Shantih."

Miss Tuke was holding the halter ropes of two mouse-dun Highlands. It was Miss Tuke's ponies they had found. Jinny stopped dead in her tracks. Not Shantih, not Bramble, but two trekking ponies that Miss Tuke would sell tomorrow if she had a good enough offer for them.

"I found them," yelled Sue, sparkling with achievement. "I spotted their legs."

Jinny couldn't make herself speak.

"I know it's not Shantih," Sue added, seeing Jinny's face. "But it proves we're right. They have brought them here. The others must be here too. We'll find them next."

A white-haired man wearing a stockman's coat was standing between the two policemen, while Miss Tuke was showing them official-looking documents.

"States there under 'Distinguishing Features'—galled in both forlegs. Rest of the description fits to a T. Without a doubt, they are my beasts," she was saying.

"Ain't nothing to do with me," stated the white-haired man. "The gaffer tells me what horseflesh to bring here and I brings it. No questions. You can't pin nothing on me. Two carthorses and these two here. Picked them up in the yards this morning. Brought them in here now. You ain't got nothing on me. The gaffer's the one you want."

"We're quite satisfied that they're yours," one of the policemen said to Miss Tuke. "I'll keep the insurance certificates and we'll be in touch with you later."

"Is it in order to put them in my box? Take them back with us tonight?"

"Under the circumstances, quite in order. You won't be selling them before the whole matter is cleared up, will you? We may need you to give evidence if we can get a case together."

"Don't forget there's two more," said Jinny. "The Arab and the black Highland. You've got to find them as well."

"Eleven o'clock, miss, and fifty per cent of the stolen property returned. We'll sort out the rest before much longer."

"They seem none the worse for it," declared Miss Tuke, after she had examined her ponies. "Not starving, either," she said, when they had watered them and loaded them into the box and the ponies were nosing, without interest, at the armfuls of hay that Miss Tuke had just given to them.

"If only they could talk, they could tell us where they've been," said Jinny, a lump choking in her throat. It should have been Shantih and Bramble who were standing there. She knew she should have been glad that Miss Tuke had rescued her ponies, but she wasn't. It was Shantih and Bramble she wanted.

"Now, let's get on with it," said Miss Tuke, thumping her hand down on one of the solid rumps. "Ken's standing duty at the ringside. Help me get this ramp up and we'll get going."

Jinny went outside to a barren stretch of waste ground at the side of the sale ground. Here the worst of the ponies and horses were standing, tethered to rails. She walked between the rows of animals, her feelings numbed by what she saw. Rheumy, dull eyes were half hidden under drooping eyelids, worn out heads hung down from slack necks, brittle stick legs supported ridged ribs and jutting hip bones. Many were galled or scarred. Hardly any of them had the energy left to look round when Jinny passed them.

She forced herself to walk along the rows of horses until she had seen them all. Neither Shantih nor Bramble were there.

Jinny went back to the covered part of the sale ground and once more went round the horses that were tied to the wall. Already there were gaps where horses had been bought and taken away. It was already possible that Shantih had been there and they had missed her.

Jinny wached at the ringside from two until three. Halfway through her hour, Ken joined her.

"Why must they hit them?" he asked, as yet another pony was chased round the ring to the accompaniment of the auctioneer's patter.

"Makes them look lively," said Jinny bitterly.

She was watching a nappy chestnut pony being ridden round the ring by a scared child, when Ken touched her arm.

"That one," he said, and drew her attention to a black pony that was next but one to come into the ring.

The pony had a hogged mane, clipped heels and a ridiculously short tail. His face had a white blaze and he had four white socks above his blue-black hooves.

"I'll get the police," said Ken. "Stop them going into the ring if you have to."

"Why?" Jinny asked, but Ken had gone.

Jinny walked over to the black pony. Ken couldn't possibly have thought it was Bramble. The pony looked almost a hand higher than Bramble. Bramble's neck was thick, short-set, and his head far heavier than this pony's. Then the pony turned round and looked at Jinny. She knew him at once. It was Bramble.

Jinny threw her arms round his neck, ran her hand over his withers and down his strong, square back. Touching him, she knew immediately that it really was Bramble. If Jinny had been blind she would have known him.

"Here, enough of that," said the man who was with Bramble.

Jinny scowled at him, wondering if he had stolen the ponies, had stolen Shantih.

"He's such a super pony," Jinny said, remembering that she had to stop them going into the ring. She ran Bramble's ears through her hands and felt the nick on the inside of his right one.

"Give over," said the man, pushing Jinny away.

"I'm only looking at him," said Jinny, in a Clare Burnley voice. "I do think he is such a super pony."

The auctioneer's hammer knocked down the chestnut pony. The scared child, wiping her eyes on the sleeve of her jacket, was led out of the ring and a piebald pony was led in. Bramble was next.

"I think he's absolutely what we are looking for," said Jinny. "I know mummy will just love him."

"Well, let your mum bid for him when I take him into the ring. You clear off."

"Do you need to take him into the ring?" said Jinny, searching desperately for any sign of Ken returning with the police. "I know we'll want to have him. He is just what we've been looking for. Can't you wait here and we'll buy him from you? Whatever price you like."

"You barmy or what?" said the man, glaring suspiciously at Jinny as the bidding for the piebald rose steadily.

The piebald was sold and still there was no sign of Ken.

"You can't," said Jinny. "You can't take him into the ring." But already the piebald was out of the ring and the man was leading Bramble in.

"No!" cried Jinny. "Stop!" But the man strode past her and the auctioneer started the bidding.

Jinny stared round the sale ring. There was still no sign of the policemen, Miss Tuke, Sue or Ken. Cupping her hands round her mouth, Jinny bellowed their names.

"Quickly! Come quickly!" she roared. "Bramble's in the ring."

Then she dashed across the ring to the foot of the auctioneer's stand.

"That's one of them," she said, shouting up at the auctioneer. "One of the stolen ponies we told you about. He can't sell it. It doesn't belong to him. Ken's gone for the police."

From the tiered seats around the sale ring, people began to stand up to get a better view of the disturbance, their voices rising in a buzz of curiosity.

The man leading Bramble told Jinny to get out or he'd get the police to her.

"You saw me this morning," Jinny shouted at the auctioneer. "I'm with Miss Tuke."

The auctioneer looked down at Jinny with obvious disapproval. For a moment she thought that he too was going to tell her to go away, but then, to her relief, two of the policemen came running into the ring. One spoke to the man with Bramble and took him out of the ring, the other explained what was happening to the auctioneer.

"He wouldn't listen to me," Jinny said, as she hurried over to where Miss Tuke was being loud and definite.

"Utterly positive," she was saying. "Bred him myself. That's my mark on his ear. All that white they've daubed over him—that'll come off. Daresay a good shower of rain would shift the lot."

To Jinny's dismay, the man with Bramble swore that he knew nothing about him. He said he was a cattle dealer and he had only brought Bramble in to the sale as a favour to a friend of his.

"Chap called Vernon, Sid Vernon. Dealer he is. Deals in anything. Told me the pony belonged to a kid and he wanted it selling, quiet like, so there'd be no fuss with the kid. He's done a few favours for me, on and off like. Wasn't doing anything special today myself so I said I'd oblige and bring the pony in for him. Don't know more than that. You check up on him."

"Might be just what we had in mind, a little checking up," said one of the policemen.

"Three of them," said Miss Tuke with satisfaction, when the policemen had got all the details they needed from her and one of them had gone with the man to Sid Vernon's yard. "But no nearer to getting to the bottom of all this—finding out who is responsible for it."

"Would you have known Bramble?" Sue asked.

When they had examined Bramble carefully they had found black roots on all his white parts, where they had been bleached.

"Known him anywhere," said Miss Tuke.

"I would never have known him," declared Sue.

Jinny said nothing. Once Ken had pointed Bramble out to her then she had known him, but not before. Earlier in the morning she must have passed him and not recognised him. "But I would know Shantih," she thought. "No matter what they've done to her, I would know her."

"Where is she?" Jinny whispered to Bramble. "What have they done to her?"

It was late afternoon before the policeman came to tell Miss Tuke that there had been no one at Sid Vernon's yard.

"Drew a blank at his house as well. Next-door neighbour said he is away a lot. But we'll get him. From the looks of his yard, I'd say he's only a middleman. We'll find out though. We're keeping the other man for questioning."

By five o'clock there were only a few animals left. The last of the bidding was over, the seats round the ring empty.

Jinny walked intently round the sale ground, moving from one horse to the next, ignoring the empty rings hanging from the walls and the empty pens. Only a few hours ago they had been full of life. The whole sale ground had been filled with men and animals, loud with voices and the ring of hooves. Now it was almost silent. A few hours ago, Jinny had been filled with hope that she would find Shantih, that by now they would have been driving home to Finmory, and by tomorrow Shantih would have been back in her own field.

Why had they found the ponies and not Shantih? Why had Shantih not been at the sale? Or had she been there and Jinny hadn't recognised her? Seen her and hadn't known her? Or had missed her? Had Shantih been one of the horses that had been taken from one box into another? Had she never been brought into the sale?

Jinny was almost running now. So clearly in her mind's eye she could see the flat curve of Shantih's cheek, the flare of her nostrils, the shell curve of her ears, and her dark eyes watching for her mistress.

"Shantih," Jinny called silently. "Shantih." And clearly in her mind's ear was the sound of Shantih's answering whinny.

Conspicuous now that the sale ground was nearly empty, Jinny dashed to and fro between the few horses that were left; avoiding Miss Tuke, Ken and Sue; refusing to admit that Shantih was not there; refusing to start on the night journey back to Finmory without her horse.

Miss Tuke appeared, marching between the pens towards Jinny.

"Well, that's that," she said, pouncing on Jinny. "Got to get back. Three out of four. Pretty good. At least you've got Bramble back."

Jinny couldn't speak. It wasn't possible. Not possible that they hadn't found Shantih.

"Right then. Off we go," said Miss Tuke.

CHAPTER ELEVEN

They drove through the city, then through the red-brick suburbs where dual carriageway changed into motorway. The wheels of the box purred along the road to the north.

Miss Tuke and Sue discussed the sale. Ken sat silently while Kelly slept with his head on Ken's knee. Behind them the three ponies shifted their weight to keep their balance as the box swung round corners.

Jinny sat staring through the cab window, seeing nothing, hearing nothing. Things had no names, were strangely flat and distant. Her touch carried no messages to her brain. There was nothing but a metal pain. The moment when the dentist's drill touched the nerve in her tooth, the flash second of unendurable agony, was locked hard and heavy and constant in her head and chest.

"Shantih! Shantih! Shantih!"

Jinny gritted her teeth to lock in the sound. If it escaped she wouldn't be able to stop the scream going on and on, wiping her out.

"Don't know about you lot," said Miss Tuke, "but I could do with a good meal, something you can get a knife and fork into. Utter disgrace having no decent catering at a place the size of that sale ground. We'll stop at the first service point."

"They're very expensive, motorway stops," said Sue doubtfully. "Dad says they're daylight robbery."

"On me," said Miss Tuke. "Left to myself, I'd still have been chasing the tinkers round Alec's farm."

"In that case, I'm starving," agreed Sue.

"What about Ken?" asked Miss Tuke. "Chips? Baked beans?"

"Miss Tuke's going to buy us a meal," Sue told Ken. "Will you have chips and baked beans?"

Ken showed no sign of having heard her. They turned off the motorway and drove into the car park at the side of the service station. Glass doors opened on to a brilliantly-lit hall, a self-service shop dazzled under neon lighting, teenage boys played slot machines and, at the far end of the hallway, concrete stairs led up to a cafeteria.

"Everybody out," said Miss Tuke.

"For lady you walk through hell," said Ken, as the glass doors opened in front of them and they drowned in the electric glare.

Jinny followed them in. If she had stayed alone in the horsebox she would have started to cry, and she couldn't do that until she was alone at Finmory.

They climbed the stairs and walked along a glass and concrete tube that crossed the motorway. It lay beneath them, a ribbon of light, constant movement that appeared to be motionless.

The self-service cafeteria was neon-lit and plastic. The tables, chairs and floor were plastic. Ranged along a metal and plastic counter were plates of food sealed over with polythene. Even the people were plastics—the night travellers, grey plastic; the waitresses who hovered behind the counter waiting to replace the plates of plastic food, were made of shiny pink and white plastic.

Miss Tuke and Sue filled their trays with food, Jinny took two egg sandwiches wrapped in polythene and Ken an apple.

"Take the seeds home and plant them. A real orchard springing up from a place like this," he said, not eating it but putting it in his pocket.

Jinny took one bite of her sandwich, chewed on the mixture of tough egg, yellow grease and cotton-wool bread. She left the rest. Miss Tuke and Sue started on their tomato soup, telling each other how hungry they were.

Suddenly Ken sprang up, angular, long-haired. He leapt through the cafeteria, out through the glass doors, and danced his way along the glass tunnel in a weird silhouette of freedom.

"Where's he off to now?" demanded Miss Tuke, while Sue stared in shocked disbelief at such behaviour.

"Fresh air," said Jinny. "He can't breathe in a place like this."

"He is unbalanced," judged Miss Tuke. "If he were a horse I'd have him shot."

Jinny waited until Miss Tuke and Sue had started on their fish and chips, then she made an excuse and went to find Ken.

She searched through the complex but could see no sign of him. Only ghost people like herself wandered in this garish wilderness. She passed a young woman crying in an older man's arms, a screaming toddler being orbited along by his running mother, a boy with a blank, stoned face sitting staring at his own hand.

"Maybe they are all like me," Jinny thought. "All the people who are here are here because something dreadful has happened to them."

She went out into the dark.

"You will never see Shantih again. Never," she told herself. Having had Ken with them had made no difference. Bramble would be back in his field tomorrow, but not Shantih. Never, ever again would she look out of her bedroom window, call "Shantih" and hear her horse's answering whinny.

"Don't cry," Jinny told herself. "Not yet. Don't start."

Ken materialised at her side. Kelly pushed his wet nose against her hand. They walked together through the car park, past the towering bulk of container lorries and tankers, trucks and cars.

"We are their prey," said Ken. "They've captured us and brought us here. While we are inside, the electricity sucks life from us," and he leapt in karate chops against the cars and lorries.

From one of the parked floats came the sound of cattle. For an instant, Jinny didn't realise what the noise meant. She only thought of it as a farm noise, a comforting, country sound. Then she felt Ken stiffen, and realised that they were cattle being taken to market, or already sold and on their way to the slaughterhouse.

Jinny shuddered and turned quickly away, not looking at the float.

"No you don't," said Ken. He caught her by the arm and forced her to turn round. "You made me come to the sale, so now you look. See what I see," he said, as Jinny struggled to escape from him, run to the other end of the car park and shut herself away in Miss Tuke's box.

The float was packed with calves. Through the open slats Jinny saw their dark eyes, doe-gentle, liquid, reflecting neon light, glistening muzzles and moving shadows cast by their bat ears.

"They are so beautiful," said Ken. "Each one perfect and this is what we do to them."

"Let me go," cried Jinny, but Ken ignored her.

"Breathe with love," he said. "Give them your silence. Let them know that there are humans who care." And he forced Jinny to stand silently, to be aware.

As Jinny stood there, it did seem that the calves knew they were there, as if they shared some dim understanding.

"They do know," said Ken at last. "We know when a God gives his attention to us; that moment, that inkling. We all know what it feels like. In the East, they know by the scent which God holds them in its hands."

Somewhere in the parking space a horse whinnied.

"Shantih!" screamed Jinny, and immediately she had broken from Ken's hold and was running through the rows of vehicles, shouting her horse's name at the top of her voice. "Shantih! Shantih!"

The whinnying that answered her was as frantic and desperate as Jinny's own voice.

"There," cried Jinny. "There. She's in that horsebox. We've found her. Shantih! Shantih!"

"You're certain it is her?" asked Ken.

"Totally positive. I'd know her whinny anywhere. It couldn't be any other horse. If there were a million other horses I'd know it was Shantih."

For a moment they both stood staring up at the box.

"Come on," said Jinny. "We've got to get in to her. Quick, before anyone comes."

The back of the horsebox was securely padlocked. Jinny sped round to the cabin. The passenger door was locked. Desperately she ran round to the driver's door. The metal handle moved beneath her hand. The unlocked door opened. Jinny scrambled inside. She saw a door at the back of the cabin and opened it with shaking hands.

For a second she stood, unable to move, hardly able to trust her eyes.

"Shantih!" she screamed, and in the instant had squeezed her way into the back of the box, to where Shantih was standing, tied to a rail at the side.

Jinny flung her arms round Shantih's neck and buried her face against her mane; tears poured down her face and her breath sobbed out of her body. She had found her horse, had broken free of the nightmare. It had not happened. It was not true.

Jinny ran her hands over Shantih's neck and head, felt her soft muzzle lipping against her cheek; her forelock and mane slipped like silk between Jinny's fingers. Quickly she checked over Shantih's legs and quarters, making certain that Shantih had not been harmed in any way. At the last minute of the eleventh hour the horror of losing Shantih had let her go.

"Is it her?" Ken asked from outside.

His voice brought Jinny back to the present and she scrambled out of the box.

"Yes," she told him. "We've got to get her out before the thieves come back." She looked hurriedly over her shoulder for any sign of the owners of the horsebox.

"Can't get her out," Ken said, "unless we've keys for the padlocks. Better get Miss Tuke."

"You go," said Jinny. "I'll stay here."

"Right," said Ken, and raced off into the darkness.

Left alone, Jinny felt suddenly vulnerable and afraid. If the horse thieves came back now she didn't know what she could do to stop them driving away. A sudden vivid picture flashed through her mind of the horsebox with Shantih inside it being driven away, while she stood helplessly watching it go.

"I've got to get inside with Shantih," Jinny thought. "If Ken gets back first with Sue and Miss Tuke I'll hear them, but if it's the horse thieves, at least I'll be with Shantih."

Jinny climbed into the cabin and then into the back of the box, carefully shutting all the doors behind her.

Shantih whickered a welcome, stretching out her head to breathe over Jinny.

"Where have you been?" Jinny whispered to her. "What did they do to you?" She stood waiting, one arm over Shantih's withers, her ears peeled for the sound of Ken bringing Miss Tuke and Sue.

"Perhaps they're phoning the police," Jinny thought, as each minute stretched out endlessly and still they did not come. "Oh, hurry, hurry. We've got to get out of here before they catch us."

The sound of footsteps came out of the darkness. Relief flooded over Jinny. It must be Ken, Miss Tuke and Sue. She waited, poised, listening for just another moment before she burst out of the box to join them; to tell Sue how she had heard Shantih; to listen to Miss Tuke's bossy efficiency taking charge of the rescue.

The footsteps drew nearer, but they were not Ken's slow stride, Miss Tuke's bustling or Sue's light step. They were strong and heavy and unknown. Biting her knuckles, Jinny waited, praying they would pass the horsebox and go on to another car or van.

She heard men's low, angry voices as they strode up to the box and climbed in.

Frantically, Jinny looked for somewhere to hide, but there was nowhere; no pile of straw or heap of rugs. She pressed herself against the back of the box where she would be hidden by the door opening from the cabin. If they only looked through the door at Shantih, there was a chance that she might not be noticed, but if one of the men came into the back of the box they were bound to see her.

The box started with a jerk as the driver swung out of the car park and on to the motorway. Standing in the darkness, Jinny could hear the sound of the men's voices. One seemed an older man with a deep sarcastic voice, while the other man, who was driving the float, sounded younger.

Now and again Jinny caught snatches of their conversation. The older man seemed to be the boss. He was called Major Fitzsimmons and obviously employed the younger man.

"All right for you," Jinny heard the younger man saying. "You're blooming calm you are, Major blooming Fitzsimmons. Picking up her ladyship and then stopping for a meal. You're O.K., you are." Then the words were lost in the crash and rattle of the horsebox.

"How do you know that Sid Vernon hasn't spilt the beans?" Jinny heard the young man demanding.

"Because, just like you, my dear boy, Sid doesn't know any beans worth spilling."

Straining her ears, Jinny tried to follow the conversation, but again the words were drowned by the noise of the box.

They seemed to have been driving for about half an hour when Jinny heard the older man beginning to open the door into the back of the box.

"I'll take a look at her," he was saying.

There was nothing Jinny could do. Only stand frozen, waiting.

The door opened, a man's head peered in at Shantih.

"Bright as the proverbial button," he said, shutting the door again, while Jinny's heart banged so loudly she was sure they must hear it in the cabin.

Suddenly Jinny heard the sound of a police siren growing louder and louder as a car scorched towards them.

"Lord, the blooming cops," swore the young man, and Jinny felt the box surge forward. The sudden movement threw her into a corner and made Shantih stagger and plunge to keep her balance.

"Slow down, you fool. What do you want them to think? That we've something to hide? They'll have us for speeding if you go on like that."

The police car drew level with the box, kept pace with it, its siren banshee above the traffic.

"Do what they want," Jinny heard the older man say. His voice without its edge of mockery was cold and rasping. "They've no evidence. Horse belongs to my daughter. Leave it to me. You're a hired driver, know nothing."

"I blooming told you we should have scarpered the minute they picked up the first two ponies," the young man muttered, as Jinny felt the box being driven on to the hard shoulder of the motorway and jammed to a halt.

She heard the police car scream in in front of them, its doors being opened and running footsteps race to the box. Holding her breath, she listened, hardly able to believe that the police had found them.

"Good evening, sir," said an official voice, as the door was opened. "Can we trouble you to take a look in the back? Reason to believe that you may be carrying something of interest to us."

"Good evening, officer," said the older man. "Rather a sudden demand. Got my daughter's horse in the back. If that's of interest to you, in you come."

Jinny heard the man jump out, the policeman climb into the cab and open the door. In a shaft of light, a helmeted head looked in at her.

Jinny stood with her arm round Shantih, opening and shutting her mouth, unable to think of a word to say. She was held in the policeman's torch like a rabbit in headlights. There was nothing in her mind but the incredible, dazed delight of the fact that now Shantih was truly safe.

The police contacted their station, where Miss Tuke, Ken and Sue had all been waiting. They arrived in the horsebox and Shantih was transferred to it. The two men were taken away for questioning.

"We thought we'd lost you too," Sue told Jinny, "when we got out to the car park and found the box had gone. Ken guessed that you must have gone with Shantih, so Miss Tuke rushed us off to the nearest police station. Ken had the number of the horsebox and the police did the rest. Whatever would you have done if we hadn't found you?"

"Dunno," said Jinny. "Hadn't thought. It didn't matter. All that mattered was that I'd found Shantih."

Back in the police station, Jinny told the policemen what she had overheard, showed them the description of Shantih signed by the vet and listened to Miss Tuke being loud and efficient. Jinny floated on a dream of delirious happiness. Shantih was safe.

"We've to thank you for tonight's work," the policeman said, as he came with them to the door of the station. "We've been on the lookout for Major Fitzsimmons, as he calls himself, for some time. We knew there was one man behind the horse thefts but we couldn't pin him down. Didn't want to bring in the little men until we'd got the brain behind them. Now, thanks to you, we've got him."

Jinny insisted on travelling in the back with Shantih. She stood leaning against the sides of the box, feeling Shantih's warm breath on her face, twisting strands of Shantih's mane between her fingers. The box rumbled into life, the ponies propping themselves on outstretched forelegs as Miss Tuke drove on to the motorway.

"Home," said Jinny, happiness bubbling in her. "Back to Finmory."

They had phoned Mr. and Mrs. Manders to let them know what had happened, and the lights were on in Finmory House as they drove up the drive. Jinny's parents and Mike were waiting at the door to welcome them.

Stiff-legged, Jinny stomped down the ramp, Shantih clattering at her side and jumping from the ramp with an enormous leap that almost dragged the halter from Jinny's grasp.

"Beyond me what you wanted her back for," said Mike, "the mad idiot," while Sue and Miss Tuke told them the details of their day.

Sue led Bramble and Jinny took Shantih, down through the garden to their field. In front of her, Jinny could just make out the bulk of Bramble, could just hear Sue chatting to him. The darkness was velvet soft about Jinny. From the shore she could make out the soft sighing of the sea. She sprang up on to Shantih's back and rode the last few steps to the field.

"I should have died if I hadn't found her," Jinny said,

leaning on the familiar field gate as Shantih thudded round the field.

"You wouldn't," said Sue.

"A bit of me would have," said Jinny. "Truly. A bit of my heart would have been torn out."

When they got back to the house, Miss Tuke was climbing into the cabin of her box.

"You're not going so soon?" shouted Jinny, who had been thinking of coffee and food, to be eaten slowly as they sat round the kitchen table reliving the day.

"Must. Trekking tomorrow. No peace for the wicked." Miss Tuke slammed the cabin door and switched on the engine.

"Thank you for everything," Jinny shouted. "Thank you."

"My pleasure," said Miss Tuke, thinking of tomorrow's trek. Then she suddenly stuck her head out of the cab window. "How are you getting to Inverburgh?" she asked.

"To where?" said Jinny, trying to think why Miss Tuke thought she wanted to go to Inverburgh.

"Saturday. The show. I'll phone you tomorrow night. See if you want a lift."

"But I can't take Shantih to the show," said Jinny. "Not after I've just rescued her."

"Why not? Day's rest tomorrow. Do her no harm."

Jinny stared up vacantly at Miss Tuke. It seemed like years since she had given a thought to Inverburgh Show.

"Can't let Clare Burnley win all the cups," laughed Miss Tuke, as she drove away.

CHAPTER TWELVE

The dew lay thickly on grass and hedgerows, diamonding spiders' webs, creating crystal palaces from last year's bracken. Jinny left a trail of dark footprints as she walked down to the horses' field in the early morning. She walked slowly, knowing there was no need to hurry, Shantih and Bramble were safe. Already she had seen them from her bedroom window, floating shapes in the morning mists.

Jinny climbed into the field and stood waiting as Shantih walked towards her, precise and delicate. The Arab's white stockings were darkened with dew, her ears listening for the sound of Jinny's voice, her nostrils trembling a welcome, her eyes under their long lashes glistened dark-silver. Jinny held out her hand and Shantih lipped gently over her palm. Finding nothing, she lifted her head, whiffled at Jinny's neck, tickling her ear.

Bramble, suspecting food, came trotting up. He still looked strangely shorn, and, despite herself, Jinny couldn't help smiling at the difference it had made to him.

"Wonder if you'll be able to jump any better without all that hair?" Jinny asked him, producing sugar lumps from her anorak pocket and giving them to Bramble and Shantih.

"Hi," said Ken, stopping on his way to the shore. "Settled in again?"

"If you hadn't come, we wouldn't have found Shantih," said Jinny.

The knowledge that Shantih was safely back in her field dazzled the whole of Jinny's being. She didn't know of anything that would have been enough to express the way she felt.

"If Miss Tuke and Sue hadn't been hungry we wouldn't have stopped at all," Ken said.

"But if you hadn't made me look at the calves I would have been back in Miss Tuke's box. I would never have heard Shantih from there. So nearly, nearly I would never have seen her again," Jinny said. "It was so lucky that she was there in the car park. Such a coincidence. Even now I can hardly believe it."

"Coincidence!" said Ken scornfully. "There's no such thing. It's a cover-up word for a chain reaction, a linking of incidents which we hardly understand. We're only beginning to be aware of them."

"What links brought Shantih to the car park?"

"Your love for her," said Ken slowly. "The tinker boy's courage. Me coming to the sale instead of chickening out? The calves? The men in the horsebox? Who knows? These and a billion more subtleties create what we call coincidence." He laughed, harsh and sudden. "We know nothing," he said, and, running his hand over Shantih's neck, he went on down to the sea.

"And what are you going to do today?" said Mrs. Manders, when the breakfast dishes had been washed up and put away.

"Lie in the sun," said Jinny. "I'm going to lie in Shantih's field and watch her. I might, just might, draw her as well."

"Hardly *Homes and Gardens'* idea of the ideal hostess," said Mrs. Manders. "What about Sue?"

"I shall sleep," said Sue. "Lie in Shantih's field and sleep."

"And there's Ewan MacKenzie's ponies. Have you to ride them back?"

"Not today," said Jinny. "We will, but not today."

Although Jinny took her drawing pad and pencils with her, her attempts at drawing soon changed into lying back with Sue, watching the horses grazing.

"If I want to," Jinny thought, "I can get up and walk across the field and Shantih is there. Really there."

To prove it to herself, she got up and walked across to Shantih to clap her neck, run her hand under her mane and sprawl over her back.

"Ten times this morning," said Sue's drowsy voice. "Ten times you've had to make sure that she isn't a mirage."

Jinny sat back down, resting her chin on her knees.

"Why do you think they stole them?"

"For money," said Sue. "Pretty easy money. We wouldn't have had a chance of tracing them if we hadn't found the *Horse and Hound*."

"And I would never have found it if Tam hadn't told us about the horses being at the Barony."

"I'd say he deserves a V.C. for coming to tell us. Jake would have killed him if he'd found out."

In the afternoon they rode bareback down to the shore. Everything that Jinny had taken for granted before Shantih was stolen was now shimmering with delight. Even putting on Shantih's halter was like some joyous miracle, some special gift from the gods, a touch of heaven.

When they reached the sands, the contentment was still there. It was enough to sit on the rocks holding Shantih and Bramble and stare out to sea.

"If only they could tell us where they've been," Sue said, as they rode back to Finmory.

"One thing, Shantih didn't do any work while she was away," laughed Jinny.

She was riding Shantih in a halter and the Arab was flirting from side to side, gravel spurting from her hooves as she kicked and shied, desperate to gallop.

They had just got back to the stables and were brushing down their horses when Mike came looking for Jinny.

"Phone," he said.

"Miss Tuke?" Jinny asked, thinking it was too early for Miss Tuke's evening call.

"Don't know. Mum answered it. She didn't say who it was."

Tipping oats and nuts into Shantih's trough, Jinny left her and went in to the phone.

"Hullo," she said.

"Hello," said Clare Burnley's voice.

"Puke, double puke," thought Jinny, as Clare's loud insincerity gushed into her ear, telling Jinny how utterly delighted they had all been to hear that she had found Shantih.

Jinny held the phone at arm's length, and, in a few minutes, Clare told her that she must fly.

"Right," said Jinny. "Do that."

"One more thing. Are you going to the show tomorrow?"

"Why?"

"I was only wondering. I mean to say, one does know how keen you are, and trying so hard with your jumping on that totally unsuitable beast. One was wondering."

"Was one," said Jinny.

"Or are you chickening out? Must fly. Bye." And Clare put the phone down.

"Well!" exclaimed Jinny. "Of all the cheek!"

"Who was it?" asked her mother.

"Clare Burnley," said Jinny. "Phoning me! Wanting to know if I'm going in for the jumping at the show."

"Are you?"

"Don't know whether it would be fair to Shantih, although she seems fresh enough."

Miss Tuke phoned in the evening. She had heard from the police that Major Fitzsimmons had been the man they were after.

"He worked through middlemen," Miss Tuke told Jinny. "Like Fred the driver, or Sid Vernon. Jake had nothing much to do with it. Only showed them where they could leave the stolen horses while they were up here. Still, he knew what was going on."

"Why wasn't Shantih at the sale?" Jinny demanded.

"Special order, you might say. They'd left her somewhere for the day. Picked her up after the sale and were taking her to their customer. A friend of the Major's. That's why he was there. He normally left the delivery to the others. The police told me to congratulate you on tracking him down. Seems he was the mastermind behind it all. They're both being charged. I've to go down to give evidence. See if we can get them behind bars. That'll stop them causing any more trouble."

At Miss Tuke's words, Jinny saw the men crouching in

a rat-trap cage, tearing at the bars, fighting to escape. She pushed the thought away. Jinny didn't want them to come back stealing horses but she didn't want to think of them shut up in prison. She wanted them to feel the way she had done all day, when everything was alive with joy. Every least thing sparkling and unique. If they felt like that they wouldn't want to steal.

"Are you still there?" demanded Miss Tuke.

"Yes. Oh, er, yes," said Jinny, coming back to earth.

"Then listen. I said, 'Are you coming to Inverburgh?' "

"Well . . ." said Jinny.

"Your horse is quite fit. I can only take Shantih. Haven't room for Bramble. What do you say? Pick you up tomorrow morning? Eightish?"

"Well . . ." said Jinny again. She had so totally forgotten the world of show jumping and shows and cups. It was enough to have Shantih. She didn't need any more.

"Brisk up," said Miss Tuke. "I can imagine the state you're in. Come to the show. Give that Clare Burnley a run for her money."

At the mention of Clare Burnley's name, Jinny felt the thrill of competition shiver through her. To go to Inverburgh Show and beat Clare Burnley. Perhaps Shantih would behave herself tomorrow. Perhaps tomorrow would be the day when Shantih would jump in the ring the way she did at home. For weeks Jinny had been preparing for Inverburgh Show. Suddenly it seemed a pity not to go. She would be sorry tomorrow if she decided to stay at home.

"Be ready for eight," said Miss Tuke, and put the phone down.

CHAPTER THIRTEEN

Shantih, groomed to perfection, stood at Finmory's front door waiting for Miss Tuke to arrive. Jinny, holding her, was dressed in jodhpurs and jacket, white shirt, tie and hard hat.

Yesterday evening had turned into a frantic preparation for Inverburgh Show—Mrs. Manders pressing Jinny's riding clothes, Jinny grooming Shantih and Sue cleaning her tack.

Sue had said she would enjoy going to a show without a horse, having a chance to look round without worrying about what Pippen was doing.

"Anyway," she'd said, "it wouldn't be fair, exposing Bramble to the public gaze in his shorn condition."

Miss Tuke's box drove into the yard.

"Get her loaded," called Miss Tuke. "Highland Ponies in Hand is the second class. Mustn't be late."

Two lady trekkers, who were entering Miss Tuke's Highlands for the Handy Horse, climbed down from the cabin and came to help. Miss Tuke had three Highlands in the box, all spruced and gleaming, hooves oiled and manes brushed out into clouds of hair. They strained against their halters, trying to see what was happening outside.

"Jinny, travel in the back with Shantih. Rather crushed in the front," said Miss Tuke.

So Jinny stayed with Shantih, watching the ramp swing up, blocking out the light.

"A day at Inverburgh Show," thought Jinny. "A day with Shantih." And it didn't matter, didn't matter in the least, how Shantih behaved. Jinny couldn't have cared less whether she won anything or not. Enough to be there, being driven to the show with Shantih.

Jinny felt the box stop at the gate of the show field. She heard Miss Tuke speaking to the men at the gate and then the box drove on, lurching over the grass until it came to a shuddering halt. The Highlands, knowing they had arrived, kicked impatiently, wanting to be let out.

"Give over," roared Miss Tuke, as the ramp swung down, revealing white tents and marquees.

Jinny ran, light-footed, down the ramp at Shantih's side. The show field was already bustling with humans and animals. The smell of trodden grass pricked in Jinny's nostrils and she stared round at Persil-white sheep, cattle scrubbed and polished, carthorses primped out with ribbons. Children on shaggy ponies cantered about, their faces serious under hard hats. A few adults rode show horses, red-faced farmers leant against the sides of their cattle floats, talking to friends they hadn't seen since the last Inverburgh Show. Jinny grinned to herself, remembering last year when she had come to the show with the Burnleys.

Sue was helping Miss Tuke with the Highlands, so Jinny mounted and began to ride round on Shantih. She had decided only to enter for the Open Jumping and that wasn't until the afternoon. Jinny relaxed, enjoying herself. As she rode about, people she hardly knew came up to speak to her, telling her how pleased they were that she had got Shantih back. Jinny nodded, smiling, saying, Yes, yes, yes she had been lucky, and feeling as if she would burst for happiness, for joy to be riding there on Shantih.

"And none the worse she's looking for her wee adventure," said Mr. MacKenzie, coming up to speak to Jinny with his cloned grandson in his arms.

"Och, but I'm pleased you were finding her. It's your madness I'd have been missing if she'd been for the sausages."

Miss Tuke's Highlands were placed first and second. Miss Tuke was chuffed.

"Did *not* expect it," she said, pinning the rosettes on her windscreen.

"Jolly well done! Congrats!" shouted Clare Burnley, as

she rode past on Jasper, looking as if she was about to show a horse at Wembley.

"Thanks," said Miss Tuke. "Pleased myself."

"Terribly sweet grey that won it," said Clare. "One was wondering if it might not be rather fun to buy a Highland down south, bring it up here and see how it would show."

"Really," said Miss Tuke, as Clare rode on. "She is an impossible girl."

Watching Clare riding into the ring for the Over 14.2 showing class, Jinny wholeheartedly agreed with Miss Tuke. Jasper, her black thoroughbred, was so obviously superior to any of the other show horses.

"To bring them all the way from Sussex!" declared Jinny in disgust.

"Just a minute," said Miss Tuke, who was standing by Jinny's side. "What have we here?"

Into the ring rode a lady on a bay horse.

"Mrs. Bowen," said Miss Tuke. "They've bought a bung. not far from us. Knew she was horsy, but not this!"

The bay the woman was riding was about seventeen hands high. He strode into the ring with an assured presence, arching his neck and trotting out with a bold courage. Beside this majesty, Jasper seemed to dwindle into little more than a blood weed. His thoroughbred head was waspish, his hocks weak and his shoulders too straight.

Clare scowled at the woman, drew Jasper together, and, when they were asked to trot, sent him on at a showy extended pace. Jinny had always thought that Clare looked better on Huston. She was too heavy for Jasper, took the light out of him. With a more sympathetic rider he might have lifted, shown his qualities of air and flame, but with Clare on top he began to resist, switching his tail, crabbing and dropping behind the bit.

"This could be it," said Miss Tuke, and she was right. The judge put the bay first, Jasper second. Clare had not won the cup.

"First time for years," said Miss Tuke, tucking in her lips, lifting her eyebrows, twinkling at Jinny out of the corner of her eyes.

With a face as sullen as late November, Clare followed Mrs. Bowen round the ring.

Mike and Mrs. Manders arrived at lunchtime, bringing a picnic basket.

"Have you done your thing yet?" Mike asked.

"This afternoon," Jinny said. "Open Jumping. There is only one show jumping class this year."

"Always used to be two," stated Miss Tuke.

"They've made the other one for ponies of 14.2 and Under. So I could only have gone in for one jumping class anyway."

"That means," said Miss Tuke, "that Clare only has one more chance to win a cup."

"She'll win it," said Jinny, not caring, as she looked up from where she lay stretched out on the grass, holding Shantih's reins, gazing at the threatening bulk of Shantih's head descending from above, wanting a bit of her cake. "She always does."

"Always *did* win the showing," said Miss Tuke.

Moira Wilson on Snuff won the 14.2 and Under jumping class with a clear round. A boy on a bay pony was second with one refusal for three faults, and a tall, spotty girl was third. Her flea-bitten grey had the pole off the second jump for four faults. Jinny, who had been riding Shantih in, came back just in time to see them cantering round the ring.

The jumps were put up for the Over 14.2 jumping class —the Open Jumping. The first jump up the side of the ring was an upright of red and white poles, followed by a stile and rails and a third jump of parallel poles. At the top of the ring there was a brush jump, then, diagonally across the ring, there was a double. Back up the opposite side of the ring there was a white gate and another brush fence with straw bales in front of it. Finally, down the centre of the ring there was a high wall of red and white bricks.

Jinny sat on Shantih, watching as a young farmer on a heavy bay rode the course. He had a pole down at the second part of the double, two refusals at the brush and bales and a brick out of the wall. He rode out, good-naturedly cursing his horse.

Last year, when Jinny had ridden in the Handy Horse, she had been tight with nerves as she had waited to ride into the ring, but today she wasn't in the least nervous. She was too glad to be riding Shantih; too glad that the nightmare of the horse sale was over, too glad that she had found Shantih, to care about her performance in the ring. She was looking forward to jumping; totally, completely looking forward to being allowed to jump.

Four more riders had rounds punctuated with knockdowns and refusals and then Clare Burnley rode into the ring. She cantered a slow circle, holding the grey, Huston, between the control of her hands, seat and legs. She was in total command. She jumped a clear round, placing Huston at every jump, telling him where to take off, gathering him back into hand whenever he landed.

"Who has been watching the Germans?" said Miss Tuke.

The next woman had two refusals at the white gate on a Highland cross, and then it was Jinny.

Shantih cantered into the ring. Jinny felt her gay and willing and laughed aloud for joy, was filled with overbrimming delight.

Over the first three jumps they went in clear, bounding arcs, and at the top of the ring Shantih came sweetly back to hand. They cantered to the brush, sailed effortlessly over it and cantered across the ring to the double. Shantih was jumping more calmly than she had ever done before, as if at last she had absorbed Jinny's schooling and it had become her own true nature. She touched down between the double and cleared the second part with inches to spare. Up the side of the field they went, red-gold in the spring sunlight. Gate and brush were behind them. Round the top of the ring, to sail over the wall and ride out with a clear round.

"You were clear!" shrieked Sue. "A clear round! She was super."

"Drugged," said Miss Tuke. "You realise there may be tests?"

Mike and Mrs. Manders were amazed.

Jinny jumped to the ground, hiding her uncontrollable

grin under the saddle flap as she loosened Shantih's girths.

"You see," Jinny said, "you never believe me when I keep telling you she is improving," and she clapped Shantih's neck, scratched her face and slipped her forelock through her fingers.

There were no more clear rounds.

"Only you and Clare for the jump-off," said Sue.

But even as she watched Clare riding into the ring, Jinny couldn't feel desperate to win; didn't need to win.

"Watch out," mouthed Miss Tuke, as Clare, riding a super, correct round, placed Huston at the brush and bales. "He's too slow to clear that spread."

Miss Tuke was right. To the groans of the spectators, the pole on top of the brush rolled off. Clare had four faults. Her face set, her mouth frozen, she rode out of the ring.

"Do it again and you've won the cup," Mike said to Jinny. "Go on, show them."

Filled with delight at having a second chance to go round the course, Jinny rode into the ring. She knew that Shantih could have jumped twice the height of these jumps, and, behaving the way she was today, Jinny knew she would go round clear a second time.

Jinny felt the rhythm of her horse flowing through her as, with pricked ears, bright eyes, Shantih bounded clear over the jumps. As they turned into the wall, Jinny let her gallop on, felt her gather herself and take wings to soar over it. They were round clear for a second time.

There was clapping and a red rosette; shaking the hand of a fur-coated lady who smelt of talcum powder as she handed the cup up to Jinny. Overcome, Jinny tried to hand it back to her.

"It's yours. Yours to keep for the year," laughed the woman. "Give us a gallop round."

The cup held awkwardly in one hand, Jinny turned Shantih to gallop her round the ring. As she did so, she caught a glimpse of Clare Burnley's defeated face.

"But I won," thought Jinny. "Shantih won it. We've won the cup."

Standing in her stirrups, Jinny held the cup above her

head, rode round the ring laughing, the sun glinting on the cup in the way she had always known it would, the red rosette fluttering on Shantih's bridle. As she rode triumphant, Jinny blocked out the knowledge that Clare had been almost crying.

The congratulations and the cup were icing on the day. It would have been enough to have known that Shantih had improved; the minutes in the ring when she had been totally at one with Shantih would have been enough.

Clare's blank, bereft face pushed itself into Jinny's consciousness, would not leave her alone.

"But it is mine. I won it," she told herself. "It's what I've always wanted—to win a cup."

"You wanted a cup, but you didn't want to beat anyone," mocked the voice in Jinny's head. "Clare needed that cup more than you. You've got Shantih back. You didn't need a cup."

"I hate her," thought Jinny, "I hate her." But she didn't, not any more, not after having seen her.

A movement at the edge of the field caught Jinny's eye. It was Tam, the tinker boy. Jinny galloped across to him.

"Don't go," she shouted, and jumped to the ground beside him. "I've to thank you. We didn't find the horses at Barony but we did get them back in the end, thanks to you coming to tell us that they'd been there."

"Aye," said the boy staring at his feet.

Jinny looked at his pinched, smeared face; his old clothes, shiny with greasy dirt; his bird bones under the man's jacket. She should have had something to give him, something with which to thank him properly.

"Will you be staying on at McGowan's farm?"

"Moving on tonight."

Jinny had only a few pence in her pocket. She couldn't offer that to him.

"Listen," she said. "If you hadn't told us about the horses, I'd never have found Shantih. I love her the way you love your dog."

For an instant the boy looked straight at Jinny. His eyes,

dark as Jake's, were flecked with golden lights and fringed with black lashes.

"You saved Zed for us," he muttered.

"Well, you saved Shantih," replied Jinny. "If there's anything I can ever do to help you at any time, you've only to come to Finmory House and ask. You know where it is?"

"Aye."

"I mean it. Honestly. For ever."

"Aye," said the boy again. Then, with the characteristic duck of his head and shoulders, he was running away from Jinny. In seconds she had lost sight of him in the crowd.

Jinny sat staring into space, her hand on the reins checking Shantih's restless movements. She thought of the tinker boy going back to Jake while she would go back to Finmory, to all the warmth and protection of her life there. She shuddered, goose over her grave. But there was nothing she could do to change things.

Pushing back her hair, Jinny rode over to Miss Tuke's box. She passed Clare standing by herself, holding Huston.

"Not much better being Clare," Jinny thought, as Clare ignored her, looking pointedly in the opposite direction.

The cup that only a week ago had mattered so much to Jinny was now only a lump of useless metal. Winning cups was Clare's thing, not Jinny's.

Jinny left the cup in the back of their car. Before, she had been planning to keep it in a special place in her bedroom, but now it didn't matter. Her mother could find a place for it and next year Clare could win it back. Jinny didn't need cups. She had Ken and her family and their life at Finmory. She had Bramble and Shantih.

Sue went home in the Manders' car. Miss Tuke dropped Jinny and Shantih in Glenbost.

Jinny stood watching the horsebox being driven out of sight. It was early evening and the day nestled like a bird in the palm of her hand.

"You are fabulous," she said to Shantih. The moments in the ring when Shantih had truly been the winged horse of Jinny's dreams, were still vivid in her mind.

For a little way she walked beside Shantih, her arm over

Shantih's withers. Then she mounted and rode over the moor, following a sheep track that would bring her to the hill behind Finmory.

Jinny was considering the possibility of cheese buns and chocolate peppermint ice cream, for it had been a special day and her mother knew they were her favourite food, when she saw Ken standing on the hillside above her, waving and pointing to the sky. Jinny stopped Shantih and stared upwards, shading her eyes.

High in the clear, evening air, two birds flew in spiralling ecstasy. "Not buzzards or eagles," thought Jinny, and then she knew they were ospreys. Although their nest had been destroyed last year, they had come back to Finmory.

Jinny gazed entranced as they rose and fell with effortless power, playing in air.

She watched them without moving until, with great flaps of their wings, they both swung down the sky in the direction of Loch Varrich. They would rebuild their nest. This time their eggs would hatch.

Ken was waiting for her.

"It's all . . ." Jinny said, meaning the miracle of having found Shantih, the ospreys coming back again, and somehow Tam and Jake, and even the suffering of the animals. "It's all so . . ."

"Yes, isn't it," said Ken.

PATRICIA LEITCH

The Magic Pony

The Magic Pony was first published
in a single volume in Armada in 1982

CHAPTER ONE

"Who bloomin' cares?" thought Jinny Manders rebelliously. "Who cares what X equals? Not me. If I sat here forever I still couldn't find out," and she stared down at the algebra text-book open in front of her, hating its smug rows of meaningless equations. "What does it matter, anyway?"

It had been the mid-summer-term holiday. Riding home from school on Thursday, four days of freedom had stretched out before Jinny, four days when she could spend all her time with Shantih, her Arab mare; and now it was Monday evening, the long weekend wasted. Jinny's plans for a picnic ride to Loch Varrich and a day's ride to Miss Tuke's trekking centre had been washed out by three days of downpour. Three days of solid, pouring rain that had made any thoughts of riding an utter impossibility.

Jinny had tried to ride on Saturday morning, but after only twenty minutes she had been soaked to the skin, rain cascading from the brim of her hard hat, her newly-cleaned tack sodden and Shantih's red-gold coat sleeked to her body. Admitting defeat she had turned back home to Finmory House.

But Monday had been fine—blue sky with placid puffs of drifting white clouds.

"Think I'll ride to Miss Tuke's today," Jinny had told her family at breakfast. "Least the forestry tracks won't be flooded."

"You can't have forgotten?" said Petra, Jinny's elder sister.

"Forgotten what? What can't I have forgotten now?" demanded Jinny, glaring suspiciously at Petra, thinking how dreary it was to be thirteen and burdened with a sixteen-year-old sister who never forgot anything, never seemed to do anything wrong and, even at breakfast, looked crisp and bright.

"Go on, tell me, what have I forgotten?"

"We discussed it before I made the appointment," said her mother. "So there wouldn't be any fuss."

"Dentist," said Mike, Jinny's ten-year-old brother, pulling a face of agony.

And Jinny had remembered. The day had been arranged about a month ago. Dentist for them all first, then school shoes and new blazers.

"But I can't come," panicked Jinny. "Not when it's been so wet and I haven't been able to ride. It wouldn't be fair. You should have told me last night." But no one was paying any attention to her.

"Be ready for ten," Jinny's father said. He was driving them in to Inverburgh then going to see Nell Storr who had a gift shop in the town and sold the pottery that Mr. Manders and Ken Dawson, a boy who lived with them, made.

Dragging herself upstairs to get ready, Jinny abandoned all hope for the day. "But I'm riding tonight," she had promised herself. "I'm going for a gallop then. Nothing will stop me."

While the dentist was filling one of her back teeth, Jinny thought hard about galloping Shantih over the Finmory moors. She heard the thunder of Shantih's flying hoofbeats, felt her horse fit and eager, the wind blowing back the drift of Shantih's mane and her own long red hair as they galloped into the wind. All about them lay the open moorland and the glimmer of the sea in Finmory Bay.

"There we are," said the dentist. "Wasn't too bad, was it? Rinse out your mouth, please."

Jinny spat with enthusiasm, avoiding her hair. That was the worst part of the day over. Only buying clothes and back to Finmory. If they all got a move on they should be back for four at the latest, which left plenty of time for a long ride.

It was well after six before they got home. Mike's feet seemed to have reached an in-between stage not catered for by shoe manufacturers, and they had had to trail round dozens of shoe shops before they found a pair to fit him.

"At last!" Jinny had exclaimed as her father stopped the car outside Finmory House. "I'm going to ride *now*. At once. So don't anyone ask me to do anything."

"What about your algebra?" Petra had asked sweetly.

Half-way out of the car, Jinny froze with dismay. She had

completely forgotten about her algebra. On Thursday night, high on the thought of her four days holiday, she had made the mistake of pouring out her troubles to Petra, telling her how foul Mr. Palmer, her maths master, had been, saying that Jinny was lazy, insolent and totally inattentive. "And he gave me two punishment excercises to do for Tuesday," she had said. "Fourteen equations, all stupid letters instead of numbers. He knows I can't do them."

"Well, you'll need to, won't you?" Petra had said. "If it's a punishment exercise, you'll need to do it."

"What algebra?" her father demanded, turning round from the front of the car to look at Jinny. "Homework?"

"Oh, just some algebra I've to do," Jinny replied. "I'll do it when I come back from my ride."

"You'll do it before you ride," Mr. Manders had stated.

Jinny stared back at her father, wondering if it was worth arguing.

"Now," said Mr. Manders. "At once."

Into Jinny's mind swam the enraged face of Mr. Palmer when he had thrown her exercise book down on her desk and begun to tell her what he thought of her. He would not be happy if Jinny arrived at his class on Tuesday without having done the two exercises that he had given her.

"Blast!" exclaimed Jinny, which was the nearest her family allowed to swearing. "All weekend I haven't been able to ride and now it's fine I've to go and do bloomin' equations."

Jinny slammed the car door shut and stomped her way into the kitchen. Ken Dawson was baking bread. Kelly, his grey, shaggy dog lay stretched in a patch of sunlight. Ken was eighteen. He was tall and lanky with fair, shoulder-length hair. His rich parents sent him a cheque every month, but apart from that they had washed their hands of him. In the kitchen garden he had created at Finmory Ken grew all the fruit and vegetables that the Manders needed. He himself ate nothing that came from animals. "How can you say you love animals when you slaughter them for food? Kill days-old calves so you can drink the milk that was meant for them?"

"Hi," he said, looking up as Jinny burst in. "Had a happy family shopping trip?"

"Do I look it?" said Jinny, fending off Kelly's welcome. "Been to the dentist, had a filling, been dragged round every shoe shop in Inverburgh and now, now when I was going to ride, I've to go and do algebra."

Jinny marched on out of the kitchen, up the broad flight of stairs, along the long corridor past bedroom and bathroom doors, until she came to the almost-vertical ladder of stairs that led up to her own bedroom. Crashing up the stairs, Jinny pushed open her door. She ran across her room, sprang on to her bed and stared out through the open window over Finmory's reach of garden, past the stables to their field where two horse shapes—dark against the green of the grass and the brightness of the sea dazzle—were grazing intently. One was Shantih, Jinny's chestnut Arab mare, the other was Bramble, a black Highland pony on loan from Miss Tuke's trekking centre.

"Shantih," Jinny called, leaning out of the window. "Shantih!"

The Arab lifted her head, ears pricked at the sound of Jinny's voice, her lustrous eyes wide as she looked around for her mistress.

"Shantih!"

Shantih whinnied with a tremble of sound and came, stepping delicately, precisely, towards the hedge closest to Finmory House. She stood at the hedge gazing up at Jinny, her nostrils still fluttering a greeting.

Next to her family and Ken, Shantih was the being closest to Jinny's heart. Two years ago Shantih had been in a circus, billed as Yasmin the Killer Horse. Now she belonged to Jinny. At first she had been wild and untamed and sometimes even Jinny had almost despaired of calming her. But now she had almost forgotten her fears of the ringmaster's whip, had stopped her frenetic rearing and mad runaways. Although she was still as fast as ever and could jump as if her heels carried wings, now she accepted Jinny's authority, shared gladly in the partnership of horse and rider.

"Dear horse," said Jinny lovingly, and with every atom of her being she longed to run into the open air and be riding Shantih over the moors.

With a great camel groan, Jinny turned away from the window. She went under the archway that divided her room into two and sat down at her table, dragged her algebra books from her schoolbag and stared despondently down at them.

The window in this half of Jinny's room looked out over the Finmory moors to the far blue mountains. The walls of the room were covered with Jinny's paintings and drawings, but on the wall facing her was a mural of a red horse.

When the Manders family had left the city suffocation of Stopton and come to live in the grey stone fastness of Finmory House, the Red Horse had been waiting for them. During the day, it was only a crude painting of a red horse with yellow eyes that plunged through a jungle of fleshy blue and green leaves and drooping white flowers, but by night there was a strange magic power belonging to the Horse. Jinny shuddered, goose over grave, remembering how last summer the Red Horse had haunted her dreams. She shrugged the memory away, determinedly opened her books and copied out the first equation.

Almost an hour later she was still staring down at the meaningless figures. Outside, the bright evening was beginning to fade. If she didn't get up and go now it would be too late to ride Shantih.

"If I stay here all night I'll never, ever, be able to do them." For minutes longer she sat wriggling on her chair, tipping it backwards and forwards as if trying to escape.

"I don't care," she said aloud. "I don't care what he says. Old potty Palmer! He can keep me in all week if he likes, but I'm going for a ride." And Jinny sprang from her chair and fled downstairs.

"Jinny," her father's voice shouted, as she passed the door of his pottery. "Have you finished your homework?"

"Done all I can," she yelled back, racing on.

In the kitchen, Petra was arranging her collections of pressed flowers.

"And how much was that?" she asked.

"No one," said Jinny, "was speaking to you."

"Bet you haven't done any."

"Wrong, as usual." And Jinny was out of the house before Petra could find out the truth.

"Whee!" she breathed, dropping to a slow loping trot. "Near thing."

Mrs. Manders jack-in-the-boxed from behind a row of raspberries.

"Remember," she said. "You must wash your hair."

"Glory hallelujah!" exclaimed Jinny. "I don't know why you can't all leave me alone. Nagging on at me."

"Jinny," warned her mother.

"But you do, you do. All the time."

"Are you going for a ride?"

"Yes, I am."

"Then come home past the farm and bring the milk," said Mrs. Manders. "And don't stay out too long."

"Don't stay out too long," said Jinny, managing to speak at exactly the same time as her mother. "Honestly, you'd think all I do is gallop over the moors at midnight."

"It has been known," said her mother, but Jinny was away.

She ran into the stables, grabbed Shantih's bridle and saddle and ran on down to the horses' field where Shantih was standing looking over the gate.

"Bet you're bored too. Stuck in that field for four days. Come on. We're going for a gallop."

As Jinny pushed the gate open, Shantih half reared, throwing up her neck, tossing her head, plunging away from Jinny into a sudden mad flurry of swirling mane and tail, a pounding drum-beat of hooves as she circled the field making Bramble gloom and glower. Then back at a full gallop to skid to a halt inches from Jinny.

"Idiot," said Jinny lovingly. "Bat brain."

Shantih lowered her head, accepting the bit and stood patiently while Jinny buckled on her bridle and saddled her. Jinny led Shantih out of the field and, gathering up her reins, sprang easily on to her back.

"The moor or the shore?" Jinny asked, gazing around her, hesitating. Then she knew. Between now and the moment when she climbed into the school bus, was marched into the prison of school, the moment when Mr. Palmer asked her for her algebra, she had to do everything, had to have such a ride on Shantih that all the boring miseries of tomorrow wouldn't matter. "Both," said Jinny. "Ride such a ride as never we rode before," and she turned Shantih towards Finmory Bay, letting her canter on with a long flowing stride.

They clattered over the bulwark of sea-smoothed boulders and the glimmering sands stretched before them. Jinny gave

Shantih her head. "On you go," she murmured, as Shantih bucked, stretched out her neck and was away.

In an ecstasy of speed, Jinny crouched low over her horse's neck. The screaming of the gulls and the brightness of the shore were all about her as they raced over the sands. She turned Shantih in a wide circle and galloped back until they came to a narrow track that climbed from the shore to the moors.

Shantih plunged upwards, digging her toes into the stony ground, humping suddenly forward as the rain-drenched earth gave way beneath her and cascades of stones made mini-avalanches down to the shore.

Over the moors they galloped. Dry-stone walls rose up before them and fell away behind them as Shantih soared over them and galloped on. There was no tomorrow, only this now of space and light. Joy in Shantih and in this flying freedom sang through Jinny's whole being. She rode entranced, the Arab mare part of her own being. On and on they went.

Then, against the skyline, Jinny saw the black fingers of the standing stones. She was back in Time. She slowed Shantih to a trot and then to a walk. Conscious now of the grey evening, Jinny knew that she had come too far. It would certainly be what her mother considered late before Jinny reached home. She turned Shantih round and began to ride back. Shantih crabbed, half rearing, wanting to gallop on.

"No way," Jinny told her, sitting down firmly, forcing her on. "We have had it. They will all be furious. We've got to get back."

They were in sight of Finmory when Jinny remembered about the milk. "Mr. MacKenzie will be in bed by now,' she thought, and wondered if her family really needed the milk, if there would be lost tempers if she didn't get it.

"Honestly," she told Shantih, as they rode down towards Finmory. "All my life is nothing but other people bossing me around. I hate them all. Why can't they leave me alone? Leave me alone to do the things I want to do. All I want is to be left alone to ride and draw, but oh no, Jinny do this, Jinny do that. Teachers shouting at me, all week shut up in that prison of a school, and then, when I do get home, I've to spend all my time running errands."

Jinny stared out balefully over the darkening moors. Black clouds lying low over the sea had turned it into dark mercury. The rocks at either side of the bay were ebony jaws poised to kill. The coming night reached long shadowy fingers over the rough moorland. Shantih's hoofs dipped into pools of shadow. And tomorrow Mr. Palmer waited for the alegbra that Jinny hadn't done. Another detention meant a visit to the Headmaster.

Suddenly Jinny gathered up her reins and urged Shantih on into a gallop. The stone wall dividing Finmory's land from the moors stretched in front of them. Normally Jinny would have ridden through the open gateway, but tonight, her black mood heavy upon her, she rode Shantih straight at the wall.

Shantih pounded up to it, and Jinny saw that it was higher than she had realised. In daylight she would never have dreamed of jumping it. As Shantih rose to clear it, Jinny knotted her fingers into Shantih's mane, saw Shantih's neck arched, her ears pricked, caught a glimpse of her forelegs tucked close into her body. Suddenly, from the other side of the wall, a sheep erupted into life. In mid-air, Shantih screwed herself sideways, eyes bulging with terror. She landed awkwardly, fought to stay on her feet, then fell. Jinny saw the ground coming up to knock the breath out of her. She lay plastered flat against it, watching helplessly as Shantih struggled to rise.

It was minutes before Jinny managed to get up and stagger across to where Shantih stood, her head almost touching the ground, blood trickling down her shoulder.

"Shantih!" cried Jinny, appalled at what she had done. "Oh Shantih! There, the horse." She rubbed the sleeve of her anorak over the cut in Shantih's shoulder and saw, to her relief, that it was little more than a scratch. Urgently, Jinny looked at Shantih's knees and legs and ran her hands over her quarters searching for any other cuts, but as far as Jinny could see in the half-dark, Shantih was unhurt.

Jinny collapsed on the ground.

"Jinny Manders, you fool, you lunatic. How could you be so stupid," she told herself.

Looking up at the wall, Jinny saw that where she had jumped it there had been an enormous drop on the landing side. Even without the sheep hazard it would have been a risky landing.

Jinny shuddered, stood up, and still shaken by her fall, didn't remount but took Shantih's reins and began to lead her downhill. Coming down in the gathering dark, Shantih seemed unsure of her footing, stumbling and tripping over loose stones and heather roots. Even when they reached the track that led to Mr. MacKenzie's farm, Shantih still seemed to be stumbling far more than usual. Twice, Jinny, plodding on ahead of her horse, nearly had the reins pulled out of her hands as Shantih lost her balance.

Mr. MacKenzie opened the farmhouse door as he heard them approach. He stood in the shaft of golden electric light that suddenly made the dim grey evening change into darkness, and watched them coming into his yard.

"I've come for the milk," Jinny said, trying to make her voice sound easy, as if it was the afternoon, wondering how late it really was.

"Would that be so?" said Mr. MacKenzie, reaching up for his cap, putting it on the back of his head and pulling it well down over his gimlet eyes. "I'm thinking it's the blessing you're not for the duck eggs, or the wee bit ducklings would have been swimming away by this time," and the old man led the way across the yard to the byre.

"It's the roll in the mud you've been having to yourselves," he said, as he picked up the full milk can and handed it to Jinny. "Haven't I been warning you until I'm sick of the sound of my own voice, not to be riding over those hills in the dark?"

"Not you too," said Jinny in disgust. "It wasn't dark when we set out."

"Is that a fact? Well, it's the dark now, I'm thinking, and from the sound of your horse's feet it's herself will be lame tomorrow."

"What do you mean? Shantih's not lame."

"And why would you be leading her? Away home with you and be listening to her ladyship as you go."

The door of the farmhouse snicked shut behind the farmer as Jinny screwed up her face at his departing back.

"What does he know?" she said to Shantih. "Always minding other people's business. You're not lame, are you? You're

O.K. Of course you're not lame." Jinny ran her hand down Shantih's sleek neck, pulled her ear through her hand as Shantih pitched forward, stumbling so badly that her muzzle touched the ground.

When Jinny had listened to her parents' angry anxiety she went upstairs and washed her hair. While she was drying it she heard her family going to bed, the house sinking into silence. She was just going to get undressed when she changed her mind, pulled on her anorak and crept downstairs. She took her father's powerful torch from the kitchen dresser and eased the key round in the back door. The golden circle of torchlight slid in front of her as she made her way down to the horses' field.

"Shantih," Jinny called, as she climbed over the gate. "Come on then, Shantih."

She swung the swathe of torchlight over the field, picked out the bulk of Bramble lying at the hedge roots, then Shantih standing close by.

"Shantih," Jinny called again, and the Arab began to walk slowly towards her, her stride uneven, plucking up her left foreleg almost before it touched the ground. Before Jinny had left her she had picked out her hooves, checked her legs for any cuts or scratches but had found none.

As the Arab came closer, Jinny saw her head nod forward with the tight, almost imperceptible grimace of pain. There was no doubt about it, Mr. MacKenzie had been right, Shantih was lame.

"And I did it," Jinny thought. "It's all my fault for making her jump that wall."

CHAPTER TWO

The next morning, Shantih was still lame. Mr. Manders had to drive Jinny into Glenbost, the nearest crofting village to Finmory. Normally Jinny rode Shantih into Glenbost and left her in a field while she caught the school bus to the comprehensive school in Inverburgh. Mike, who went to the Glenbost primary school, rode Bramble, leaving her in the field with Shantih. Petra, who was a weekly boarder at Duninver High School, was collected on Monday mornings by a school taxi.

"Come on, Jinny. Hurry up!" said Mr. Manders irritably, as he waited, still gritty with sleep, for his daughter to organise herself into the car.

"I have to be out every morning at this time," Jinny told him, climbing in beside her father and slamming the car door.

" 'The hoar necessitous horror of the morning'," quoted Mr. Manders.

"Will you phone the vet?" asked Jinny urgently.

"Don't panic. Couldn't we leave her for a day or two? Might only be a twist. It might get better by itself."

"No. Of course not. She's really lame. Say it was something that needed treatment right away and we didn't get the vet. Then when he came he said she'd never be sound again because we hadn't called him in earlier? How would we feel then?"

"Or, of course, she may have dropped dead in the field by now so there's no point in worrying."

"It's not funny," said Jinny. "Not anything to make jokes about."

"Sorry," said Mr. Manders. "Blame the hour. I'll phone when I get back. Better if he comes tonight when you're there to hear what he has to say." He slowed the car to a crawl as Mr. MacKenzie and two sheepdogs came towards them, a froth of sheep filling the road.

"Aye," Mr. MacKenzie greeted them. "A fine morning."

"Grand," agreed Mr. Manders impatiently, as the farmer stopped and leant an elbow on the open window of the car.

"It's yourself has the chauffeur this morning?" he said to Jinny. "And it's surprised I am that you're even fit to be driven to the school after your madness on the hill last night."

Jinny scowled up at him.

"What madness?" demanded Mr. Manders.

"Sailing over walls that would have stopped Red Rum himself. And I'm thinking from the mess of the good ground, it's the wee tumble you had to yourselves. She'll be lame this morning, I'm thinking."

"Oh yes," said Jinny. "You're thinking right as usual. Shantih's lame. And if we don't get a move on, I'm going to miss the bus."

"No foot, no hoss," said Mr. MacKenzie, savouring the thought. "No foot, no hoss."

"And what was all that about?" asked Mr. Manders as they drove away.

Reluctantly, Jinny told her father about last night's fall. "Though how Mr. MacKenzie found out about it, I don't know. Must have been up at dawn searching the moors for hoofprints."

"Honestly Jinny, at times I utterly despair of you. What makes you do such stupid things?"

"The bus," cried Jinny, catching a glimpse of familiar red bus on the road from Ardtallon. "Oh quick, hurry up. Dougal won't wait for me if I'm not there."

Mr. Manders put his foot down and they reached Glenbost at the same time as the bus.

"We'll meet you," he called. "If there's no one there, start walking."

"Be sure to phone the vet," Jinny reminded him, as she scrambled out of the car and ran towards the bus.

"Lucky you are that you weren't late this morning," Dolina Thompson said, squashing up on her seat to make room for Jinny beside her. Dolina had gone to Glenbost School and was in the same class as her at Inverburgh. "It's the black dog Dougal has sitting on his shoulder this morning."

"Not the only one," said Jinny, flopping down beside her.

"Aye," said Dolina, turning flat cod eyes to survey Jinny's

turned-up collar and uncombed hair. "It's the look of the jumble you have on you yourself."

"Shantih's lame," said Jinny, and told Dolina what had happened.

"Och, I wouldn't be worrying yourself about that. When we'd the old pony for the ploughing, he was lame all the time, but a wee bit work soon took his mind off it."

"Honestly!" exclaimed Jinny. "Fancy working a lame pony."

"What's more to the point," said Dolina. "Have you done the algebra for Mr. Palmer? I'm thinking he'll be having the wee turn if you haven't it finished for him."

"Well, I haven't," said Jinny. "So he'll just need to have a wee turn. I can't help it. Bad enough Shantih being lame without worrying over stupid things like algebra."

"You know the maps we've to do for the geography? Well, I was just thinking I could be doing the algebra for you and you could be copying it out before we reach the school, and maybe you could be drawing the map for me before Thursday? It's the wee arrangement we could have?"

Jinny hesitated. She knew what her parents would think about Dolina's wee arrangement, but it would save so much trouble. Save all that shouting when Mr. Palmer discovered that Jinny hadn't done the wretched algebra.

"Oh, O.K." agreed Jinny, opening her schoolbag. "Need to be quick. He gave me two excercises to do."

As if they had been simple additions, Dolina worked her way through the equations and Jinny copied them down into her exercise book.

"It's the kindness we're doing him," said Dolina smugly. "You can see to look at him that he has the raging blood pressure. It'll be much easier this way."

"Dolina was right," Jinny thought at the end of the algebra lesson when Mr. Palmer had taken her excercise book, glanced at it to make sure that she had done the work, grunted and put it on top of the pile of books on his desk.

Jim Rae, the vet, came that evening, listened to Jinny's explanation of Shantih's fall, then told Jinny to trot Shantih up and down keeping the halter rope loose. As Jinny ran at Shantih's head she felt the uneven beat of Shantih's stride.

"She's worse," Jinny thought, as several times Shantih

stumbled, nearly coming down on her knees as she tried to avoid putting any weight on the left foreleg.

"She's lame, O.K." said the vet. "Near fore. No doubt about that. Poor woman. Now, let's see if we can find out what's causing it."

Jinny stood holding Shantih as the vet ran his hand down Shantih's leg, his strong, sensitive fingers searching for unusual lumps or swellings. He picked up Shantih's hoof, examined it thoroughly, felt the wall of the hoof for heat and tapped it with a small hammer, but Shantih showed no reaction. She stood staring out over Jinny's shoulder, apparently feeling no pain.

At last the vet straightened up.

"Can't see a thing," he said. "She doesn't seem to feel anything in her foot. No heat, no swelling in her leg. Nothing showing. Could be her shoulder, but from the way she was moving I'd swear it's her leg or foot. Just need to wait and see."

"You mean you can't do anything for her," demanded Jinny aghast.

"Could be a sprain, a twist. Leave her out and don't ride her until the weekend. If she's still lame, give me a phone and I'll come out and take another look at her. Meanwhile I'll give her a shot in case there's any poison in her. She's had an anti-tet., hasn't she?"

"Yes," said Jinny, watching the sure, automatic movements of the vet's hands as he injected Shantih.

"That's the woman," he said, clapping Shantih on the neck, turning to go. "Dare say she'll sort herself out in a day or two."

But Shantih didn't. A week later she was still as lame as ever. The vet had been back but couldn't find any reason for the lameness. There was no heat, no swelling, but Shantih was dead lame. Jinny spent her time leaning over the field gate watching her horse limping about.

"Even a slightly twisted ankle can take weeks to stop hurting," he mother reassured her. "Give her time."

But Jinny's heart was heavy with guilt. She knew that if she hadn't jumped that wall Shantih wouldn't be dragging round the field, the light and fire gone from her.

Jinny had phoned Miss Tuke to see if she could give her

any help, but Miss Tuke was too busy organising her trekkers to have any time for Jinny.

"Told you before you'd break that mare's leg galloping her about the way you do. If Jim Rae can't find out what the trouble is, there's no point in me coming over. Hock-deep in trekkers. Haven't a sec. to spare."

"Thank you very much, Miss Tuke," said Jinny, when she had put the phone down.

The blacksmith, who always came on to Finmory after he had shod Miss Tuke's trekkers, had taken the shoe off Shantih's near fore. But he too had shaken his head.

"I wouldn't be saying it's the shoe, though if the vet wants it off, off it will come. There's not a thing I can see wrong with the poor brute's leg. Probably a twist, though she's feeling it, a blind man could see that."

"There must be someone else who knows about horses," Jinny complained to Ken. "Must be."

"Heard about someone who treated animals with homoeopathic medicine," said Ken.

"Where?" said Jinny, clutching at straws, not even too sure what homoeopathic medicine was.

"Amsterdam," said Ken.

"A-plus for useless, pointless information," said Jinny, swinging away from him.

It wasn't until the next Wednesday afternoon that Jinny heard about someone who might be able to help. Dolina had persuaded Jinny to help with the tea for a choir from St. Margaret's, private girls' school in Inverburgh, who were giving a performance at the comprehensive school on Wednesday.

"We'll miss double science," coaxed Dolina, and Jinny had agreed to volunteer.

She was standing behind the long table making sure there were enough cups and saucers, filling up the milk jugs and sugar bowls, when one of the St. Margaret's girls spoke to her.

"You must be Jinny Manders?" the girl said.

"Yes," said Jinny, looking suspiciously at the tall, dark-haired girl who had spoken to her.

"The one who has an Arab and rides it to school?"

"Well, into Glenbost and then bus, but not at all just now. She's lame."

"Oh, that's a pity," said the girl. "I'm Joyce West. My aunt is friends with one of your staff. And when she heard about you she told me, seeing I'm horse-daft. Sorry to hear your Arab's lame. What's wrong?"

"Don't know," said Jinny, welcoming a sympathetic ear. "Even the vet doesn't seem to know. She's been lame for nearly two weeks now and she's not getting any better. The vet just keeps on saying it's a twist and to give it time."

"Front leg?"

"Yes. Near fore."

"How maddening. Especially when there's nothing you can do."

"I know. And she isn't getting any better. It's dreadful not being able to ride her and utterly dreadful watching her limping round the field and not being able to do anything to help her."

"Do you know what could have caused it?"

"She came down after we'd jumped a wall," Jinny muttered, feeling her stomach clench cold and tight with guilt.

"Could easily have sprained it," comforted Joyce. "Or it might be a puncture. Could it be a nail? I knew a horse who was bedded on woodshavings. There was a nail left in them and she got it right into her foot. It took the vet weeks to find out what was wrong. No sign at all from the outside."

"Shantih hasn't been near any nails so I don't think it could be that," said Jinny. "If only I knew someone really horsy who could come and look at her for me." Jinny looked hopefully at Joyce.

"Not me. Sorry. Horse-daft but I'm no expert. I just ride at a riding school."

"Near here?" asked Jinny.

"Not far. About three-quarters of an hour's walk. Bit grotty, but we get quite a good canter along the edge of a golf course."

"Is there anyone there who might come and look at Shantih?"

"Brenda Digby. She runs the riding school. Been around horses all her life. She might, if you asked her. Look, why don't you come for a ride? I ride on the eleven o'clock ride on a Saturday morning. Come then."

"This Saturday," said Jinny eagerly.

"Oh no. No use. I'll not be there. How about the next? Or go yourself. Listen, I've to phone up to cancel. Shall I tell Brenda you'll take my place?"

"Right," said Jinny, suddenly seeing Brenda as a tall, elegant horsewoman who would gladly come out to Finmory and, after years of horsy experience, know instantly how to cure Shantih's lameness.

"It's called the Arran Riding School. Here, I'll draw you a map of how to get there." Taking a pen from her blazer pocket, Joyce drew a quick sketch-map on a paper napkin of how to reach the riding school from Inverburgh bus station.

"Could I have some money, please?" Jinny asked her father. "I'm going for a ride at a riding school on Saturday morning."

"Riding school?" said Mr. Manders. "What on earth for? You can ride Bramble, can't you?"

"I met this girl who told me about it. The woman who runs it has worked with horses all her life, so I thought if I went for a ride I could get to know her and I could ask her about Shantih."

"But surely she won't know more than the vet?"

"She might," said Jinny. "Jim Rae doesn't see all that many horses. All sheep and cows he deals with."

In Jinny's mind was a clear picture of Brenda Digby. After her career with horses she was bound to know more than the vet. Probably she had worked with hunters and show ponies; even possible that she had worked in racing stables. Jinny saw her with short wavy hair, dressed in an elegantly-cut hacking jacket and cord slacks, striding across the field to Shantih, picking up Shantih's leg and saying, "Nothing to worry about here. I'll tell you what to do. Have her sound in no time."

"Rather a long shot," said Mr. Manders dubiously. "Isn't the vet coming on Saturday?"

"No. Friday night. So please may I have some money?"

Rather reluctantly, Mr. Manders handed over five pounds. "There had better be change," he said.

"Bound to be. Thanks." said Jinny, pocketing the note quickly before he changed his mind.

Jinny rode Bramble into Glenbost early on Saturday morning.

"I know it's not a work day," she said, kicking on the stubborn pony. "But just for once you are going to have to work overtime and lump it."

Bramble pinned back his ears and switched his tail.

"Be thankful," Jinny told him, "that you're not Shantih." Sitting down hard in the saddle, she forced him into an unwilling trot.

"Still no improvement," the vet had said the night before. "Can be the dickens to find out what's wrong when it's their feet. I'll pop back at the beginning of the week and give her an injection that will stop all feeling in her foot. If she goes sound after that, we'll know it *is* her foot."

"And once we know it is her foot," thought Jinny, kicking Bramble harder than ever, "What then? What's he going to do then to cure her?"

Jinny caught the Inverburgh bus by the skin of her teeth. Trying to follow Joyce's map, she took a wrong turning and took ages finding her way back.

"Going to be late," she thought, as she raced along the road to the stables. "Not going to have time to talk to Brenda before the ride."

Now that she was nearly there, Jinny's stomach was beginning to turn over. She had only been to one other riding school in her life. That had been Major Young's place in Stopton. It had been very superior, with an immaculate yard, well-groomed horses and equally well-groomed riders. But as Jinny turned down a lane by the side of a golf course and saw a huddle of ramshackle buildings in front of her and a weather-faded riding-school sign nailed to a tree, she realised that the Arran Riding School wasn't going to be at all like Major Young's. Half of Jinny was relieved that it wasn't going to be a posh place, but half was already beginning to realise that if Brenda worked in a place like this she wasn't likely to be much help with Shantih.

Jinny went through a gateway, gingerly opening and shutting a gate that threatened to fall to pieces when it was touched. On her left was a small cottage, its paint peeling, its walls stained green where rain had poured down from the broken guttering, its small windowpanes grimy with dirt. Over the porch at the front door, rambler roses swarmed in unpruned confusion.

Jinny walked along the hedge that encircled the wilderness cottage garden, following it round to a small field where several jumps were set up in the middle of a rutted schooling circle. At the field gate, oil drums and broken poles were piled in high battlements but there was no sign of any life.

Jinny hesitated, listening. Then, hearing the sound of voices, she retraced her steps and followed a muddy track through a narrow opening between two outhouses that seemed to be made of old doors and sheets of corrugated iron. She came out into a stable yard.

Along one side of the yard were four looseboxes in the same state of disrepair as the rest of the buildings. On the opposite side was a long, low building and, through its open door, Jinny glimpsed a row of narrow stalls. More rusted oil drums were piled in a corner of the yard, a water trough was half-filled with stagnant water, and heaps of dung were swept into corners.

Jinny saw these things but hardly noticed them. She had eyes for nothing but the ponies and horses. There were two bay fifteen-hand horses—one that looked almost a thoroughbred. Its coat was sparse and staring, stretched tight over ribs and gaunt hip bones. Its neck was so thin that Jinny could clearly see the ridging of its larynx. Its hocks and elbows were capped and its knees badly scarred from an old fall. Its tail hung down in a fouled wisp of hair and its quarters were deeply grooved with poverty lines. The other looked as if it had been put together from parts of several different horses—its heavy head too large for its long neck, its slab-sided body supported by four misshapen legs—legs which were lumped and bumped with splints and spavins and old scars.

Of the four ponies, one was a heavy Highland, its shrunken body still covered in patches of winter coat, its blubbery lower lip hanging open almost touching the ground as it stood with its head drooping lifelessly. One was a 12.2 dark brown pony with fine-boned legs and a world-weary face. Its long feet were turning up with laminitis. One was a fourteen-hand chestnut; its fiddle-face on an upside-down neck was strapped in with a tight standing martingale attached to a drop noseband. The fourth pony was a black 14.2 with a white face. It had an open girth gall, rubbed raw by an iron-hard, leather girth.

All the tack was dried and cracked. Some of the ponies were unshod, with cracked, breaking hooves, while others had thin, smooth-worn shoes, the risen clinches sticking up from their hooves.

Jinny felt sick. She couldn't believe it possible, couldn't believe that anyone could work horses like these. They were worse than the ponies that had pulled carts in Stopton, worse than the blackest of Jinny's imaginings. She stood staring, the scream that was always inside her when she really thought how cruelly people treated animals, tightening her throat, crushing her skull. Yet the girls holding the ponies were smiling, chatting, excited at the thought of going for a ride.

"Hi!" called the girl holding the two horses. "You must be Jinny. I'm Moira. Joyce told me you were coming. Think you're to ride Sporty." She gestured towards the jig-saw horse. "I'm riding Queenie. Those two always stick together so you'll be O.K. Better wait until Brenda comes out before you get on."

Jinny hardly heard her. She wanted to turn and run from the horrors of the place, but she stood unable to move.

A girl in smart riding clothes came along the path behind Jinny. For a second Jinny thought this must be Brenda, then saw that she was too young.

"Hi!" Moira shouted to the smart girl. "You've to ride Easter. Brenda said to get her out when you arrived."

The girl smiled a thin-lipped, nervous smile and, crossing the yard, went into the row of stalls. She came out leading an aged white pony of fourteen hands. She was poor, as all the others were poor, with ridged ribs, sunken quarters and scarred legs. Her dark eyes, fringed with black lashes and long, straying hairs, were lustrous in her skeletal head. Her mane was a tangle of witch-knots and her long tail twisted into cords of hair. All the others were old, but this pony was like a ghost—so old she seemed hardly there, unable to stand against the assault of the light.

The scream tore out of Jinny in a sudden gasp of sound. For the spirit that was almost visible in the white pony was that of a top-class show pony, fleet and beautiful beyond the singing of it.

"What's up?" demanded Moira. "Are you feeling sick? You've gone dead white."

Jinny stammered for words to shield her, and Brenda came out from one of the sheds.

"Everyone ready?" she asked. "Get up then."

Brenda was small and dumpy. Faded jeans stretched over a broad bottom, short fat legs squashed into wellingtons, a dirty blue anorak strained at its fastenings. Her hair was dyed red with henna, her face was pink with make-up, orange lipstick spread over her lips.

"You the girl instead of Joyce?" she asked Jinny, a cigarette bobbing in the corner of her mouth.

Dumbly, Jinny nodded.

"Ride Sporty. Moira will keep an eye on you."

As if in a trance, Jinny took Sporty's reins, tightened his girth, pulled down the rusty stirrups and mounted.

Riding a bay horse with a Roman nose, Brenda led the way out of the yard. The horses, as if they were programmed automata, turned and followed her.

They rode along the track at the side of the golf course in a slow straggle, except for the girl on the chestnut, who had quickly been carted past Brenda and was struggling to hold back her pony as it fought, half rearing, to break away from her control.

"Are you O.K.?" Moira asked. riding at Jinny's side. "You'll need to kick him on a bit. Get him going. Good job we're not in the paddock. He'd just stand still with you there. What you need is a stick. Pity we didn't think of it before. There's plenty old ones lying about the tack room."

Jinny closed her ears to Moira's chatter. She had never ridden anything like Sporty before. His sides were completely dead, without feeling, and his lips so calloused that he hardly seemed to notice the bit in his mouth. Jinny ran her hand down his scrawny neck, making much of him, talking gently to him, but he plodded woodenly on, giving no sign that he knew Jinny was riding him.

When they reached the end of the track, the ride turned round and headed back to the stables. They reached the stables, turned, and rode back alongside the golf course.

"Do you always just ride up and down here?" Jinny asked.

"No. 'Course not. Sometimes we go for road rides or in the paddock. Are you getting bored? Well, you needn't be. Next time back, we trot and then we canter.

Jinny wanted to say, "Big deal," but she bit the words back as she longed desperately for the ride to be over so that she would no longer be part of the dismal procession.

When they trotted back, the chestnut pony took off at a mad tearaway gallop.

"Always does that," confided Moira. "Brenda gets furious. Says we can't ride or we could stop him. Still, doesn't matter, he always does stop at the stables."

Sporty's trot threw Jinny up and down in the saddle. Each leg seemed to be doing its own thing as he battered along. When at last they cantered, Jinny, used to Shantih's smooth paces, was tossed about in the saddle like a cork on a rough sea.

"You haven't ridden much, have you?" stated Moira. "Bet you're not bored now."

Jinny thought of telling her about Shantih, but changed her mind. There was no point. Moira wouldn't have believed her.

Once, Jinny glanced back and glimpsed Easter, the white pony, moving with a showy, toe-pointing stride. Her thin neck was arched and her head tucked in, a pathetic echo of her past. Quickly, Jinny looked round again, tears stinging behind her eyes, a lump hard in her throat.

"Any use?" asked Mr. Manders, when at last Jinny was home again.

"The end," said Jinny, giving him back two pounds. "Terrible, terrible place. The horses were awful—worn out, ancient. They should all have been retired years ago. There was one white pony—I'm sure she must have been a show pony once, years ago. But now . . ."

Words failed Jinny, but Ken nodded, understanding, sharing her heartbreak and useless fury. Out of all the people Jinny knew, Ken was the only one who really cared about animals. Not as pets or show objects or for their speed or usefulness to humans. He cared that they should be free to be themselves. Ken was the one person who would really understand how Jinny felt about the white pony.

"They shouldn't be allowed to run a place like that," said Jinny. " The R.S.P.C.A. should close it down."

"Can't you do something about it?" asked Mr. Manders. "If it's as bad as you say it is, I'm sure something could be done about it."

"I'll ask the vet," said Jinny, "the next time he's here. He's bound to know it."

Jinny went out and down to Shantih, the blackness of the riding school still filling her mind. She gave Shantih an apple and ran her hand down her horse's firm neck, over her withers, and stretched her arm over her broad strong back. She straightened the fine hair of Shantih's forelock so that it lay in a silken tassel along her white face.

"You will never become like them," she promised, as Shantih lipped at her hand hoping for more titbits. "When you're old you'll have the moors and a warm stable when you want it."

Then into Jinny's head came Mr. MacKenzie's voice. "No foot, no hoss," it said. "No foot, no hoss."

CHAPTER THREE

It was the Thursday after Jinny's visit to the riding school and Jinny was sitting at the back of Mr. Palmer's algebra class. Presumably Mr. Palmer was standing at the front teaching algebra. Jinny wasn't listening. She was thinking about Shantih and drawing a picture of herself jumping Shantih over a stone wall. Jinny had got into so much trouble over drawing in her school exercise books that now she carried a drawing pad with her and drew on that. With an exact, precise line, Jinny's pencil moved over the blank page and Shantih, full of grace and joy, came to life. Jinny found it easier to think while she was drawing.

The vet had injected Shantih's leg on Sunday morning and by the afternoon she was going sound, proving that the lameness was in her foot. He had told Jinny to try hosing Shantih's foot with cold water, so in the mornings before school and in the evenings after school Jinny was hosing Shantih's leg, but with no result. The vet was coming back on Saturday morning.

"He just doesn't know what to do," Jinny thought miserably. "He doesn't know any more than I do and all this time Shantih's suffering. He doesn't really care either, not the way I do . . ."

"Jinny," hissed the boy sitting next to her. "Wake up."

Jinny started back to the reality of the classroom, automatically covering her drawing with her algebra book.

"Now that you've condescended to give me your attention, for the third time of asking, will you come out to my desk?"

Watched by the rest of the class, Jinny made her way uncertainly to Mr. Palmer's desk. She couldn't think what he wanted. The punishment exercises she had copied from Dolina had come back to her with all the equations ticked correct and "is light beginning to dawn?" written at the foot of them. Jinny had spent nearly two hours struggling through the six equations that had been Monday's homework and, although she didn't think they would be correct, she had got them all finished and handed them in on time.

"Now, Jinny," said Mr. Palmer, looking up from Jinny's algebra exercise book which was open in front of him. "Perhaps you can explain something for me. Here are the punishment exercises you did for me. All correct. And here is Monday's homework. Every one wrong, showing not even a basic understanding of equations. What happened between one exercise and the other? Eh?"

Staring, mesmerised by Mr. Palmer's bulging blue eyes, Jinny struggled to find an explanation.

"The first lot just seemed easier," she muttered lamely. "I could do them."

"Or somebody else could do them? Eh? Isn't that nearer the fact?"

Jinny felt herself blush scarlet—the whole class was listening. She could feel their staring prickling her spine. Memories of her primary school, when, without meaning to, she had got Dolina into trouble, swam back into Jinny's mind.

"Ken helped me," Jinny blurted out, changing her story in mid-stream. "He's a boy that lives with us."

"So you didn't find them easy? You needed help? Take a look at this."

A nicotine-stained forefinger directed Jinny's attention to one of the equations. At first it was only a jumble of meaningless letters and figures, and then Jinny saw what was wrong. Somehow in the workings she must have jumped from one equation to the next, then copied the correct answer.

"It's that rickety old school bus," Jinny thought. "Jumping about."

"I don't think anyone helped you. I think you copied them. I think someone in this class did them for you and you copied them down?"

Jinny paused to test the soundness of her lie, then, looking Mr. Palmer straight in the eye, said: "Ken did them. I copied them after he'd done them for me."

"I do not believe you," stated Mr. Palmer, "but I don't intend to waste any more time over you. You'll go to detention tonight and do the first of the punishment exercises then bring it to me in my room."

"Not detention. I can't. Mum or Dad meet me at Glenbost

because Shantih's lame. They'd be mad if I wasn't on the school bus."

"Give me your phone number and I'll let your parents know that you're being detained. Though, from the look of the detention book, I should think they must be quite used to your non-arrivals."

"Oh, you can't. There's no one at home today," said Jinny, panicked into instant lies by the thought of her maths teacher actually speaking to her father.

Without words, Mr. Palmer's look conveyed that once again he did not believe Jinny.

"Very well," he said. "Tell your parents that you will be in detention tomorrow. Now sit down and have the good manners to pay attention while I am teaching you."

As Jinny went back to her seat, Mr. Palmer's gaze picked out Dolina's bright pink face.

"Whoever did the equations for Jinny to copy was not doing her a favour. She is here to learn how to do algebra, not to learn how to cheat."

"Now Jinny, read out the next equation and we'll work it on the blackboard."

The girl in front of Jinny turned round and pointed out the equation. Jinny stood up and read it out.

"You could teach monkeys to read," she thought as she sat down. "You don't need to understand what you're reading to be able to read it." Then she thought "Shantih". Who would hose her foot on Friday evening and was it doing any good anyway? Jinny's eyes filled with sudden, infuriating tears.

The detention hour was almost over on Friday afternoon and Jinny was still struggling with the third equation, when Mr. Palmer came to the door of the detention room and beckoned her out.

"Right," he said. "Come along to my room and we'll go over them together."

Following Mr. Palmer down the corridor, Jinny glanced at her watch. It was five to five. If she missed the six o'clock bus there wasn't another one until eight o'clock. "Please don't let him keep me too long," she prayed. "Let me catch the six o'clock bus."

"I think," said Mr. Palmer, when he had looked at Jinny's

attempts to work out the equations, "we had better go back to basics."

Jinny groaned aloud.

Going back to basics took until a quarter to six. Dragging on her anorak, Jinny ran full pelt out of the school, across the yard and raced for the bus station. She was just in time to see her bus drawing away.

"Stop!" Jinny yelled. "Wait for me!" But the driver paid no attention to her.

"Doom and double doom," swore Jinny in a fury of utter frustration. "Oh curses, curses, curses. Two hours to wait when I should be at home hosing Shantih's leg. Bloomin' algebra. Bloomin' school. Blast it all."

For minutes Jinny stood fuming, but there was nothing she could do about it. The bus had gone and that was that. Slowly she wove her way through the people pouring into the bus station.

"All going home," thought Jinny, "and here I am stuck here for two hours."

She was going into a shop to buy a bar of chocolate when suddenly she changed her mind and went into the fruiterers next door.

"I'll buy two apples," she decided, "and take them to the white pony."

Now that Jinny had thought of something to do, the two hours she had to wait didn't seem nearly so long. She bought the apples and began to walk briskly out to the riding school, thoughts of Easter filling her head.

"If only they could talk," Jinny thought. "If only they could tell us what has happened to them. When she was a show pony what went wrong?" And Jinny imagined all the different things that could have happened to the white pony to bring her down in the world. Bought by rich parents for a daughter who was scared of her, then sold on as a dangerous runaway? Or kept until she was too old to win in the ring then sent to a sale? Or maybe when she was young she had been difficult to ride; perhaps only one girl could show her, and when the girl had to go abroad with her family the pony had reared in the show ring coming down on top of her rider, injuring her for life. Perhaps the pony had been sold cheaply to get rid of her.

Jinny had nearly reached the riding school when the sound of hooves made her stop and listen. Then, coming down the road towards her, was a ride being led by Brenda on her bay.

Jinny's heart sank with disappointment. Now she wouldn't be able to give the apples to Easter, for she could see the white pony trailing along behind the ride. The chestnut pony behind Brenda was already frothing at the mouth as the girl riding him tried to hold him back. Of all the horses, the chestnut was the only one who showed any life. The others walked slowly along, heads down, eyes half-closed, the clink of loose shoes ringing against the road as the ride dragged its way past Jinny.

Easter was being ridden by a heavy man sitting far back in the saddle, his legs stuck out in front, his elbows wide. In one hand he held the reins in a muddled twist of leather. In the other he held a long cutting whip.

"Get on, you lazy cow," the man shouted, kicking his feet against Easter's shoulders as he saw Jinny watching him.

The gaunt weariness of the white pony never changed. As if she moved through a nightmare, she walked on with a slow stride. Her harsh coat stretched tightly over her protruding bones as she moved.

The man jangled the rusty bit in Easter's mouth. "Gee up. Get on," he said, and hit the pony with his whip.

The white pony shuddered through her whole frame. For a second she seemed about to break into a trot. Almost, her head lifted, her eyes brightened and her worn-out limbs carried her sweetly, lightly, into an effortless trot. Almost, but not quite. Before she actually changed from her slow, dragging walk, she fell back into the reality of her age, the reality of what it meant to be an old pony at the Arran Riding School.

"Don't hit her! Oh, don't hit her!" cried Jinny, dashing forward to the pony's head. "She can't go any faster. She's too old, too tired."

At the sound of Jinny's voice, Brenda turned and came trotting to the end of the ride.

"What's up?" she snapped.

"Can't get this brute to move," said the man.

"He was hitting her," said Jinny, "and she's tired and old and shouldn't be working. She should be retired."

Brenda reached down and grasped Easter's rein. "Keep your legs back," she said sharply to the man. "You kick behind the girth not in front of it. And as for you, Miss Busybody, buzz off with you and mind your own business."

"It *is* my business . . ." began Jinny, but Brenda, urging her own horse forward, was dragging the white pony with her.

As Jinny watched helplessly, Easter turned her head to look back at Jinny, looked straight at her with wise dark eyes. As vividly as if Easter had spoken, Jinny knew that the pony was asking for help, asking Jinny to rescue her.

Jinny stood stock-still, watching the ride trail away from her. The moment of communication with the pony had been direct, undeniable, as if there was no such thing as sight known to humans and for a split moment Jinny had been able to see.

"It's all your imagination," said Petra's voice in Jinny's head. But Jinny knew it wasn't. The white pony had asked Jinny to save her, to free her from the torments of the riding school.

"I will, of course I will," Jinny promised. "I'll find a way. Even if I have to steal you, I'll find a way to rescue you."

There was no one at Glenbost to meet Jinny.

"Abandoned I am," she thought and, shrugging her shoulders, she began to walk to Finmory. Her mind was full of plans to save Easter, to bring her back to Finmory. "She can share the field with Shantih and Bramble. It wouldn't cost any more. Dad couldn't object. Maybe they'd be glad to let her come here."

"We've been looking for a good home for her, somewhere where she can retire. Thank you for taking her," said the Brenda in Jinny's head. But when Jinny thought about the real Brenda, with her painted mouth and hard, calculating eyes, Jinny had to admit that it wasn't very likely. "If I don't save her, they'll work her until she dies," thought Jinny, and saw Easter collapsing in the road, fighting to get to her feet again, then, exhausted, letting her head sink back into the gutter

Again Jinny saw the quick, urgent turn of Easter's head, saw, as clearly as if the pony was standing in front of her, the lips pulled back by the rusty bit, the hard leather of the bridle biting into her skin, her skull almost visible under the harsh coat, and again Jinny experienced the desperation that pleaded from the dark eyes. Again Jinny saw the pony as she must once have been, vibrant with life and energy, red rosettes flickering from her bridle as she was cantered round the show ring.

"I swear," said Jinny, "I swear I'll save you. And bring you to Finmory. I'll find a way."

When Jinny reached home she left her schoolbag at the stable and went straight down to Shantih. Ken was sitting by the gate, Kelly lying beside him.

"I hosed her leg for you," Ken said, pushing open the gate for Jinny. "Had a few soothing words with her."

"Thanks. That foul man kept me in for ages. I was going to start and hose her now," said Jinny, suddenly feeling too worn out to do anything except flop into an armchair, eat her supper and go to sleep.

Shantih limped across the field to Jinny, hardly able to put her foot to the ground.

"She's worse, isn't she, and the vet doesn't seem to know what to do next. He only said hosing wouldn't do any harm. Not as if he thought it would cure it."

"Give her time," said Ken gently.

"Time's no use if she's getting worse," stated Jinny, as she ran her hand down Shantih's neck and, stooping, picked up Shantih's lame foreleg. There was no swelling and no heat. Not a thing to show what was causing the lameness.

The chestnut Arab blew gustily over Jinny's head.

"What's wrong with it?" demanded Jinny. "What's wrong with your foot?"

But Shantih only flurried her nostrils again and nudged Jinny for titbits.

As Jinny straightened up she had the spine-tingling sensation that someone was watching them from behind the hedge.

Suddenly, Kelly, barking madly, scorched across the field. He charged at the hedge, lips wrinkled up from his teeth, his hackles raised.

"Kelly," shouted Ken. "Come back!"

But the dog fought his way through the hedge. At the other side, his barking changed to a deep growling.

"Kelly, come back!" Ken commanded.

Unwillingly, growling and grumbling to himself, Kelly came back.

"There was someone there," said Jinny, fear of horse thieves springing full-blown into her mind. "I felt them too."

But although they searched around the hedge and looked across the fields that reached down to the sea, there was no sign of any intruders.

"Probably only rabbits," said Ken.

"He doesn't get worked up like that about rabbits," said Jinny.

"Angels in disguise, then, waiting to be entertained, and we've driven them away?" said Ken.

Jinny ignored his suggestion.

"There was someone there," she said. "I'm sure there was."

CHAPTER FOUR

That night Jinny hardly slept at all. When she did fall asleep it was only to dream of Shantih, Bramble and the white pony being led away by night thieves to be sold to a racehorse trainer, who forced them to gallop endlessly, round and round the Grand National course. Screaming, Jinny would wake herself up, but each time she fell asleep again the same dream was waiting for her.

Twice she crept down to the field just to make sure that Shantih and Bramble were safe. The second time, her father was waiting for her.

"Where have you been?" he demanded crossly.

"To make sure Bramble and Shantih are still in their field," muttered Jinny.

"It is half-past two in the morning. Get back to bed and stay there."

"We told you there was someone lurking behind the hedge tonight. Kelly went for them."

"Ken said it was only rabbits," replied Mr. Manders, shepherding Jinny upstairs. "Kelly would know if there was anyone suspicious. He'd give the alarm."

"He gave the alarm and none of you listened to him," said Jinny, climbing back up to her room. "Fat lot of use having a guard dog and when he barks saying it's only rabbits. Bet he feels like Little Dog Turpie."

"Bed," said her father. "And stay there till the morning."

"I will do," said Jinny. "Even if I hear the hobyahs carrying you off."

For the rest of the night, Jinny tossed and turned restlessly. Once she got up, went through to the other half of her bedroom and stood in front of the Red Horse.

"Cure Shantih," Jinny murmured. "Make her foot better."

But tonight the Red Horse was only a painting on her wall. Its yellow eyes stared back blankly at Jinny. No spirit charged it with the strange power. Jinny was speaking to herself.

"And the white pony. Help me to save the white pony,"

pleaded Jinny, but the painting remained only a painting.

"Pretty faded, too." Jinny thought as she turned away. "I'll need to repaint it."

But she knew she wouldn't. Several times before, Jinny had planned to repaint the Horse, but when she had actually stood in front of it with her paints and brush she had been unable to touch it. Mr. MacKenzie had told her that once the Red Horse had been painted on a stone at Finmory's gates and every spring the tinkers had repainted it.

When the stone was blown up by the owners of Finmory who were making more flowerbeds, the tinkers had come in the winter when the house was empty, and a girl with long red hair, like Jinny's own, had painted the Red Horse on the wall, while an old woman of the tinkers had watched her. "Moaning and chanting while the lassie was painting the Horse on the wall," Mr. MacKenzie had said, remembering it from his unbelievable boyhood.

"Maybe that is the only way it can be repainted," Jinny thought, as she went back to bed. "Only the tinkers can do it."

At six o'clock Jinny decided that it was most definitely morning. Now it was daylight she could see Shantih and Bramble grazing safely in their field but, nevertheless, Jinny felt a vague sense of unease. Stray wisps from her dream still wandered through her mind and she couldn't shake off the certainty that there had been someone watching them last night.

She dressed and went out into the still, early-morning world, the grass heavy with dew, the grey sky washed with primrose and violet lights, the mountains beyond the moors bulked against the luminous morning light.

Filling a bucket with pony-nuts, Jinny took them down to the horses. At her approach, Bramble came bustling to the gate, smelling the nuts.

"You don't need any," Jinny told him, pushing past him to get into the field.

"I'm starving," exclaimed Bramble in sharp pig-squeals of greed, as he swarmed round Jinny trying to wedge his face into the bucket.

Jinny tipped half the nuts on to the grass and left Bramble suctioning them down while she went to feed Shantih.

The Arab blew over the bucket then picked out one or two nuts and rolled them round her mouth fastidiously, swallowed them, then rested her head on Jinny's shoulder.

"Why are you still lame?" Jinny asked her, as she pulled Shantih's ears and scratched along the root of her mane. "What is wrong with your foot? Oh, why can't you tell me what's wrong? The vet's coming again this morning—fat lot of good that will do . . ."

Suddenly Jinny knew that this time there was someone watching her. She didn't turn round but went on talking to Shantih.

"Why can't he find out what's wrong? If you hurt your foot when you jumped, why isn't it better by now?" Jinny mouthed, wishing she had Kelly with her.

She heard Bramble swing round, positioning himself between the intruder and his few remaining nuts. Straining her ears, Jinny could just make out the light, almost silent footsteps coming towards her. In Shantih's dark eye she could see the reflection of a small figure walking towards them. It was too small to be a man and yet it didn't look like a child.

Jinny sprang round. "Tam!" she cried, and dashed across to where the tinker boy was standing. "How super to see you again. I thought you said you were all going away, that you wouldn't be back here?"

The tinker boy stood without speaking. He was about nine years old, a pick of bird bones draped in a man's jacket and old jeans cut short to fit him. His white face was sugared with dirt and his greasy hair was tucked back behind his ears. He stared straight at Jinny from eyes so black that she could see no pupil in them, only an intensity of purpose.

"Are you back staying at Alex McGowan's farm?" Jinny asked, wishing Tam would speak. "How's Zed?" she tried, asking for Tam's dog.

But still he only stood, fixing Jinny with his commanding collie eye.

"Would you like a cup of tea?" Jinny asked. "Some breakfast? I'm just going in for mine. Come on, come with me."

The boy flinched away. For a moment, Jinny thought he was going to make off without telling her why he was there. She put her hand out to catch his arm and the boy ducked away from her, lifting his arm to shield himself from an expected blow.

"Don't be silly. I'm not going to hurt you," said Jinny. But she had seen Jake, the man of the Brodie tinkers, knock a young woman to the ground. She knew why Tam had cringed away from her.

Last Easter, when Shantih and Bramble had been stolen, Tam, risking Jake's fury, had come to tell Jinny where to find the horses. If it hadn't been for Tam's courage, Jinny knew that she would never have seen Shantih or Bramble again.

"What's wrong? What can I do for you?"

Tam knitted his lips together, twisted his fingers.

"You've got to help me get her out," he said, the words, hard stones, painful to utter.

"Who? Get who out?"

"It's the old woman, Keziah. They've got her and locked her in."

"Prison?" demanded Jinny. She remembered the old woman she had seen when she had ridden to the tinkers' camp; her eagle-face and thick, steel-grey hair; the strength in her claw-like hand when she had gripped Jinny's knee, trying to force her to buy wood-chip flowers.

"The old woman I saw at your camp? They couldn't put an old woman like that in prison."

"In the hospital," said Tam.

"Is she ill? She must be if she's in hospital."

"She heard her call," said Tam. "She knows it's her time. Yon woman from the Social came. Brought an ambulance and took her off."

"You mean she's dying?"

"Aye."

"Then she's better in hospital. That's the best place for her if she's very ill," said Jinny. "Honestly."

"We've got to get her out."

"But they'll be trying to cure her."

"She's ninety-two. She's ready to go, but she'll no die shut in there without her folk round her."

"But where could she go? You mean back to your camp?" Jinny remembered the broken-down vans and black tarpaulin hump that had been the tinkers' camp. "Back to Jake?"

"Naw," said the boy. "He's gone off. Left her. Keziah said I was to tell you."

"Tell me? But what can I do? You can't leave hospital

until the doctors let you out. And where would she go to if she did get out?"

"You said you'd help me. You said to come and ask. Well, I'm asking."

"I will help," said Jinny. "You saved Shantih and I will help. I promised. I want to help, but what can I do.?" Jinny saw Tam, the old tinker woman and herself standing in a busy Inverburgh street. Keziah, still wearing a white hospital gown and wrapped in a flannel dressing gown.

"She said to bring you to see her. Will you come? Aye?"

"When?" asked Jinny, shrinking from the thought of going into the grim Inverburgh Hospital; knowing in her heart that she was afraid of seeing the old tinker woman. In Jinny's life, people were either alive or else you heard they'd died. You didn't visit them, knowing they were dying.

"Today."

"Not this morning," said Jinny. "The vet's coming to see Shantih. She's lame, but the vet doesn't know what's causing it."

"Aye." Tam agreed. "Come this afternoon."

Excuses skipped through Jinny's mind. "Jinny Manders," she told herself severely, "I am disgusted with you. You promised you'd help Tam—anything, anytime, and here you are trying to wriggle out of it."

"O.K." she said.

"Three o'clock. That's when they let you in."

"Outside the hospital?"

"Aye," said Tam, and he swung round and ran across the field.

"Don't you want some breakfast?" Jinny shouted, but he ignored her, running faster, diving through the hedge at the place where Kelly had barked last night.

It was after eleven before the vet came. Jinny had haltered Shantih and was grooming her at the kitchen door when she heard his car coming down the drive.

"And about time too," she said to Shantih. "If I miss the half-past one bus I'll not be at the hospital to meet Tam. He'll think I'm not coming." Knowing how easily she could miss buses when she didn't want to go somewhere, Jinny was keeping a close watch on the time.

"Any improvement?" asked Jim Rae, coming to stand

beside Shantih, running his hand down her shoulder.

"None," said Jinny. "And I've hosed it night and morning. Every day."

"It's worth trying. Still, can't say I've much hope. Run her up for me again."

Jinny did, but after a few strides the vet stopped her.

"We know it's her foot," he said, and yet again examined Shantih's hoof—tapping the hoof wall and the sole, pressing her frog. "Doesn't seem to feel a thing."

"But she does when she's walking. She feels it then," said Jinny urgently. "No good saying she doesn't feel anything when she does."

"A twist or a strain should be showing signs of clearing up by this time. Need to have it X-rayed. See what that shows up."

"And what will that cost?" asked Mr. Manders, coming to the kitchen door.

"The vet smiled ruefully. "Transports the thing. She'll need to go up to the Vet College in Glasgow. Nearest place.

"Cost a mint," groaned Mr. Manders.

"I've another horse going up. One of Danny Sargeant's prize Clydesdales. Got a kick on the shoulder. Fractured the bone and been standing in for six months. Needs to go back up for an X-ray in about a fortnight. I could arrange for Shantih to go with it. Danny'll not mind. You could share the cost."

"Sounds a good idea," said Mr. Manders, looking at Jinny. "Will it make any difference, Shantih having to wait?"

The vet shook his head. "May have cleared itself up by then. These mystery lamenesses sometimes do. And if it's the worst, time won't make any difference."

"The worst?" asked Mr. Manders. "You mean it may be something you can't cure?"

"Could be a fractured bone in the foot, and you can never rule out . . ."

The vet, catching Jinny's desperate expression, stopped himself in mid-sentence.

"But no point in worrying ourselves about these things until we get the result of the X-ray."

"You'll fix it up then?" said Mr. Manders.

"Will do," said the vet. "Though I'm quite sure Danny will be delighted to share the costs."

Jinny stood with her arm over Shantih's withers, feeling

the warm, strong bulk of her horse. Alive. Now. Shantih. The horror of the journey to the Vet College, the X-ray, the waiting to find out, to be told. Jinny shook back her hair, squared her shoulders.

Suddenly she remembered that she had to ask the vet if he knew the Arran Riding School.

"Mr. Rae!" Jinny shouted. "Wait a minute."

Leaning out of the car window, hand on the wheel, Jim Rae waited.

"Do you know the Arran Riding School? The horses are in a terrible condition. Absolutely dreadful."

The vet frowned and nodded. "So Martin Post's back to his old tricks is he? Used-car dealer by trade. The stables are a profitable sideline, and I dare say he uses them to fiddle his income tax. About two years ago, Miss Tuke got the R.S.P.C.A. to him. They took him to court, almost lost his licence, but he promised to clean the place up. Bought a few better horses, got rid of the worst ones. Wasn't too bad after that. I expect he's slid back into his old ways. If I'd anything to do with it, that Martin Post would never be allowed near another animal in his life."

"Martin Post?" Jinny said, "I thought it was a woman called Brenda something who owned it?"

"Is that what the current one's called? Been dozens of girls doing all the work for him. Lured by the thought of a cottage to themselves. I blame the idiots who pay him money to sit on his old crocks as much as anyone. I'll give you a phone when I've fixed up for the Vet College. Bye."

Jinny watched his car purr down the drive. She would need to phone the R.S.P.C.A. and tell them about the white pony, tell them that if they rescued Easter she could give her a good home.

"Jinny," called her mother. "If you're going to catch that bus, you'll need to get a move on."

"Double oats," Jinny promised Bramble, as she trotted in to Glenbost. He glowered, switching his tail. "I know you're mad," she told him, running her hand down his shaving-brush mane, "but it's no good sulking. I don't want to go any more than you do. But we've got to, so come on."

The bus was a half an hour late reaching Inverburgh. "Tam will think I'm not coming," Jinny told herself, as she scuttled through the hordes of Saturday afternoon shoppers crowding the pavements. "I know. I saw you," Jinny said, scowling furiously at a driver who had sounded his horn at her when she made a road detour round a crowd of boys. She ran on, panicking in case she should be late, desperate to reach where she didn't want to go.

As the soot-blackened walls of the hospital came into sight, Jinny slowed down, her flesh clinging more tightly to her bones at the sight of the high-barred windows through which she could glimpse hospital beds and screens; the stone steps leading up to the Ionic columns and on into the hospital itself. For a moment she couldn't see Tam and then she spotted him standing close to one of the columns, looking like a small, terrified animal crouching at the roots of a tree.

"Hi," said Jinny. "Bus was late. Do we just go in?"

Tam nodded but didn't move.

"Come on then," said Jinny, trying to sound as if walking into hospital was no more to her than walking into Finmory kitchen. "I expect she'll be pleased to see you." And Jinny marched on up the steps and pushed open the swing doors.

The hospital smell leapt out at her, hitting her with a wave of fear.

"Don't be a fool," she told herself. "Nothing is going to happen to you. You're only going to visit an old woman." "An old dying woman," mocked an echo in Jinny's mind. "Don't," Jinny warned herself. "Don't let it start." But it was too late, all the other things that she was worrying about came bursting out. The fear of the X-ray; the thought of the white pony that somehow HAD to be rescued from the riding school; and the thought of school where her last visit to detention meant that some time next week the Headmaster would want to see her.

"Well, don't just stand there," Jinny said, turning on Tam. "Come on, we'd better see her now we're here. Do you know which ward it is?"

Tam, cowering into his jacket, shook his head.

"Then we'll have to find someone to ask." And, holding the basket of fruit which her mother had given her for Keziah well in front of her, Jinny pushed open another swing door and marched down a brown, tiled corridor, Tam scuttling in her shadow.

CHAPTER FIVE

"And where are you two off to?" asked a woman in a green overall who didn't look much like Jinny's idea of a nurse. She thought her mother would have things to say about her fingernails.

"We want to see Keziah Brodie," said Jinny.

"You're far too young to be in here by yourselves."

"We've got permission," said Tam.

"And who gave you permission?"

"The doctor," said Tam, fishing a dirty-looking piece of paper out of his pocket. "He said I could come. There's nobody else to visit her."

The woman took the paper, holding it disdainfully between fat thumb and fat finger, and read it. She blew down hairy nostrils and handed it back to Tam. "In my day, rules were rules. Children stayed outside. Ward 29 you want." She pointed down the corridor. "Turn to your right at the end. Up the stairs. Left, then right again. Ward 29. And don't go poking your noses in. Ask if you can't find the way." Turning, she flapped off on flat feet.

"Come on," said Jinny. "Before someone else tries to stop us."

Jinny led the way down the long corridor, looking straight ahead, trying not to look past the curtains that half covered entrances to the wards, trying not to see the medical posters stuck on the walls, or the torture machines parked in alcoves. She found the stairs, climbed up them, looking through leaded windowpanes over the city streets.

"To be shut in here. To be waiting to die . . ." thought Jinny, and wanted to turn and run, back to Finmory, to feel the wind and the sun, to breathe fresh air again.

They turned left, along the corridor, then right.

"This is it," said Tam. "I know it now."

Written above an archway was "Ward 29". Jinny breathed in hard and pushed past the curtain that hung from the arch. She found herself in a long ward, the beds arranged along the walls on either side. For a second Jinny thought that nearly all the beds were empty and then she realised that the old women lying in them were so thin that their bodies were invisible under the bedclothes, only their heads sunk back on the pillows showed that the beds were occupied. Here and there sat a few palsied visitors.

Jinny didn't know what to do next. She stood awkwardly, trying not to stare at the parchment skins, gaping mouths and white wisps of hair. They were like skulls and Jinny couldn't keep her eyes away from them.

"Hulloa there," said a breezy voice, and a nurse came out of a doorway behind them. "Can I help? Looking for someone?"

"Oh yes," said Jinny, her relief sounding in her voice. "We've come to see Keziah Brodie."

"Why, that's right. I've met Tam." The nurse beamed down at them. "Keziah will be really pleased to see you. She's in the day room. I'll take you there." And the nurse walked down between the rows of beds, opened a door at the end of the ward, crossed a passage and opened another door. "In here, that's it."

The day room was a small carpeted room. At one end, a gaudy colour television set blared out a full-blast commentary on a football match. Grouped around it in a semi-circle sat half a dozen old women. Two were droolingly asleep; the others sat in a drugged dream, staring from themselves into nothing, their fingers knitting and knotting, their lips working, their bodies twisted by age into grotesque shapes.

Jinny was back in the yard of the riding school. She felt the same hopelessness, the same empty endurance as she had felt from the riding-school horses. But these were people. Some day her mother? Some day herself?

For a moment Jinny wondered which of them was Keziah. Not one of them looked the least like the old woman Jinny had seen at the tinkers' camp. Then Jinny saw her. She was sitting alone, staring through a barred window. Her back was erect, her steel-grey hair drawn away from the strong profile of her face; her lips were firm, her tanned skin deeply wrinkled. Despite the destructive noise of the television, there was a stillness, a silence in Keziah Brodie. The other old women had reached an end, were worn out, their days over. They had taken refuge from the reality of pain and the fear of death, had abandoned themselves to this doped infancy. But Keziah Brodie looked from herself with the assured air of a traveller about to start on an eagerly-awaited journey.

"Look who nurse has brought to see you," said the nurse, in a pink marshmallow voice quite different to the voice she had used when she had been talking to Jinny and Tam. "Isn't that nice now? There now, we'll feel so much better now we've got visitors, won't we? Someone to chat to? There now. That's my girl. Ups-a-daisy we go."

The nurse fussed around, straightening the rug over Keziah's legs, easing her up in the chair, tidying back her hair. But Keziah paid no attention to her.

"You'll hear the bell when visiting's over," the nurse said to Jinny. "You're rather late. Not much time left." And with a brisk tidying up of two of the other old women she left the room.

When the nurse had gone, Keziah slowly turned her head, her dark eyes set in their web of wrinkles acknowledged Tam and Jinny.

"You'll be the lass from Finmory," she said. "Tam brought you then."

"Yes," said Jinny. "How are you feeling? Mum sent you this fruit. She hopes you'll be much better soon."

"I'm ready to go," said Keziah, brushing aside the polite froth of Jinny's words. "The call will be for me in a week or two. I know that well."

"Oh no. Don't say that. You'll get better. That's what hospitals are for—to help you to get well."

Keziah laid her claw-hand on Jinny's arm.

"But before I go, there's one thing still to be done. Tam told me you gave him your word to be helping him when he was asking?"

"That's right," said Jinny. "I did."

"Then it is now we're needing you. You have to get me out of this place. It was only them with their interfering that brought me here. I'm helpless now with my age upon me. It's you must arrange the car to take me to Jock MacKenzie's. He has the bothy on the hill. He'll not be refusing Keziah Brodie the use of it."

"Oh, but you couldn't. Couldn't possibly leave hospital and go to live in Mr. MacKenzie's bothy. It's only a ruin. No one's lived in it for years. And you have to stay in hospital. They'll be treating you. You can't just leave," prattled Jinny anxiously.

"And where would the pride of Keziah Brodie be if she were to die in a place like this?"

"But you're warm here and comfortable," said Jinny in her mother's voice.

"Never to breathe the free air again, never to see the hills or the sea. To die without my folks around me. I see it in your eyes that you know the truth of it." The old woman's hand tightened on Jinny's arm.

"But aren't you having tablets and pills and things? You can't just stop taking them."

"Their filthy poisons," said Keziah, and she spat contemptuously on to the turquoise carpet. "I've cured myself all my days with the herbs of the hill. What would I want with their poison?"

"You just can't do that. You have to take medicine. You have to stay in hospital."

The grip of Keziah Brodie's talons bit into Jinny's arm. "You with the red hair and knowledge of the Red Horse speak the truth that is on your heart."

Jinny felt herself forced to look straight into the old woman's eyes, her gaze drawn to meet Keziah's. The voice she spoke with was her own true voice.

"I couldn't bear to be shut away in here. It's a foul place. I don't know how anyone ever gets well in places like this. There's no air. Just being here makes me ill. I couldn't bear it. Not to die in here and never breathe the hills again. I'll find some way of getting you out."

"Tomorrow," demanded Keziah. "Come and take me away tomorrow."

"Well . . ." began Jinny. "I'll try . . ."

"You'll tell Jock MacKenzie to be expecting me."

"Yes, but . . . I'll need to arrange a car. And I'll need help. I really don't know if I'll manage to get you out tomorrow."

The bell for the end of the visiting time shrilled through Jinny's fumbling excuses.

"Be bringing Maggie with you," Keziah told Tam. "She'll have the care of me for the few days I'm on the hill."

"Please," warned Jinny. "Don't get too worked up about it. Honestly, I may not manage to get you away tomorrow. There's a lot to be arranged."

"You must be taking me out of here tomorrow. I have the work that must be done."

"Well . . . I will do my best, but . . ."

"Ah, still here," said the nurse, coming in to make sure that Jinny and Tam were getting ready to go.

"Weren't you the lucky girlie to have two young friends to visit you like this," the nurse twittered. Then, without warning, she stepped forward, grasped Keziah's nose tightly between her finger and thumb, tipped back the old woman's head and dropped a red and black capsule into her mouth. Deftly she held Keziah's mouth firmly shut until she had swallowed the capsule.

Jinny stared, utterly appalled. She wouldn't have given Kelly a pill like that, not without speaking to him first, explaining to him what she was going to do.

"Come along now. Off with you," the nurse said to Jinny and Tam.

Keziah had turned from them and was again staring out of the window, distant and remote, a stillness upon her as if the assault had never happened.

"Don't worry," said Jinny. "I will be back tomorrow. I promise."

They found their way out of the hospital and Jinny organised Tam into a café.

"We've got to get her out tomorrow. She can't be left in there," Jinny told Tam when they were each seated in front of a glass of orange. "I've got to find someone to help. You weren't much use at all. Never opened your mouth, did you?"

"I couldn't be talking to Keziah. It was only yourself she had the eye for."

"Well, you'll need to buck up your ideas tomorrow," Jinny told him. "We'll need a car to get her to Mr. MacKenzie's. No good asking at home. Mum would have a canary at the thought, and Ken can't drive."

Suddenly Jinny thought of Nell Storr. She'd help. Nell owned a gift shop in Inverburgh. Not a trashy, tartan-touristy place but a special shop, more like an Aladdin's cave than a shop. She only bought things directly from the craftsmen who made them—weavings, carvings, jewellery, embroideries, paintings and pottery. When the Manders had first come to live at Finmory it was Nell who had encouraged Mr. Manders and Ken by selling their pots, and even now that Mr. Manders' first book had been a huge success he still made pots for her. She sold Jinny's pictures as well, was always looking for more, but Jinny wasn't very keen on giving them to her. Once a painting reached Nell's shop, Jinny never saw it again.

"I'll ask Nell Storr," Jinny told Tam. "We'll go and ask her now. I'm sure she'll understand and she's got a car."

"I'd better find our Maggie," said Tam. "Keziah will need someone to mind her. She'll be mad at me if I don't get Maggie."

"It's not absolutely sure that I'll get it all organised," said Jinny, faltering under Tam's certainty. "The car's one thing, but we've got to make them let Keziah come with us."

"The likes of them wouldn't be stopping Keziah," said Tam.

He stood up in a swift, furtive movement.

"You'll be there tomorrow?" he said, and with a quick duck of his head, Tam fled the café.

To Jinny's relief, Nell Storr was in her shop.

"Ah, Jinny. Joy to see you," cried Nell, flinging her arms around Jinny. "Weeks since I've seen you."

"Shantih's been lame," said Jinny, recovering from Nell's embrace. She felt the tightness that had cramped vice-like on her head begin to ease under the warmth of Nell's presence. Today Nell's hair was striped brown and blonde and plaited in a myriad of tiny plaits. She had glitter sprinkled on her eyelids and high cheekbones and two jade earrings hanging from one ear. Her nails were painted gold and she wore a scarlet kaftan, wide and flowing, caught in at her neck, wrists and ankles. Heavy gold and jade chains hung round her neck.

"So that's why you're looking so wretched. Ken did tell me, but I forgot. Still, I've got ten pounds for you. Money for your last two pictures."

"Oh, thanks," said Jinny. "Really it's not Shantih I'm worried about. Well, I am worried about her, terribly worried all the time, but that's not why I'm here. I need help."

"Wait a mo," said Nell. "Mrs. Lindsay, keep an eye on things. I'm going to brew up." Leaving her assistant in charge, Nell took Jinny into the back of the shop

"Herb tea," she said, giving Jinny a steaming mug. "Ken's been getting at me. Now, how can I help?"

Jinny blurted out her story while Nell listened intently.

"Are you sure she is dying?"

"She's positive. Says there's work she still has to do and only a week or two left. We can't leave her there. We must find a way to get her out. All her life she's lived outside and to be shut in there . . ." Jinny spread open her hands. "We can't leave her there. We can't."

"If there's nothing more they can do for her we'll take her out," said Nell confidently.

"We'll need a car."

"No problem. I'll pick you and Ken up about twelve tomorrow. You'll need to speak to Mr. MacKenzie. Make sure she can go to his cottage."

"It's not," said Jinny. "Just an old ruin. But if it is where she wants to go . . . How will we get her out of the hospital? Say they won't let her go?"

"Must do," said Nell. "Can't keep you in against your will. She can sign herself out."

Jinny sat beaming at Nell, a smile stretching her face. It all seemed so much easier now that Nell had understood, now that Nell was on their side.

Nell smiled back, her ugly, honest face strong and comforting.

"That's fixed then. See you tomorrow. Now I'll need to go, or Mrs. Lindsay will be having a sit down—as in strike, not chair."

"Thanks very much," said Jinny.

"Feel free," said Nell.

Jinny was just about to leave the shop when Nell called her back.

"Hey, don't forget your cash. Ten pounds," she said, giving Jinny two five-pound notes. "And I'd like some more drawings whenever you feel you can spare a few."

"Thanks," said Jinny, pocketing the money but not committing herself about the drawings.

Outside again, a clock in a bank window said five past four.

"The story of my life," thought Jinny. "Doomed to wander the streets of Inverburgh until it's time for a bus. Still, 'spose I might as well go and try to see Easter again. This time I'll wait. If she is out on a ride, I'll wait until she gets back then give her the apples."

Feeling rich, Jinny bought two pounds of the juiciest-looking apples and a pound of spring carrots and, crunching an apple, walked smartly out to the riding school.

When she reached the yard, a ride was getting ready to go out. Two young women were mounted on Sporty and Queenie, and a girl of about twelve years of age was making feeble attempts to haul herself on to the chestnut pony while he swung away from her each time she got her foot into the stirrup. A little girl in brand-new riding kit was clutching the reins of the 12.2. dark brown pony in her brightly-gloved hands and, to Jinny's dismay, the man she had seen riding Easter was standing at her head, obviously waiting to mount.

"No!" screamed Jinny silently. "No!" She wanted to dash forward and drag Easter away from the man. To shout, "You're far too heavy for her, you and your whip. Leave her alone. Can't you see she's worn out? Can't you see all she wants is a warm stable at night, and days of rest and sun? Can't you see?"

But Jinny bit the words back. If she made a fuss, Brenda would only order her out of the yard. It wouldn't stop the man riding Easter.

Brenda came into the yard talking to a man walking at her side. He had a smooth face as if his features were sinking into melting mounds of flab and his greasy hair was gradually being pushed off his head by the fat. He was wearing a tight navy-blue suit, pointed leather shoes, and from his double chins sprouted a red tie painted with a go-go dancer. He didn't look to Jinny as if he was going to ride.

"I'll be back on Tuesday to check over the books with you," he was saying to Brenda as he turned to go, making Jinny wonder if he was the Martin Post that the vet had told her about. His tiny pigs' eyes smeared over the neglected yard, the wretched horses, the riders, and inside his mounds of fat Jinny could almost hear the mini-computer checking up their value. He was Martin Post. He was the man who made money from this misery. And Jinny knew that nothing but money, the kind of money Jinny didn't have, would ever make this man part with Easter while she still had the strength to go on carrying customers on her back.

"Oke," said Brenda, and as the man turned to go, she came across the yard to take her horse from a girl who was holding it for her. On her way, she stopped to hold the chestnut pony's head while the girl, almost pulling the saddle over the pony's back, at last managed to mount.

"Get up, Mr. Broadbridge," she said to the man with Easter. "Let's get going."

The man grabbed his reins, pulling back Easter's mouth in a cruel grimace, the toe of his booted foot gouging against her ribs as he tried to mount.

Jinny knew what she was going to do. She ran across to Brenda, taking one of the five-pound notes out of her pocket as she ran.

"Please, please can I come for a ride. I'm sorry I'm so late. It was the bus. I've just got here. Look, I've got five pounds. I sold one of my paintings for five pounds!" Jinny tried to make it sound as if it was the most absolutely tremendous thing that could ever happen to anyone. "When I got the money I came to see if there might be the chance of a ride."

Brenda's lightless eyes stared suspiciously at Jinny. "Aren't you the one who rode last Saturday instead of Joyce? You're that kid who was making all the fuss over Easter."

"Only because I think she is such a super pony," enthused Jinny desperately. "She's the one I want to ride."

"You're too late," said Brenda. "We're ready to go now."

"Oh, please, please. Of course I realise that when you want to ride a special pony you have to pay more. That's why I've brought five pounds. That's what I'd expect to pay to pick the pony I want to ride."

Brenda checked over her shoulder, making sure that Martin Post had gone. She plucked the money from Jinny's hand and stuffed it into her anorak pocket.

"Bring Beech out," she said to a group of children who were hanging around the stable doorway, and to the man with Easter, "Swap over, will you? This kid's crazy to ride Easter. You take Beech."

"Oh. Right. I don't mind as long as it's got a bit more life in it than this stubborn brute."

Jinny dumped her apples and carrots in a doorway and took the iron-hard reins from the man. "You're welcome," he said. "I reckon it's spurs that one's needing. She's bone-idle if you ask me."

Jinny said nothing. She ran her hand over the blade of Easter's withers and down over her flat bony shoulder and concave neck. Gently, Jinny smoothed her face, feeling the skull under its thin covering of harsh coat, the great hollows above her eyes. The pony's eyes were nearly closed, the corners of her lips cracked, her nostrils drawn back, even standing in the yard her breathing was distressed.

"Sweet pony," murmured Jinny. "It's all right. There the pony. There Easter." A lump choked in Jinny's throat. Tears of fury filled her eyes. She dug her nails hard into the palm of her hand to stop herself crying.

"Don't stand about," shouted Brenda. "Get on." And Jinny realised that the man was mounted on the moth-eaten Highland and Brenda was looking down from the back of her bay.

"Can't you get on? Here, Wendy, help her up."

"It's O.K." snarled Jinny, and lightly swung herself up on to Easter's back.

"Keep her up with us," Brenda instructed, as she led the ride out on to the golf-course lane.

As Easter moved forward, Jinny could hear her bones creaking together, could feel the excruciating effort of each step the pony took.

"Oh Easter," mourned Jinny. "Easter." She hated Martin Post, hated Brenda, hated everyone who paid to ride Easter. Hated their total lack of awareness, that they could be so blind to such obvious suffering.

Jinny followed the ride for two or three minutes, then she took a deep breath and let out a loud groan. She slumped forward on Easter's neck, heard the man on Beech shout to Brenda and heard the bay horse being cantered towards her.

"Now what's wrong with you?" demanded Brenda.

"I think I'm going to be sick," said Jinny, and she slid slowly to the ground and stood with her head against the saddleflap.

Brenda waited an impatient minute.

"Are you all right?"

"Bit better," croaked Jinny, in what she hoped was the voice of someone struggling not to be sick.

"Well, stay there," said Brenda, "till you feel better. You can join us when we come back."

"I couldn't ride," gulped Jinny.

"Then take her back to the yard," snapped Brenda. "And don't you ask for your money back. You paid for your ride and that's that."

Jinny waited until they had ridden away then she straightened up.

"There," she said to Easter. "At least you can have a rest for an hour."

She loosened the webbing girth that was gummy with sweat and hairs; took off Easter's bridle, holding her by the loop of the reins over her neck.

"Wouldn't you like some grass? Looks super grass at the edges here. Bet you don't often get a chance to eat grass like that." And Easter began to snatch greedily at the green turf.

"Better take you back to the yard," Jinny said after a minute or two. "Before they see us. I've brought apples for you, and carrots, and I can take your saddle off there."

"Have you a halter?" Jinny asked one of the girls in the yard after explaining why she wasn't riding. The girl brought a halter.

"I'll take her tack off," said Jinny. "Does she go into a field?"

"Easter? At night she does, but we do evening rides on a Saturday. I expect she'll be going out on them so leave her in the third stall."

"Where's the field?" asked Jinny. "I'll hold her there until the ride comes back."

The girl pointed to a path. Collecting her apples and carrots, Jinny led Easter along it, to a smallish field, foul with droppings and almost as bare of grass as an Inverburgh street.

When Jinny opened the paper bags, Easter pricked her ears, her eyes brightening.

"All for you," promised Jinny, halving an apple and holding it out to Easter.

The pony lipped the apple from Jinny's hand and stood mumbling and mouthing it until it fell on to the ground.

"Come on," encouraged Jinny, picking it up and holding it out again.

When Easter took it from her this time, Jinny realised what was wrong. She had expected the pony, being old, to have the long teeth of an aged horse, but Easter was so old that her teeth were worn down.

Jinny bit the apple into little bits and fed them to Easter. She ate them greedily, pushing at Jinny's hand for more, her ears pricked and her eyes bright.

"When you're at Finmory," Jinny promised her, "I'll make special food for you—bran mashes with treacle, flaked maize and boiled oats. You can have whatever you want. And no more work. Never, ever again will you have to cart people about. You can have a rest with Shantih and Bramble for company."

Almost as if she understood Jinny's words, Easter lifted her head. Her dark eyes looked straight at Jinny and, for a moment, the wave of communication passed between the pony and the girl.

"I'll rescue you. I'll phone the R.S.P.C.A. tonight, and if they won't do anything, I'll come at night and take you home with me to Finmory. I promise."

But although Jinny phoned the R.S.P.C.A. four times that evening there was no reply.

"Flippin' closed for the weekend," muttered Jinny, banging down the receiver.

"Who are you trying to phone?" asked her father.

"Oh, nobody," said Jinny vaguely, not wanting her parents to know what she was planning just in case the R.S.P.C.A. weren't interested and she had to rescue Easter herself. "It doesn't matter."

She went to bed to toss and turn, thoughts of Shantih, Easter and Keziah boiling in her mind.

CHAPTER SIX

Jinny woke early the next morning, dressed quickly and went out to Shantih. The Arab came limping to meet her.

"I'll hose you now," Jinny told her. "Then I've done it. Today is going to be one of those days."

Shantih danced at the end of the halter rope, her neck arched, head high and tail kinked over her back. After her weeks in the field she was wild to escape, to be galloping over the moors again. Her trumpeting whinny rang out to the mountains.

"Shut up! You'll wake them all," Jinny warned, trying to hold on to the halter rope with one hand, while she aimed the jet of water at Shantih's lame leg with the other. "I'm only doing it so I feel as if I am *doing* something instead of only staring at you. I don't really suppose it will cure you. The vet doesn't think it will. Why can't he find out what's wrong. Why?"

Jinny had been meaning to ride Bramble down to the farm, but Bramble said he would like a day in his own field, if it was all the same to Jinny.

"Only to get the milk," Jinny assured him, but Bramble, turning his quarters on Jinny, said he did not believe her and would she stop bothering him and leave him alone.

"Be that way," said Jinny, and set off for the farm on foot.

On the Sabbath the old farmer milked the cows, then changed into his Sunday black and attended church in the morning and evening. Much to Jinny's relief, he was still working about the yard when she reached it. Asking him about the bothy would be tricky enough without disturbing him when he was getting ready for church. Jinny didn't know what would happen if Mr. MacKenzie said no.

"It's yourself," Mr. MacKenzie said. "I was thinking it might be when I saw the early worms careering past. That horse of yours still lame? I'm thinking it will be the bullet for her." His sharp eyes in their spearmint sockets quizzed Jinny from the shadow of his cap. "A relief to you it would be to be rid of her."

"Milk," said Jinny, clattering down her can. "And when you've filled it, I have something very serious to ask you."

"Is that so now," said Mr. MacKenzie, and went to fill Jinny's can.

"Now, let's be having your very serious request."

"You know the tinkers? Well, the old woman, Keziah, is in Inverburgh Hospital. She's dying. I went to see her yesterday and it's a terrible place. So hot you can't breathe, and stinking, and she's stuck in there with all those other doped old women, and nurses bossing her about. It was terrible."

"Aye, it's a bad business. I was thinking Keziah Brodie would be dying with the open sky above her, not in yon killing bottle. It's the terrible hard life she's had, and a bonny woman she was in her day. Not a farmer that didn't set his cap at her for all she was a tinker lass. But she was true to her own folk. One of the last of the true tinkers before they were eaten by the greed like the rest of us."

"She wants to get out," said Jinny, her hopes rising at Mr. MacKenzie's words. "She told me to ask you if she could come to your bothy. Tam and someone called Maggie will look after her. She said there's something she must do before she dies."

Mr. MacKenzie sucked on his short-stemmed, blackened pipe and stared out over the moors. Jinny waited in silence. She knew Mr. MacKenzie would make up his mind and that would be that. He was not one to be persuaded. Her parents had been most unsympathetic about the whole business, Mrs. Manders repeating all the arguments about why they couldn't possibly bring a ninety-two year-old woman out of hospital and leave her in a bothy.

"If she is as seriously ill as you say," Jinny's father had said, "she's probably on drugs. You can't suddenly take her out. What will you do if she's in pain? Real pain? In hospital they can stop that pain. Can't do that if she's left in that old ruin."

But Ken had understood. He'd pushed his long, bony hand over his eyes and forehead as he listened to Jinny.

"I'll be with you," he'd said. "If I had my way, I'd close all hospitals."

"And when *you're* ill? When *you* need doctors and hospitals? What then?" asked Mr. Manders.

"All the money they spend on their insane bombs and weapons. I'd take it all and build sanctuaries where the sick would be made whole. Places of love, so that even to be in them brought wholeness. Where people could discover who they are."

"Nell's coming about twelve," Jinny had said quickly, to stop any of her family telling Ken that he was talking impossible nonsense. For what was nonsense—the way the world ran things, or Ken's visions?

"I'll be there," Ken had said.

"Aye," said Mr. MacKenzie at last. "She can come here if she has the mind for it. I'd not be turning her away, though it's the tinks will be swarming over my land like the locust when the old yin dies."

"Oh, thank you," breathed Jinny. "We'll bring her here this afternoon. Thank you."

"Aye. I'll take a wee walk up to the bothy myself and be leaving them a few things."

During the morning, Jinny had tried the R.S.P.C.A. number three more times, but still there was no reply. By the time Nell Storr arrived at midday, Jinny had given up hoping for an answer. She had decided that they really must close down for the weekends.

Nell was driving a low-slung Bentley, not Jezebel, her own sports car.

"What a car!" exclaimed Jinny, as she and Ken climbed into its vastness. Normally Jinny thought of all cars as killers and could hardly tell the difference between a Mini and a bus.

"Rather dishy," agreed Nell. "Borrowed, naturally, but better than Jezebel for bringing home the ancient."

"Now," said Nell, when they were purring along the road to Inverburgh, "Plan of action—first we must see her doctor. Then, if it seems at all possible, out she comes. They can't stop us. She can sign herself out."

Tam and Maggie—a young woman with jet-black hair—were waiting for them at the hospital steps. Maggie was dressed in a smart suit and high-heeled shoes. She stepped forward to meet them.

"Good afternoon," she said. "Tam's told me you think you can bring Keziah out of hospital. I'm Maggie McVake, Keziah's great-niece."

Jinny introduced her to Ken and Nell.

"And I'm Jinny," she added.

"Aye. If Keziah has the mind to be finishing her days in the bothy, I'll come and see to her. It's a few years now since I was living in the open, but I'll not care if it's what the old one wants."

Jinny, who had been expecting Maggie to be someone younger but much the same as the other tinkers she had met, couldn't help feeling relieved. Even her mother would approve of Maggie.

They walked up the hospital steps together; Nell, in a fringed black dress, high boots, and with a scarlet and gold shawl over her shoulders, and Ken in his usual black sweater and faded jeans, going first. Then came Maggie and Jinny, with Tam walking in their shadow. Ken pushed open the swing doors and the hospital smell engulfed them. With a shudder, Jinny imagined how it would have been if there had only been herself and Tam. Walking behind Nell and Ken, Jinny felt protected and secure.

"Which way to Keziah?" Nell asked, turning to Jinny, and Jinny stepped up beside them leading the way.

"Remember this feeling," Jinny told herself. "Remember this when you're rescuing Easter. When you feel like this, people can't stop you. Be afraid in yourself and that's when things go wrong. When you're afraid, you're wanting people to stop you."

"Visiting is not for another half-hour," a nurse told them when they reached Ward 29. "You'll have to wait outside."

"Could I see the Sister?" said Nell. "We want to see the doctor who is looking after Keziah Brodie, but I think we had better have a word with the Sister first."

"You must have an appointment to see a doctor."

"Nonsense," said Nell. "There isn't time for that red tape."

"You must have an appointment. You certainly can't demand to see a doctor on a Sunday afternoon."

"What's the trouble, Nurse?" demanded a full-blown, official woman in a blue uniform.

"They want to see a doctor about Keziah Brodie."

"I'll deal with it, Nurse."

"Right, Sister." Casting curious glances over her shoulder, the nurse padded away down the ward.

"Now, what is this disturbance all about. I cannot have shouting in my ward."

"Words, man, words. Let the silence be," murmured Ken.

"We've come," explained Nell, "to take Keziah Brodie home. This isn't the place for her."

"Are you aware that Keziah Brodie is a dying woman?"

"Oh yes. This makes it all the more important that we take her out today with as little disturbance as possible."

"I think," said the Sister in acid tones, "you had all better come into my room till we sort out this nonsense," and she led the way into a small room.

"Now, tell me first of all who you all are."

"This is Mrs. McVake," said Nell briskly. "She is Keziah's great-niece who will look after Keziah, and this is Tam, Keziah's grandson. We are their friends. We're here to help them and unless there is a valid reason why Keziah should not leave the hospital we're here to take her home."

"Keziah Brodie is dying. At the most she has a fortnight to live."

"Yes," said Nell firmly. "We know that and she has the right to choose where she will spend her last days."

"I utterly refuse to consider your taking Keziah away."

"We wish to see her doctor," stated Nell.

For seconds, the Sister and Nell glared eyeball to eyeball. Electricity zizzed between them. Jinny dug her nails into the palms of her hands, clenched her teeth in support of Nell. Ken moved, almost imperceptably, forward. The Sister held her ground, battallioned behind the power of her uniform and her ridiculous little headdress.

"If you please," said Nell.

"There is absolutely no question of Keziah Brodie leaving this hospital today."

Nell's silence waited unmoved, commanding.

"But if you insist on wasting Doctor's precious time . . ." the sister shrugged contemptuously. She picked up a phone and asked for Dr. Gupta to come to her room.

"Thank you," said Nell, as the sister replaced the receiver, ignoring them.

In the minutes of waiting, Jinny felt the hospital smells reach to the very marrow of her bones. She hated the regulated rows of beds, the power of the uniformed men and women, and the white-coated doctors who knew things you didn't want to hear.

"It'll be like this at the Vet College," Jinny thought, "when I'm waiting to hear the result of Shantih's X-ray. Please God. Please God, let her be all right. Let me be able to ride her again."

There was a light tapping on the Sister's door, and an Indian doctor with little hands and neat feet in patent-leather shoes twinkled in.

"Are you having trouble?" he asked, smiling about him. His glinting eyes unfocused.

The Sister explained the situation. "And of course I have already told them that the whole thing is out of the question," she finished.

"Indeed yes. She is a very, very, old, done woman. No more we can do, I am most sorry to say."

"But we can take her home?" insisted Nell.

"I would not advise that course of action. I could not give my sanction for such a foolhardy act."

"She wants to die in her own place," said Ken.

"In my own country we would understand this wish, but here it would not be allowed to take her away."

"No medical reason why she should not come with us?" asked Nell.

"As I have said, she is a very old lady . . ."

"Far too ill for you to remove her," snapped the Sister.

"She will sign herself out," said Nell, her words in the future tense, her tone of voice stating something that had already happened.

A nurse brought in Keziah in a wheelchair. She sat erect and proud, her gnarled hands folded on her plaid rug, her hawk-eyes hooded.

"It is my wish to leave this place," she said, when the doctor explained to her that if she signed the book discharging herself and left against the hospital's advice she would not be readmitted.

"This is no place for me," stated Keziah, her eyes fixed beyond the confines of the room, beyond the prison walls of the hospital to where the winds scoured the bleak moorlands that she had loved all her life.

When they brought the book, Keziah signed it with a firm hand. She was free to go.

The nurse wheeled Keziah out of the room, then a short time later wheeled her back dressed in her own clothes. Ken took the wheelchair.

"The responsibility is entirely yours," said the Sister. "You are removing a dying woman from the only place where she could be properly looked after."

But as they took Keziah down in the lift, she didn't look like a dying woman. She looked like a queen coming again into her rightful kingdom.

Keziah dozed for most of the journey back to Finmory, and when they reached Mr. MacKenzie's yard, the farmer was waiting for them.

"Aye, Keziah," he said, opening the door of the car. "You've come to visit me."

"I have so. And it's grateful I am to you for the use of your bothy."

"Aye," said Mr. MacKenzie solemnly. "You be having the use of it, but keep those thieving fingers away from my eggs and my hens."

"Never did I touch the least feather of one of your hens and I'd sooner be supping the arsenic than be putting one of your eggs to my lips."

Jinny grinned with delight. She caught the fleeting shadow of a smile brush over Tam's pinched face. It had worked. They had rescued Keziah. She was back with people who spoke her own language, who knew her.

Mrs. MacKenzie insisted that Keziah came in for a cup of tea before she went on to the bothy.

"I've put some things up for you," she told Maggie. "And be sending Tam down for milk and eggs as you're needing them."

"It's good of you," said Maggie, "but I'll be paying for them. I've a fine man now. No need for charity. It's only for Keziah's sake that I'm back on the hill."

"There now," soothed Mrs. MacKenzie. "I'm seeing for myself the change in you—but don't be too proud to ask for help if you're needing it."

Ken, Nell and Mr. MacKenzie supported Keziah along the stony track that led to the bothy. Although, wrapped in her swaddlings of dark clothes, Keziah appeared a tall, strong woman, Jinny could tell from the way they helped her over rough patches of ground that she must weigh little more than a child, and once, when they had to cross a burn, Ken swung her into his arms and carried her easily across it.

The bothy was a small, two-roomed cottage that had once been used by shepherds who worked on the farm. Now one gable wall had collapsed, the rusty corrugated iron that was tied over the roof clanged in the wind. The glass of the windows had long since fallen to the ground and been overgrown by nettles. The outside door stood open. Running ahead of the others, Jinny looked in and saw that one of the rooms was still reasonably intact. A peat fire glowed in the open hearth; on a broken-down bed-settee were blankets and pillows; two buckets of water stood by a large pan and a blackened kettle, and a wicker basket was full of milk, eggs, bread and vegetables. On the wooden floor was a thick woollen rug, and two other old chairs stood against the wall.

"To have somewhere like this," Jinny thought longingly, "of my very own. Where I could ride and paint and no one to bother me."

She ran across the room and looked out at the back of the bothy. There was a small overgrown garden, then about an acre of land fenced off from the hill, the grass in it growing lush and sweet.

"For Easter," thought Jinny at once. "She can come here. Mr. MacKenzie will think she belongs to the tinkers. Mum and Dad don't need to know anything about her—least, not straight away." It seemed almost too good to be true.

They settled Keziah on to the bed-settee, wrapping the blankets about her, putting pillows at her head. The old woman sank back, her eyes closing, the bone in her beak nose sharp, her mouth sunken. For the first time, Jinny saw the resemblance between her and the other dandelion-headed women they had left lying flat and thin in their regimented ward.

"Best leave her to herself," said Maggie. "I'll be here."

For a moment, Ken and Nell stood looking down at Keziah.

"I'll be pleased if I ever make half the woman she is," said Nell.

"Aye, she's the bold one," said Maggie. "Many's the battering I've had from that one."

"Anything else you need?" asked Jinny.

"No," said Maggie. "It's fine we'll be now. Thanks to you all."

Keziah opened her eyes, fixed her dark gaze on Jinny. "It's well you've done by me," she mouthed. "It's the true word you have." Her eyes closed again, her hands relaxed and she slept.

"The minister will not be holding back his sermon for the likes of her," said Mr. MacKenzie. "I'll be going, or the church will be without one of her finest singers this night."

Nell went with Mr. MacKenzie to where she had left the car in his yard, while Ken and Jinny made their way back to Finmory. As they reached the house they saw a van parked at the door.

"The Tuke," said Ken, recognising Miss Tuke's Pine Trekking Centre van.

"Thought she was too busy trekking to be bothered with me," Jinny grumbled. "Wonder what she wants?"

Mr. and Mrs. Manders, Mike and Miss Tuke were all sitting round the kitchen table, empty coffee mugs in front of them and the remains of one of Mrs. Manders' cream sponges in the middle of the table.

"At last!" exclaimed Miss Tuke, pushing back her chair and slapping her palms on her jodhpured knees. "Been waiting for you. Come along."

"Come where?" said Jinny in amazement. "To have a look at Shantih? I thought you were too busy trekking to care."

"Well, you were wrong. Had a look at your nag when I got here. Could be anything. Get her X-rayed. See what that shows."

After the high of bringing Keziah out of hospital and taking her safely to the bothy, Miss Tuke's words were clouds suddenly blotting out the sun. Desperately Jinny wanted Shantih to be sound again, ached to be riding her, galloping over the sands, but she was terrified of the X-ray, terrified of what it might reveal.

She twisted a strand of hair through her fingers, not looking at Miss Tuke, half listening to Ken telling her parents what had happened at the hospital.

"So we'll go now," finished Miss Tuke.

"Go where?" demanded Jinny, suddenly realising that Miss Tuke had been speaking to her.

"Always suspected it," said Miss Tuke, speaking to Mr. Manders. "Your younger daughter is bananas, clean loco. Now, listen this time. We're going to the Arran Riding School. Heard from Jim Rae that you'd been hanging round the place and were pretty shocked. It's a year or two since I checked up on that Post character. Last time we crossed swords he nearly lost his licence. So come along, we'll take another little look round."

Jinny grabbed the last piece of her mother's sponge and hurried after Miss Tuke. In no time they were rattling down the road to Inverburgh.

"Let's hope it's not as bad as you think," said Miss Tuke, when Jinny had finished describing the state of the riding school. "But knowing Martin Post, anything is possible, and the worst, probable."

CHAPTER SEVEN

Miss Tuke swung round the lane leading to the riding school, jammed on her brakes in front of Brenda's cottage and bounced out of the van.

"We'll have a recce round first," she announced, striding down the path to the stable yard.

Two girls were sitting in front of the looseboxes sharing a picnic of sandwiches and lemonade, but apart from them the yard was deserted. Hands on hips, Miss Tuke glared around.

"Absolutely filthy. Total neglect," she said loudly, as her gaze took in the fouled concrete, the fungused dung swept into corners, the scummed water trough and the broken-down buildings.

She turned on her heel and marched across to the looseboxes. Queenie and Sporty were in the first boxes, Brenda's bay and the chestnut pony were in the other two. All the animals were still tacked up and damp with sweat from their day's work. Only the chestnut pony had the energy to lift its head to look at the strangers. It was obviously days since the boxes had been brushed out.

"Are you looking for Brenda?" asked one of the girls. "Do you want to book a ride?"

"How long," demanded Miss Tuke, "have these poor brutes been standing there? And why on earth is their tack still on?"

"We never take it off between rides," said the girl. "Brenda says it's not worth it. They'll be going out again at seven."

"How many rides have they done today?" asked Miss Tuke.

The two girls looked at each other uncertainly.

"The men's ride in the morning—that's a two-hour ride—and three rides this afternoon," said one of them.

"Five hours," said Miss Tuke grimly. "And they're going out again?"

"Oh yes. It's always very busy at the weekends. There's always night rides."

"I don't suppose," said Miss Tuke, "that you bother to feed them? Live on air, do they?"

"They get hay at lunchtime, and Brenda used to give them hay just now but Mr. Post caught her. Told her they didn't need it, not when they'd all that grass."

"What grass?" said Jinny. "I've seen their field and there's no grass at all."

"How do you know?" asked one of the girls suspiciously. "What business is it of yours, anyway?"

Miss Tuke ignored her and strode across to the doorway that led to the row of stalls where the rest of the ponies stood in a weary line.

"Can't believe it," said Miss Tuke, as she walked down the row of ponies. "How anyone could work animals in this condition! I'd shoot the man myself. The brute."

Furiously, Miss Tuke kicked the bales of mouldering hay piled at the end of the stalls.

"And if that's what she's feeding them she needn't bother."

"This is Easter," said Jinny, going up to Easter's head. "She's the white pony I was telling you about."

"Poor old woman," said Miss Tuke, casting her experienced eye over the pony. "You've come down in the world, haven't you?"

Miss Tuke ran her hand gently down Easter's neck. "You're quite right," she said to Jinny. "She has been a beauty once."

"Bet she was a show pony," began Jinny, and she was on the point of blurting out how she planned to save Easter and bring her back to Finmory, but for once managed to stop herself in time, to remember that it was Miss Tuke she was speaking to.

"I don't suppose," said Jinny cautiously, "that there is anything you could do for her now? She's too far gone, isn't she. I mean if, just if, I could take her home and feed her up it wouldn't make any difference, would it?"

"Rubbish," said Miss Tuke briskly. "She must be as tough as old boots to have survived this place. Given a chance she might pull through."

Jinny's face lit up at Miss Tuke's words.

"You mean it?" she demanded. "Really mean it?"

Miss Tuke had stopped thinking about Easter.

"Come along," she said. "Let's get weaving. We're off to see Martin Post. Put the fear of death into him and get this shambles cleared out."

When they got back out into the yard, Brenda and the two girls were coming to meet them.

"Can I help you?" said Brenda, sounding as if help was the very last thing she was likely to offer.

"Dear girl," said Miss Tuke, "the only way you could help me is to start and get this place gutted. Get some food into those horses, get them groomed, shod and cancel all rides for the rest of the summer and see . . ."

"Just a minute," interrupted Brenda, "this is a private yard you're in, and before I listen to any more of your interference—get out."

"Oh, we're getting out. Straight out and straight to Martin Post's. That's where we're going, and unless he gets this dump cleared up in the next few days, private yard or not, you'll be having a little visit from the R.S.P.C.A. my dear."

Before Brenda could answer, Miss Tuke and Jinny were across the yard and making for Miss Tuke's van.

Crashing gears, foot hard down, Miss Tuke drove like an avenging fury to Martin Post's detached bungalow where it stood in landscaped splendour in the shrubbed outskirts of Inverburgh.

"That girl's bound to have phoned him," said Miss Tuke, as they got out of the van. "No point in trying the front door. We'll go round the back. Know the place well. Sunday evening our Martin will be entertaining his friends to drinkies. We'll give him drinkies!"

And with Jinny close behind her, Miss Tuke charged up the path and round the side of the bungalow.

Martin Post and five plastic people were sitting on a patio arranged round a table of drinks, looking like a T.V. commercial.

"Ha, ha!" snorted Miss Tuke, warhorse smelling battle, "so this is where you are! Slothing as usual. Excellent. You'll have plenty of time to listen to what I have to tell you."

The plastic people twittered uneasily—Miss Tuke was not the sort of person that should have appeared in their commercial—while Martin Post blubbered to his feet, a glass of gin in his hand.

"What the devil are you doing here?" he demanded.

"To warn you," said Miss Tuke. "Your riding school is in a worse state than it was when I saw it two years ago. I dare say you'll remember the outcome of that visit. Eh? Filth and neglect everywhere. Hardly a horse fit to work. Ponies that should have been put out of their misery months ago. If I'd had my box, I'd have brought the worst of them with me, made you look at them. None of my business what you do with your second-hand cars, but while I'm around you're not treating animals like that. I'll be round tomorrow with the R.S.P.C.A. and the police to investigate the place. And don't think a court will let you keep your licence a second time."

Miss Tuke swung round and began to stride away. Martin Post heaved his bulk after them, catching up with her at the front of the bungalow.

"Calm down," he said. "Cut out the hysteric female act. You're jumping the gun as usual. Not a thing wrong with the stables. Sunday evening, end of the weekend. Place is bound to be a bit untidy. It'll be cleared up by Monday morning."

"Pull the other one and it'll play Annie Laurie," said Miss Tuke contemptuously. "Horses miraculously renewed every Monday. Mouldering hay turned into best feeding. Full oat bins appearing out of nowhere. Good. Then you'll not mind a visit from the R.S.P.C.A.?"

"Give us a week. I'll get the place squared up by then. It's that girl's fault. Can't trust her to do a thing."

"And how much do you pay her, I wonder? Dare say that could do with a spot of investigating as well."

"Listen, give me a week, O.K. Then you can come and poke your nose in where you like. I'll grant you some of the horses aren't all they might be. I'll send the worst off to the knackers. Give the place the once over. How will that be?"

Since Jinny had rounded the corner of the bungalow she had felt as if she had been watching a play, a performance. Only now did Martin Post's words really reach her—"Send the worst off to the knackers."

"But not Easter," she cried. "You mustn't send Easter to the slaughterhouse!"

As if noticing Jinny for the first time, Martin Post focused his piggy eyes on her.

"Heavens," he said. "You don't think I know the names of the donkeys, do you?"

"The white pony. The one that used to be a show pony. You mustn't send her to be killed."

"That old crock? It'll be the first to go." He laughed, his breath stinking in Jinny's face, watching her closely to see her reaction.

"You can't. Not Easter. Let me take her home. I've got a field where she can retire. I'll pay for her. Please let me have her."

Martin Post's thick lips drew back from his yellowed false teeth.

"Darling," he sneered, "If you were to offer me a thousand nicker for her, I wouldn't let you have her. Thursday morning the meat man will be there to collect her. There's a little thought to sweeten your dreams."

"Please!" cried Jinny.

"Please away," said Martin Post. "You don't think you can come here with that old hornet and expect favours from me?"

His fat hand reached out to pinch Jinny's cheek, and she sprang back just in time to stop him touching her.

"I'll give you a week," stated Miss Tuke. "Not up to standard by then we'll see what a court has to say about it. And you know I mean it."

All the way back to Finmory, Jinny sat without speaking, her mind full of plans to save Easter. She had thought that if the riding school was improved it would be the best thing for Easter, but it had turned into the worst. Now she must rescue her before Thursday or it would be too late.

"Would you drop me at Mr. MacKenzie's," Jinny asked as they approached Finmory.

Miss Tuke nodded and stopped at the farm to let Jinny get out.

"Don't start a nonsense over Easter," Miss Tuke warned. "Best thing for her to be put down."

"That's not what you said before. You said she'd a chance."

"More fool me. You can't save all the old ponies in the world. Not if you aim to stay sane."

"Think I'm mad already," said Jinny, as she got out of the van.

Jinny waited until Miss Tuke was out of sight then she made her way up to the bothy. Tam was sitting in the doorway. Jinny called him over.

"Listen," she said urgently. "I've helped you now you must help me."

Tam looked at her warily.

"You couldn't have got Keziah out of hospital by yourself, could you? And I organised it all, didn't I? Well, there's an old pony in a riding school in Inverburgh. She's been a super pony once but she's old now. They think they're going to slaughter her on Thursday but it's not going to happen. I'm going to rescue her."

Tam's face remained expressionless.

"I've thought it all out. We'll go on Wednesday night and take her away. We'll bring her back here and she can stay in the bothy field. They'll all think she's a tinkers' pony. No one will bother. You will help me, won't you?"

"Aye," Tam agreed unwillingly.

"Right. Wednesday night then," Jinny stated. "I'll give you the bus fare and we'll meet in Inverburgh after school."

Straight after school on Monday, Jinny went up to the bothy to see Keziah. The old woman was sitting up on a chair taking a plateful of soup. Jinny's heart lifted at the sight of her. They had done the right thing bringing her to the bothy; she was back where she belonged.

"Aye, she's fine," agreed Maggie. "We've had Jock MacKenzie up cracking memories with her the whole afternoon."

When she reached home, Jinny told her parents that she was going to spend Wednesday night with a school friend who had asked her to her birthday party.

"Rather short notice," said Mr. Manders, "asking you on Monday when the party's on Wednesday."

"She did ask me before, but I said I couldn't go because of not being able to get back to Finmory. Then at the weekend her mother said why didn't I stay the night. So she asked me again today. I can go, can't I?"

"Yes, of course you can," said Jinny's mother. "You'll enjoy it."

Wednesday was the longest day that Jinny had ever

known. From the minute she woke up and looked out to where Shantih was standing resting her foreleg, the day dragged, second by leaden second.

"Have a nice time at the party," her mother said.

"Will do," said Jinny, drowning in guilt. "It's for Easter," she told herself, summoning up behind her eyes a vivid picture of the white pony. "If I don't rescue her, she'll be dead tomorrow.

Even double art, which always made Wednesday afternoons Jinny's favourite, dragged interminably. They were meant to be painting a jungle scene after listening to jungly music. Jinny was drawing Easter. She saw Mr. Eccles the art master, approaching and quickly flipped her paper over.

"Not started yet?" Mr. Eccles asked. "No jungle vibrations?"

Jinny shook her head without looking at him.

"Come on. Let's see what you've been drawing."

Reluctantly, Jinny turned over her paper.

"Surprise! Surprise!" said Mr. Eccles. "Horses!"

"Stubbs," said Jinny, as she always did when Mr. Eccles teased her about drawing horses. "And Munnings and Skeaping."

"And no doubt Manders, given a year or two. But now, how about a jungle. You may include a tapir if you wish."

Jinny didn't wish, but unwillingly daubed her paper with greens and browns and blues as she thought about the night ahead.

When the bell went, Jinny tore down to the cloakroom. She hurriedly changed out of the dress Mrs. Manders had considered most suitable for a birthday party, and into the jeans, sweater and anorak which Jinny considered most suitable for rescuing Easter. In her canvas shoulder bag, Jinny had a halter, food for Easter, her own torch, which wasn't as powerful as her father's and therefore less likely to attract attention, and all the money she had in the world—seventeen pounds from her box and the three pounds she had left from the money Nell had paid her on Saturday—just in case she should need it.

There was an hour before Tam's bus was due to arrive at the bus station. Jinny wandered round the streets staring into shop windows, then sauntering on, thinking all the time of Shantih and Easter.

So far the vet hadn't phoned about the arrangements for Shantih's visit to the Vet College and Shantih was as lame as ever—it was weeks since she had been sound, weeks since Jinny had been able to ride her, weeks since her disastrous fall. Over and over again Jinny had relived that jump—the moment when she had turned Shantih and ridden her at the wall.

"It's all moments," Ken had said. "If you can catch the moment and stop yourself then the rest doesn't have to happen, but if the moment gets away from you all the rest follows on."

Worry about Shantih was a stone in the pit of Jinny's being.

Tam was first off the bus, his eyes darting from side to side, searching for Jinny. When he spotted her waiting for him he dived to her side.

"Good," said Jinny, glad of even Tam's support. "I'm jolly glad you made it."

"Where's the pony?" asked Tam, as if he expected Easter to be tied to one of the bus shelters.

"Good bit from here, but we can't go to the stables until it's dark. We'll wait until we're sure that Brenda has gone to bed and then we'll find Easter and take her back to Finmory.

It was almost dark before they set off for the riding school.

"If Brenda sees us hanging around she'll guess we're up to something," Jinny had insisted when Tam nagged about the waste of time, but at last she agreed that it was dark enough.

They found a place in the golf-course hedge where they could hide and watch the light in Brenda's cottage windows.

"Ten past eleven," said Jinny, shining the torch on her watch as at last the cottage lights went out. "We'll wait till midnight. Brenda should be asleep by then!"

Tam, crouching on his hunkers, his man's jacket doubled round him, his arms crossed over his chest, his sparrow hands holding his shoulders, showed no sign of having heard Jinny. He waited without movement, as settled as an animal.

"Honestly," thought Jinny. "He's useless." She longed for Nell Storr or Ken to be with her. But Jinny knew that they wouldn't have come. What she was going to do she had to do herself.

"It's nearly twelve," Jinny announced. "It's now or never. Come on."

They got up, stretching numbed limbs, and crept along the golf-course lane, which led through a gate then between sheds into the stable yard. The smell of horses and dung filled the darkness.

"Right," said Jinny. "We'll check the boxes first."

But they were all empty. The weak pencil beam of Jinny's torch only picked out unswept stone floors and the cobwebbed shadows that textured the wooden beams. In one box, something that was much too big to be a mouse flowed across the floor and up the wall at the side of the manger. Jinny shuddered convulsively.

"Now the stalls," she said, trying to make her whisper sound full of confidence.

At first Jinny thought that the big double doors leading into the stalls were locked by a huge padlock. "If Easter's in there and we can't get to her . . ." thought Jinny, then realised that the padlock was hanging uselessly from the hasp of one door. They weren't locked at all. Jinny freed the clasp and began to inch the door open, the wood screeching against the stone floor.

"Gorn! You'll have her up," said Tam, and taking the door from Jinny, moved it slowly and silently until there was enough space for them to squeeze through. All the stalls were empty.

"Must all be in the field," muttered Jinny, quickly swinging her torch away from the bales of hay at the foot of the stalls that seemed to be alive with vermin. She swung round, pushed her way out and stood clutching at herself in the yard, while Tam silently closed the door.

"Our Jake, he'd batter you one for your din," said Tam.

"That's all we need," snapped Jinny. "Your Jake."

"He'd have had the pony away by now," sneered Tam.

"I dare say," said Jinny. "He's used to taking things but I'm not. Come on, they must all be in the field." Following the light of her torch, she led the way down the track to the field where she had held Easter on Saturday.

They climbed over the gate and stood peering into the dark.

"Horses, horses," called Jinny in a low voice. "Easter, Come on, Easter."

For a second there was no response. Only the darkness pressing tightly against them.

"They must be here," said Jinny, straining her ears.

Then she heard the sound of trotting hooves, high pig-squeals of anger, the unmistakeable sound of a kick finding its mark, and suddenly the riding-school horses were crushing around them, necks snaking, jostling, pushing; hind legs lashing out to keep other horses away; a sudden power of horses bursting out of the darkness. Jinny realised that they thought she was going to feed them. Tam clutched at her as Jinny, throwing up her arms, growling in as loud a voice as she dared, tried to drive them off. But they pushed closer, desperate for food. The whites of their eyes glistening, yellow teeth terrifyingly close, as for split seconds they were caught in the beam of Jinny's torch. The smell of the titbits Jinny had brought for Easter made them wild for food. Brenda's bay reared above Jinny. In the darkness she could hardly see it, was only aware of the bulk of horse balanced over her, then the crash of its hooves just missing her head as it plunged to earth again.

Holding Tam firmly by the arm, Jinny made for the gate. The horses stampeded after her. She pushed Tam over the gate first, then climbed over herself. Safe on the other side, Jinny stared at the cottage, waiting for a light to appear in the bedroom window, for surely Brenda must have heard the noise. To Jinny it had sounded like an earthquake.

But no light shone into the darkness. Brenda couldn't have heard. Gradually Jinny's heart slowed back to normal. The horses, abandoning the hope of food, began to turn away from the gate.

"Thought we'd had it," said Tam, his voice a thin bleat of sound. "I'm not for going in there again."

"We won't need to," said Jinny. "Easter wasn't there. The chestnut pony wasn't either. They must be somewhere else. There must be another field. We'll need to search for it."

They crept back to the yard and followed muddy paths that led to a midden, out on to the golf course, to a rubbish dump and to a rotted coal shed that had sat down years ago.

"The pony'll no be here," suggested Tam.

"Of course she's here. She must be here somewhere. I should have made sure I knew where to find her," said Jinny, as they stood in the yard not knowing where to look next.

"Had we no better be going?" asked Tam hopefully. "We'll not be finding her tonight."

Jinny was cold with terror; the terror that she was too late, that the meat man had come early and taken Easter away, that the pony she was searching for was already dead.

"There's a field by the side of the cottage," Jinny remembered. "The first time I came here I wasn't sure where to go. I saw it then. Come on."

Tam hitched up his jeans and followed Jinny along the track between the outhouses. When they emerged, Brenda's cottage seemed menacingly close.

"Say she did hear the horses?" Jinny thought. "Say she's standing now at one of the windows listening?"

Jinny pushed back her hair, squared her shoulders and forced herself to walk on. "As if Ken and Nell are in front," she thought. "Remember how it was walking through the hospital." But try as she would, Jinny didn't feel like that now. She felt scared.

Along the bottom hedge they went, and there was the tiny field Jinny had seen on her first visit to the stables. Oil cans and smashed poles were piled at the gateway, three twelve-inch-high jumps were standing in the middle of the field, and two pony shapes lifted their heads and stared curiously at the intruders. One was the chestnut pony and the other was Easter.

Jinny flung herself over the gate and stumbled across the rutted earth to Easter. For a split second as she stood, white in the darkness, Jinny saw her again as the show pony she must once have been—the delicate-boned face, the unblemished legs, the proudly-arched neck—but it was only an illusion. Jinny's hand stroked a harsh neck and sunken back. The days of Easter's triumphs were lost in the past.

Jinny dragged the halter out of her bag and put it on Easter, while the pony stood like a block of wood, almost without life.

"You're not going to be slaughtered," Jinny whispered. "You're coming home with me. We're taking you home."

Jinny shared out the titbits between Easter and the chestnut.

"There's a lot more for you at Finmory," Jinny promised. "And a field full of grass just for you! Come along, we're going home." The old pony moved stiffly as Jinny led her across the field to where Tam had opened the gate.

At the gate Easter stopped, and Jinny, turning to see what was wrong, shone the torch beam over Easter's wasted body, her scarred legs and sunken quarters. Seeing her like that, Jinny didn't care how wrong other people might think it was, taking Easter away when she belonged to Martin Post. Jinny hardly cared whether they called it stealing or not. Her one thought was to save Easter from the slaughterer, to take her home to Finmory and see her grow fit and well again.

On an impulse, Jinny buried her face in Easter's neck, throwing her arm over her withers.

"It's all right now," she whispered. "You're safe now."

"Here," grated Tam's voice. "Stop that messing. We've to be getting her out of here before we're nabbed."

Jinny roused Easter into reluctant life and urged her through the gateway. Then she turned, closing the gate.

As Jinny struggled with the bolt, her foot caught against an empty trough. For a moment she fought to keep her balance, then fell into the piles of rusty oil drums. With a reverberating crash the cans became alive, like rows of dominoes they sent each other rolling and banging, filling the silent night with thunderous din.

CHAPTER EIGHT

Jinny and Tam froze with terror. This time Brenda must have heard them. No one could have slept through such a commotion.

"Oh no you don't," Jinny cried, catching at Tam's sleeve. "You're not running off. I came into that foul hospital with you, so you're staying here with me."

No light appeared in the cottage. The silence of the night settled back. At the first crash of the falling oil drums the chestnut pony had high-tailed it to the other end of the field, but Easter had stood, hardly moving, while the cans rolled about her.

"Come on, then," Jinny said at last, and together they began to creep back along the hedge. Tam was silent as a fox, Jinny shuffling and stumbling with the sharp click of Easter's joints sounding like gunfire behind them.

When they reached the end of the hedge, they paused for a moment level with Brenda's cottage. Suddenly Jinny saw a figure standing half-hidden by the overgrown rambler roses of the porch.

"Look out!" she screamed, her voice ripping the darkness. But her warning was too late. Brenda leapt from the porch, grabbed Jinny's arm and the scruff of Tam's jacket.

"So it wasn't just the horses kicking the cans about," Brenda said.

Tam twisted from her, ducked expertly, and Brenda was left holding his jacket while Tam vanished into the night.

"Little blighter!" swore Brenda, tightening her grip on Jinny's arm.

Jinny scowled furiously up at her, Easter's halter rope held tightly in her clenched fist. She knew that she could probably wriggle free from Brenda and escape too, but if she did that it would mean leaving Easter behind; her last chance of saving her would be gone.

"Here, give her to me." Brenda prised Jinny's hand from the halter rope, left Easter standing at the doorway and, twisting Jinny's arm behind her back, frog-marched her into the cottage.

"Let me go," Jinny yelled, as Brenda forced her through a small hallway and into a stone-flagged kitchen.

"Stay there," Brenda ordered, pushing Jinny into a chair. "I'll deal with you in a minute."

Jinny heard the key turn in the kitchen door, the slam of the front door, and the sound of Easter's hoofs as Brenda led her back to her field.

Jinny stayed sitting in the chair, clutching her arms about herself, staring from her at the dim shapes in the unlit kitchen. She had failed to rescue Easter. Had mucked it all up. Now she was only another of all the humans who had let the pony down.

"Right then," said Brenda coming back into the kitchen, switching on the fluorescent light so that Jinny could see the dirty dishes piled in the sink, the remains of a meal spread on a table covered with a dirty, plastic tablecloth. An ancient fridge wheezed asthmatically, a calor gas cooker stood iced with grease, and an electric fire with one of its bars broken crouched in the middle of the floor.

"Here, I know you, don't I? You're the kid who made all the fuss to ride Easter and then was sick. And it was you nosing about with that old bag, wasn't it?"

Brenda switched on the electric fire and stood in front of it. She was wearing corduroy trousers rolled up at the ankles and a heavy sagging pullover. Her grimy, painted toenails poked through open-toed sandals. The make-up on her face had set, after a day's endurance, into patches of greasy colour, and her eyes were like a panda's black-rimmed with rubbed mascara. Her hannaed hair hung round her head in lank tails. She folded her arms and stared at Jinny through strangely dead eyes.

Jinny scowled back at her.

"Out with it then. What were you doing stealing one of my ponies?"

"I wasn't stealing her. I was rescuing her so that she wouldn't be sent to the slaughterer's tomorrow. I was going to pay you for her." Jinny scrabbled in her bag and laid her money on the kitchen table.

"That's all I've got just now, but I was coming back to find out how much more you wanted for her. Honestly I was. I couldn't ask you before I'd rescued her. You wouldn't have let me buy her. And that rotten Martin Post who owns all this mess, he would do anything to stop me saving her."

"So you decided to steal her?"

"No! No! I had to rescue her. What difference does it make if I take her and pay you what you would have got for her from the slaughterhouse? But it would make all the difference to Easter. It would give her a year or two of peace and comfort. Just a bit of happiness at the end of her life. That's all I wanted."

Brenda listened without changing her expression.

"You don't care, do you? You're as bad as Martin Post. How can you work in a place like this? How can you? You don't care how cruel it all is as long as they make money for you. When did Easter last have a decent feed? When was she last groomed? Or her feet seen to? This whole place is the same. It stinks of dirt and neglect, and if Martin Post doesn't clean it up, Miss Tuke will bring the R.S.P.C.A. in and they'll make him close it down this time."

Suddenly Jinny couldn't go on. It was useless. Shouting at Brenda wasn't going to stop them sending Easter to the slaughterhouse tomorrow. Now she had been caught there was nothing else Jinny could do. She had failed. Easter was not to have her summer by the waters. This time tomorrow she would be dead, would be dog meat.

"But I hate you!" Jinny screamed. "I hate you!" Burying her face in her hands, Jinny burst into tears.

For a minute Brenda stood without speaking, then, slowly, she crossed the kitchen, filled a kettle and, setting it to boil, put instant coffee, milk and sugar into two mugs. She took a bottle of whisky from a cupboard and poured some of it into her own mug. When the kettle had boiled, she filled the mugs and took one over to Jinny.

"Here," she said, touching Jinny's shoulder. "Wipe up and drink this."

Jinny flinched away from her.

"You've had your say. I asked for it. Now you listen to me."

Reluctantly, Jinny pushed back her hair revealing her mottled face. She groped in her pocket and dabbed at her eyes and nose with the ineffectual remains of a paper handkerchief. Then, without looking at her, she took the coffee from Brenda and sat holding the mug in both hands.

"That's how it all looks to you, doesn't it, Little Miss Busybody?" Brenda asked, going back to stand by the electric fire, taking a deep slurp of her coffee.

"That's how it is," muttered Jinny.

"Not how it looks to me," said Brenda. "How old are you? Twelve? Thirteen? Well, I'm forty-nine. Remember tonight when you wake up and find you're nearly fifty. See what you think of it then." Brenda took another slug of her coffee.

"I'd never work in a place like this," stated Jinny. "Never."

"When I was your age I'd have said the same thing. But there we are—things change. Here, I'm more or less my own boss. Martin Post doesn't bother me much and I've got my own house. What would I be doing if I wasn't here? Working in a shop or an office, going back to a furnished room, or dancing attendance to a family that was rich enough to keep me along with their dogs, being bossed about by spoilt kids. No thank you. This suits me O.K."

"Don't you care about the horses?"

"Got used to them. They don't have all that bad a time. If I'd to choose, I'd rather be one of them than a showjumper—carted about, forced to jump impossible heights over and over again."

"But you can't *like* working here?"

"Oh, I'd fancy dreams of my own riding school. Or a Fell pony stud. But they're old photographs now. Faded. Pretty ridiculous really. It's O.K. here; a load of old crocks, I'll grant you that, but they suit the people who ride them.

"There's always one or two of the nags go to the knackers at the end of the summer, so they're only going a few weeks earlier than usual. What were you going to do with her, anyway? Keep her in your back garden? She'd have starved there all right."

"'Course not," said Jinny scornfully. "I live in Finmory House, past Glenbost. We've masses of grazing, and I'd got a special field for Easter. Super grass."

"I've been to Finmory Bay," said Brenda. "D'you mean that mausoleum where the hippies used to live?"

Jinny nodded. It didn't matter now.

Brenda turned to rinse out her mug, holding it under the tap, setting it down on the draining board. She stood staring at it then turned to face Jinny.

"How much cash have you got?"

"Twenty pounds."

"Martin will get eighty from the knackers. Could you get the rest in a month?"

Jinny heard Brenda's question but for seconds she couldn't make herself answer, for if Brenda was asking her that, did it mean . . .? Could it possibly mean . . .?

Jinny nodded furiously, for of course she would find the rest of the money somehow, some way, if it meant saving Easter.

"Will it be all right with your parents?"

Again Jinny nodded, unable to speak.

"Then you can have her. I'll tell Martin she's gone to a friend of mine who'll pay him the knacker's price for her. Always had a soft spot for Easter. Something about her."

Jinny sat motionless, staring dumbly at Brenda.

"It isn't true. It can't be true. I'll wake up and it will all be a dream," Jinny thought, digging her fingernails into her arm.

But nothing had changed. The dirty kitchen was still there. Brenda was still standing there, her mouth twisted into a wry grin as she watched Jinny.

"You mean," Jinny stammered at last. "You mean I can take Easter back to Finmory? Now? Tonight?"

"That's what I said."

"Oh, thank you! Thank you! I'll find the rest of the money, I promise, and there's masses of grass and plenty of food for her. Oh, thank you, Brenda."

"Don't thank me. I'm not doing you any favour. You'll never be able to make anything of her. She's beggered, that's for sure. Could drop dead in a week's time and you'll still have to pay me."

Brenda's cynical laugh cut through Jinny's delight.

What happened to make her like this. Jinny wondered suddenly. What changed her when once her dreams were almost the same as mine—her own riding school, her own Fell ponies.

"Don't," Jinny warned herself, and aloud she said, "Shall I go and get her now? Shall I just take her home?"

"Lord," said Brenda. "You weren't thinking of leading her all the way to Glenbost? Still, I suppose you were. I'll drive you over in the morning."

"I've to be at school," said Jinny.

"We'll leave early. Fiveish. You can crash down here for the night. What about the boy who was with you?"

"Tam!" exclaimed Jinny, jumping to her feet. "And you've got his jacket."

Jinny ran outside shouting for Tam. She ran down the golf-course lane, yelling his name at the top of her voice. There was no sign of him. She ran into the yard, still shouting. Tam, wrapped in sacks, appeared from one of the outhouses.

"Did she get you?" he demanded.

"It's all right," said Jinny. "Brenda's O.K. She's letting me take Easter. I've to pay for her, but she's mine. Come on in."

Reluctantly, Tam allowed himself to be persuaded into the cottage. He sat perched on the edge of one of the chairs, his dark eyes fixed on Brenda.

"You'll need to spend what's left of the night in here," said Brenda doling out horse blankets.

Tam took his and curled down on the kitchen floor. Jinny, wrapped in hers, tried to make herself comfortable on two chairs.

Even when the sound of Brenda going back to bed had faded into silence, Jinny's mind wouldn't stop galloping on. It whirled her from thoughts of Shantih's lameness to what Mr. MacKenzie would have to say about Easter occupying his field. "But he can't mind," Jinny thought. "He's not using it and it's only to begin with. When she gets a bit stronger, I can put her in with the others."

At five, the outside world was chill and grey. Jinny, going to catch Easter, found her standing close against the hedge, her eyes closed, her coat glistening with moisture. When Jinny spoke to her, she seemed to have to come back from a far place before she could lift her head and acknowledge Jinny's presence.

"You're coming home with me," Jinny told her, leading her out of the field. "It is true this time. It is happening now. You're mine. You'll never have to work again, never be hungry again."

The horsebox that Brenda had driven into the yard was as old as everything else at the riding school, but Easter went up the loose boards of the ramp without any protest. Brenda turned down Jinny's suggestion of hay for the journey.

"Don't worry," Jinny told Easter as she tied her up. "It wouldn't have been up to much, and there's a whole field of lovely sweet grass just for you, where you're going to."

Tam travelled in the box with Easter. Jinny sat in the front with Brenda. When they had safely negotiated the empty Inverburgh streets and were rattling along the road to Glenbost, Jinny broached the subject of paying for Easter.

"I'll bring you the rest of the money just as soon as I possibly can," Jinny said.

"You've a month. No longer. Remember that now," warned Brenda, her words shaking the ash from her lip-hanging cigarette all over Jinny.

"If I haven't got enough by the end of the month, what then?" asked Jinny, risking the unthinkable, for it was better to know definitely than to keep on imagining things.

"I'll come for her, take her to the knackers myself and give the money to Martin. Any longer than a month and Martin will start to smell a rat. If he finds out, there'll be hell to pay, especially when he doesn't want you to have her. Reckon he'll be around the yard a lot after Friday. He's away this week on business. Starting Friday, he's tarting the place up for Miss Tuke's inspection."

Jinny stared out at the barren countryside. The only way she had any hope of making eighty pounds was by selling pictures to Nell. Jinny had tried that before when she had been desperate for money, tried to draw dozens of pictures of Shantih, but because she had forced herself to draw them when she wasn't feeling like it they had turned out so badly that Nell had refused to take them. They would have to be better this time.

Brenda drove the box up to the gates of Finmory House.

"Straight through?" she asked Jinny.

"We'll take her out here and lead her over the hill. It's not far and it's a lovely field for her."

"I'll come with you," Brenda said. "I'll see her settled in."

Jinny led Easter along the sheep track that curved above Mr. MacKenzie's farm, then on to the bothy. It would have been quicker to have parked the horsebox in Mr. MacKenzie's farmyard, but Jinny hadn't wanted to risk meeting him. She would see him this evening and explain. Much better than trying to explain at this time in the morning.

At first, Easter walked wearily at Jinny's side, but gradually, as they climbed the hill, her head came up, her eyes brightened, and with pricked ears she began to look about her. Her step quickened and once, for no reason other than joy, she broke into a trot.

"It has been worth it," Jinny thought—all the hassle and the explanations that still lay ahead; worth it even for these few moments of seeing Easter coming alive again.

There was no sign of Keziah or Maggie. The bothy was still closed against the world. Tam opened the gate of the enclosure and Jinny led Easter in. She took off her halter and stood back.

"On you go," Jinny said. "It's all for you."

Easter raised a foreleg and pawed at the grass; she lowered her head and wuffled her muzzle through it. Then, with a high-pitched whinny, she trotted forward, stood for a second, then stiffly lowered herself to the ground, swung over onto her back and scrubbed herself luxuriantly into the grass, kicking her legs awkwardly into the air in an effort to roll. She struggled to her feet, shook herself, then dropped her head and began to graze.

"What are we standing here for?" Brenda demanded hoarsely. "I've got a day's work ahead of me."

Reluctantly, Jinny turned to follow her, saw her surreptitiously drag the back of her hand across her eyes before she lit another cigarette.

"I'll come up straight after school," Jinny told Tam.

"Aye," said Tam. "I'll have my eye on her."

"And tell Mr. MacKenzie I'll see him this evening."

"Aye."

"All right for some," said Jinny. "He'll probably spend the whole day watching Easter."

"You're not so badly off yourself," said Brenda, pointing down to the field where Shantih and Bramble were model horses from a child's toy farm. "Are they yours?"

Jinny explained. "But Shantih is lame," she finished despondently, a little of her joy over Easter leaking away.

"She's been lame for weeks and the vet can't find out what's wrong. That's why I came to the riding school. I wanted to ask you if you knew what it might be."

"Then you saw the set-up and didn't bother to ask," Brenda said, finishing Jinny's sentence. "It figures. Still, tell me now."

Jinny did.

"Don't like the sound of it. You'll know definitely after the X-ray."

"The vet said it could be a hairline fracture in one of the bones of her foot."

"Could be," said Brenda dubiously. "It's a possibility. Bad enough if it's that. She'll be lame for life but the odds are she won't get any worse; you could keep her and breed from her. But if it's navicular, nothing else for it but . . ." and Brenda put her two fingers to the side of her head and clicked her tongue.

"What do you mean?" cried Jinny. "What do you mean, navicular?"

At the word, the brightness had gone from the morning. Navicular. The word chill as cancer in a human being. It seeped like poison gas into the very core of Jinny's being. Its cold fingers of dread clutched at her heart. When she had been reading through her horsy books trying to discover what could be causing Shantih's lameness, her eyes had flicked away from the horror of navicular. She had locked it away at the back of her mind with other unthinkable things. But Jinny knew exactly what her book had said. It had said: "Navicular—an incurable disease of the navicular bone in the forefeet."

White-faced, her nostrils pinched, her lips tight, Jinny turned on Brenda.

"Don't talk such bloody nonsense," she swore. "Of course Shantih hasn't got navicular. It comes on slowly. Shantih went lame suddenly. Of course it isn't navicular. Of course it isn't"

"Pardon me for breathing," said Brenda, shocked by Jinny's visible terror. "But surely the vet's mentioned navicular? He must suspect it when he's having her X-rayed. I know of a case where it came on suddenly. The nerve had been blocked, and when the horse landed heavily out hunting it went dead lame and it was navicular."

Jinny opened her mouth to tell Brenda that the vet wasn't an idiot, that of course he didn't think there was any possibility of navicular, and then she remembered how Jim Rae had stopped in mid-sentence. His voice echoed in Jinny's ears: "You can never rule out . . ." and then he had stopped suddenly and told her not to worry until they got the result of the X-ray.

At once there was no doubt in Jinny's mind. She was sure. He had been going to say navicular. Jinny shuddered uncontrollably. The joy of seeing Easter come alive again as she breathed in the freedom of the moors, had gone; it was less than a memory now.

"It couldn't, it couldn't be," said Jinny, staring at Brenda.

"Could," said Brenda.

"Do you think we could hurry or I'm going to be late for school," said Jinny's voice, empty, polite.

She couldn't bear to go on talking about Shantih. When the vet phoned with the date for the X-ray she would have to ask him if it could be navicular. He would say there was a chance—a chance that when they saw the result of the X-ray, some time in the future Jinny would have to say "Yes," say "Yes" to Shantih being put down; would have to be sensible about it because it would be the only thing possible.

"Please could we hurry," said Jinny again.

The bell for them to get into line was ringing at school as Jinny jumped down from the cabin of the box.

"You'll bring the rest of the money to the riding school?" Brenda said.

"Will do," said Jinny. "The very minute I have it."

"Jinny Manders!" exclaimed Dolina, as Jinny joined her line. "Would you be looking at yourself. Is it sleeping under the hedge you've been at?"

"Don't worry, I'm going straight to Miss Lorimer. 'Miss Lorimer,' I shall say, 'I've come to save you the trouble of hunting me down. My appearance is a disgrace to the school, my homework is undone and I expect I'll fall asleep in class. Please may I go to detention now?' "

"If you hadn't gone belting off last night you'd have seen Miss Lorimer then. She was looking for you. You've to go and see the Headmaster this morning."

CHAPTER NINE

When Jinny got off the school bus that evening, Mr. Manders was sitting in the car waiting for her.

"This is it," thought Jinny grimly, as she took the letter the Headmaster had given her to give to her father out of her schoolbag. "Here goes."

She walked across to the car and got in.

"Bus was on time tonight," said her father, starting up the engine. "How was the party?"

Jinny swallowed hard. "There wasn't a party," she said. "I made it up. It was all lies. I took Tam with me to the riding school. I was going to rescue Easter, but Brenda caught us."

"Oh, Jinny," said Mr. Manders, looking at his daughter's woebegone face. "Oh, Jinny." And he reached across, putting his arm round her shoulders, hugging her to him. "You crazy coot. You'll never learn, will you?"

"Doubt it," agreed Jinny ruefully. "But don't worry, I'm not for the juvenile court this time. In the end, Brenda agreed to let me have her. She's going to tell Martin Post that a friend of hers has taken Easter and they'll pay him the same money as he would have got from the slaughterhouse."

"How much will that be?" asked Mr. Manders, releasing his daugther.

"Eighty pounds. I've paid twenty and I've to give the rest to Brenda within a month."

"But you haven't got sixty pounds."

"I will have. I'll paint pictures for Nell. I'll get it somehow. I will."

"And where is the pony now?" asked Mr. Manders, abandoning the question of paying for Easter in the face of Jinny's certainty.

"Mr. MacKenzie's field. The one by the bothy."

"And does he know about it?"

"I'll see him tonight. If he's mad, I'll need to bring her down to our field. Don't really want to put her in there in case Bramble bullies her. You should have seen her when we let her go in the field. She couldn't believe it was true. All that grass to herself. She was quite different. Not old and wooden but young again."

"Put on its rose again," came into Jinny's head from a poem she had read, and she lit up inside. The miseries of the day, her interview with the Headmaster, the things Miss Lorimer had said to her were completely wiped out. For the instant, Jinny's whole world was white light, was joy.

"You should have seen her. If only you all could have seen her."

"It's quite good having you to tell me about it," Mr. Manders said, looking resolutely ahead through the windscreen.

"The next bit's not quite so good," said Jinny, deflating. "That's a letter from the Headmaster. I'd to go and see him today. I should think it's about me being in dentention so much and not working."

"Not at all good," agreed Mr. Manders. "We'll talk about it after I've read the letter."

"I think he wants you to check up on my homework every night. Sign it to say I've done it. Take an interest in me."

"I hope you told him that at least fifty per cent of Manders' family conversation is about you and your homework?"

Jinny didn't reply. She felt a small silence would help to change the subject.

"The vet phoned today. He said he'd spoken to Danny Sargent and they could take Shantih for the X-ray this Saturday or the next. I said this Saturday was out because we're meeting the Wrights, so we arranged the next. You've to phone him tonight, after nine, just to let him know that it's O.K."

"I'm not meeting the Wrights," stated Jinny positively. "I said when you got the letter from them that I wasn't coming. Petra was there, you can ask her. I cannot stand Belinda Wright. But the next Saturday will be best for the X-ray."

"If you're sure you're not coming to Inverburgh with us why not make it this Saturday? Get it over with. The sooner you find out what is wrong the better?"

Jinny shook her head. Once Shantih was X-rayed, Jinny would know. She wanted to put it off for as long as possible. Wanted it never to happen.

"Shall I go in and see Mr. MacKenzie now?" Jinny asked as they approached the farm.

"Better come home first. You can tell us what actually did happen at the riding school last night, and we'll see what the Headmaster has to say about you."

The Headmaster's letter was mostly about Jinny's inattention in class and her undone homework.

"Right," said Mr. Manders. "What homework have you tonight?"

"English essay," said Jinny. "French sentences and a drawing of a stone-age village."

"Well, finish your tea and straight upstairs. When you've done all your homework bring it down and I'll check it."

"But I've to go and see Easter and Mr. MacKenzie and I've hardly spoken to Shantih. Couldn't I do it after I've seen them?"

"Certainly not," said Mr. Manders sharply. "Your school work is far more important than all this nonsense."

Subdued, Jinny went on eating her salad. Her mother had been most unenthusiastic about Keziah being left in the bothy. Although she had approved of Maggie when she had gone to see if there was anything she could do to help, she still thought that the best place for Keziah would have been hospital. And she had listened to Jinny's confessions with a serious face.

"How can we trust you when you do things like this?" she had said. "You're always telling us to leave you alone and then you do this sort of thing."

Mike went upstairs with Jinny.

"I'll help," he said. "What could I do?"

"Stone-age village," said Jinny. "It's only to be copied from this book. Thanks."

The essay was on Shylock. Jinny wrote three pages and then turned her attention to the French sentences. A quarter of an hour later she had finished.

"Super village," she said to Mike. "I'd better just touch it up a bit in case they guess I didn't do it." Taking her wax crayons, Jinny began to colour Mike's drawing.

Mike sat back on his heels watching enviously as his picture came to life under Jinny's hands. She added several hunting dogs, drew a herd of wild ponies looking down at the village from the hillside, two or three skin-clad people standing about the huts, then put a huge sun into the sky dominating the whole picture, its rays beating down on the village as they did in Egyptian pictures Jinny had seen.

"You didn't need me," said Mike.

"I did. It would have taken me ages to copy it correctly and really that's what Mrs. Crowther wants."

When her father had seen her homework, Jinny ran down to the stable and mixed a feed for Easter. She paused, wondering if she should go and see Shantih first.

"No," Jinny decided. "I'll see her last. Then I can spend all the time I've got left with her. Mr. MacKenzie first."

The farmer was sitting on the bench in front of his farm, his feet in their tacketty boots stuck straight out in front of him, his shirt sleeves rolled up, his waistcoat buttons undone, his cap pulled down over his nose and his short-stemmed blackened pipe held between his teeth. He didn't look up as Jinny approached.

Jinny sat down beside him, waiting for him to speak to her. Mr. MacKenzie puffed away, ignoring Jinny.

"You've seen Easter?" asked Jinny at last, forced into speech.

"Aye, if that's the name you've given to that skinful of bones that's eating my grass. Grass I was keeping for the heifers I'm buying from Charlie Moss next month. Aye, I've seen her."

"Oh no!" gasped Jinny. She had never once imagined that there might be anything special about the field by the bothy. It had just looked to Jinny like any other grass, only longer and sweeter.

"I never thought it was special grass!"

"You'd have been doing better to have been asking my permission first, before you went putting a beast like yon on my land."

Mr. MacKenzie never looked at Jinny; he went on staring straight ahead and smoking his pipe so that Jinny knew he was really annoyed.

"I didn't mean to do any harm."

"Oh, I'm sure of that. Here and there like a flea in a colander, minding other peoples' businesses, that's the style of you and, 'So sorry, Mr. MacKenzie,' when the damage has been done. 'I didn't know, Mr. MacKenzie.' 'I didn't mean it, Mr. MacKenzie,' " mocked the farmer in Jinny's voice.

Jinny stood up. There was obviously no point in wasting any more time. Mr. MacKenzie was umbraged and intended to stay that way.

"I'll take her down to Shantih's field," Jinny said.

"Och, be leaving the poor thing where she is now. Keziah has taken the bit fancy to her. Though next time," warned Mr. MacKenzie, taking the pipe out of his mouth and pointing it at Jinny, "be asking my permission first."

"I will," said Jinny. "Don't worry."

Jinny left the farmyard and began to climb up to the bothy. She felt so tired that she thought she could have lain down in the bracken and slept. It was an effort to walk, to lift one leaden foot and place it down in front of the other; the bucket of food was a dead weight in her hand.

Events of the past day and night flickered through Jinny's mind as she plodded on. Brenda's gaudy face became Miss Lorimer's prim disapproval; Mr. MacKenzie's fixed basilisk gaze became the Headmaster's bald authority; Shantih became as poor as Easter, the flesh withering from her, great hollows sunk above her eyes, the beauty of her proud bearing and arrogant breeding fallen into the gaunt frame of Don Quixoté's mare Rosinante. Her lameness became Easter's broken, shuffling gait. Jinny's mother and father watched, and Petra's starling voice asked endless questions that Jinny couldn't answer. The man in the white coat at the Vet College said that the X-ray showed navicular.

Jinny rounded a corner of the track and the bothy came into sight. In the doorway sat a wise woman; her long grey hair fell to her shoulders, her black robes covered her feet, and a cloak patterned with mystic symbols was brilliant about her. A white beast crouched at her side, its head resting on her knee. Unicorn or hart or mare. Jinny couldn't tell. She stopped, stared, held by the vision.

"It's yourself has been the long time coming," said Keziah.

Blinking, shaking her head, Jinny walked towards the old tinker woman and the white pony lying beside her. Keziah's hair was loose, her rusty black clothes grew on her and round her shoulders was a brightly-patterned shawl.

"I thought . . ." began Jinny vaguely.

"Be sitting you down," said Keziah, pointing to a wooden stool.

Thankfully, Jinny collapsed on to the stool. "Do you know, I thought . . ."

Easter, disturbed by Jinny's arrival, got to her feet and stood looking out over the moorland.

"Tam was telling me it was yourself saved the pony."

"Well, Brenda really," said Jinny, standing up again and holding out the feed to Easter. "Brenda said I could have her. I've to pay for her before the end of the month. If I hadn't saved her, she would have been dead by now."

For a moment, Jinny thought about the other horses from the riding school who would have been loaded into the slaughterer's float that morning, but there was nothing she could have done for them. She had done all she could. She had saved Easter.

"It was the right thing to do," said Keziah gently.

At her words, Jinny felt the turmoil inside her head begin to settle and grow calm so that she could reach the deep, still place within herself, and Keziah's voice was the voice of this stillness. It had been the right thing to do.

When Easter had finished her feed she began to graze, and Jinny sat down again sharing the evening silence with Keziah, gazing down over the reach of moorland to where the sea lipped and clipped in a quicksilver quiescence. Somehow it was as if she had always known Keziah, or had found her after searching for her all her life. She was someone who understood how it was for Jinny. Ken did in a way, but he was still searching himself. Keziah had a peace about her. She knew and rested in the knowing. If she only would, she could tell Jinny all she wanted to know.

"It's your family will be all away on Saturday?" Keziah asked.

Jinny looked up, startled back into present things.

"Why, yes," she said, wondering why Keziah should care.

"But it's yourself will be there?"

"I'm not going with them. I can't stand that Belinda Wright. I'm staying at home."

Keziah nodded as if it mattered to her, then Maggie and Tam, carrying bags of shopping, came round the track.

There was chatter and fussing when Maggie saw Keziah still sitting in the doorway. Bustling, she helped Keziah into the bothy, demanding to know why Jinny hadn't had the sense to put peat on the fire.

"Was Mr. MacKenzie mad when he saw Easter in his field?" Jinny asked Tam.

"Aye. Said he'd be dealing with you when he saw you."

"He's seen me. Still, he said she could stay."

"There'll be no trouble with her now," said Tam. "It's herself that has taken to the pony. I'll keep the eye on her, be seeing that she's not eating too much of the rich grass. I'll be bringing her out here to graze."

With her hand on Easter's neck, Jinny walked beside her back to the field, talking to her, feeding her bits of bread.

"She can't be," Jinny told herself. "It really is my imagination this time." For to Jinny's loving eye, Easter looked a bit better already. Her eyes were brighter, her ears flickered to the sound of Jinny's voice, and when she left Easter in the field and went down to Shantih, Jinny looked back and saw Easter with her head down grazing steadily.

"You've to go to the Vet College," she told Shantih, standing still while the Arab blew over her hair. "Not this Saturday but next. It's more or less all fixed up. Oh, why are you lame? Why can't you get better?"

Jinny stood gazing into the greying evening. She did not know how she could ever bear to take Shantih to the Vet College knowing that her lameness might be incurable. Leading her into Danny Sargent's float, knowing where they were taking her, what they would do to her—and Shantih not knowing.

"Oh, please, please Shantih, couldn't you get better then we won't need to go?" Jinny pleaded uselessly.

Jinny went straight to the phone when she got into the house. She stood staring down at its black toad waiting, then she drew in a deep breath, grasped the receiver and dialled the vet's number.

Jim Rae was sharp and businesslike. The Manders would pay for half of the petrol, and she was to mention to her father that a bottle left in the float for Danny would be acceptable.

"There's absolutely nothing else we could try?" Jinny asked.

"Brisk up," said the vet. "You're only taking her for an X-ray, not an execution. Be ready seven o'clock, a week this Saturday."

"Yes," said Jinny and almost, almost she didn't ask.

"Right," said the vet, ready to put the phone down.

"It could be navicular, couldn't it?" Jinny demanded, her voice high-pitched and anxious, pleading with the vet to say no, of course it couldn't, not to be so silly.

There was a moment's pause.

"Whatever put that into your head?"

"But it could be, couldn't it?"

"We can't rule out the possibility, but don't upset yourself about it. Wait until we see what the X-ray shows. We'll cross that bridge if we come to it."

Jinny went upstairs to her room. She sat on her bed, staring down the garden to the horses' field. Bramble grazed steadily, walking smoothly, but Shantih stood still, stretching her neck to reach as much grass as she could without moving, then she stumbled forward and stood still to graze again.

"You must want them to find out what's wrong with her. She can't go on like this," Jinny told herself.

"No!" Jinny said aloud. "No!" She could not bear the thought of taking Shantih to the Vet College that would smell the same as Inverburgh Hospital; could not bear the thought of the suave, self-assured face above the white coat telling her that it was a fractured bone, that it was navicular.

Jinny jumped up, sweeping the terror out of her head. She swung through to the other half of her room, laid out paper, sharpened a pencil and sat down to draw pictures for Nell Storr, pictures that would sell for enough money to pay for Easter.

But the pictures refused to come. The pencil in Jinny's hand was a clumsy piece of dead wood not a living extension of her being, the way it usually was. It was no good, she could not draw anything tonight. There was no magic.

At last Jinny gave up trying.

"Are you in?" called her mother's voice.

"I'm in," replied Jinny. "And getting ready for bed."

"Good," said Mrs. Manders. "Sleep well."

Jinny got up and went to stand in front of the Red Horse.

"Cure Shantih's lameness," she begged. "Let her be fit again. Make her fit to gallop and jump. Let me find out what's wrong with her foot before I need to take her to the Vet College."

The mural of the Red Horse was without power. Jinny stretched out her hand towards it, ran her fingers over the arched line of its neck, the bulk of its chest, its plunging legs and blocked hooves. With her forefinger Jinny traced the outline of its yellow eyes and trumpeting nostrils. But it was only a lifeless painting, a crude drawing with its paint flaking away in places.

If Jinny had stood there all night it would have made no difference. She turned away and, undressing, got ready for bed. She pulled the clothes over her head and buried her face in the pillow. There were too many challenges in Jinny's life for her to start and think about them tonight.

Just before she slept, the pressure of the Red Horse, as it had once been when it had haunted Jinny's dreams, strayed into the edge of her consciousness. It was like the sun that Jinny had drawn above Mike's stone-age village; the rays from the Horse reached out encircling Keziah and Easter, Jinny and Shantih. It stayed, brilliantly waiting, for them to approach it. Waited, knowing that they would come.

CHAPTER TEN

The noise of Petra having a bath woke Jinny on Saturday morning. She sat up in bed, checked automatically that Shantih and Bramble were in their field, then thought how satisfactory it was that she wasn't going to have to go into Inverburgh with her family and spend the day with Belinda Wright. Positive action obviously paid off. Jinny noted the fact for future use. If she had said weakly that she really didn't want to meet the Wrights again, never having been at all fond of Belinda when they had been in the same class in their Stopton school, and would her family mind if she stayed at Finmory and didn't meet them, they would probably have persuaded her to go with them. A strong "No" had made everything quite definite from the start.

Before breakfast, Jinny went down to see Shantih and Bramble.

"You might have been going to the Vet College today," Jinny told Shantih, shivering suddenly at the thought. "At least the Wrights have done some good going home through Inverburgh. They've put that off for a week."

Shantih listened with alert ears to Jinny's voice.

"You'd give anything to be sound again, wouldn't you?" Jinny murmured. "So we could go for a ride again." And Jinny thought of all the rides they had shared—quiet rides along the beach in the early morning, rides over the moors, the race to the standing stones when Shantih had jumped the waterfall.

"What will I do? What will I do if it is navicular? If it is a fractured bone? I couldn't bear to let them shoot you. Couldn't. Not ever. Not ever. Please God, no. No. They'll tell me to be sensible about it. Tell me it's the only thing."

Shantih, sensing Jinny's distress, gazed at her through solemn eyes. Listening to her. Trying to understand.

For a brief moment, Jinny laid her face against Shantih's neck.

"It would have been today," she murmured. "If Dad

hadn't thought I was going with them to see the Wrights, I'd have known by tonight."

A bit of Jinny knew that she couldn't go on like this. In the end, Shantih would have to go to the Vet College, Jinny would have to know, but just now she couldn't face up to it. She pushed it out of her mind, spun round away from Shantih and ran back to the house.

Her family were having an early breakfast, all looking smart and unlike their usual Saturday morning selves.

"It would have been so much nicer if you'd been coming with us," said her mother, as Jinny sat down and spooned muesli from the big bowl on to her own plate. "Mrs. Wright will think it very odd."

"She thinks I'm odd no matter what I do," stated Jinny.

"I'm dying to see Susan again," said Petra, making sure that nobody thought she was odd.

"Surprise, surprise," mocked Jinny.

"I don't see why I have to go when you're letting Jinny stay at home," said Mike. "I don't want to go a bit. It's not fair, dragging me into Inverburgh."

"Silence," ordered Mr. Manders. "Eat."

"Jinny would have been far better coming with us," insisted Petra. "All you'll do is moon about over Shantih. As if that's doing her any good. What you should be doing is getting her X-rayed as soon as possible. That's what would do her some good. Find out why she is lame."

"Shut up," said Jinny, scowling at her sister. Never in a million years would Petra understand why Jinny couldn't bear the thought of taking Shantih to the Vet College. Petra's world was crisp and smart, held together by time tables and examinations successfully passed. It was black and white and Petra intended to keep it that way.

"A good chance for you to get on with your homework," said Mr. Manders. "I'll look at it tomorrow morning and if it's not done properly you're not going out until it is."

"Say nothing," Jinny told herself. "Another hour and they'll all have gone," and she bit her tongue between her teeth.

It was after ten before Mr. Manders drove out of Finmory drive. Jinny stood on the steps waving, Kelly at her side, for Ken had gone too, taking the chance of a lift to see Nell.

Jinny waited until she knew they would all be well past Mr. MacKenzie's, then she danced through the house, swinging her arms, stamping her feet, in and out through every room, making the house her own.

"First," thought Jinny, when she eventually threw herself flat on the kitchen floor in utter exhaustion, "I'm going to mix a feed for Easter, then bring her down here and try to groom her a bit. Then I shall do some pictures for Nell."

Jinny went down to the stables and mixed oats, nuts and two handfuls of the mixture into a bucket. She had brought apples and carrots from the house and she cut these into long strips, added them to the feed, then stirred it round with her hands.

"Better damp it," Jinny thought, going outside to where a rain barrel stood by the stable door. A movement on the hillside caught her eye and instantly, calling Kelly to heel, Jinny dodged back into the stable.

"Knew there was something going on," she thought, as she crouched down by the stable window and peered up the hill. "This is why Keziah wanted everyone out of Finmory."

Down from the hill came Easter being led by Tam. Keziah, supported by Maggie, was sitting sideways on her back.

"What on earth can she be doing," Jinny wondered, as she watched the shabby procession descending from the hill. Maggie's days in the bothy had changed her plastic, new-housing-estate image back into Maggie of the tinker days. A man's anorak covered a rough dress, she wore heavy wellingtons, and her hair was drawn back into a knot at the nape of her neck. Keziah was slumped almost double over Easter's neck. In her black cowl of shawl and plaid, she looked like a shelled woman, hunched against fate, her gnarled face indomitable. Easter was worn out, pathetic, and Tam was sleekit, furtive. Jinny saw them through Miss Tuke's eyes. They were tinkers, not to be trusted, coming to steal.

At Jinny's feet, Kelly snarled, his hackles rising. Jinny silenced him. Crouching down, she gripped his collar, told him to be quiet, but the dog growled in his throat, wrinkling his muzzle over white teeth.

"It's all right," said Jinny. "You know them. It's OK."

She looked up out of the window again. Keziah was tall and stately, the robes she wore about her shoulders trailed to the ground. She rode a white mare, proud-stepping with eye imperial and cascading mane and tail. A hand-maiden walked by her side, and a page boy walked at the head of her palfrey. All the fairy-tales Jinny had ever read, all the illustrations she had ever seen of queens upon white horses, or wise women, of elfin lands, took hands and danced in Jinny's sight. She watched spellbound.

For a minute they dropped out of sight as the track looped downhill and when they reappeared the spell was broken. They appeared tinkers and an old pony again.

Tam led Easter up to Finmory's back door. Maggie helped Keziah down from Easter then supported her into Finmory. Minutes later, Maggie came out alone and she and Tam took Easter back up the hill out of Jinny's sight.

"Take the food to Easter," Jinny told herself. "Go up the hill to Maggie and Tam. Ask them what Keziah is doing." But she put the bucket of food down on the stable floor and went towards the house, Kelly padding at her side. She stood outside the back door, the familiar door-handle smooth and comforting in her hand. Then she turned it and went in.

Jinny walked up the wide curving staircase and the empty house seemed to vibrate to a strange low keening. The chant, the mouth music, the vibration, grew stronger as Jinny walked slowly along the corridor and stopped at the stairs that climbed up to her own room. The chanting was coming from there.

Jinny climbed the steps, opened her door, walked in and under the archway. Her table and chair had been pulled towards the window. Keziah knelt on the floor in front of the Red Horse. Smoke rose from a stone bowl, sweet-smelling herbs that somewhere in a lost dream Jinny had smelt before. The chanting of the old woman filled the room, changed it,

Jinny stood uncertainly until Keziah turned to her and gestured her forward.

At Keziah's side were seven earthenware pots each containing a different colour of paint, a jar of water and two paintbrushes. She handed the pot of red paint and the larger of the two paintbrushes to Jinny.

Jinny opened her mouth to speak, to ask Keziah what she

was doing, what she wanted her to do, but words were out of Jinny's reach. Her mind couldn't get back to where speech was possible.

Now there was only the vibration of Keziah's chanting.

Jinny stood in front of the Horse, felt the chanting resonate through her body, lift her being clear from her mind. She dipped the brush into the red paint and, with a sure, steady stroke, began to repaint the Red Horse; the body glowing red; mane, tail, hooves, black; the leaves green, blue and purple ; the fleshy blossoms white. Jinny re-created the Horse. She knew she was doing it, yet it was not herself, her everyday self, but some vital force that flowed through her. Last of all, Jinny painted in the Horse's yellow eyes.

Keziah rose up from the floor. Taking the other paint-brush, she dipped it into the red paint, touched pupils into the yellow eyes, and the Red Horse could see again. The room was filled with its presence. Keziah's chant grew louder, more urgent. Jinny crouched down, shielding her face until the chanting faded into a silence as sweet as the taste of true water. Jinny opened her eyes.

The freshly-painted mural was luminous and somehow, in the light that came from the Horse, Jinny could see Shantih galloping, free in her element, made whole again.

"Shantih, Shantih," Jinny cried into the silence. But the vision had gone. There was only Keziah lying amongst the shrouds of her black clothes, her eyes closed, her weathered skin stretched tight over her eagle-nose, high cheekbones and ridged jawbone. The pots of paint were empty, the brushes and the water soiled, the herbs burned out.

Jinny sat up, swung her hair back from her face, shaking her head to clear her mind, to come back into herself again. The power that had possessed her had gone. Jinny couldn't even begin to understand what it was. Something to do with the mystery of the Red Horse, Jinny's own red hair and Shantih, glowing chestnut—all fire things, flaunting, magic. And somehow it was close to the way Jinny felt when one of her paintings was going so right that not Jinny but something else was painting it.

She sat beside Keziah, supporting the old woman until she was sitting, leaning against Jinny. There was no substance to her body, brittle bones under slack skin, as if only her clothes held her together. Gradually Keziah opened her eyes.

"Are you all right?" Jinny asked anxiously, as Keziah turned her face to the Horse.

"You did well," she said. "It is the work well done before I go."

Jinny helped her to her feet. For a long moment the old woman stood before the Horse, then she turned and without looking back made her slow way through the arch and out of the door.

"I'll not be seeing it again with these eyes," she said, as Jinny helped her down the stairs. "I will not be staying long in this body now."

All her mother's easy reassurances sprang to Jinny's lips, but she couldn't say them. They would be too false. Keziah was dying. There was no need for pretence.

When at last they reached the kitchen, Jinny helped Keziah into a chair then busied herself making tea. Keziah sat as still as Tam.

"I've made it really sweet for you," said Jinny. "Could you eat anything? There's scones or biscuits."

Keziah took a biscuit and drank the sugary tea without speaking. When she had finished, she placed the mug firmly on the table in front of her.

"If you bring the Arab to me," she said, "I will be finding out for you the reason for her lameness."

"You what?" demanded Jinny.

"Bring her to me," repeated Keziah.

"But how could you tell what's wrong with Shantih? How would you know when there's nothing to see. She's just lame . . ." Jinny's words trailed into silence. Keziah sat as if Jinny hadn't spoken.

Jinny stared at her unbelievingly. How could Keziah know what was wrong with Shantih? An old tinker woman couldn't find out why she was lame when the vet had failed. Or could she? Could she know?

"I'll bring her," said Jinny and, hair bannering behind her, she wheeled round out of the kitchen and down to Shantih's field.

CHAPTER ELEVEN

Jinny fumbled the halter on to Shantih, led her through the gate, and slowly, limping and stumbling, Shantih followed Jinny up to the house. At the back door Jinny stopped. She pushed the door open and called into the kitchen that Shantih was there.

"Be bringing her in," replied Keziah.

"But I can't," shouted Jinny. "My mum would have a thousand canaries—a horse in her kitchen!"

"Bring her in to me."

Shantih stepped into the kitchen at Jinny's side, her neck arched, eyes goggling, nostrils flared. She was tight with panic, ready to leap away, shying from the strange objects that surrounded her, the sense of a prison, a cage.

Keziah spoke in a low, lilting voice, crooning and gentle, and Jinny felt the tenseness leave Shantih as she stretched her neck and blew over Keziah. The old woman's stiffened hands moved over Shantih's head and neck, her voice murmuring as she did so.

Shantih lowered her head on to Keziah's shoulder, and the old woman laid her face against the Arab's flat cheekbone. Lifting her arms, Keziah laid a hand on either side of Shantih's neck. She spoke gently, soothing Shantih, breathing peace and love into her.

At last Keziah straightened up and, lifting Shantih's lame leg, held the foot in both her hands. Jinny watched as Shantih stood perfectly still, allowing Keziah to examine her foot, making no attempt to draw it back from Keziah's control as the old woman carefully examined the sole and frog of Shantih's foot.

As Jinny stood holding Shantih she felt lost in a sense of total unreality. All the things that told her who she was, kept her safely linked to her pattern of everyday life, seemed to have fallen away leaving only the repainting of the Red Horse vivid in her mind. And now, the unreality of Shantih being in their kitchen, standing so peacefully while Keziah examined her foot; Shantih, who normally would have reared and plunged away if Jinny had suggested she should come into the house.

Keziah's eyes closed. She sat motionless, her hands cradling Shantih's hoof, and still Shantih stood without the least movement.

"In a way," Jinny thought suddenly, "It is the same as if I'd taken her to the Vet College. When Keziah tells me what's wrong it will be the same as the vet in the white coat confirming a fractured bone or navicular. I'll know any minute now. If Keziah says she can't be cured, that's it, final."

Ever since the moment when Shantih had laid her head on Keziah's shoulder and the old woman had bent her head to meet the Arab, Jinny had known that Keziah's power that had held her while she repainted the Horse, now bound Shantih in its spell. More surely than any veterinary diagnosis, Keziah would know what was causing Shantih's lameness.

At last Keziah's eyes opened. She freed Shantih's foot and Shantih placed it back precisely on to the kitchen floor. Keziah laid her hand on Shantih's shoulder, lowered her face for a last moment of communion with the horse, then sank back in her chair.

Jinny couldn't speak to ask what she was desperate, yet terrified, to discover. She could only wait.

"Do not be distressing yourself," said Keziah. "It is a poison deep in her foot. I felt something sharp—a piercing in her foot."

"Not navicular? Not a fractured bone?" cried Jinny.

"There is no disease," stated Keziah. "It is an injury. Not a broken bone for I was feeling the poison. Be taking her back to her field and come yourself to the bothy, and I will find the herbs to be drawing the poison out of her."

"You're all right, you're all right," Jinny cried, as she led Shantih back to her field. "It's not navicular. You'll be all right. I'll be able to ride you again. She can cure you. You don't need to go to the Vet College. Oh, Shantih, Shantih."

Jinny let Shantih go and stood watching her as she made her slow way across to Bramble. "Thank you. Thank you," said Jinny aloud. She stood for a long moment, freed from the terror of the unspeakable thought that Shantih might have had an incurable lameness, that she might never have been able to ride her again.

They brought Easter down to Finmory, and Maggie and Jinny helped Keziah up on to her back. Jinny could see that Maggie was concerned for Keziah and yet she said nothing, no reproaches or selfish fussing. The work that had brought Keziah to the bothy had been done.

When at last they reached the bothy, they had to carry Keziah inside and lay her on the couch. She sank back, her breath harsh, her face toned in yellows and greens, the great shadows around her eyes and nostrils, black purple. Jinny was appalled by the change. It seemed to have happened so suddenly.

Before she fell into a heavy sleep, Keziah told Tam to bring her bag to her and, from the black sack, Keziah drew out crumpled packets of dried herbs. She chose three of them, gave them to Jinny and told Tam the names of the herbs he would find growing on the moor.

"Be waiting here and Tam will bring them to you," Keziah told Jinny, her voice weak, used up, a harsh wrack of sound that Jinny could hardly hear as she told her how to make a poultice, apply it to the sole of Shantih's foot, binding it tightly into the frog and leaving it in position for a week.

"Do not be touching it for seven days," she warned. "By then it will have drawn the evil from her foot."

By the time Tam came back with the plants Keziah had told him to collect, Keziah was asleep. Maggie put the dried herbs and the ones Tam had brought, into the saucepan, added water and put the pan on the peat fire.

"They'll be ready by the afternoon," she told Jinny. "Be coming back then."

When Jinny went back there was no sign of Maggie or Tam. Keziah was lying as she had been when Jinny had left, closed into a heavy sleep. The pot of herbs simmered on the fire.

"Better wait till they get back," Jinny decided, and she took the feed she had brought for Easter out to where the pony was lying dozing in the shade.

When Jinny approached her, Easter got stiffly to her feet, shook herself and stepped towards Jinny, her eyes bright, her nostrils wiffling a welcome.

"Dear pony," said Jinny, setting the bucket of feed on the ground and watching as Easter buried her head in it, eager for the oats.

When Easter had finished feeding, Jinny put on the halter that she kept by the field gate and, using the dandy-brush that she had brought up with her from Finmory, began to groom the pony. Clouds of white hairs flew up from Easter's harsh coat.

"Bet it's years since anyone groomed you properly," Jinny told the pony. "You'll feel a lot better when I've finished."

As Jinny worked, happiness sparked electric through her. Shantih didn't have navicular, wouldn't have to go for an X-ray; in a week she would be sound and Jinny would be riding her again. Soon Easter would be coming down to the Finmory field; already she was coming alive again, beginning to be herself. Once she was at Finmory, Jinny would get her feet attended to and ask the vet to have a look at her.

Jinny brushed out her mane, patiently teasing out the tangles, sweeping it from one side of her neck to the other until it fell in a silver sheen almost as silken as Shantih's. After a few attempts to do something with the corded mat of Easter's tail, Jinny gave up.

"That can wait for another day," she said and, taking off Easter's halter, she sat down on the grass. The pony waited beside her.

"Where did you come from?" Jinny wondered, reaching up to scratch Easter's face. "To be here today to carry Keziah down to the Red Horse. When you were a show pony all poshed up with rosettes, did you know then that you would be here today? When was then? How were you young then and old now? What changes us?"

Jinny lay flat on the grass staring up at the sky, conscious of Easter beside her; of Keziah asleep in the bothy knowing that she was soon to die and seeming not to mind, not trying to cling on to breathing but letting it happen; of her family somewhere in Inverburgh being polite and plastic with the Wrights; and of Shantih who, by this time next week, would be sound again. And again Jinny felt the presence of Easter as clearly as she had done when she had seen her being ridden through the Inverburgh streets. As if the pony communicated with her through a sense that Jinny hardly knew she possessed, but that this time the sharing was of contentment and peace.

It was late afternoon before Tam and Maggie came back. Several times Jinny had looked in to the bothy to check that Keziah was still asleep and the herbs were still bubbling in the pot.

"We were sending the word," said Maggie. "It'll not be long now. Only the few days."

Jinny shivered, asked quickly if the poultice would be ready yet. When she went in with Maggie and Tam, Jinny kept close beside them, but Keziah lay without moving, sleeping deeply.

Maggie gave Jinny the pot to take down with her.

"Be binding it tight now," she cautioned. "And mind the old one's words—not to be touching it for the seven days."

To Jinny's delight, Ken was back home. She told him what had happened.

"You repainted the Horse?" said Ken, his eyes lighting. "Whee! Really nice. Can I see it?"

Jinny looked down at the soggy mess of herbs in Maggie's pot.

"Help me do Shantih's foot first," she said.

"Right," said Ken, "what do we need?"

"Cotton wool, bit of that green oilskin stuff that Mum used for Mike's arm, bandage—that's in the stable—and a sack. Oh, and scissors and Elastoplast."

"I'll get the things from the house," said Ken.

"I'll bring Shantih into her box. Be best to do her foot there. We can tie her up."

When Jinny led Shantih into her box, Ken had already assembled the things they needed to hold the poultice of herbs in place against the sole of Shantih's foot.

Even with Ken's calming influence, getting the poultice in place on Shantih's foot wasn't easy. First Jinny washed Shantih's hoof, then packed the green, strong-smelling mess of herbs into the sole of her foot. She laid a thick covering of cotton wool over the sole, held this in place with strips of Elastoplast, then put a covering of the green oiled skin over it. With Ken's help, she cut sacking into a rough boot shape and put the whole hoof into the sacking shoe. But even when she had bandaged it securely, it did not look as if it would stay in place for one day, let alone seven.

"Whoa lass, whoa Shantih," crooned Jinny, soothing the restless Arab.

"It won't do," said Ken. "She'll have it off in an hour."

Despondently Jinny agreed, but she couldn't think of any other way of keeping the poultice on.

"She needs a proper shoe," said Ken. "Know any horse shoe shops?"

"Oh, dozens," said Jinny. "There's two in Glenbost."

"Nip down and buy . . ."

"But I do know where I can get one," interrupted Jinny, remembering suddenly the leather poultice boots for horses that stood in a row on one of the shelves in Mr. MacKenzie's back porch. "If he'll lend me one, I'll get one at the farm."

Jinny left Ken holding Shantih while she raced down to Mr. MacKenzie's trying to think of the best way to ask for a loan of one of the boots. She hadn't seen Mr. MacKenzie since he had told her off for leaving Easter in his field. He might well refuse to lend her one of his poultice boots.

Luck was on Jinny's side. As she ran into the yard, one of Mr. MacKenzie's Shetlands, with a rope trailing from her neck, came bucketing out.

"Shouldn't be loose," thought Jinny, and flung herself at the pony, grabbing its rope, then its muzzle, as the Shetland, doing its very best rocking-horse imitation, struggled to escape.

Mr. MacKenzie, scarlet-faced, came stomping across the yard in hot pursuit.

"How many times," said Jinny, as Mr. MacKenzie pulled a halter on to the Shetland, "have I to tell you no to be leading a beast about on a wee bit rope? It's no safe."

"Aye," said Mr. MacKenzie. "It's quick you were there."

"Jet-set Jinny," replied Jinny, knowing it would be O.K. —Mr. MacKenzie would lend her a boot for Shantih.

When Mr. MacKenzie had returned the escapee Shetland to its stall, Jinny told him what she wanted.

"Och now, is that not an improvement, to be asking before you're taking?" said Mr. MacKenzie. He led Jinny round to the back porch and brought down two of the leather boots, knocking the spiders out of them before he handed them to her.

It's one of those two should be fitting her," he said.

"Thanks," said Jinny.

"It's honoured you were that Keziah was curing your horse. Her father, he was a whisperer. Could speak the healing words into a horse's ear. Some said it was Old Nick was putting the speech on his tongue, though my father aye said it was the herbs he used that did the healing. The gift passed on to Keziah, but she took against it and no money would make her use it. Only the tinkers' horses would she be treating, though it's the gentry themselves I've seen pleading at her."

"She whispered to Shantih."

"Aye."

One of the boots fitted Shantih's foot perfectly. Jinny buckled it securely into place. Leading Shantih back to the field, the Arab seemed more lame than ever with the clumsy boot on her foot.

"Only a week," Jinny assured her. "A week and you'll be sound again."

In the kitchen, Ken had made apple and carrot juice and cut slices of his home-baked bread, covering them with honey.

"Delish," said Jinny. "Haven't eaten since breakfast. Oh! Better phone the vet first."

"Vet?"

"To tell him I'll not need to take Shantih for the X-ray," Jinny called back, already on her way to the phone.

It was Mrs. Rae who answered, said she was glad to hear that Shantih was sound again, that Jim had been worried about her.

"Will be," said Jinny.

"Pardon?"

"Will be sound next weekend," said Jinny and, thanking her, put the phone down. It would have been too difficult trying to explain to Mrs. Rae.

When they had finished their snack, Jinny took Ken up to see the mural.

Ken stood in silent admiration in front of the Red Horse. The colours from Keziah's earthenware pots could not have been ordinary poster paint, or any other paint that Jinny knew of. They glowed from the wall as if light vibrated in them; they made the mural luminous.

"Whee!" exclaimed Ken at last, with a long drawn-out breath. "And you painted it?"

"In a way," said Jinny uncertainly. "In a way it was Keziah. I don't know how it did it. Not really. I couldn't have painted it without Keziah."

"I'm taking Kelly down to the sea," invited Ken, when at last he turned away from the mural.

"Better do some homework," said Jinny, but she didn't. When Ken had gone, she took out paper and paints, spread them out on the floor and, sitting back on her heels, stared at the white paper. For Jinny, no experience was ever complete until she had drawn or painted it in some way.

First she painted the tinkers coming down the hillside. Tam crunched into his caddis shell of clothes, Maggie supporting an old bent woman who hardly had the strength to cling on to the worn-out pony. Then the vision she had had of them—Keziah, the wise woman on her pacing palfrey attended by a young girl and a page. But they weren't enough. The first was too ordinary, the second too romantic. Jinny held both paintings in her mind's eye, tried again, screwed it up and started again. At her third attempt, she got what she wanted. They were tinkers, and Easter was old, but being themselves they were also the vision. It was there in the angle of Keziah's neck, her hands, her cloak; in Tam and in Maggie, as the bright shadow of Easter's past was visible in her. When she had finished it, Jinny hardly glanced at it.

She put it up on her table and quickly did a pencil drawing of Shantih—Shantih sound again, the wind in her mane and tail.

Then Jinny took a piece of her precious pastel paper and with wax crayons drew the Red Horse, pressing the wax colour hard on to the black paper until it had a thick enamel quality.

Her family came back just as Jinny had finished it. For minutes Jinny listened to the banging of doors, their voices loud after the silence.

"Jinny, are you in?" called her mother.

"I'm in," Jinny replied, and went tearing down the staircase to tell them her day.

The phone rang before she reached the kitchen. Jinny doubled back into the hall and answered it. It was the vet.

"That's right," Jinny assured him. "No, I really don't need to take her to the Vet College now. She will be quite sound by next weekend. I'm perfectly sure."

Jinny held the receiver away from her ear so that she couldn't quite hear what the vet was saying, only knew when he had stopped talking.

"Fine," said Jinny into the phone. "Right then. Thank you," and she put the phone down.

"Belinda was most upset you weren't there," said Mrs. Manders.

"Who was it on the phone?" asked Mr. Manders.

"Susan had six-inch heels, at least," said Petra.

"The vet," said Jinny. "I'd phoned up earlier to tell him that Shantih wouldn't need to go to the Vet College."

"Not go for the X-ray?" interrupted Mike in amazement.

"But it was Mrs. Rae I got and that was Mr. Rae. Just checking, I suppose."

"You mean Shantih's sound?" demanded Mrs. Manders. "That's great. Tell us."

"Well, not exactly sound," said Jinny. "But she will be by next weekend." And Jinny told her family what had happened.

"You mean," said Petra, "just because that mad old tinker woman boiled up some plants into a poultice you think that's going to cure Shantih's lameness? You don't, Jinny? Even you couldn't be a naïve as that!"

Jinny stared in horror at her sister. Until Petra had spoken there had been utterly no doubt in Jinny's mind. To Jinny, Shantih was as good as cured. For seconds the shock of Petra's words was so great that Jinny could hardly believe what she had heard. How could anyone doubt that Shantih would be sound in seven days?

"Keziah knew what was wrong with her foot," said Jinny, "and she knew how to cure it. Shantih will be all right by next weekend."

"Well, we'll hope so," said her mother. "But I don't think you should have cancelled the arrangements with the vet."

"Better phone back and explain," suggested Mr. Manders. "Tell him you've discussed it with us and decided that Shantih had better go for the X-ray after all."

"No," said Jinny.

"Don't be so daft . . ." began Petra.

"I'm not daft and I'm not naïve, whatever that means," Jinny shouted. "Shantih is not going to the Vet College. She doesn't need to go. She will be sound by next weekend."

Jinny turned and dashed out of the room and up to her own bedroom. She looked down to where Shantih stood, resting her poulticed leg.

"They know nothing," muttered Jinny. "Nothing. By next week I'll be riding you again. Then they'll see that I'm not daft."

CHAPTER TWELVE

On Monday lunchtime Jinny took her paintings to Nell to see if she would buy them. She was making a discreet escape from school, for although it wasn't actually forbidden, pupils who took school dinners weren't encouraged to roam around Inverburgh at lunchtime, when Mr. Eccles spotted her.

"Jinny! Jinny Manders" he called.

Jinny turned, ready to defend her right to go to the shops if she wanted to.

"Glad I caught you," said her art teacher. "Have you a minute?"

Unwillingly Jinny admitted she had.

"Was having a word about you with the Headmaster this morning. Seems you're up to your neck in detentions and undone homework?"

Jinny said she supposed she was.

"Well, I told him that the art department had no complaints whatsoever. That your work is outstanding."

Jinny squirmed inwardly, as she always did when anyone praised her painting.

I'm not saying you won't have to apply yourself to your maths, but I thought I'd let you know you're not entirely unappreciated. Spent grim years myself struggling with science because my family thought it was the only thing for a boy. So I know what it's like."

Jinny twisted her hair not knowing where to look.

"O.K."

"Yes," said Jinny.

As she trotted through the crowded street, Mr. Eccles' words rang pleasantly in her mind. "Outstanding". "Not entirely unappreciated". Despite herself, she smiled as she hurried on to Nell's shop.

"I've got to get the money to Brenda before the month is up to pay for Easter," Jinny explained to Nell. "So could you put them somewhere where people will see them easily?"

Nell was looking intently at Jinny's pictures spread out on

her counter. There were the three of Maggie and Tam bringing Keziah down the hillside on Easter, three pencil drawings of Shantih, two of Kelly, and three other pastel drawings of Bramble and Shantih. Jinny had kept the one of the Red Horse for herself.

"I'll do better than that," said Nell. "I'll pay you in advance. Sale or return to begin with, but once a supplier is established I always buy the goods from them. Consider yourself established. Five pounds a picture—fifty-five pounds."

"But will you be able to sell them?" asked Jinny, feeling embarrassed by taking so much money from Nell.

"Picked up a rather nice selection of frames from a house clearance. I'll frame your pictures and make a filthy profit," Nell assured her. "Don't worry, I'm not giving money away."

Jinny took the money to the riding school on Tuesday after school.

Brenda was out with a ride, and Jinny had to hang about the yard waiting for her to return. Jinny wondered if Miss Tuke had been out yet to inspect things. There was no doubt about it, the place had been smartened up. The yard had been thoroughly swept and someone had started to repair the stabling. Jinny looked into the stalls and saw that the chestnut pony who was standing in had been thoroughly groomed and had hay in his manger. At the end of the row of stalls, instead of the rotten hay, there was a fresh load of sweet smelling bales and three brand-new, galvanized bins. As usual, Miss Tuke was effectively seeing to things.

It was almost half an hour before Brenda, accompanied by two men riding Sporty and Queenie, arrived back.

"How's tricks?" asked Brenda.

"I've got fifty-five pounds for you," said Jinny, holding out the money to Brenda. "So that's seventy-five altogether. I'm bound to get the other five in time, so she's quite safe."

Brenda took the money, flicking the notes through her fingers.

"Call it square," she said. "Your Miss Tuke got me a rise. Threatened to report Martin for not paying me a living wage. She's a one she is. Seventy-five will satisfy his lordship."

"Oh thanks. That's great."

"And how's Easter?"

"Super. She really is. Still in the field by the bothy, but I should think I'll take her down to the others next week and then I'll ask the vet to look at her."

"Get her wormed," said Brenda.

"Will do," said Jinny. "I made her a bran mash with treacle and oats and chopped apple on it. She smelt it and came cantering to the gate for it," Jinny's face was bright at the memory.

"I'll come and see her some time," said Brenda. "If it's O.K.?"

"'Course," said Jinny. "Do come. You can see Shantih. She's getting better too."

For a moment before Brenda turned away she smiled at Jinny, her mask drawn back, and, for a second, Jinny saw quite clearly the girl who had once shared her dreams.

Jinny raced for the bus and caught it by the skin of her teeth, but by the time she got home it was too late to go up to the bothy.

"I was up this morning," Mrs. Manders assured her. "Keziah's very weak. There's nothing you could do. You'll see her tomorrow night."

"But Easter—I should be feeding her."

"She was stuffing herself with grass. Shouldn't think she'd be thanking you for any other kind of food."

"Must go down and see Shantih, then," insisted Jinny. "I'll go now. I'll be very quick, then I'll come back and do my homework."

"Quarter of an hour," said her father.

"Oke," said Jinny, and went.

Shantih came hobbling to the gate, her hoof still safely inside its leather boot.

"Dear horse," said Jinny, rubbing Shantih's neck, straightening her mane and feeding her lumps of sugar. "How does your foot feel now? I can't see how it is now you're all cluttered up with that boot. Only another three days and I can take it off. Then you'll be sound again. Then we can go for rides again." To Jinny, not having Shantih to ride was almost like being lame herself. It seemed so long ago, the last time she had ridden Shantih on the moors. So long ago since she had galloped and jumped, felt Shantih winged beneath her as the moorland fell away under Shantih's flying hooves. "Soon you'll get out of this field, get down to the shore again," Jinny told her.

But Shantih was pushing at Jinny's pockets, pawing the ground, asking for more sugar-lumps.

It wasn't until Jinny was getting ready for bed that it suddenly struck her that Shantih had been standing on her lame leg and pawing the ground with her sound foot.

On Thursday night, Jinny only had English and French homework.

"Test my vocabulary," she said to Mike.

"I learnt it at lunchtime," she told him, when she'd got it all right.

"And that's my English essay," she said to her father, holding out her exercise book for his approval.

"Good," said Mr. Manders, when he had finished reading it. "Spelling original but A-plus for content."

"Am I free?"

"Miss Manders, you are absolutely free."

Jinny mixed a feed for Easter, putting in apples, sliced carrots, turnip, oats, maize and pony nuts. "Oat cocktail," she thought, setting off to the bothy.

Easter was grazing in the far corner of the field. When she saw Jinny she gave a shrill, trembling whinny and came eagerly to the gate.

"By the end of the summer you'll be quite fit again," Jinny thought optimistically, as she watched Easter wolfing down the feed. "Wonder if I could ride you? Or you could be a pack pony. We could go on a trek and you could carry the tent. Kelly could be a watch-dog."

Easter finished the feed, tipped the bucket over with her nose, then shied away from it's rattling menace. Jinny grinned, remembering how Easter had hardly noticed the oil drums and poles clattering about her legs.

For a while, Jinny stayed just watching Easter. At the end of her life, things were going right for her again. She would never leave Finmory. She would stay there with Shantih and Bramble until she died. The best had happened for her.

Reluctantly, Jinny turned away and walked across to the bothy. Inside, Keziah was lying on the couch, propped up with pillows, covered with blankets. Her eyes were closed and her breathing harsh. Maggie and two other tinker women Jinny hadn't seen before were sitting over the fire. They looked up uneasily, waiting for Jinny to go when she had just arrived.

"How is she?" Jinny asked awkwardly, feeling an intruder.

"Do not be disturbing her," cautioned Maggie. "She's sleeping easier now. Be leaving her in peace."

The gaunt face with its heavy grey hair was indrawn, not to be reached by Jinny's polite enquiries.

"I'll come back tomorrow night," said Jinny.

"Don't be upsetting yourself now," said Maggie kindly. "Keziah would not be wanting to stay here when she is ready to go."

Jinny went down to Mr. MacKenzie's to collect the milk. As she reached the yard, two rackety vans drove in, their doors opened and several tinkers unloaded themselves. One of the men spoke to Mr. MacKenzie, asking where Keziah Brodie was. The farmer pointed to the track. Children and dogs, women and men, came out of the vans and made their way up the track. Mr. MacKenzie stood watching them, smoking his pipe and spitting. Saying nothing.

"Not like him," thought Jinny. Normally the farmer would have been shouting after them, warning them to keep to the track, to shut gates and not to interfere with his stock. "Or chasing them off his land altogether," Jinny thought, and the strangeness of Mr. MacKenzie's behaviour shivered through Jinny like a cold finger laid on her spine. For the tinkers had come to be there when Keziah died.

"Aye, she was the bold one," said Mr. MacKenzie, giving Jinny the full can of milk. "The same Keziah Brodie. It's the sleepness nights I've spent tossing on my bed thinking of that one. Aye. So it is."

Jinny took the milk and hurried away. She didn't want to know.

As she came in sight of the horses' field, Shantih and Bramble were grazing. Jinny paused, changing the milk can to her other hand. Then she stood perfectly still, staring intently.

"If being sound was the worst thing in the world to happen to Shantih, the thing you most absolutely dreaded, so you would pretend she wasn't sound for as long as you could, what would you think now?" Jinny asked herself. "You couldn't pretend she wasn't sound, could you? No matter how badly you wanted her to go on being lame, you'd have to admit she's not so lame."

Excitement welled up in Jinny, for Shantih, grazing beside Bramble, was moving easily, keeping pace with the Highland, taking her weight evenly on each leg as she walked.

"Not yet," Jinny warned herself, banking down the brimming joy that threatened to overflow inside her. "It's too soon. I can't be sure yet. Not till Saturday morning. Not until I take the poultice off."

On Friday afternoon, Mr. Manders was taking a load of pottery in to Nell and he had arranged to pick Jinny up outside her school.

"I'd have been quicker on the bus," Jinny thought irritably, as she waited, watching the hands of the school clock creep towards half-past four. "And I've so much to do."

It was almost a quarter to five before Mr. Manders appeared, and to Jinny's dismay there was someone sitting next to him in the car.

"Sorry," he said, opening a back door of the car for Jinny. "Got held up at Nell's."

Disgruntled, Jinny clambered in.

"I've been waiting for bloomin' ages," she grumbled, which was as far as she dared to go with a stranger in the car.

"Peter," said Mr. Manders, "this is Jinny, my daughter. Jinny, meet Mr. Drennan."

"How do you do?" said Jinny, wondering who Mr. Drennan was and why he was in their car. Most of all she was hoping that it didn't mean more wasted time before they got back home.

"Mr. Drennan was delivering some carvings to Nell, so I'm giving him a run back to his house," said Mr. Manders. "Save him hanging around waiting for a bus."

"Where to?" asked Jinny.

"Rashburn," said Mr. Manders.

Jinny sat back utterly defeated. It would be after seven before they got back to Finmory.

"Just when I wanted to be home as soon as possible," she thought. "Curses. Curses. Curses."

Mr. Drennan insisted that they should come in for coffee.

Coffee turned into beer for Mr. Manders and it was half-past eight before they were back at Finmory.

"Look at the time!" ranted Jinny. "I'll need to go up now to see Easter. I'd have caught the six o'clock bus if I'd known we were going to be as late as this."

"It wouldn't have made any difference what time you'd got home at, so calm yourself," said Mrs. Manders, who had come to the door when she heard the car. "Even if you'd been home at your usual time you couldn't have gone up to the bothy tonight."

"Why? I must go up and see Easter."

"Ken saw her this afternoon and she's fine. He took a feed up to her."

"But why can't I go up?"

"Too many tinkers up there," said Mrs. Manders. "No place for you tonight."

"Oh Mum, don't be so ridiculous . . ."

"Settled," said Mrs. Manders. "Even Mr. MacKenzie came round to tell me to be keeping the hems on you tonight."

"Final," said her father. "That's it." And Jinny knew there was no point in arguing.

"First thing tomorrow then," she promised herself.

Tomorrow. The seventh day. The day she could take off the poultice.

CHAPTER THIRTEEN

The buckles of the leather boot were so stiff that Jinny could hardly loosen them.

"Whoa, steady, steady horse," soothed Jinny, as Shantih, tied to the gate-post, pulled back against her halter rope, yet again snatching her hoof out of Jinny's grasp.

Jinny turned her sideways against the gate and patiently tried again. Kneeling in the dew-wet grass, she struggled to push the leather strap through the buckle. Time stood still. Jinny's world had shrunk to nothing but her concentration on the obdurate leather. In minutes the poultice would be off and Jinny would know.

At last Jinny managed to undo one buckle, which eased the tightness of the boot, and the other buckle opened easily. She took the leather boot off, untied the bandage, and the poultice with its paddings fell away from Shantih's foot. Lying on the mess of the poultice was a shard of stone about an inch long and sharp as a needle. It had been embedded in Shantih's foot and the poultice of herbs had drawn it out. Jinny wiped the sole of Shantih's foot clean, but there was no way of telling where her foot had been punctured.

Jinny untied Shantih, took off her halter and let her go free, her movements still slow and concentrated as if her actions were not linked by time, had no past, would have no future.

For a second the Arab stood poised, unmoving, and then she reared up, swung round on her quarters and charged full gallop round the field. Mane and tail fanned back by her speed, she charged round, a red-gold force. Her white hoofs beat a furious tattoo on the drum-skin of the earth; her speed sleeked the contours of her face into a precious, carven icon; the force of her quarters drove strength into her shoulders and chest. Round and round she went in power and glory. Shantih was sound again.

As Jinny watched, the weeks of misery dissolved, the dreaded threat of navicular or a fractured bone faded away.

For it had not happened, was not true. Shantih was sound. Jinny would be able to ride her again.

"Yarhoo, gaudeamus," yelled Jinny at the pitch of her lungs. She flung herself over the gate and went racing through the grey stillness to tell her family, to tell Keziah that Shantih was cured. No one was up in Finmory, but Jinny ran through the house shouting that Shantih was sound, that she had been right, that Keziah had cured her.

She slammed the back door shut behind herself and was about to run up the moors to the track that led to the bothy when suddenly she remembered that she didn't need to walk. She could ride. She could ride Shantih.

Jinny ran down to the stable, taking great leaps into the air, flinging her arms wide, shaking her hair for joy. She had to tell Keziah as soon as possible.

She grabbed Shantih's bridle from its hook, feeling its smooth leather familiar in her hand. She ran on down to the field where Shantih snatched mouthfuls of grass, then reared up, striking out with her forelegs before she bucked violently and tore round the field, flat out, the enclosure of the field turning her speed into a red-gold flame.

"Don't need to worry about whether I should ride her or not," Jinny thought. "She's sound O.K."

Jinny called her and Shantih flung up her head, stood for a moment taking in the bridle in Jinny's hand and then, knowing it meant a ride, came trotting to Jinny, her mane and tail bannering about her, high spring-stepping, bounding from a molten earth, her eyes lustrous with memory and expectation. Dour and stolid, Bramble grazed ignoring her.

Jinny slipped the reins over Shantih's head, slid the bit into her mouth and gently lifted the headpiece over her ears. She could hardly fasten the buckle of the throatlash her hands were shaking so much.

Jinny stood for a long moment, her hand laid flat on Shantih's neck, her being expanded with love. Never such a morning as this. Shantih was sound again.

Jinny gathered up her reins and sprang on to Shantih's back. Turning Shantih towards the moors, she touched her legs against the Arab's sides.

"We've got to tell Keziah that you're sound," Jinny said, as Shantih cantered on the spot, her tail kinked over her quarters, her neck and head high, her nostrils trumpeted into blood pits.

Jinny felt her drop behind the bit, her weight sink back on her hindlegs as she reared, struck out with her forefeet, then with an enormous bound was galloping up the track to the moor.

Shantih was all captured things flying free, was spirit loosened from flesh, was bird again in her own element. Jinny circled her once in a wide sweep over the open land then she turned her back to the path that lead to the bothy. In a way, Keziah already knew that Shantih would be sound, but Jinny wanted to see her again, to tell Keziah and to thank her.

As they reached the bothy, its air of stillness, of indrawn waiting, reached out to Jinny, striking cold against her jubilation. She dropped to a walk, remembering in a rush that there would be other tinkers there, not only Tam and Maggie and, with a chill tightening of her stomach, that Keziah was dying. But still her exultation carried Jinny on. She had to tell Keziah.

The door of the bothy was almost closed. Slipping down from Shantih, Jinny pushed it open. She had to let Keziah know that Shantih was cured.

The darkened room seemed crowded with tinkers standing about the couch, sitting on the floor. The only sound was the rasp of Keziah's breath as her lungs pushed out the unwanted air. Her eyes were closed. There was no flesh on her face, only her bones straining against the taut skin. Keziah was dying.

Jinny stood, clutching the buckle of Shantih's reins in her hand, desperate to escape but unable to move. Maggie came from Keziah's side and put her hand on Jinny's arm to take her out. At the disturbance, Keziah's eyes opened. It seemed to Jinny that they looked straight at her, and from somewhere beyond her eyes Keziah acknowledged her, knew that Shantih was cured.

Maggie steered Jinny out of the bothy.

"Be off home with you," she said. "There's no place for you here."

Tears running down her face, Jinny turned away. Leading Shantih, she walked round to the bothy field. Easter was standing four-square, her bony head stretched out towards the bothy, her ears sharp. She was so intent on what held her there that she seemed oblivious of Jinny's presence, did not even turn her head or flick an ear at Shantih but stood statue-still, gazing wistfully towards the bothy window.

Jinny waited by the field, arms folded along the top bar of the gate, her chin resting on them, Shantih's reins looped over her arm. Shantih, too, seemed caught in this spell of silence; her exuberance forgotten, she stood patiently waiting.

The sun brought back colour into the bleak moorland, to the mountains, to the dazzling rim of the sea. Still Jinny waited, unmoving. She did not understand death, its strangeness, its totality; that when someone died you would never see them again. When Jinny had been painting the Red Horse, Keziah had seemed like a part of herself. As if it was Keziah who had painted the Horse through Jinny and now . . .

Easter gave a sudden whinny and from the bothy came an indrawn shadow of sound, growing from it a high-pitched searing grief as the tinkers' keening mourned Keziah's death.

Now, even if Jinny were to search the whole world, over and over again, she would never find Keziah; never see her or hear her speak, not ever again. She was dead. Jinny stared out numbly across the moors, for it was not only Keziah who was dead, not some strange, special thing that had happened to her alone. This dying was a common thing, it happened to everything that lived; some day all her family would die, Jinny would die and even Shantih.

Jinny laid her arm over Shantih's withers, felt the strong, comforting presence of her horse close beside her.

Easter came slowly towards them. She reached out her head and breathed over Jinny's tear-stained face, exchanged curious questioning breath with Shantih, then stood waiting.

"Keziah's dead," said Jinny bleakly. "She's gone. No more. Dead."

Shantih rested her head on Jinny's shoulder, and Easter gazed at Jinny through eyes as wise as Keziah's had been. It was as if they understood more about death than Jinny could ever understand; that they knew death and life to be part of the same weaving, not in the easy way that humans used these words to cover over their fears, but deep in the very centre of their being. All their living was a part of this acceptance and they searched for a way to share this wisdom with Jinny.

Tam came out of the bothy, hesitated, looking about him. Seeing Jinny, he came towards her holding out a box.

"What is it?" Jinny asked, rubbing her arm across her face.

"For you," he said. "From Keziah."

Jinny opened the box. Inside were the seven earthenware pots of paint, each one refilled, carefully sealed, and the two paintbrushes and the stone bowl in which Keziah had burned the herbs while Jinny had painted the Red Horse.

"I'll keep them," she promised. "I'll put them in a safe place."

Tam nodded. "I'm away then," he said.

"Where will you go now?" Jinny asked.

"When we've buried the old one we'll be moving on."

"But where to?"

Tam shrugged.

"Don't you mind?" questioned Jinny. "Don't you mind that Keziah's dead?"

"She was ready to go," said Tam. His pinched face showed no sign of grief. "She died with her own folk. That's what she wanted."

And Jinny knew he was right. Keziah had been ready to die. To upset herself over this was only selfishness, wanting what she couldn't have.

"Will you be back?" Jinny asked.

Again Tam shrugged, not caring. "You'll keep the paints until an old one comes? Don't be showing them to anyone or using them."

"'Course not."

Tam turned, walked back to the bothy and, without looking round, went inside. Jinny waited a long, last minute then she put on Easter's halter and, mounting Shantih, led the pony down the track to Finmory.

"You're coming home," she told Easter. "You'll stay with us for always."

Catching Shantih's freshness, Easter walked freely at Jinny's side, looking eagerly in front of her, and when Bramble whinnied she answered with a clarion blast and broke into a trot, tugging at the halter rope.

"Easy, easy," cried Jinny, as she sat astride Shantih, laughing to see Easter so full of life again.

Ken was waiting for them by the stables. "Keziah?" he asked.

"She's dead," said Jinny.

"She'll know everything now," said Ken, smiling wistfully. "Once we all used to think that the world was flat, go too far and you fell over the edge. Now we all know it's round."

Jinny let Ken's words stay in her mind as they walked down to the field.

"The way we see it isn't the way it is? No edge to fall over?"

"Something like that," agreed Ken.

"Well, anyway," said Jinny, "Easter isn't going to fall over any edge. She's getting better." Reaching the field, she took off Easter's halter and turned her loose.

Bramble came bustling up to her, giving sharp little whickerings of welcome. They stood for a second, nostrils touching, then, standing side by side, began to nibble along each other's necks and withers giving shrill squeals of delight as they did so.

"They know each other," cried Jinny in amazement. At the very least, she had expected Bramble to have a kick or two at Easter. "They do. They must."

"Looks like it," agreed Ken.

Jinny took off Shantih's bridle and the Arab circled the ponies. Tail high, mane bannered, she cast a red-gold ring round them before she began to graze.

Jinny gave a long sigh of relief. Things were back as they should be—Shantih sound, Easter saved; even Keziah's death amongst her own people was the right thing to have happened.

Carrying the paints carefully in her hand, walking backwards so that she could see the ponies and Shantih for as long as possible, Jinny followed Ken back to the house. All manner of things were well.

PATRICIA LEITCH

Ride Like the Wind

Ride Like the Wind was first published
in a single volume in Armada in 1983

CHAPTER ONE

The dream gripped Jinny Manders, pulling her down into its depths. Although she struggled to wake, as a drowning swimmer fights for air, it held her down in the place where there was nothing but a nameless, total, terror. An evil force crashed about her, and Jinny held up her arms to drive it away. But she was not strong enough. There was nothing she could do against it. She cowered away, still screaming; felt the ground move beneath her feet, so that there was no place of safety in the whole universe, and nowhere for Jinny to be except curled into herself, wrapped in her own screaming fear forever.

Jinny woke smothered in a web of her own long red hair, the echoes of her screaming still disturbing the security of her bedroom. For seconds she lay pinned down by the memory of her dream, then slowly let her gaze slide round her room. Nothing had changed, all was as it should be, dim in the early grey light of a summer morning.

Then Jinny thought of the horses. She leapt from her bed to the window in one panic-swift movement. Vivid in her mind's eye was the morning last spring when she had woken, gone to her window as she always did to call a greeting to Shantih, her beloved chestnut Arab, and looked out on to an empty field. But this morning the horses were all there – Jinny's Arab, Bramble, a solid black Highland the Manders borrowed from Miss Tuke's trekking centre, and Easter, an aged white pony whom Jinny had saved from a cruel riding school. They were all safe. Jinny sat down on the edge of her bed, too scared that she might fall back into her dream to risk going to sleep again. Even to think about it dragged her back into its power. She shivered uncontrollably. "Don't let it happen," she thought. "Please don't let it happen." But she didn't know what it was she was afraid of, what it was she dreaded.

"Now look here, Jinny Manders," she told herself, speaking aloud to hear the normality of her own voice. "Stop all this nonsense. You've finished with school for six whole weeks. Weeks and weeks of freedom and here you are getting your knickers in a knot because of a stupid dream."

But the darkness was still there. All the things on the surface of Jinny's life were as good as they had always been since her family — Jinny's mother and father, Petra, Jinny's sixteen-year-old sister, and Mike her ten-year-old brother — had left their city lives behind them in Stopton and come to live in Finmory House, a grey stone house that stood alone, four-square between the moorland and Finmory Bay. But now, underneath the surface of things, there was an uneasiness, a sense of autumn in the summer air that wouldn't leave Jinny alone. Although she hardly knew what it was, it followed on her heels like a shadow, was always there under the surface of her mind.

"Can't think about it here," Jinny decided and knew what she would do. She would go down to the horses and tell Shantih, her Arab, the things that were worrying her. Shantih would understand.

Jinny scrambled quickly into her clothes but before she left her bedroom she went through the archway that divided her room. The window in this part of the room looked out over the moors to where mountains shouldered up against the sky. The walls were covered with Jinny's drawings and paintings. There was a table and a chair, in term time used for Jinny's reluctant homeworking but now holding paints, pastels and piles of paper.

On the wall was a mural of a red horse. It had been there, painted on the wall, waiting for Jinny when she had arrived at Finmory two years ago. Jinny and an old tinker woman had repainted it and now it stared out at Jinny, harsh and bright, its yellow eye commanding as a collie's eye. It was a being of power, held a strange magic force that linked Jinny to her own depths; but this morning it was too close to Jinny's nightmare.

She turned swiftly away from it, skeltered down the steep ladder of stairs that led from her room to the long upstairs corridor. She sped past doors that closed in her sleeping family, down the main flight of stairs, along the hall to the stone-flagged kitchen and out through the back door.

The world was without life, waiting, breath indrawn.

"My world," thought Jinny as she ran through wet grass, down past the stable, feed house and tack room that had been decaying outbuildings when the Manders had first arrived at Finmory. On she went, down to the horses' field, sea in front of her, glimpsed metallic and glittering between the black jaws of rock that held Finmory Bay within their bite.

"A dewdrop world that could vanish in a split second — all my family doing safe, correct things. Petra playing her piano, passing her music exams; Mike over the moon because Mr. MacKenzie is letting him drive his tractor; and me — Jinny and her pony."

As she ran, Jinny saw herself as if she were the beginning of a film where a skinny girl with long red hair ran through the grey morning, not knowing that these were the last moments of her old life; that in a moment the necessary action of the film would change everything, carrying her on against her will into an unknown future where nothing would ever be the same again.

"We have so much," Jinny thought. "Mountains and sea and freedom. So much. We're not real in our fairy-tale world."

But Shantih waiting at the field gate was real. No dream horse, but the Arab who had once been billed in a circus as a killer horse and now belonged to Jinny. She had found a bit in a book about a sheikh praising his Arab horse and it was how Jinny felt about Shantih. "Her face is a lamp uplifted to guide the faithful to the place of Allah."

Jinny flung herself over the gate and threw her arms round Shantih's neck, pressing her face against the warm bulk of horse.

"Dear horse," she murmured. "Dear real horse." And the threatening shadow of her nightmare drew back a little as Shantih turned her head and blew sweet-scented breath over Jinny's neck.

Easter, the white pony, lay flat on her side, spindle legs stretched from the coarse-coated barrel of her body. Her quarters and shoulders were no more than bones beneath her skin. Her long neck, almost without muscle, looked as if there was not enough strength in it to lift her fine-boned head from the ground. Only her tail and mane, lovingly brushed by Jinny into silver cascades of hair, showed no sign of the extreme age that blurred away the last traces of the top-class show pony that Easter had once been. At first, when Jinny had brought her from the Arran Riding School, Easter had flourished, and Jinny had been filled with the certainty that Easter had a long retirement ahead of her — summer days grazing with Shantih and Bramble, winter nights bedded down in deep straw while the gales stormed outside her thick stable walls.

"Blooming miracle she's still alive," the vet had said

when he had wormed Easter. "Forty if she's a day. Hardly worth worming her."

"But she is so much better," Jinny had declared.

"Give her a last summer and then . . ." the vet had said, leaving his death sentence unfinished.

"Don't talk nonsense. Easter's going to live at Finmory for years."

Then Jinny had been certain, but now she could hardly bear to look at the pony as she stood long hours without moving, head hanging, hardly bothering to even pick at the grass. She had refused all Jinny's offerings of treacle-laced bran mashes, oats mixed with chopped apple, milk pellets or sugar beet begged from Mr. MacKenzie whose farm was close to Finmory. Even when Jinny had grated a plateful of carrots for her, Easter had only breathed over it then walked slowly away.

Jinny pressed her face harder against Shantih's shoulder to blot out the thought of Easter, for surely, surely she had earned just one summer at Finmory to make up for the life she had led at the riding school.

Bramble stood close beside Easter. He was solid as a tank, self-willed and dour. When Easter had first been turned out into the field at Finmory, Bramble had welcomed her with gusty whickerings and urgent neck-nibblings. Jinny was sure that at some time in their past lives they had known each other. Now they were always together.

"But not for much longer," Jinny thought, turning to face the ponies, leaning back against Shantih's shoulder.

For most of the year Bramble lived at Finmory and Mike rode him to school in Glenbost village, but during the summer holidays Bramble went back to Miss Tuke and resumed his true role of trekking pony.

"Perhaps this year she'll forget. It will be September

before Tukey remembers, and we'll all be back at school."

"But of course we don't mind keeping him. Really we look on him as ours already," said Jinny, speaking to Miss Tuke inside her head.

"Strange you should say that. Just decided I'd give him to you. From now on he is yours. Bramble Manders."

"But how very kind," said Jinny's voice.

"Don't," Jinny warned herself. "Don't go on. It's not true."

Jinny knew that it was more likely for Shantih to grow wings than for Miss Tuke to give Bramble away. Any day now the phone would ring and Miss Tuke's foghorn voice would be telling Jinny it was time that black beggar was doing some honest work for a change.

"But Easter will miss him so much. What will she do without him?"

But Jinny had no answer.

She walked slowly across to the ponies. Bramble bustled to meet her, nudging her pocket, hoping for a titbit.

"Wait your hurry," Jinny told him, pushing him away. "You'll soon have dozens of trekkers to spoil you. You can bully them to your heart's content but not me."

Bramble swung round, ears pinned back, turning his quarters against Jinny.

"Get on with you," said Jinny sharply.

"As if I would," said Bramble, turning to face Jinny again, pricking his ears and instantly changing his expression from Roman-nosed ferocity to dish-faced innocence.

"Clown," said Jinny, giving him a bit of carrot from her pocket.

At Jinny's approach, Easter had lifted her head and was

watching Jinny through dull, lack-lustre eyes. Jinny crouched down on the grass beside her, gently stroking the gaunt head, dry ears and the harsh hollowness of her neck under its long mane. She dug into her pocket offering Easter sugar lumps and carrot, but Easter moved her head away with a small movement of rejection and a cold tightness settled in Jinny. She got to her feet and stood looking down at the pony. She wasn't getting any better.

Suddenly Easter surged upwards, forelegs stretched awkwardly in front of her she strained for purchase. For a long moment she balanced there then, with a final struggle, she lifted herself and stood with her head hanging. She took a few steps away from Jinny and began to pluck listlessly at the grass.

Instantly Jinny was filled with hope. Easter was only old, had only been resting.

The sound of Shantih's hooves made Jinny look round. Ken Dawson was standing at the field gate, Kelly, his grey dog, lying beside him.

Ken Dawson lived with the Manders. He was eighteen, tall and angular with fair, shoulder-length hair. Every month his rich parents sent him a cheque but, apart from that, they had nothing to do with him. Jinny went cold when she thought about it — your own parents not loving you.

In his kitchen garden Ken grew all the fruit and vegetables that the Manders needed. Ken was a vegetarian, eating nothing that came from animals. "How can you say you love animals when you slaughter days-old calves so you can drink the milk that was meant for them?" And to this Jinny had no answer. She knew what Ken said was true.

Ken stood at the gate causing no stir, no disturbance. If Petra had been standing there her eyes would have been accusing Jinny of fecklessness, of untidyness. Her father, even standing still, would only have been pausing from getting on with something more important. But Ken was there, being not doing.

"Manders on the move," said Ken, as Jinny climbed over the gate to stand beside him. "Tom's up making himself tea. You down here. On the stir, all of you."

Jinny knew only too well why her father was up so early. She pushed the thought out of her head, for this was the blackest of all the things that waited restlessly under the surface of Jinny's life.

"Easter's up too," she said hurriedly. "And she's grazing."

Ken nodded, not saying as almost anyone else would have done that the few blades of grass held between Easter's slack lips could hardly be called grazing.

Colour had come back into the world – greens of myriad shades; the sea, turquoise ice, knife-grey, the sky so space-blue there was no lid on the world.

"What's Tom going to do if they send his book back again?"

A time warp from her dream engulfed Jinny. For a moment outside the present the ground moved under her feet. There was nowhere for her to stand.

"Of course they won't send it back. Of course they won't," she almost shouted. "They only wanted him to make a few changes in it, and he's done that. When they read it this time, it will be exactly what they want."

"And if it's not?" asked Ken, turning to look straight at Jinny. "If they won't publish it, what then?"

"He'll go on making pots, selling them to Nell, the way you've always done."

Mr. Manders had been a probation officer in Stopton but, when they had come to live at Finmory, he had become a potter, selling his work to Nell Storr who owned a craft shop in Inverburgh, their nearest town. He had also written a book about the conditions which destroyed young people living in a place like Stopton. It had been a success, selling foreign rights and having a television documentary based on it. A month ago his publishers had sent his second manuscript back to him, wanting part of it changed. Mr. Manders had changed it and returned it to them. Like Jinny, he was waiting for a letter.

"Tom go on being a potter?" mused Ken. "It's not how he sees himself now. His pots are a hobby. He sees himself as someone who can get things changed through his books; a sand witch fingering the dreams of others, shaping destiny, does our Tom."

Jinny didn't answer. She still didn't really see her father as a person to be criticized. He was her father and that was that. In a way she didn't want Ken to speak about him like that, in a way it fascinated her.

"They won't send it back," said Jinny.

"If you say so," said Ken.

They walked down to the sea, Kelly feathering ahead of them, turning bright eyes through the denseness of his hair to check that they were still with him. Where the sea drew back from the sand it left a shimmering stretch of white light; dazzling, moving quicksand. As they walked over it, each step they took left dark prints, yet when Jinny glanced back the shining level was smooth again; no trace remained of the way they had taken.

"I'd a nightmare," began Jinny, breaking the silence. "I dreamt . . ." and then she couldn't go on. She couldn't remember what she had dreamt, couldn't find words to tell Ken.

Breakfast was over before they heard the sound of the postman's van.

Mr. Manders went to the door and came back in with a parcel. It was from his publishers. They had sent his book back.

They all waited while he opened the parcel, laid his typescript on the table and took a letter from an envelope, reading it quickly to himself before he read part of it aloud.

"'. . . and taking into account these varied opinions we have decided that your manuscript, as it stands at present, is not suitable for publication. Should you feel able to make major changes along the lines we have indicated, we would be more than willing to reconsider it.

Yours sincerely,
Stephen Jones.'

"I met Stephen when I went to London," said Mr. Manders, glancing up. "He's added a hand-written PS. 'For myself, I found parts of your book stimulating and insightful. A common criticism, which I must say I shared, was that it lacked the immediacy of your first work which was so obviously alive with personal experience of the teenagers you were writing about. In chapter five you comment at some length on an act which is no longer in force. A minor point, but seized upon by those who gave your book the thumbs down.'

"And that," said Mr. Manders, "is that. The thumbs down."

"Would it be quite impossible to change it?" asked Mrs. Manders.

"Totally. They don't want it changed. It would be a complete rewrite, and I can't do that."

"It can't be as good as your last one," said Petra, wiping down the draining board with smug efficiency.

Jinny glowered through her hair at her sister, hating the way she shone with cleanliness. Her hair was neat and tidy, her clothes were crisp and smart. "Bad enough having your book sent back, without Petra going on at you," she thought.

"The maddening thing is," went on Mr. Manders. "they're right in what they say. It is years since I had anything to do with Stopton kids. Stuck out here in this wilderness."

Jinny turned away quickly. She went down to the stable, took Shantih's bridle and went on down to the field. She bridled Shantih, not looking too hard at where Easter was standing dozing in the shade of the hedge, and springing up on to Shantih's back, rode her past Finmory and over the moors.

Jinny touched her legs against Shantih's sides and felt her surge forward into a gallop. Their speed wiped Jinny's mind clear. There was nothing but this ecstasy of space. Jinny rode centaur-like, growing from her horse; Shantih's strength and power her own, all the glory her own. Loose stones clipped beneath Shantih's beating hoofs, heather roots and bracken had no hold against her. The track of air she followed lifted over stone walls and burns running peat-clear through the heather. Jinny rode like the wind.

At last Jinny steadied Shantih to a walk, slackened her reins, clapped her hard neck. There would always be Shantih.

"Fire horse," praised Jinny. "Desert dancer. Joy of my being."

She turned Shantih and stood looking out over the folded sweeps of moorland and suddenly, in the mid-distance, there was a girl riding a black horse. Jinny stared in blank amazement. The girl was tall and slender, dressed for riding in expensive jodhpurs, boots and black jacket. The sun glinted on blonde hair beneath her hard hat. It was certainly not Claire Burnley, and Claire Burnley was the only other person who might have been riding on the moors.

Jinny opened her mouth to shout to the girl but for seconds only a croak of sound came out.

"Hi!" Jinny yelled, finding her voice at last. "Hi, wait a minute. Hi!"

Shantih flinched at the noise, but the girl never looked round. She cantered on, away from Jinny. In another moment she would be out of sight.

"Wait for me!"Jinny roared and clapped her heels against Shantih's sides. The Arab reared, and Jinny clutched at insubstantial handfuls of mane.

"Stupid idiot! It's Shantih you're on, not Bramble," Jinny told herself as she fought to stay on top of Shantih, to urge her on as Shantih's forefeet touched down. But she couldn't manage it. Shantih's neck disappeared, head tucked between knees. Her quarters bulked skywards. Her hind hooves lashed out at the sun, and Jinny shot from her back and crashed down into the heather.

When Jinny scrambled to her feet, both girl and horse had gone. The moor was empty again.

CHAPTER TWO

Jinny rode home through Mr. MacKenzie's yard and, hearing Shantih's hoofbeats, Mr. MacKenzie emerged from the byre.

"Guess what I saw on the moors," Jinny called.

"A fancy bit lassie riding a black horse," he said, fixing Jinny with the gimlet gaze of his washed-blue eyes.

"Typical," exclaimed Jinny. "I might have known you'd be sitting on a wall watching."

"Is it yourself has been at the hibernation not to have heard the news?"

"Tell me. I haven't heard a thing."

"Have you not heard it is the rich strangers we have staying at Hawksmoor? Friends of the banker man who owns it. The Mr. Dalton is a fat old gnome with the chain of discos raging away all over England, and his wife is an old boiler done up like a spring chicken. But the lassie, Kat Dalton she is after calling herself, will be ages with yourself, I'm thinking, and as wasted, being driven up here in a brand new horsebox. They're saying it is the racehorse she has, those that have seen it."

"Could be," said Jinny, seeing the black horse in her mind's eye. "Looked fast enough."

"No doubt you will be finding out for yourself."

"Well," said Jinny. The summer holidays stretched before her to be lived through without Sue. Sue Horton, Pippen, her pony, and her parents had camped at Finmory Bay last summer. This year they were going to Greece.

"And if it is not yourself that is chiselling them out, I'm

thinking they will be knocking at your door themselves."

"Why?" said Jinny, thinking it unlikely when they were rich enough to buy their daughter a horsebox with a racehorse inside it.

"Mr. Dalton was in Mrs. Simpson's shop telling her the terrible problems he has getting rid of his money before the tax man pounçes. Does he not spend his holidays going round the Highlands looking for the likely houses to buy, offers the big money for them, does them up fancy and sells them again. And leaves the poor tax man fair muddled with it all. Or so he was after telling Mrs. Simpson."

"But why would that make him come to Finmory?"

"With the cash in his hand. It's the fair notion he has taken to the place. Wasn't he asking Mrs. Simpson the Mastermind questions about you all."

"Dad would never sell Finmory."

"And him with his new book like the homing pigeon?"

"Honestly!" exclaimed Jinny in disgust. "I do not know how you find things out."

"It's the big money he would be offering for Finmory."

"No," said Jinny. "Definitely no."

When Jinny told her family about the Daltons, Mr. Manders said, "Dalton? Dalton's Discos. There was one in Stopton. Wonder if it is the same lot."

"He wants to buy a holiday house here. Told Mrs. Simpson that he liked Finmory!" and Jinny waited for her father's indignant laughter. "Imagine thinking he could buy Finmory!"

But Mr. Manders didn't laugh.

"He would pay something for Finmory," he said.

His words laid icy fingers along Jinny's spine for they

weren't casual, paper-handkerchief words. He was speaking directly to her mother, meaning what he said.

The next morning Jinny rode Shantih towards Hawksmoor.

"I'm not actually going to have anything to do with them," she told herself. "But if it *is* a racehorse. . . And the girl might be O. K. She doesn't have to be like her family."

Hawksmoor lay in the opposite direction to Glenbost village, so that Jinny seldom passed it. Even when she was riding that way she hardly ever went along the narrow road that led to Hawksmoor, for it stopped at Hawksmoor's high iron gates, didn't go anywhere else. The house belonged to an English banker who came up sometimes to shoot things, then went back to England taking the creatures he had killed with him.

Shantih was fresh — her head high, her tail lifted and her trotting hooves drumming the road, desperate to be galloping.

"We are not," Jinny told her severely, sitting down hard in the saddle and turning her up the road to Hawksmoor. "This is a road ride, control yourself."

But Shantih danced sideways, challenging the silence through trumpeting nostrils. A sheep erupted from the roadside, her grown lamb bleating behind her. Shantih leapt into the air. Four feet off the ground, she humped her back and starfished skywards. Jinny dug her knees into the saddle rolls and gripped the pommel to stay on top.

The car coming down the road towards them hardly slowed down. Jinny just managed to control Shantih before it drew level with her. A bald man was driving it. The woman sitting next to him was wearing a dress of purple silk, so obviously expensive and fashionable that even Jinny noticed it. In the back of the car was a girl with straight, shoulder-length fair hair cut in a long fringe. As the car passed Jinny, the driver sounded his horn. Shantih leapt the ditch at the side of the road and in a mad flurry of fear, half real, half used as an excuse for a gallop, she was storming over the moors with Jinny crouched over her neck totally out of control.

At last, swinging her round in wide circles, Jinny managed to bring Shantih to a halt.

"Idiot mare," she told her guiltily, knowing that it was weeks and weeks since she had schooled Shantih, and that Shantih had been slipping steadily back into her old tearaway madness. But Jinny had been too worried about Easter to do anything about it. When she had been riding Shantih all she had wanted to do was to gallop, urging Shantih on to greater speed to help her leave her worries behind.

"Making a fool of me like that," Jinny muttered, jumping to the ground. "They were the Daltons. He's the man who thinks he can buy Finmory. Just the kind of thing he would do, blasting his horn when he was passing us. You could have broken a leg or anything, getting a fright like that. And that girl staring at me!"

From where she stood, Jinny looked down on to Hawksmoor House — its Sleeping Beauty tangle of overgrown grounds, its stone turrets surfacing from the surge of ivy, lay beneath her. But although it looked neglected from the outside, Jinny knew that the banker had renovated the inside, bringing up an interior decorator from London to design it for him.

"Huge place," thought Jinny, imagining herself living there. She would take Bramble, Easter and Shantih inside with her. She imagined the horses and herself eating from the same table, sitting round the fire at night while the gales stormed over the moors.

But today it was summer sky and sun. Both Mr. and Mrs. Dalton and their daughter had been in the car, and if there was anyone working for them they would be from the village and Jinny would know them. Without actually admitting to herself what she was planning to do, Jinny remounted and turned Shantih down towards Hawksmoor.

Both gates stood wide open. Jinny hesitated.

"Even if they are only going into Glenbost they won't be back yet," Jinny told herself. "And I'm not doing any harm, only looking."

Jinny straightened her shoulders, flicked back her hair and rode Shantih determinedly up the drive. Pine trees lined an avenue that led straight up to Hawksmoor's steps. Shantih walked light-hoofed on a dense carpet of decaying pine needles.

Heart in her mouth, Jinny rode past the house and round to the outbuildings at the back. Shantih's head came up, with goggling eyes she looked about her, then with a trembling whicker of sound she carried Jinny round the side of a broken-paned greenhouse and into a neglected stable yard. On one side were what had once been tack rooms and feedhouses, but now doors hung from their hinges, crookedly awry; nettles and dockens invaded rotten wooden floors. But on the other side of the yard, from one of the decaying looseboxes, a black head looked out. Shantih kinked her tail and pranced on the spot, blowing through wide nostrils.

"Steady," warned Jinny. "Steady Shantih." But all her attention was taken up by the black mare. She had a white star, a fringing of pulled mane, a wisp of forelock, and the sweetest, most gentle expression that Jinny had ever seen in a horse. Her thoroughbred head lacked the carven quality of Shantih's dished Arab face. It seemed smooth and silken, a melting quality in her bones. Flames of white light glistered her satin coat as she moved, and ears, fit for silken purses, pricked with mild curiosity at the intruders.

Jinny slipped to the ground and spoke to the black horse, holding out her hand for the tickling caress of her velvet lips.

"Aren't you a beauty?" she said, running her outstretched hand down the mare's muscled neck. Her hard body gleamed jet in the shadows of the box. She was about sixteen hands high and finely built. Jinny didn't know enough about horses to be able to judge her conformation, but she knew instinctively that every line of the black horse was bred for speed. Standing still she was like an arrow held in a drawn bow, only waiting to be set free, to fly faster than the eye could follow.

"As fast as Shantih," Jinny thought, and for a second she was astride Shantih racing the black mare.

Suddenly Jinny realised how long she had been standing talking to the mare.

She said a hurried good-bye to her, promising to see her again soon. Then, mounting Shantih, she cantered down the drive, her nerves still jangling, expecting the Daltons' car to appear through the gates with every second. Even out on the road leading from Hawksmoor, Jinny hurried Shantih on.

Within minutes of turning on to the broader road the Daltons' car came into sight.

"Timing excellent," Jinny thought, congratulating herself as she turned Shantih off the road and on to the moor, just in case Mr. Dalton should sound his horn again.

The car sped towards her and again, to Jinny's fury, the

driver blasted his horn. Shantih half reared, but this time Jinny was ready for her. She steadied her, speaking soothingly, telling Shantih to pay no attention to such bad manners.

The woman sitting in the front twinkled scarlet nails at Jinny, but the girl stared from the back window with an expression of superior disdain on her face.

"Nasty little snob," thought Jinny, as she rode back home. "If I was somewhere and I saw a girl riding an Arab I'd be out of the car speaking to her. I'd be wanting to get to know her."

"She could have been shy," suggested Mrs. Manders, when Jinny told her about the meeting. "Perhaps she thought the same about you."

"That will be right," said Jinny. "She looked at me as if I'd just crawled out from under a stone."

"Probably thought you had," said Petra, "if you were wearing those jeans."

"Ha, bloomin' ha," said Jinny, refusing to be drawn. "And she has such a super horse. I think she really might be a racehorse."

"How do you know what her horse is like?" demanded Petra suspiciously.

"Saw her on the moors yesterday, didn't I?" said Jinny quickly and went out before her sister had time to ask any more questions.

Jinny mixed a small feed and took it down to Easter.

"Just eat a little," Jinny pleaded, holding it out hopefully to Easter.

The pony was dozing, standing with her eyes closed, head hanging. At the sound of Jinny's voice she started awake, coming back from some far place to find a bucket of food being held beneath her nose. Automatically she reached out to the feed, opened her mouth and then, just when Jinny thought she was going to take a mouthful, she seemed to slip back into her dream and turned away without eating anything.

"Oh Easter, don't. Please eat something. You must eat."

Jinny tried feeding the pony from her hand, running the feed through her fingers and rattling the oats against the side of the bucket, but nothing she did made any difference.

"It's no use," thought Jinny. "I must get the vet. Dad will need to pay for him. There must be something he could do for her."

Yesterday evening Jinny had told her father that Easter would need to have the vet. Mr. Manders had grunted and gone on reading his book. When Jinny asked again, he told her not to make such a fuss, that the vet had seen Easter once and told Jinny that there was nothing he could do for the pony, that she was too old.

"I'll need to ask Miss Tuke," Jinny decided, but she didn't want to remind Miss Tuke of her existence. She wanted to lie low and keep Bramble for as long as she could. But she would need to ask Miss Tuke for advice and if she got in touch with Miss Tuke. . .

"That's how I think. Round and round in circles getting nowhere."

Jinny gave up trying to make Easter eat and tipped the feed out for Bramble.

"All right for some," she told him as he hoovered it down.

The phone rang while the Manders were having supper. Mr. Manders jumped to answer it. Petra raised her eyebrows at her mother.

"He phoned his publishers," said Mrs. Manders. "Stephen Jones is phoning him back this evening."

Before Jinny could ask any questions, her father called her to the phone.

"It's Miss Tuke for you. Don't be on all night. I'm expecting a call from London."

"Bet she wants Bramble back," Jinny thought dismally as she answered the phone.

"Jinny?" checked Miss Tuke's foghorn voice. "Good show. Now listen carefully. It's all fixed up. Tomorrow night. Six o'clock. You'll have heard that there's people staying at Hawksmoor? Dalton's their name. Arrived at my place tonight demanding cross-country instruction for the daughter. I told him Saturdays were my only free days while we were trekking, and he offers me fifteen pounds for an hour's instruction, so I'm taking her tomorrow night."

"So what," thought Jinny. "I don't care what Kat Dalton is doing."

"Next he demands company for his daughter. I suggest Sara and Pym, but when the girl heard Pym is a Highland pony she said he wouldn't be fast enough. You were acceptable. They liked the sound of an Arab."

"I can't pay fifteen pounds!" exclaimed Jinny.

"They are paying for you."

"But . . ." objected Jinny, not at all sure that she liked the idea of being paid for. "I don't . . ."

"My cash flow needs all the fifteen pound booster shots it can get. You're coming. No excuses. Give you some competition. Sharpen you up. You've to phone them. Glenbost 735."

Jinny found pencil and paper and wrote the number down.

"See you six o'clock," said Miss Tuke. "Be in good form. The girl is quite a rider. She told me so herself." And Miss Tuke put the phone down before Jinny had a chance to ask her about Easter. "But at least she never mentioned Bramble," Jinny thought as she put the receiver down.

She stood thinking about the way Kat Dalton had looked at her, the Daltons' road-hog killer car and the cheek of them, thinking they could buy Finmory. Jinny didn't want anything to do with the Daltons. She would phone Miss Tuke back, tell her she wasn't riding with Kat. Then Jinny remembered the black mare. She wanted to see her out of her box being galloped over the moors, wanted to race Shantih against her.

Jinny picked up the receiver and dialled the Daltons' number. A man's voice replied.

"Hullo," said Jinny. "I'm Jinny Manders. Miss Tuke told me to phone you."

"Hold on." Jinny heard the man shouting for Kat. Jinny waited.

Mr. Manders had come out of the kitchen and was standing beside Jinny and tapping his watch.

"I'm holding on," mouthed Jinny.

"Hard earned," said Mr. Manders, meaning the money that was paying for the phone call.

"Can't put it down now," said Jinny, scowling at her father.

"Hullo," said a girl's voice. "Kat Dalton here."

"It's Jinny Manders. Miss Tuke told me about riding with you."

Kat Dalton said nothing.

"Is it tomorrow night?" said Jinny, floundering. "She said I was to phone you about it, that you wanted me to have a lesson with you."

"It was Paul, actually. He's paying for you, isn't he? So I suppose it is all arranged. Will you ride over here? We'll box them to Miss Tuke's. Your horse will have been boxed before?"

Kat's voice was distant, supercilious; it held no interest or enthusiasm. It filled Jinny with instant dislike.

"Of course," said Jinny, wanting to tell this Kat Dalton that she didn't care if she never rode with her, never met her, that she wanted nothing to do with her.

"Be here for five," said Kat. "Oh, hold on a moment."

Jinny heard muffled voices and tried to look as if she was listening intently. It helped her to ignore her father's watch-tapping routine which was becoming more and more demented.

"Helen says you are to come for lunch. She says it will give us a chance to get to know each other. Be here for twelve, then we can ride in the afternoon. I'd like to see what your riding is like before we go to Miss Tuke's. Bye," and Kat hung up before Jinny had a chance to reply.

"About time," said her father.

"Rude!" exclaimed Jinny. "Rude and super rude! She must be the rudest person I've ever met. Like to see what my riding is like! That's what she said. She did. I've a jolly good mind not to go at all. Blooming cheek."

"You'd better do something about your appearance then," said Petra, when Jinny had finished giving her family a word by word account of her phone calls.

For once Jinny didn't argue.

"I'll wash my jodhs," she said, going to look for them.

CHAPTER THREE

"But whatever did you do to them?" Mrs. Manders exclaimed next morning, as Jinny held up a shrunken pair of jodhpurs for her inspection.

"I put them in the sink, sprinkled soap powder over them, poured in the boiling water and left them to soak. Is there nothing you can do to stretch them?"

"Nothing, I'm afraid."

"Then I shall need to go in my jeans. They will see me as a character."

"Oh, Jinny!" exclaimed Petra, coming in and viewing the shrunken jodhs with amazement.

"Cheap rubbish," said Jinny, disclaiming all responsibility. "They were too small anyway. I was always getting cleg bites in the gap between them and my jodh boots," and she went out to catch Shantih.

Easter was standing nose to tail with Bramble. Last night she had eaten a few more handfuls of feed but this morning she had turned her head away refusing to eat.

"Least I'll be able to ask Miss Tuke about her," Jinny thought, sitting down on the grass. "If Miss Tuke says I should get the vet, Dad can't argue with her. I'll get her to speak to him."

Jinny had no money to pay for the vet herself. Normally she could make money by selling her pictures to Nell Storr. Nell had bought eleven of Jinny's pictures so that she had been able to buy Easter, but last time Jinny had been in Nell's shop there were still four of her pictures left and Jinny didn't like to ask Nell to buy any more until they were all sold.

"Think of her well again," Jinny told herself. She tried to imagine Easter young again, bright-eyed, with rounded quarters and arched neck; tried to imagine the rosettes that must once have fluttered from her bridle. Jinny's imagination built the show ground around her — the smell of crushed grass, the hooves of the horses, the incredible striving for cups — and Jinny was sitting on Easter while the judge presented her with a red rosette.

Jinny went back to the stable, found the pad of paper and the pencil which she kept there and returned to the field. Staring at the real Easter, Jinny drew her as she must have been in her days of praise. Jinny was filled with the intuition that if she only knew the secret, her drawing could make Easter young again; could bring back taut muscle and satin coat; that there was some trick about time. It was a monkey god, an aging magician, and when Jinny drew she could see through his pathetic trick and, having seen that it was only a trick, she could re-shuffle time to suit herself, any way she wanted.

"You're not still here," said Mike. "Mum sent me to see if you'd gone without telling us. It's nearly eleven o'clock. If you've to get there for lunch you'll need to belt."

Jinny shuddered back to normality. She hadn't heard Mike coming across the field. If Mike hadn't disturbed her, could she have done it? Could she?

"That is terrific," said Mike, taking the drawing from Jinny. "It is Easter, only years ago when she was young."

Jinny would have hidden her drawing from almost anyone else. Ken, Nell and Mike were the only three who understood about her drawing, who didn't gush, embarrassing her.

"Not really eleven? Oh glory!" And Jinny, catching

Shantih by the forelock, bustled her out of the field and up to her box.

"Late," Jinny told her as she attacked her with a dandy-brush, scrubbing at muddied hocks and grass-stained legs. "Always late. Wanted to have you looking really special but I never manage it. Still, they'll see that we're not the type for Kat and that will be that."

Jinny dragged a body-brush through Shantih's mane and tail, took care over her saddle patch and elbows. Then, with final sweeping strokes from neck to quarters, she tacked her up and dashed into the house to get herself ready.

"Aren't you going to wear your jacket?" asked Mrs. Manders, catching Jinny as she was on her way out again.

"Too small," said Jinny. "It looks ridiculous. I keep telling you I need a new one."

"And that anorak is filthy," said Mrs. Manders as Jinny dashed past.

Catching Jinny's excitement, Shantih burst from her box. Tail kinked, head high, she whirled dervish-like around Jinny as she tried to tighten her girth.

"Stand still," beseeched Jinny, muffled under the flap of her saddle. "Shantih, stand still!"

Even when Shantih's girth was fastened and Jinny was trying to mount, Shantih refused to stand.

"What's up with her this morning?" asked Mike, coming to Jinny's rescue. "Haven't seen her messing about like this for ages." Mike caught hold of Shantih's bit ring just in time to stop her rearing.

"Don't know," lied Jinny, trying not to think about the huge feed she had given Shantih the night before to make sure that she would be fit for Miss Tuke's cross-country. "She's just fresh. I like her like this."

"Rather you then me," declared Mike, watching his sister as she was carried out of the yard and down the track to Mr. MacKenzie's on a prancing, plunging Shantih.

Jinny turned Shantih along the road that led to Hawksmoor.

"Never," said Shantih, forefeet tittuping, her weight sunk back on her quarters. "We never go that way."

"Oh yes we do," said Jinny, insisting with seat and hands, remembering just in time not to use her heels. "Get on with you."

Shantih spun round and charged into the farmyard, scattering hens and sending the farm dogs into hysterics.

"What would you be at now?" demanded Mr. MacKenzie, coming out from the hayshed.

"I'm going to Hawksmoor," Jinny shouted back, furious that the farmer should have seen her making such a fool of herself. "Shantih doesn't want to go."

Mr. MacKenzie grabbed a stick and advanced on them with waving arms.

"Don't hit her," warned Jinny, knowing from grim past experience that any kind of whip or stick brought back fearful memories of the circus, triggering Shantih into violent terror.

But Jinny was too late. Shantih had seen the stick. Jinny felt her horse bunch tight beneath her, then, head down, Shantih bolted from the yard at full gallop. Knees tight against her saddle, sawing at her reins, Jinny just managed to steer Shantih's crazy runaway in the direction of Hawksmoor. After that there was nothing she could do except sit tight.

They had almost reached the turning to Hawksmoor before Shantih began to slow down and pay any attention to the bit in her mouth or Jinny on her back.

"Oh, horse," mourned Jinny, when at last Shantih came to a walk and Jinny was able to jump to the ground. "It's all right. You'll never, ever go back to that circus. That's all past now," and Jinny turned Shantih, head into the wind, gazing in dismay at her lathered sides, foaming mouth and wild eyes.

Half an hour later, when Jinny was leading her up the drive to Hawksmoor, Shantih was still rust red with sweat; eyes rolling she pranced at Jinny's side. Ringmasters lurked behind every tree trunk, every branch was a whip.

"Wait till I see Mr. MacKenzie," Jinny thought grimly.

Before they reached Hawksmoor House, the door opened and Kat Dalton came down the steps. At least, Jinny supposed it must be Kat, for the person coming towards her had straight blonde hair cut in a long fringe above her black eyebrows, hair that fell in a curtain of glinting gold.

For seconds Jinny thought that this must be some relation of Kat's, maybe an older sister or aunt. She was wearing a white linen dress and jacket, gold sandals that were no more than high heels and a jewelled strip of leather. She was tanned a smooth honey-gold as if she had just been taken out from under a toaster, and her face was skilfully made up.

"Manders," thought Jinny, dismounting, "drop dead. Earth open and swallow me up."

Kat came slowly down the steps.

"It is you," she said. "You *are* in a muck sweat. Are you all right? When Miss Tuke said you had an Arab, I told Paul you would be the girl we'd seen from the car. Do you always gallop about like that?"

"She got a fright," muttered Jinny, scowling back at

Kat, on the defensive, thinking that Kat saw her as a stupid child who couldn't control her horse.

"Really? Is she nervous? She looks as if she would be. You'd better take her down to the stables. We've been waiting to start lunch." Kat led the way down the side of the house and round the greenhouse to the stable yard.

Shantih, remembering the black horse, pranced at Jinny's side, whinnying.

"Put her in there," said Kat, indicating the box next to her own horse. "I only hope she won't upset Lightning."

"She won't," snapped Jinny. "She's used to other horses."

"Really," said Kat, turning her back on Jinny.

"Go home," thought Jinny. "Just get back on Shantih and go home. She doesn't want me. I don't need to stay here and be spoken to like this."

But Jinny didn't. She took Shantih's tack off, gave her a quick wisp down and, telling her to behave herself, left her in the box.

"At last," said Kat. "Do come along." She turned nonchalantly on her six inch heels and began to walk back to the house.

Jinny paused to make sure that Shantih had water, then to stroke Lightning's gleaming neck, run the silken ears through her hands and scratch under the mare's neck.

"Do leave Lightning alone," Kat called, without looking back. "And don't feed sweets to her. Paul didn't pay six thousand for her to have you spoiling her."

"Spoiling her!" exclaimed Jinny indignantly, trotting after Kat, conscious of her muddied jodh boots, sweat-stained jeans, the sticky mess of her anorak sleeves where she had tried to dry Shantih's head, and the utter impossibility of anyone paying six thousand pounds for a horse. "I wasn't going to feed her. You never even spoke to her."

Kat glanced back and, for a moment, it seemed to Jinny that her expression had changed, as if something that Jinny had said had touched a half-healed wound.

"If you knew what . . ." began Kat, but stopped herself almost before she had begun to speak. Her face hardened again. "I should think," she said, "you'd want to wash before lunch."

"And I said," repeated Jinny, catching up, "you never even spoke to her."

Kat turned, her hair a silken curtain, a swinging shampoo commercial. She opened her eyes wide, staring at Jinny, and her eyes under their black lashes were yellow as a cat's. Black eyebrows in sharp contrast to her blonde hair arched above them. She lifted pink-painted lips from the whitest teeth that Jinny had ever seen.

"And *I* said, I hoped you were going to wash before we had lunch."

Jinny did her best to clean herself up in the pale lemon cloakroom where Kat had left her. She took off her anorak, scrubbed her hands, arms and face; combed her hair with a huge comb that was lying beneath the mirror and was probably meant to be an ornament, and rubbed her jodh boots clean with toilet paper.

"We are waiting," said Kat's voice from the other side of the door.

Jinny ignored her. She was staring in dismay at the dirty footprints on the pale lemon carpet. There was nothing she could do about them.

"Don't care," she thought. "Don't care what they think about me. After today I'll never see them again." And Jinny picked up her anorak and walked out of the cloakroom, shutting the door quickly behind her so that the footprints would be a surprise for whichever Dalton went into the cloakroom next.

The walls of the high hall and the corridor were encrusted with the heads of dead stags, foxes, roe deer and badgers. From the first landing a pair of stuffed, moth-eaten golden eagles peered down at them.

Kat opened a door, stood back so that Jinny had to go in first. Where the hall and corridor had been dark and old this room had been transformed into a Homes and Gardens confection. Walls, woodwork and carpet were white; huge easy chairs were covered in floral loose covers, and the wooden furniture was a light, good wood colour. For a second Jinny stood blinking in a haze of cigar smoke.

"Do come in," welcomed a female voice, and a slim woman eased herself gracefully from one of the chairs and came across to Jinny, glass in hand.

"This is Jinny. Jinny, this is Helen," introduced Kat.

"Kat is so pleased you are going to be riding with her," said Helen, holding out limp fingers.

"Hasn't been talking to Kat recently," thought Jinny as she grasped Helen's dead-fish hand.

"And Paul," said Kat, gesturing to where the cigar smoke was densest.

Sitting in the armchair was a bald, fat Humpty Dumpty. His legs stuck out in front of his egg-shaped body, hardly reaching the floor. The backs of his broad hands were carpeted with curling black hairs. His eyes, lost in their own reflections, stared blindly from behind pebble lenses. He had a squat nose and thick lips. On the arm of his chair was an empty brandy glass. When he shook hands with Jinny he held on to her too long. A moment longer and Jinny would have snatched her hand away.

Kat had perched on the arm of Helen's chair and was

leafing through a magazine, ignoring Jinny. At first Jinny had thought Helen was a young woman but now, with Kat sitting so close to her, Jinny saw that, as usual, Mr. MacKenzie had been right. She was like a puzzle picture, where cubes of black and white flashed into different shapes as you blinked.

At first sight Helen's hair was as blonde as Kat's but, when Jinny looked closely, its perfect colour glinted with a chemical sheen. Flawless make-up flashed to a slackness at her throat; her slim figure couldn't disguise her scrawny elbows; her feet, in sandals almost more miniscule than Kat's, were spread and horny. She was an old boiler. Jinny grinned, remembering Mr. MacKenzie's words and felt Kat's yellow eyes staring at her.

"Lunch, don't you think," twittered Helen. "Jinny must be starving, riding all that way. Next time we must come and collect you."

"There won't be a next time," vowed Jinny silently, as they went in to lunch.

They had melon, served by Mrs. Haddon from Glenbost, who Jinny supposed must be cooking for the Daltons while they were staying at Hawksmoor. Carefully watching Helen, Jinny picked out from the array of cutlery the correct implements for eating melon.

Beside each place were wine glasses. "I suppose they weren't too sure where I'd be sitting," Jinny decided, keeping her eye on the waiting wine glass while Paul crouched over his melon and Helen chirruped.

Mrs. Haddon served the next course. Paul got up, crossed to the sideboard and uncorked a bottle of wine.

"Of course," said Kat, smiling at Jinny with her mouth, "we would all rather have a dry wine, but Paul chose a sweet wine especially for you."

Jinny began to say that he needn't have bothered

because she didn't drink wine, that her father didn't even let Petra drink wine, when she saw Kat's mocking smile.

"She knows I'm going to refuse it," thought Jinny. "She's waiting to laugh at me, make me feel stupid."

A round, convex mirror on the wall sucked the room into its single eye. At this glossy-magazine dining table, amongst these beautiful people, there sat a scruffy girl, tousled hair pushed behind her ears, her face set in a scowl.

Before Jinny had recovered from the shock of seeing herself looking so out of place, Paul had filled her glass.

"And where do you go to school? Do you have to travel miles every day or do you board? Kat goes to boarding school."

"Terston Manor," said Kat as if she expected Jinny to be impressed, but Jinny had never heard of it.

"Inverburgh Comprehensive," Jinny replied. "I ride to Glenbost, leave Shantih there and get a bus in to Inverburgh."

"Oh, quaint," said Kat. She lifted her glass and drank from it, her eyes challenging Jinny.

"Dad will never know," thought Jinny, as she took a mouthful of wine. "It wasn't my fault. I was going to say no, but he didn't give me the chance."

The wine was pleasant tasting, icy cold. Jinny took another mouthful. What she would really have liked was a long drink of limeade, but she supposed the wine would have to do. She tipped her glass up and gulped the wine. Paul refilled her glass. Jinny drained it. Paul refilled it.

"We were sure you would enjoy a sweet wine," said Kat.

Jinny smiled broadly at her. She felt the smile stretched

across her face, the corners of her mouth hooked up in a vast grin.

"It's smashing," she said. "Super. Super-duper," and hiccuped loudly.

Kat's laughter seemed to get caught in Jinny's ears, like an irritating fly that would not leave her alone. Jinny shook her head, trying to dislodge it, and glowered across the table at Kat's hazy face. She took another gulp of her wine.

"You'll be one of the locals by now?" asked Helen.

"Goodness no!" exclaimed Jinny loudly. "We've only been here for two years. We used to live in Stopton. Yuk! Was that yukky!"

"Paul has a disco there," said Helen. "Did you go?"

"Me?" said Jinny. "Never."

"Do you like living here?" asked Paul. "Don't you find it rather dull?"

"Finmory is the most wonderful place in the world."

"That's where you live?" asked Paul.

"Finmory House. It's a great big house. The front windows look right down to the sea and at the back it's all moorland. There's a mountain, Finmory Beag. You can climb it easily if you go round the back of it. The view from the top is forever — standing stones, Loch Varrich and miles out to sea."

"All your land?" asked Paul.

"Mr. MacKenzie rents most of it from us," said Jinny, not sure how much of Finmory's land did belong to her father. "But a lot of it is ours."

Paul nodded. His pebble glasses looked like lighthouse lenses to Jinny, dazzlingly bright.

"Is the bay sand or shingle?"

"Oh, sand. Most of the shores round here are rocky bays, but Finmory is sand."

Jinny paused for another mouthful of wine. She had been wrong about the Daltons. They weren't stuck up. They liked her. Even Kat was listening to her.

"How does your father feel, leaving Stopton to come out here?" asked Paul.

"Really," thought Jinny, "he is a most friendly man." She couldn't remember her own father taking such an instant interest in any of her friends.

"I'll tell you this," said Jinny confidentially, leaning across the table towards Paul. "He's a worried man. They've sent his book back. They are not going to publish it."

"I'm not surprised he's worried," said the lips beneath the flashing lenses. "Come to the end of a fairy tale. Thinking about getting back to reality, is he? Nine to five and a pension looking attractive again?"

"Oh no," said Jinny sagely. "He will never leave Finmory. NEVER!"

"How many bedrooms did you say?"

"A lot," stated Jinny. "There are a lot of bedrooms."

Again Kat's laughter was stuck in Jinny's ears. She considered putting her head down on the table but discovered a plate of peaches and cream had appeared at her place.

"Sounds as if you've found what you're looking for," said Helen.

"Yes," said Jinny. "I am always looking for peaches."

Kat's laughter chimed in Jinny's head like unruly bells. With great effort Jinny turned her head and focused on Kat's glinting hair.

"Shut up," she said. "Bloomin' shut up."

Half way through the peaches Jinny couldn't eat any more. She put her spoon down firmly.

"I've finished," she announced. "Absolutely finished."

When Helen gave her black coffee, Jinny took it without mentioning that she always took milk.

"Are you both riding this afternoon?" Helen asked.

It was the very last thing Jinny wanted to do. She felt absolutely terrible.

"We're going to school," said Kat.

"Oh no," exclaimed Jinny. "I'll just watch. Shantih has done enough for today. She wouldn't be fit for tonight if I ride her again now."

"I don't suppose you're fit to ride, either," said Kat, regarding Jinny through slit eyes.

"Perhaps that would be best," said Helen anxiously. "You should have told us that you aren't used to wine. You could have had lemonade."

"Too late now," thought Jinny bitterly. She had made a total and utter fool of herself. She felt sick, a headache throbbed behind her eyes, and she knew that Mrs. Haddon was bound to carry the tale of her behaviour back to Glenbost.

"I'm all right," muttered Jinny, feeling Kat's yellow eyes staring at her.

Half an hour later, Kat, wearing a black jacket, breeches and boots, was mounting Lightning. Her horse was being held by a dark-haired young man whom Jinny recognised as being a farmer's son from one of the neighbouring farms.

"We were so lucky to get Sam Marshall," Helen said, standing beside Jinny, watching Kat. "He's looking after Lightning for us and he can drive the horsebox. He'll drive you over to Miss Tuke's tonight. Mr. Vernon, who owns Hawksmoor, found him for us. So lucky."

Looking at Lightning's gleaming perfection and her

shining tack, Jinny had to agree with Helen, but she knew that she wouldn't have wanted someone else looking after Shantih.

Helen and Jinny followed Lightning and Kat down a path until they came to a flat lawn already tracked with a schooling circle.

Jinny collapsed on the grass. She sat staring at Kat, trying to keep her eyes open despite her throbbing headache.

Lightning moved at a balanced, long-striding, extended walk. Kat sat looking like a copy-book illustration of the correct seat. Yet there was something not quite right about her riding. She was too stiff, too perfect, as if she would come off if Lightning shied.

"I expect you'll be looking forward to riding round the cross-country," said Helen kindly, and the thought of Miss Tuke's cross-country obstacles hit Jinny like an engulfing wave. She didn't feel as if she would ever be fit to sit on Shantih again, let alone ride her round a cross-country course.

CHAPTER FOUR

"Magnificent," breathed Miss Tuke, as Kat led Lightning down the ramp of her brand-new horsebox. "That one didn't come from the Horse and Pony Home."

Jinny, still inside the box hanging desperately on to Shantih, wasn't in the least surprised to hear Miss Tuke's praise. She knew Lightning was superb. Standing watching Kat schooling her that afternoon, Jinny had known that Lightning was probably the best horse she had ever seen. She was beautifully schooled, well balanced and smooth in her paces. Kat had ridden her sitting stiffly upright, looking as if someone had bent her into the correct position and perched her on top of Lightning. "Not like me," Jinny had thought. "All over the place. Bet she knows far more than I do — half passes, turns on the forehand and all that sort of thing. Really I don't know anything about riding. I just know Shantih. Bet Kat has had lessons all her life. The best lessons Paul could buy."

"Jinny," roared Miss Tuke. "Move it."

Shantih hovered on the edge of the ramp, gazing down its slope as if she was being asked to descend from the moon.

"It's all right," Jinny assured her. "Go gently. Steady now."

With an outstretched hoof, Shantih tested the insubstantial wood, drew back snorting. Miss Tuke shouted something about all night, and the next second Shantih leapt, tearing the reins from Jinny's hand as she landed far out in the yard to be pounced on by Miss Tuke.

"What an exhibition," sneered Kat, sitting cool and correct on Lightning.

"She is too much for you," warned Miss Tuke, holding Shantih while Jinny mounted. "She'll break your blooming neck for you if you don't pull yourself together."

"Are you really going to ride dressed like that?" Kat asked, as they followed Miss Tuke down to the paddock.

Jinny couldn't be bothered replying. Her headache seemed to have spread in a dull, cold ache all over her. "They can say what they like," she thought. "I don't care. In an hour it will all be over. I'm never, ever riding with Kat Dalton again. Never ever. I don't care if Miss Tuke goes bankrupt."

"We'll do some schooling on the flat first," said Miss Tuke, opening the paddock gate. "Then some jumping."

"Then cross-country," stated Kat. "That is why I am here — to ride over cross-country obstacles. Lightning knows it all, but I've never ridden cross-country. Paul bought Lightning from Alice Moss. She rode her at Badminton. I'm going to ride her in all the big events. That's why Paul bought her for me."

"If whoever you said had won Badminton on her, we would still start with schooling on the flat. How would you feel if you were hauled out of bed and made to jump? Walk on."

"Actually . . ."

"Walk on," boomed Miss Tuke, and Kat did.

Jinny rode round suffering. Dregs of trekkers standing at the gateway gave Shantih the excuse to spook and shy every time she passed it. When Miss Tuke told them to trot, Shantih leapt forward into a canter that turned into a gallop when Jinny fought to steady her. Twice Jinny was carted round the paddock before she could bring Shantih back under control again.

"Don't blame you," Jinny thought, staring down at her hands, not watching as Kat took Lightning round at a collected canter. "You've had a beastly day too. Shut up in a strange stable, shoved into a horsebox and rattled all the way here. You hate it as much as I do. Wish Sue had come and then we wouldn't be here." From Sue, Jinny's mind drifted to Easter. "Wish. Wish. Wish," she thought.

"Right," said Miss Tuke, organising the trekkers to set up three cavalletti poles and a jump of about two feet. "Get your timing right, through the cavalletti, one stride and then over the jump. Round and repeat it."

On both circles Lightning bobbed through the cavalletti, took one exact stride and arched fluid over the pole.

"Knows it all," said Miss Tuke, admiration glowing from her. "She can teach you."

Shantih cleared the cavalletti in one bound and jumped what felt like six feet over the pole. On her second gallop round, she tried to clear the cavalletti and the jump in one leap and landed on the pole with an ominous cracking sound.

"What the dickens has got into you tonight?" demanded Miss Tuke, dragging away the broken pole. "Take her over there and work her at a sitting trot. She'll be jumping over the gate next and smashing it to smithereens."

Jinny took Shantih to a corner of the field, trotted a few desultory circles, then stood watching as Miss Tuke set up different combinations of cavalletti and jumps, making

Kat count Lightning's strides, encouraging her to ride her horse more actively.

Jinny thought about Easter, wondering if Ken had managed to persuade her to eat anything, wondering what Miss Tuke would say when she asked her about the pony.

"One thing for sure, I couldn't have chosen a worse time," Jinny thought, and stared dismally over the hillside dotted with the grazing shapes of trekking ponies.

"We're going out on to the cross-country course," Kat informed her, riding up beside Shantih. "I suppose that will suit you better. At least she won't be able to smash solid obstacles."

Normally a retort would have been blistering Jinny's tongue before Kat had finished speaking, but tonight she had no answer. A leaden weight pulled her down. She turned Shantih, conscious of hand and leg speaking to her horse, conscious of Shantih's stride, her reaching neck, her delicate mouthing on the snaffle. And conscious of the thought of Easter, lying in the field at home with Bramble standing guard over her.

"Of course, as Paul says, mountaineering is the real challenge. He used to climb a lot when he was younger. Still, I think cross-country riding is quite a challenge too."

Jinny had been going to say that with a horse like Lightning that knew it all, nothing was a challenge, but something in Kat's voice stopped her. It couldn't be that Kat was scared. And yet . . .

"We'll ride out to the sheep pen," Miss Tuke said as, riding bareback on a dun pony, she caught up with them. "Take each obstacle as a separate jump. Time enough to be thinking of them as a course."

Jinny remembered the sheep pen from the time she had ridden the course in Miss Tuke's cross-country competition. By the time they had reached it, Shantih had been going so fast that Jinny had hardly noticed it. She remembered it only as a neatly timed double.

Tonight when they reached the sheep pen it looked solid and menacing. Once you jumped in you had to jump out. After the sheep pen, flags showed the course sloping downhill over an enormous spread of poles with a ditch on the take-off side. Despite her gloom, Jinny felt her heart lift at the sight of the jumps. A shiver of excitment zigzagged through her. She glanced round at Kat, expecting to see the same brightness answering her, but Kat Dalton's features showed no expression. Her mask was firmly clamped in place. If eyes were gateways to the soul, Kat's were barred and padlocked, allowing no entry to her thoughts.

"Now," said Miss Tuke. "Imagine the sheep pen is in the paddock. Get your stride, timing, and throw your heart over it. No stride in the middle. In and out. Go too fast and they'll be too close to the second part to be able to take off, too slow and they'll stop. Don't let that happen. I do not want to start and take my jump down to let you out. You've got to get it right. Kat, canter Lightning in a circle. When you feel you're ready, another circle, knowing that this time you are going to jump. Then, keeping your rhythm, over you go."

Kat rode Lightning at a steady canter then, increasing her impulsion on her last circle, rode her at the sheep pen. Lightning's ears flicked forward, all her attention on the jump. Her timing perfect, she lifted over the first part of the sheep pen, touched down and sailed effortlessly over the second part. Kat had only sat there. Lightning had done it all.

Jinny watched entranced, half of her filled with delight at the grace of the black mare, half of her tight with jealousy that she should belong to such an arrogant snob as Kat Dalton. Jinny's imagination spun daydreams of how it would have been if Kat had been friendly, for Lightning would have been a perfect pair for Shantih.

"Jinny!"

Miss Tuke's irritation broke through Jinny's dream. She grabbed at Shantih's reins, urging her forward, realising that both Kat and Miss Tuke were waiting for her to jump.

The little bit of attention that Jinny had been paying to Miss Tuke's instruction vanished. Jinny rode Shantih straight at the sheep pen.

"Circle her first! Circle her!"

But it was too late. Shantih, as bored as her rider, snatched at her bit. Head down, she tore at the sheep pen, her torrent of speed scorching the still evening.

"Steady her! Bring her back! Circle her!" roared Miss Tuke.

Jinny was fighting to do just that but there was no time. No time to yell back to Miss Tuke that she was trying to stop Shantih but couldn't. The sheep pen rushed furiously at her. She felt the impact of Shantih's soaring leap connect with her spine, shooting her out of the saddle. Her face was buried in the harshness of Shantih's mane as she glimpsed the second part of the sheep pen beneath her and realised that Shantih was jumping it as a spread. She felt Shantih strain to clear it and then, with drum-beat fury, Shantih was storming downhill back to the paddock.

They raced past a jump of railway sleepers that loomed

its barricade frighteningly high, and flew on at the wall. Flags marked where it was to be jumped. Pulling wildly at Shantih's mouth, Jinny managed to steer her between them and over the wall.

Even to Jinny, used to Shantih's speed, they were going at a break-neck gallop, a roller coaster of uncontrollable power where there was nothing else that Jinny could do except hold on.

One more wall lay between Shantih and the paddock but, by the time she reached it, she had raced out of steam. Of her own accord she chose the lowest part to jump, and by the time they were back at the paddock Shantih was trotting, and Jinny, arms and legs chewed string, was back in control again.

"No point in going back up there," Jinny decided. She walked Shantih into the yard, dismounted and gazed ruefully at her blown, muddied horse. The second runaway in one day.

Jinny loosened Shantih's girth, sat down on the edge of a half-empty water trough and waited for Miss Tuke and Kat to come down the hill. She didn't like to think what Miss Tuke would have to say about her performance and she didn't care what Kat said. After this evening Jinny would never see her again.

The Daltons' car swung into the yard, spraying gravel as it skidded to a halt. Paul got out.

"Good evening," he said gruffly. "Where's Kat?"

Jinny looked up the hill and saw Kat and Miss Tuke riding down towards them.

"There," she said, pointing, glad that she wouldn't have to explain why she was sitting there alone.

Paul strode irritably backwards and forwards, turning sharply, digging his heel into the gravel, hands thrust deep into his pockets. When Kat was in earshot he called to her and she came, trotting Lightning into the yard.

"Get in," Paul said, nodding curtly towards the open car door. "We're going out. Helen wants to see you back before we go."

For a second, Jinny could have sworn that Kat's expression changed, her blank mask of sophistication slipped. Whether it was loathing or fear that showed in her eyes, Jinny couldn't be sure, for by the time Kat had sprung down from Lightning her expression was under control again.

"Evening," said Miss Tuke, following Kat into the yard and dropping like a ripe plum from the dun pony. "Some horse you've got there."

"Should be. Paid enough for it. What's the rider like? That's more to the point. Got the guts to ride across country?"

"Did very well," said Miss Tuke.

But Paul Dalton wasn't listening. It was almost as if he hadn't spoken to Miss Tuke, as if his words had been aimed at Kat.

"It's quite a course," said Kat. "Can I come again tomorrow night?"

"If it's not going to be another of your fads that end up with nothing to show for it."

"Tomorrow night?" Kat asked Miss Tuke.

Miss Tuke agreed enthusiastically, and Jinny knew she was thinking about her cash-flow problems. But it didn't matter — it had nothing to do with Jinny.

"Sam will come for you," Kat said, turning to Jinny. "I don't suppose you'll want to risk having lunch with us again."

"I'm not coming. You don't need me."

"Of course I do. It's better for Lightning to be schooled with another horse."

"I can't come tomorrow night. I'm going to Inverburgh tomorrow." It was the first excuse that came into Jinny's head and she supposed it was possible. It was always possible that she might be going into Inverburgh. And she was not riding with Kat Dalton.

From the car, Paul sounded his horn, commanding Kat.

"I will see you tomorrow evening," Kat said to Miss Tuke and ran to the car, her hard hat in her hand, blonde hair rippling. She did not run the way Jinny ran — striding out, elbows eating the air — but as if her breeches were a hobble skirt, her hands with outstretched fingers balanced on air.

Kat got in next to Paul and he revved the engine, fought the steering wheel and drove away without glancing at her.

"Are you going to Inverburgh?" Miss Tuke asked.

"Probably," said Jinny.

"You'll be riding with Kat next time then?"

Knowing that she was just about to ask Miss Tuke for help, Jinny said she might, it depended when Kat was having a lesson.

"Fifteen pounds," said Miss Tuke. "And don't forget I can be doing with it."

"Fifteen pounds for telling me to trot Shantih in circles! Pretty good," Jimmy thought. But she said, "I'm very worried about Easter," and went on to tell Miss Tuke about the pony.

"The trouble is, Dad's not keen on paying any more vet's bills, and I thought if you told him that Easter must have the vet, he would listen to you."

"Don't like the sound of it," said Miss Tuke. "She is very old. Well into her thirties. It's a bad sign when they stand about a lot, half sleeping. You can't get her to eat?"

Jinny shook her head, her teeth digging into her lip, fighting to control the tears filling her eyes.

"Tell you what," said Miss Tuke. "I'll come over with you now. Cast my ancient and experienced eye over Easter, then ride Bramble back. I could do with him for tomorrow's trek. Holly's cast a shoe. Ask me, she spends the nights picking them off, the varmit."

"Bramble!" exclaimed Jinny. "Ride Bramble back tonight? But you can't. Easter needs him. Please, please, you can't. What will she do without him to keep her company?" Jinny was back in her nightmare where all safe, secure things would not stay still but changed their shape, grew menacing; she was back where the ground moved.

"What rubbish! She'll have Shantih. It's not as if she'll be left alone," and Miss Tuke marched off to return the dun pony to his trekking colleagues.

"Would you be putting your horse into the box?" asked Sam. "That's her Ladyship's tied up."

Jinny turned blind eyes on him, heard his words but could make no meaning from the noise.

"Here, I'll take her up for you. It's the man she's needing to knock some behaviour into her," and Jinny felt the reins taken from her hand, heard Shantih's hooves skittering on the ramp and Sam shouting at her.

"Not Bramble. Not tonight," beseeched Jinny. "I'll ride him over. Honestly I will."

"I'm coming with you," Miss Tuke shouted up to Sam,

ignoring Jinny. "Room for two of us in there beside you?"

"It is the whole of Glenbost would be fitting in here with me," said Sam, leaning over to open the cabin door for Miss Tuke and Jinny.

"Please don't . . ."

"Now look here, you know perfectly well that Bramble comes back to me in the summer. I never heard such nonsense," snapped Miss Tuke, turning on Jinny. "Get in and be your age."

As they drove back to Finmory, Miss Tuke and Sam talked about the price of hay and the harvest prospects, while Jinny stared straight ahead, willing herself not to cry.

Sam drove to Finmory first. They unloaded Shantih who again sank back on her hocks and cleared the ramp in one leap.

"She is totally out of control," said Miss Tuke, as Jinny led a dancing Shantih down to her field. "Back to her old ways. You wouldn't win anything at Inverburgh Show on her the way she is just now."

Jinny didn't care. She was too worried about Easter.

"Have you stopped schooling her?"

"'Course not."

"If you ask me, all you've been doing is galloping her about. Worst possible thing for a sputnik like her," and Miss Tuke regarded the flaunting Arab with definite distaste.

"I like her the way she is," said Jinny.

"Like her making a fool of you in front of Kat Dalton?"

Jinny didn't answer. The last person she wanted to talk about just now was Kat Dalton.

Bramble and Easter were standing together at the far end of the field. Seeing Shantih, Bramble whinnied a welcome but stayed with Easter. Miss Tuke strode across to them while Jinny took off Shantih's tack and set her free to roll.

"Bramble's looking well," said Miss Tuke, as Jinny joined her. "Fat as a pig. A few weeks trekking will soon turn that into muscle."

"Easter?" demanded Jinny urgently.

"You don't need me to tell you. You've only to look at her to know. It's cruelty keeping her alive any longer. She's a walking skeleton. You've done all you can for her. No way is she going to get any better."

"But if I make Dad get the vet?"

"You'll need to get the vet. Tell your father I said so. He'll put her down for you. It's the only thing you can do for her now."

Jinny couldn't trust herself to speak. She wanted to shout at Miss Tuke, telling her that there must be something the vet could do to help Easter. That never, never, would Jinny let Easter be put down.

"I'll hear how it goes," said Miss Tuke, running her broad, short-fingered hand down Easter's neck, resting it for a moment on her bony withers. "It's hard, but the only thing when they reach this stage."

"Let Bramble stay with her."

"Right, my man," said Miss Tuke, grasping Bramble by the forelock. "Trek forward. Remember?" so that Jinny didn't know whether Miss Tuke was ignoring her or really hadn't heard her. "We'll get him tacked up and I'll be off."

Bramble plodded after Miss Tuke. Half-way across the field he turned and whinnied to Easter. Without moving to follow him, Easter lifted up her head and answered him with a high, thin tremble of sound. Bramble plunged to go back to her, but Miss Tuke, hand over his nostrils, elbow in his shoulder, urged him on. "Please couldn't you let him stay? Just till the vet has been?"

"We've all got to work," said Miss Tuke, forcing Bramble on. "I'll be riding him myself until he gets back into the way of things. Expect you'll be wanting him again in the autumn?"

But to Jinny the autumn was too far away to be thought of. The total fear of her nightmare pressed upwards against the edge of her mind. Sheer cliffs of fall lay between Jinny and the autumn.

Jinny held Bramble while Miss Tuke tacked him up and mounted.

"Tell your parents I'll drop in the next time I'm passing. Haven't time tonight."

Jinny stood and watched Bramble being ridden away.

"Really he's mine," she thought. "Mine, and I stand and watch him being ridden away when Easter needs him. If I were Kat, Paul would buy him for me. He would have offered a price that Miss Tuke couldn't refuse, and Bramble could have stayed with Easter."

Jinny went back to Easter, but the pony turned away, didn't want to be bothered with Jinny's attentions.

"I'll get the vet tomorrow," Jinny promised. "He will know some way of helping you. I'll go and ask now."

Jinny walked quickly up to the house. Through the lighted window she could see her parents sitting one on either side of the kitchen table, talking. She could tell from their attitudes that it wasn't the usual evening chat. They were talking about something that mattered.

"Don't care what I'm interrupting," thought Jinny. "I must get the vet for Easter."

She went in through the kitchen door, making a noise so that she wouldn't overhear what her parents were talking about.

"Jinny," said her mother. "How did it go? Did you enjoy yourself?"

Her father glanced up; his elbows were on the table, his fingers interlaced. He twiddled his thumbs, waiting for Jinny to go so he could get on with what he had been saying before she came in.

Her head full of Easter, Jinny could hardly think what her mother was talking about. Her day at Hawksmoor had almost faded from her memory.

"Terrible. Kat Dalton is a stuck-up snob. And I got drunk at lunch. You're bound to hear about it from Mrs. Haddon, so you're better to know now."

"Drunk?" echoed Mrs. Manders incredulously. "How?"

But Jinny wasn't to be side-tracked by such trivial happenings.

"Miss Tuke came back with me. She's taken Bramble away and she says we MUST get the vet for Easter. MUST." Jinny was speaking directly to her father, trying to break through his preoccupation. "It's not just me. It's Miss Tuke says it's urgent. We must get the vet tomorrow."

"Then let Miss Tuke pay for him," said Mr. Manders. "The vet's been and he's told you there's nothing he can do for Easter. She's too old."

"But when he sees her now he may be able to think of something," Jinny insisted. "Honestly, we must get him."

"What's he going to do? Perform a minor miracle? Bring back the dying? And what will he charge for that?"

"Tom," warned Mrs. Manders.

"You MUST get him," said Jinny.

"Money! Money! Money!" roared Mr. Manders. " Do you ever think what it costs to keep Shantih in food and shoes? Never mind Bramble and that old wreck you've installed in the field now."

There was a moment of shocked silence.

"How could you?" gasped Jinny. "How could you say such a thing about Easter?"

"Because I have to pay for it all, that's how."

Jinny and her father stared furiously at each other. Tears welled in Jinny's eyes.

"I hate you," she said. "Hate you."

"Now don't upset yourself. Your father's worried," began Mrs. Manders.

"I don't care what he's worried about. I'm worried about Easter. I've been worrying for days about Easter and not one of you cares. I'll tell you what Miss Tuke said. She said Easter should be shot, and you won't even let me get the vet."

Mr. Manders pushed his splayed fingers through his beard, raised his hands to heaven.

"I have not got the money," he said.

Jinny rubbed eyes and nose on the sleeve of her anorak.

"I'll pay for the vet myself," she said. "I've got pictures Nell has never seen, and when she sees them she'll want to buy them. They're the best I've ever done. And the vet will know how to help Easter. He will. I don't want your money. I'll pay for the vet myself."

Jinny flung herself from the kitchen, diving headlong

for the security of her own room. The phone rang as she passed it. Automatically she picked it up.

"Could I speak to Jinny?" said Kat's voice.

"What?" demanded Jinny.

"We are going into Inverburgh tomorrow. Shall we pick you up about ten?"

"I never. . ." began Jinny, then checked herself. She had been about to tell Kat what she thought about her, to tell her that she never wanted to see her again, when she had thought how much easier it would be if she could get a lift into Inverburgh. Probably the Daltons would bring her home as well. She would be able to phone the vet before lunch.

"Be ready at ten and do wear something a little more respectable than those jeans," and Kat's mocking laughter rang in Jinny's ears.

CHAPTER FIVE

Jinny sat next to Kat in the back of the Daltons' car. They had come for her at ten, and for once Jinny had been ready in time. She had set her alarm for five and when it had gone off she had got up straight away and gone down to the horses. She had said a quick good morning to Shantih, spent a few minutes with Easter who was standing in quietness, her head turned in to the hedge as if she wanted to block out the world, and then come quickly back to her room.

Last night she had taken her folder that held her best drawings out from its hidden place behind the wardrobe, and had just been going to spread her pictures out on the carpet to decide which ones she would take to Nell, when she had heard her father's footsteps on her stair. By the time he knocked on the door, Jinny had the folder hidden again.

"Sorry," her father had said. "Lost my temper. Not at you really. Just everything. They're definitely not taking my book. So money will be less flush than it's been recently. We'll all need to pull our horns in. Okay?"

Behind her hair, Jinny had nodded; had wanted to say she understood about the money being scarce and that of course it didn't matter. They could all live on the vegetables Ken grew and the eggs Mr. MacKenzie gave Mike now that he was more or less working on the farm. Jinny understood about the money.

"Go on," said Mr. Manders, sitting down on the bed

next to Jinny. "Don't bottle it up. Tell me what you're thinking."

"It's what you said about Easter," muttered Jinny.

"About Easter?"

"You called her an old wreck."

"That was only words. I didn't mean to say it."

"You were thinking it," said Jinny, "or the words wouldn't have been there for you to use."

Mr. Manders stretched back his neck, staring at the ceiling.

"You're right," he said eventually, looking back down at Jinny. "But I am sorry I said it. Wish I didn't see her that way. Wish I could see her the way you do."

"I love her," said Jinny.

"Love," said Mr. Manders hopelessly. "Is it too late to send for the vet tonight?"

"Suppose so. It's not really an emergency. But it's all right. You don't need to pay. I'm going into Inverburgh tomorrow with the Daltons to sell my pictures to Nell. I'll pay for the vet myself."

Mr. Manders slapped his palms down on his corduroy-covered knees and stood up.

"If Nell doesn't buy your drawings get the vet all the same. Another ten pounds isn't going to make much difference to the Manders' economy, not with the state it's in at the moment."

When her father had gone, Jinny hadn't felt like sorting out her pictures. She had stood in front of the mural of the Red Horse, staring at it.

The Red Horse plunged from the wall, bursting through the blue-green leaves and white flowers, its yellow eyes blazing. Since Jinny and Keziah, the old tinker woman, had repainted it, the Horse glowed vibrant with colour.

Although the Horse still linked Jinny with the dark, hidden side of herself, she was no longer afraid of it as she had been last summer. Sometimes she would choose not to go into the strange, haunted world of the Horse, would choose to stay in her safe, everyday world, where Petra knew best and doing your homework mattered. But now Jinny saw the Horse more as a messenger of power from that other world; a guide, weird and awe full but a friend as well.

Coming in from Shantih and Easter, Jinny had made a mug of sweet coffee and a peanut-butter sandwich for comfort and taken them up to her room with her. She took the folder from behind the wardrobe, opened it and carefully laid out her best pictures on the floor. They were the very best she had ever done.

"I'll choose four," Jinny had decided and picked up her absolute favourite—a watercolour of Shantih's head with her mane fanned out in the wind. She was about to put it back in the folder when she knew that that wouldn't do. She had to take the best to Nell.

Jinny chose the watercolour of Shantih's head, an ink drawing of Finmory House with her family, their animals and their most prized possessions ranged around it. The third picture was an Indian ink drawing of Bramble standing against a bare hedge in the snow, and the last one Jinny picked was another watercolour of Shantih grazing. Jinny was certain Nell would buy them.

She sat in the Daltons' purring, low-slung car, holding them, carefully wrapped, on her knee. Kat was staring out of the window, Helen chirruping to herself, for no one else in the car was listening to her, while Paul, like Toad in *The Wind in the Willows* was crouched over the wheel. When they reached Inverburgh, Paul bent even closer to the wheel, swearing at other traffic, sweat beading his bald head.

"Now let's see," twittered Helen, when Paul had parked the car. "Paul and I are going to the bank. What have you to do, Jinny? How long will you be?"

"Only one shop," said Jinny. "Nell Storr's craft shop. Shall I come back here when I've finished?"

"Craft shop?" said Helen. "A real craft shop?"

"Oh yes. A super shop. Nell only buys things directly from the people who make them. It's quite different to any other shop."

"Absolutely my thing. Shall we go too?" Helen grabbed Paul's arm, gazing up into his face as if she had been a child begging for sweets.

Paul shook her off irritably.

"After the bank?" pleaded Helen, and Paul grunted, which Helen seemed to take for agreement, clapping her hands and fluttering her eyelashes at Paul.

"Tell us how to get there," she said to Jinny.

"It's not far from here," said Jinny, telling Helen how to reach Nell's and, at the same time, hating the thought of the Daltons getting to know Nell or of them seeing her pictures.

"We'll see you both soon," said Helen, as they all got out of the car.

"Both!" exclaimed Jinny.

"I'm coming with you," said Kat.

"No you're not," said Jinny, horrified at the thought of Kat being there when she was trying to sell her pictures.

"You don't think I want to go with them to the bank, do you? Banks are Paul's drug. He starts getting high whenever he sniffs one and when he's actually speaking to the manager! Wow, is that something!"

"Bye bye," called Helen, twinkling her nail varnish at them as she teetered, high-heeled, in Paul's wake.

"Well, come on then," said Jinny. "But I've something private to talk to Nell about so you'll need to keep out of the way."

"Don't forget we gave you a lift."

"Thanks for reminding me," said Jinny. "Thought I'd flown in on my hang-glider," and before Kat had time to answer, Jinny had dashed across the road just as the lights changed, stopping Kat.

"I expect," said Kat, as she caught up and trotted along beside Jinny's striding walk, "you're wondering about Paul."

"The very last thing I'm wondering about," said Jinny. "So last, I'm not wondering about him at all."

"Why I call him Paul?"

"So what?"

"He's not my father," said Kat. "He's my stepfather. I couldn't call him Dad so I just call him by his first name. He prefers that. And I call Helen, Helen. It makes her feel younger."

"Oh," said Jinny, hardly hearing what Kat was telling her. "Here's Nell's shop."

Nell was standing at the counter wearing a long scarlet skirt and a white top that looked more woven than knitted, with tails of knotted wool and glinting mirror chips. She turned at the sound of the shop door, her ugly, interesting face beneath its afro halo lighting up at the sight of Jinny.

"Ah, Jinny," she said. "I was just hoping some of your clan might drop in."

"Dad's got a load of pots ready for you. Expect he'll be bringing them in next week."

"That is going to be the hard part," said Nell.

Jinny didn't know what she meant, couldn't stop to ask her, for Kat had gone across to the far end of the shop. It was Jinny's chance to show Nell her pictures.

"I know you've not sold all the drawings you bought from me last time," Jinny said, hurriedly unwrapping her pictures. "But I must have some money to pay for the vet for Easter. These are my best pictures, special ones that I was keeping for myself. Please would you buy them. For Easter."

Nell picked up the pictures, holding them with reverence in her heavily ringed hands. She looked at them in silence. When she had seen them all she said, "You would really sell these?"

Jinny nodded.

"Find some other way to make money."

"I need money this morning," stated Jinny. "Please take them."

"They're far too good to sell. And I can't take them. I'm closing down. That's what I wanted to tell your father."

"Closing down?" said Jinny, looking at Nell in blank dismay. "You mean you won't have a shop any more?"

"Been thinking about it for a bit. Sky-high rates. More or less have to be here fifty-two weeks in the year. So I've made up my mind. Closing down. Packing up. Offski."

"But you can't! What will we do without you?"

Ever since they had come to Finmory, Nell had been part of Jinny's life. Someone to be relied on. Someone who was always there. She had bought pictures from Jinny and pottery from Mr. Manders and Ken.

"NO! Oh no!" gasped Jinny. "You can't go."

Another part of the jigsaw that made up Jinny's life had fallen away. No Nell.

"But you can't," insisted Jinny desperately, hardly noticing Kat coming across to the counter and picking up her pictures. "You can't go."

"Can," said Nell. "To the Carmargue in France. Blissful place. An old farmhouse. Trite, I suppose, but in the end if it's trite it's right, or, as Iris Murdoch puts it, 'The human heart is ultimately drawn to consolation,'" she quoted. "And I'm getting married."

"Married!"

"To the owner of the farmhouse. You'll meet him at the party on Wednesday night."

Jinny stood small and cold; an alien surrounded by the once familiar delights of Nell's shop that were now so much rubbish — useless bits of wood, clay or stone.

Nell came round the counter and hugged Jinny to her.

"It's right for me to go," she said. "Things have to change."

Conscious of Kat, Jinny wriggled free. "I want things to stay the same," she muttered.

"You'll want then," said Kat, staring yellow-eyed straight at Jinny. "Wanting won't get you anywhere. Are you selling these pictures? I'll buy the one of Shantih's head."

"They're not for sale. Not to you."

"Twenty pounds," said Kat.

"No. I'm not selling them."

"Thirty pounds."

Jinny stared at her in disbelief. "You haven't got thirty pounds."

Kat took three ten pound notes out of her purse and laid them on the counter.

"Thirty pounds," thought Jinny, staring at the notes. "For one picture." She had only to pick up the money and she could phone the vet whenever she got home. He would come to see Easter that afternoon. She wouldn't need to ask her father for money.

Without looking at Nell, Jinny picked up the money. "For Easter," she thought and thrust it deep into her jacket pocket.

"Have you got a bag I could put this in?" Kat asked, as Paul and Helen arrived.

Helen spent two hundred and thirty-six pounds. Paul wrote a cheque. Jinny watched enviously. So much money when her family needed it so badly. For now Nell was closing down, who would buy Mr. Manders' pots?

Nell's party was to be in her flat above her shop. Ken and all the Manders were invited, and by the time they left, Paul, promising a case of whisky, Helen and Kat had managed to get themselves invited too.

"I'll come in and meet your father," Paul said, switching off the car engine in front of Finmory. Mrs. Manders had seen them arriving and came to the door to welcome them in.

Jinny went straight to the phone.

"I sold my picture," she told her father as he passed her in the corridor in answer to his wife's call. "I'm going to phone the vet," and Jinny hesitated, wondering if she should tell her father about Nell closing her shop or wait until the Daltons had gone. Waiting would make it false. It was the kind of news you told someone immediately you saw them.

"Nell's getting married," said Jinny, "and she's closing her shop."

"Oh Lord," said Mr. Manders. "That is it."

"You'll find some other shop. When Nell could sell your

pots, other shops will want to buy them," but Mr. Manders had walked on past Jinny, not listening to her.

The vet's number was engaged and Jinny sat on the stairs, waiting until she could try again.

Her mother and Helen came out into the hall.

"I must admit," her mother was saying, "it was rather overwhelming when I saw it at first. Carpets and curtaining seemed impossible, but we got it together eventually."

"I think it is absolutely gorgeous," enthused Helen. "Not too terribly big. Some of the places Paul buys are mausoleums. I'm only too relieved when he sells them again. We've such a pretty place in Sussex. I couldn't bear to leave it. But something the size of this would be ideal for little breaks."

"As long as you took your little breaks in the summer," clipped Mrs. Manders, so that Jinny knew she didn't think too much of Helen.

"Oh, we'd have central heating installed first thing," smiled back Helen. "If Paul were to buy it, I'd love to decorate it myself."

"You're welcome," said Mrs. Manders.

"Blue, I think," said Helen, half closing her eyes and gazing around. "Powder-blue walls, gold brocade hangings and midnight-blue carpeting. I can just picture it."

"Needn't bother, just picturing it," thought Jinny darkly, as Helen and her mother made their way upstairs.

The third time Jinny tried the vet's number, Jim Rae, the vet, replied. Jinny told him about Easter.

"Miss Tuke phoned me last night. Told me she was pretty done. I'll fit you in this afternoon. Straight after lunch."

"But not to shoot her," Jinny said urgently, knowing what Miss Tuke would have told the vet. "Come and look at her. There must be something you can give her."

"We'll see," said the vet.

"Thank you," said Jinny. "Come down to the field. I'll be there."

Jinny put the phone down and walked quietly towards the front door, intending to go out and down to the field without seeing any of the Daltons again. From the pottery came her father's voice charged with electric excitement.

"But that's an utterly ridiculous price," he said.

"Worth it to me. The minute your little girlie told us about it, I knew it was a more than possible choice. And now I see it, I like it."

"But I tell you, Finmory is not for sale. Absolutely not."

"Dare say you wouldn't mind selling off some of your overheads?"

Mr. Manders laughed. "I'll give them to you."

"There you are. I'm offering to pay you for them. Dare say you got this place dirt cheap, and I'm offering a hundred and fifty thousand plus for it. Think about it."

Jinny stood listening, breath indrawn.

"Definitely not. No question of it," said her father's voice.

Jinny recognised the tone. It was the way she had said No to Kat before she had let her buy the picture of Shantih; before she had picked up the thirty pounds and allowed Kat to take away the painting of Shantih that was the closest Jinny had ever come to capturing the essence of Shantih's being.

Pressing her feet into the receiving floor, Jinny crept to

the front door, cradled the handle in both hands and, easing the door open, went out. She walked down to Easter, blotting out the conversation she had overheard. Never, never, never would her father sell Finmory. Never.

Kat came down to the field looking for Jinny.

"You'll come to Miss Tuke's tomorrow evening?"

"Okay," said Jinny unwillingly, thinking about Miss Tuke's cash flow and the fact that she had gone to the trouble of phoning the vet about Easter.

"I'll send the box round for you. Six o'clock," and the sound of Paul blasting his car horn sent Kat running back to him.

Easter was standing head down, eyelids wrinkled shut, nostrils pulled back. Jinny sat down close beside her, but leaving her alone, not troubling her.

When the vet came he sounded Easter, shaking his head. "Lord now lettest Thou Thy servant depart in peace," he chanted. "Afraid there's nothing else for it."

"I do not want her put down," said Jinny. "You are not to kill her."

Waiting for the vet, she had practised the sentences so that they would come out sounding like statements not like feeble pleadings.

"Why?" said the vet. "What are you keeping her alive for?"

"Just one summer," said Jinny. "That's what I want her to have. There must be something you could try."

"There is something," said the vet. "If you insist."

"Yes," said Jinny.

"Far out chance that it might work," said the vet as he set up his syringe. "It gives a boost to all the organs —

kidneys, liver, heart — but whether she's strong enough to stand it..."

Jinny put a rope halter on Easter and held her while the vet injected her.

"There," he said. "I'll come back, not tomorrow but the next day, some time in the morning. That'll give it time to work if it's going to do her any good. If not I'll have to put her down. It's cruelty keeping her alive in this state."

The vet waited for Jinny's consent, but although she heard him and knew that what he said was true she couldn't speak.

"I'll need someone to hold her for me. Could you do it?"

Hidden by her hair, Jinny nodded, tears pouring down her face.

"That's it then," said the vet.

He clapped Jinny on the shoulder and walked away, leaving Jinny with Easter, holding the halter rope in her hands.

CHAPTER SIX

The next day, immediately after breakfast, Jinny took a feed of oats, bran, chopped apple and carrot down to Easter. She had seen the horses earlier in the morning when she had been on her way to Mr. MacKenzie's for the milk. Shantih, as usual, had come to the gate, eager to welcome her, and although Easter had only turned her head to watch Jinny pass, there had been a brightness in her eye; her ears had been pricked with an interest that Jinny had not seen for days.

"It's working," Jinny had thought. "The injection's going to work." For an instant her old dream of Easter fit again began to build itself up in Jinny's mind. "Stop it," she told herself. "Stop it. Don't go imagining things. It's too soon to tell," and when her family asked her at breakfast how Easter was, Jinny only said, "Much the same," and went on eating her toast.

Now Jinny rattled the feed bucket. "Easter," she called as she climbed over the gate. "Easter. For the pony. A feed for Easter."

Easter looked up at the sound of her name, whinnied, and came towards Jinny. Her bones creaked in their sack of harsh skin, her head was stretched out on its clothes-pole neck, but her eyes were bright, her nostrils quivering. Jinny stood transfixed, hardly able to trust her eyes. It was the first time for days that Easter had shown any interest in food.

"It really is working," Jinny thought. "She really is a bit

better," and chasing off Shantih, she went to meet the pony, talking low, sweet talk to her.

Easter plunged her gaunt head into the bucket, snatching at oats, chomping mouthfuls of the feed, scattering apples, carrots and half-chewed oats in her desperation to eat. Holding the bucket, Jinny couldn't believe her eyes, couldn't believe that Easter could be so much better.

Jinny set the bucket on the ground, ran her hand down Easter's neck and huge-boned withers. She felt a turn of joy deep inside herself. For it was true, Easter was eating, was hungry. Perhaps ... Perhaps ... And for a long moment the dread of tomorrow eased in Jinny's mind. Maybe there was a chance, a chance after all, that Easter wouldn't have to be shot.

Then, as if a switch had been clicked off, Easter stopped eating. She turned away from the bucket, half-chewed food falling unnoticed from her mouth.

"Don't stop," pleaded Jinny. "Eat a bit more. If you eat you'll get strong again. Just a few more mouthfuls. Please, Easter," and Jinny followed the pony, rattling what was left of the feed. "You've only eaten half. You must eat more."

But Easter's eyes closed. She stood still, her head low, and even when Jinny held up handfuls of feed to her mouth she showed no interest, did not even move her head away. Jinny could have been offering food to a wooden rocking horse.

"But she did eat half of it," Jinny kept telling herself as she went back to the house. But no matter how often Jinny told herself that this was true, she knew that there had been something strange about Easter's greed; as if it had taken over Easter, had nothing to do with the pony herself.

"I'll tidy my room," Jinny thought, on the vague

principle that to do something that you really didn't want to do would attract good luck.

"If I do it now, no one will start nagging at me about it," she thought and walked firmly through the hall towards the stairs. She was just about to start the climb to her bedroom when she remembered that a clay model she had made of Bramble should have been biscuit fired by now. "I'll just have a look at it first," Jinny thought. "I'll not glaze it, only look, and then I'll do my bedroom."

The pottery was empty. Jinny walked along the shelves of drying pots, bleaching as they dried from slug grey to brilliant bone, until she found her model. It was a concise statement of Brambleness, solid and self-centred, a nugget of Bramble, weighty in the palm of her hand.

"Now I'm here it wouldn't take long to glaze it and then it could go into the next firing," Jinny decided.

She wandered down to the other end of the pottery. Here her father's desk was littered with papers — invoices, accounts, notes of firing times for different glazes all jostled together. Jinny sat down in his chair and wondered what it would be like to be her father, to have to cope with all the figures that demanded attention, with delivery times that had to be met and accounts that had to be paid. Pushed to a corner of the desk was her father's manuscript still in its shrouds of brown paper wrappings. Jinny tilted back her chair and stared at the paper storm that covered the desk top.

Just in front of her was a typewritten letter. There was a crest printed on the top of the letter, a familiar crest, but for a second Jinny couldn't place it. Then she knew. It was the Stopton coat of arms. It had been at the top of all the official notepaper that her father had used when he had been a probation officer.

A cold clench of fear tightened on Jinny's spine. What

was it doing at Finmory? They had left everything to do with Stopton behind them. Stopton was the past. Her father had left Stopton because he had grown to hate its meanness and dirt; had stopped being a probation officer because he could no longer cope with the stress of being part of a system that trapped people into the squalor of degrading housing, compulsory education that led nowhere; could no longer stand by, watching the rebels being crushed into conformity by legal power.

Because Jinny could read, when her eyes looked at print she couldn't help knowing instantly what the print said.

"Glad you've come to your senses." "Just the job for you." "The interview should be no trouble. Jon Brady is as keen as anyone to have you back." "Rinsed out the Manders coffee tankard." The letter was signed Bill, typewritten beneath the signature — Bill Wright. The Wrights had been friends with Jinny's family when they had lived in Stopton. Bill Wright had worked with Mr. Manders.

Suddenly Jinny realised what she was doing — reading someone else's letter, a letter that certainly wasn't meant for her to see. She sprang guiltily to her feet and dashed upstairs to her room.

She slammed her door shut and stood pressing her back against it. Her whole being was numb with shock, for the letter from Mr. Wright must mean that her father had applied for a job in Stopton.

"To go back to Stopton," thought Jinny in horror. "To do it without telling me, without discussing it with us." Jinny wondered if Ken knew, if Petra knew. Maybe they all knew except her. Maybe for days they had all known; every time they looked at her they had all been thinking, "Jinny doesn't know yet. Doesn't know that we're all going back to Stopton."

"But Shantih," thought Jinny. "What about Shantih?"

The tightness ballooned in Jinny's head and chest. She was back in the Stopton world of unending traffic, roads, city houses, soot-darkened parks and maggot-many hordes of people. No place for Shantih. No free land. Nowhere for Jinny to be.

"Oh no! No!" she cried. "It can't be true. It can't be. We could never leave Finmory. Never."

To leave Finmory would mean that the house would have to be sold. "I'm offering a hundred and fifty thousand plus," treacled Paul Dalton's voice in her head. Did her father mean to sell Finmory to Paul Dalton?

Jinny went back to the pottery to look for her father. She had to find out what was happening.

Mr. Manders was standing by his potter's wheel. A quick glance showed Jinny that the letter she had read was no longer on the desk.

"Is it today the vet's coming back?" Mr. Manders asked.

"For something to say, not because he cares," thought Jinny. "All he's thinking about is going back to Stopton."

"Tomorrow," she replied, and wanted desperately to go on to tell her father she had seen the letter from Mr. Wright.

"He must think there's some hope for Easter or he wouldn't have bothered with the injection."

"I made him try it," said Jinny, and again she searched for words to tell her father that she knew.

"Going over to Miss Tuke's again tonight? Kat seemed pretty full of herself. She was telling us how she is planning to ride at Badminton."

"He's scared of me," thought Jinny in amazement. "He's scared in case I have found out about Stopton, scared in case I ask. Maybe not scared, but not himself, not straight."

"Well," said Mr. Manders, "better get started," and Jinny turned away without having asked what she was desperate, yet terrified, to find out.

Having failed to ask the first time, the second opportunity slipped past more easily. Jinny was washing up the lunch dishes with her mother. There was no one else in the kitchen. She could easily have told her mother that she had seen the letter. But she didn't.

In the afternoon when she was grooming Shantih, Ken stopped to ask about Easter. Jinny didn't mention Stopton. By then it had become something that she didn't dare mention. Perhaps, if no one talked about it, it might go away. Perhaps Jinny might forget that she had ever seen the letter, had ever known anything about it. Maybe she hadn't read it properly, had taken the wrong meaning from it. Jinny didn't think these things clearly, in precise words; somehow they just seeped into her mind and made it seem the best thing to do, not to say anything about Stopton, when really all she wanted to do was to scream at the pitch of her voice, "Why haven't you told me we might be going back to Stopton?"

Her mother had washed and ironed Jinny's anorak, jeans and shirt. Jinny had polished her jodh boots. Regarding herself in the mirror, Jinny decided that on the whole the effect was worse today than her previous appearance had been. Seeing her old clothes carefully laundered, the Daltons would know that they were all she had. Dirty, they had had a certain style about them, and the Daltons must have thought that she was only wearing her old things, her good riding clothes being kept for more important occasions.

Kat had said that Sam would bring the float for Shantih

and Jinny at six o'clock. At half-past five Jinny called good-bye to her family, and yes she had got her hard hat to her mother, and went down to the stable. Earlier in the afternoon she had brought Shantih in, groomed her and cleaned her tack.

Shantih clattered the door of her box with impatient forefeet.

"Get up with you," said Jinny, tacking her up. "Don't know what you're grumbling about. Off for another special lesson." But Shantih was unimpressed. She would rather have been going back to her field.

Since the morning, Easter had refused to eat any more food.

"You're only annoying her," Ken had said when he had seen Jinny holding a cupped handful of oats under Easter's muzzle. "Leave her alone."

And Jinny had had to admit that he was right.

She went out now with a few oats in a bucket, so that they whispered dry and, Jinny hoped, appetizing, against the bucket's sides.

"Easter," Jinny called, crossing the field. "There's a girl. Come on the pony."

Easter turned slowly round and stepped towards Jinny.

"She is going to eat something," Jinny thought, the sudden hope sparking inside her. But even as she thought it, Easter staggered; her front legs buckled and she collapsed to the ground.

Jinny dashed forward and crouched down beside Easter, but now that she was lying down Easter seemed all right, only worn out.

"She hadn't the strength to walk," Jinny thought as she got up and stood looking down at Easter. It was going to happen. Tomorrow the vet would come back and Easter would be killed. "Oh, pony, pony," murmured Jinny, and felt the unavoidable certainty of it choking her.

There was the crashing roar of the horsebox coming up the lane from Mr. MacKenzie's. Jinny ran her hand gently over Easter's neck, over her flat cheek bones, the hollows above her eyes, down the skin-covered bone of her forehead to her dry muzzle. "Oh, Easter, Easter." But there was nothing more she could do. Turning, Jinny left her and went to get Shantih.

Miss Tuke, mounted on a fifteen-hand, overgrown Highland, was waiting for them as Kat's horsebox drew into her yard.

"Action this evening," she called. "We're going for a cross-country ride. Get the gees out and let's get weaving."

"Thank goodness," said Jinny. "At least we're not going to school."

"But I want a lesson," said Kat when they had unloaded their horses. "I need instruction on how to jump cross-country obstacles."

"And that's what you're going to get," said Miss Tuke. "Lightning is going to instruct you."

"Paul's paying you to teach me."

"And I am going to allow Lightning to instruct you on my land. What's more, I'm coming with you."

"That's not . . ."

"Jinny, up you get."

Jinny sprang on to Shantih. If she had to ride at Miss Tuke's, this was the best possible riding it could be.

Miss Tuke, followed by Kat and a prancing Shantih, led the way through the paddock and up the hill.

"You'll have heard the old hoary that nothing improves an eventer like a season's hunting?" Miss Tuke asked. "Well, don't think it's cutting up foxes into little bits that improves the nags. It's galloping on, taking jumps as you come to them, loosening up, enjoying yourself."

Jinny could see from Kat's face that she wasn't paying any attention to Miss Tuke. She was staring straight ahead, her lips tight, her black brows drawn together, her fingers gathering up her reins although Lightning was only walking out with her usual calm stride.

"She is nervous," thought Jinny in surprise. "Probably she's not used to riding across country." She smiled at Kat, trying to tell her that it was okay, a bit stomach churning at first if you weren't used to it, but great once you got going; fantastic on a horse like Lightning.

"You've to keep behind Guizer. He knows the way. Jump where I jump. If you think your horse is going to pass me, circle it. You're completely safe as long as you follow me. Right?"

"I should think it's Jinny that you want to warn about not passing you," mocked Kat.

Instantly Jinny wondered why she had bothered trying to be nice to Kat.

"I'm telling both of you," stated Miss Tuke, and she kicked her Highland into a battering trot.

"Easter," thought Jinny. "Leaving Finmory. The impossibility of going back to Stopton. No Nell. The vet tomorrow," and she let the black thoughts stream from her, did not hold on to them as she set herself to follow Guizer's carthorse rump.

They trotted on until Miss Tuke pushed Guizer into a rolling canter. Jinny sat down hard in the saddle, struggling to keep Shantih to a collected canter. Suddenly Miss Tuke twisted to the right, was cantering downhill and over a dry-stone wall. Shantih galloped behind her. Yards before the stone wall she arched into the air, landing far out beyond Miss Tuke on the other side.

"Circle her," yelled Miss Tuke, stopping Guizer.

Jinny hauled on her left rein, swung Shantih round and saw that Kat was stuck on top of the hill.

"Stop holding her back, " yelled Miss Tuke. "Let her come down."

Tight-lipped, Kat held Lightning to a slow trot, clutching at her mane as her horse cat-jumped the wall.

"Terrible," raged Miss Tuke. "There'll be broken bones before tonight's over if you both go on like this. You must not hold her back, Kat. Keep up with us. Frustrate her like that and you'll be in real trouble. Even Lightning won't put up with that sort of treatment."

The make-up stood out from Kat's blood-drained face like a clown's paint. The knuckles on her hands shone through her skin as she clutched her reins. Her lower lip was gripped tightly between her teeth.

"And if you let that idiot career about with you, you'll end up laming her again. Understand?"

Jinny wanted to say that Shantih wasn't used to being kept behind other horses, but she only nodded.

"Great," said Miss Tuke. "Now, next time I'm not stopping. You'll have to sort yourselves out." Guizer, irritated by the delay, shook his storm of black mane, clinked his bit and pounded the peaty soil with his forefeet. "Okay?" and Miss Tuke was away.

Jinny set herself to follow, sat down firmly in the saddle, weighted her feet in the stirrups as she fought to control Shantih. A wall rose from the bracken and Guizer bucketed over it. Shantih stretched and sailed, but Jinny was ready to check her as she landed, to bring her back behind Miss Tuke. Close behind Shantih, Lightning cleared the wall and came back sweetly under control.

But Jinny had no time to pay attention to anything except Shantih. Another dozen strides and Miss Tuke seemed to fall over the edge of the moor as she vanished over a wall with a drop on the landing side. Shantih plunged to follow. Jinny, sitting well back, let her reins slip through her fingers to the buckle, felt her stomach suspended above her as if she were in a dive-bombing lift. Kat screamed. Miss Tuke glanced back, and Jinny knew from her expression that Kat was still on top.

Shantih quickly realised what was happening and understood that if this game of jumping and galloping was to go on she had to follow Guizer, so Jinny was able to sit down and enjoy herself.

Dodging this way and that, swinging her heavy Highland round on his hocks and galloping to left or right, Miss Tuke rode like the Pied Piper over her land. Sometimes the jumps were poles on cans set cunningly in the heather; a brush jump that pounced on them just as they rounded a corner; downhill spurts; walls with wide ditches on the landing side; streams with mired take-offs; and three of the solid cross-country obstacles, which they took without pausing as if they had been no more than the dry-stone walls.

"That shook up the molecules," laughed Miss Tuke, when at last she brought Guizer to a trot and, reins in one hand, turned to look at Jinny and Kat. "There's life in the old bat yet, eh? How did that grab you?"

Jinny was without words, her head a shaken kaleidoscope of images — stone walls flying beneath her, cross-country obstacles held for a fleeting second between Shantih's pricked ears, mud from Guizer's pounding hooves sailing past her face, and the zap of action without thought.

"It was absolutely super," Kat enthused, her voice high with nervous excitement as their mounts walked level with each other again. "It was the most exciting thing I've ever done."

Kat's make-up was no longer perfect, her riding clothes were splashed with mud, but Lightning was her usual calm self, as obedient as ever.

"Wonder what she would be like on Shantih?" Jinny thought. "Wonder if she's always ridden perfectly schooled horses? Wonder how she'd manage if Lightning was really fresh and forgot all her schooling?"

Twice, when Jinny had looked back at Kat, she had been holding on to Lightning's mane, and once, when Lightning had drawn level with Shantih over a wall, Jinny had seen Kat's face puckered with utter terror.

"Oh, it was super. Can we do it again tomorrow night? Jinny, can you come tomorrow?" said Kat, full of enthusiasm now that the ride was safely over.

And Jinny was back drowning in the material world. "Tomorrow" — the word clanged its goblin change. The moors became Stopton's city streets. Where would there be in Stopton for Shantih to gallop and leap? Did Miss Tuke know that they might be leaving Finmory? Had everyone been told except herself?

"Well, even if Jinny can, I can't," said Miss Tuke. "It's the trekkers' film show."

"And the next night is Nell's party," said Kat.

"To say good-bye to Nell," and Jinny thought how much she owed to Nell. Nell had not only said her drawings were good, she had bought them. Say Nell a last good-bye. How she would miss her.

"Couldn't we go over a few more jumps now? Paul won't mind paying."

"It's after eight," said Miss Tuke. "Think of your horse. She's not clockwork. Though from the way she was jumping tonight I wouldn't like to bet on it."

Soon she would be home, Jinny thought. Soon she would be in bed. Soon it would be tomorrow. Tomorrow when the vet was coming back.

"I MUST ride in a real cross-country competition," declared Kat. "Paul would be so pleased if I won something. Couldn't you fix it up? There must be somewhere round about that's holding a cross-country event. Oh, couldn't you?"

"We're hardly in the Home Counties where these things grow on trees," declared Miss Tuke. "But I'll see what I can do for you."

"Cash flow," thought Jinny cynically. "Miss Tuke's fixing will cost you." But she only thought it with the froth of her mind; with all the rest of her being she could only think of Easter, that tomorrow the vet was coming to put her down, to kill her, and he would need someone to hold Easter for him.

"Paul would really be impressed if I rode in a real cross-country event before we go away," Kat went on. That would show that I'm really interested in cross-country. And Lightning could do it, couldn't she?"

CHAPTER SEVEN

Jinny woke early, knowing at once what the day held for her. She sat up, stared out of the window to the horses' field. Shantih was still lying down, Easter standing thrust against the hedge in the far corner of the field. By lunchtime she would be dead. Without calling Shantih, Jinny lay down again. She lay on her back, flat and completely still, waiting. Tears ran out of the corners of her eyes, dripping on to her pillow. Yet in a way, she wasn't crying. She was waiting, tight and hard, somewhere inside herself, knowing that it had to happen. There was no other way, Easter had to be shot. But the tears went on flowing out of her.

Much later she heard Mike getting up and going out to the farm, then her mother.

"It's time," Jinny told herself. The cold, isolated waiting was over. She had to get up now and go down to Easter, stay with her until the vet came.

When Jinny went through the kitchen, her mother was cooking breakfast. The smell of food gagged in Jinny's throat. Slices of dead pig. Slices of dead Easter.

"Morning," said her mother.

Jinny roboted on to the door.

"Where are you off to? Breakfast will be ready in a few minutes."

"Don't want any," said Jinny. "I'm going out."

She had reached the kitchen door.

"It's far too soon to go down to Easter," said her mother. "The vet can't possibly be here yet. Hasn't he a surgery until ten?"

Mr. Manders came into the kitchen, frowsy from sleep, looking for coffee to lure him back to life.

"Far too early," he said, agreeing with his wife. "Have something to eat and I'll come down with you and wait for the vet."

"Perhaps if you'd let me get the vet sooner he wouldn't be coming today to shoot Easter," Jinny said, choosing her words carefully, wanting to hurt her father, saying them because something had to be said between herself and her father. There had to be some noise across the gulf that had opened between them. Really, Jinny wanted to scream at him, demanding to be told what was happening behind her back, why she hadn't been told that they might be going back to Stopton. "Perhaps you should think about that."

Mr. Manders hunched his shoulders, reached for his coffee mug.

"I'll come down when I've had breakfast," he said.

"No," said Jinny. "I don't want you. We don't need you," and she banged the door behind herself.

Jinny walked slowly down to the field. On her way she took a rope halter from the tack room — a rough, knotted halter that Mr. MacKenzie had given to her — and went on to the horses. She spoke to Shantih, watching herself speaking — the film about the skinny, red-haired girl had reached an exciting bit, the cinema audience was sitting on the edge of their seats. As if she sensed the fear in Jinny, Shantih turned away and went to graze in the far corner of the field.

Jinny went over to Easter. The pony didn't even turn her head. She gave no sign that she knew Jinny was there.

Jinny sat down by the hedge and waited. The words, "Thus it is to be an old pony," came into her head. She repeated them over and over again — "to be an old pony". The spell of the words stopped other thoughts from reaching her — the thought of what exactly the vet would do to Easter. Would she groan or scream, rear away from the vet, try with her last energy to escape? Could she bear to hold the halter rope, the hanging rope? "To be an old pony." Even now was there not some way out? Somewhere Jinny could take Easter where they could cure her. If Jinny took her away now and hid her from the vet, perhaps tomorrow she could find someone who could cure her. "Thus it is to be an old pony." The reality of Easter's worn-out body denied all such false hopes. There was nothing Jinny could do except wait. This was real. This was not drawing pictures.

The vet arrived just after eleven. He vaulted over the gate, came striding across the field. Jinny got up to meet him.

"I'm afraid it's no use," he said as he saw Easter. "Well, you've done all you could. Let's get it over with. Poor old lass, you're ready to go, aren't you?"

Easter made a slight movement of her head.

"Not pleasant but it has to be done," said the vet. "Can you put her halter on and we'll take her over to the gate. I'll drop her there. I gave the hunt kennels at Brighill a phone last night. Told them there might be a carcass for them today. They'll come for her this afternoon."

Somehow Jinny fumbled the halter on to Easter, tugged at the rope to try and lead her to the gate. Easter took one step, swayed and stood still again.

"She doesn't want . . ." began Jinny, and saw the vet float liquid before her, the grass pound in waves about her head. She heard herself scream, "No!" before the sea of land swept over her.

When Jinny came to, she was sitting on the ground and the vet was holding her head down.

"How's that?" he asked, as Jinny swam back to the sound of his voice and struggled to sit up. "Easy now. Sit still for a minute."

"I'm okay," insisted Jinny and got shakily to her feet. "What happened?"

"You fainted."

"Fainted?" said Jinny, then she saw Easter and remembered what she had to do.

"Nip over and get Jock MacKenzie," the vet told her. "He's used to these things. No point in torturing yourself like this."

Jinny turned and ran. Blinded by tears and hair, she fled across the field, through the gate and towards the track to the farm.

Panic raged in her. No spell of words now to keep her separate. She hadn't been brave enough to see Easter through. Now Mr. MacKenzie would do what she was afraid to do. Would shout and bully Easter to the gate. His hands the last things Easter would know. "But I can't, I can't," cried Jinny.

Ken caught her and held her as she ran full tilt into him.

"Has he shot her?" Ken asked.

"No," sobbed Jinny. "I've to get Mr. MacKenzie to hold her."

"I'll do it," said Ken.

"But you never do. You never have anything to do with killing animals."

"That's why I can hold Easter," said Ken, and he went on down to the field.

Jinny ran through garden and house to her room, threw herself face downwards on her bed and bit hard on her clenched fist. She wanted to stay with her face pressed into her pillow but she couldn't, she had to look.

Through the window she saw Ken standing at Easter's head, his hand on her neck. Saw the vet hold the humane killer to her forehead. Saw Easter crumple and fall. The vet brought a tarpaulin and they covered her body with it.

Even watching from the safety of her room, Jinny felt a flooding sense of relief. It was over. What had to be done had been done. They had reached the other side, and Jinny knew more about herself. She hadn't been able to hold Easter. The courage to have done this was something that she didn't have. Jinny buried her head in her hands and wept.

Ken's footsteps came up Jinny's stairs.

"That's it over," he said. "She was glad to go."

"Thank you."

"I meant to come down before the vet arrived, but Tom caught me. Had something to tell me."

Watching Ken's face, Jinny guessed what her father had told him. She waited, wondering if Ken was going to tell her or if her father had warned him not to mention it.

"So," said Ken, turning to go.

"Wish we could bury her," said Jinny.

"Only a body left. You don't go round worrying what's happened to the clothes you were wearing last year. That's all Easter's left — old clothes."

After lunch, two Hunt servants arrived in a pick-up truck with a crane on it. They fitted a sling to Easter's body and lifted it into the truck. Mr. Manders went down with a bottle of whisky and gave them both a dram. In the late afternoon, when Jinny went down to catch Shantih and ride her, there was only the crushed grass at the gateway and the wheel tracks of the Hunt's pick-up to show that anything had happened. Jinny led Shantih through the gate and the field was empty.

She saddled Shantih and rode down to the beach. Most she wanted to go to bed and sleep, but to go to bed so early would rouse her mother to sympathy or worry and Jinny didn't want either. She let Shantih pick her way over the boulders and then walked her on across the sands. The tide was far out, and Jinny rode Shantih to its frothing, laced edge. She sat staring out at the glittering expanse of sea.

"She's dead," Jinny said aloud. "Easter's dead." Shantih flickered her ears, but Jinny's words meant nothing to her. While the vet had shot Easter, Shantih had gone on grazing. "Like the torturer's horse scratching its innocent behind while his master went about his gainful employment," thought Jinny, remembering a poem by Auden they had read at school. Like the innocent sea that would go on pulsing over the sands when she was back in Stopton. Soon there would be nothing left of Jinny's world. No sign left to tell the strangers that she had been there. No trace. Leaning forward, Jinny threw her arms round Shantih's neck, leant the side of her face against Shantih's shoulder and stared backwards at an upside-down world.

Clattering over the sea-smoothed pebbles, trotting over the sand, came Kat on Lightning. Jinny groaned aloud but she had no will or energy left to escape. She sat and waited.

"They told me I'd find you here," said Kat, bringing Lightning to a halt at Shantih's side.

"Then they were right, weren't they?" said Jinny.

"Your mother said I wasn't to bother you because you were upset. Something about having some ancient old pony put down. Sounded to me like the only sensible thing to do. Nothing to make a fuss about."

"Go," said Jinny, "and play in the traffic."

"You won't say that when you hear what I've come to tell you."

Jinny ignored her, stared out to sea.

"Miss Tuke has fixed it. She's found a riding club that's having a cross-country event next Saturday, a week today, and she's fixed it so that we can ride in it."

"Brandoch Riding Club?" asked Jinny, knowing that it was the only one anywhere near Finmory. "The one attached to the Country Club?"

"Yes."

"It would be a good idea if you were to ask me what I want to do before you and Miss Tuke go fixing things. And anyway she can't have fixed it, the entries had to be in weeks ago."

"We can't compete against the others but we can ride the course. 'Hors concour' Miss Tuke called it — she says it's often done. Paul was delighted when I told him. He likes competitions. Likes me to win things."

"Then Paul can ride in it if he's so keen. Miss Tuke can hire out Guizer to him. She can give him lessons."

"Goodness, we are in a tizz-wizz," said Kat. "You don't really think Paul would ride, do you?"

"Joke," said Jinny. "J. O. K. E. Joke."

"Climbing was his thing."

"You told me. Everest, I expect, when he wasn't so fat."

"He has climbed in the Himalayas. He was down here with your father last night having a look at the bay." Kat clapped her hand to her mouth in exaggerated dismay. "Hush my mouth," she mocked in a deep-south accent. "I am not to talk to you about Finmory being sold. You is not to be worried about such things, being too refined in your nature."

Despite herself, Jinny felt her stomach lurch at the thought of Paul Dalton buying Finmory, the thought of the Daltons living in her home.

"They were down here, and your father showed him a rock that hardly anyone has climbed, called the Chimney. That's the kind of challenge that Paul likes."

"That's the entrance to it , beyond the bay," said Jinny, pointing. "You can only see it because the tide's right out."

"Doesn't look anything special to me," said Kat scornfully. "When I was climbing in Wales we tackled far harder things than that."

"Surprise! Surprise!" said Jinny. "You've to go into the cave and look up. It's not just climbing it. It's getting out to it, climbing it and getting back. You can only reach it at very low tide and you've got to climb up and get back before the tide comes in again. A man was drowned in it once. The current at the headland is so strong it would sweep you away if you tried to swim back, and if you're trapped in the Chimney at high tide you've had it. Drowned dead," and Jinny shuddered at the thought. "Dad says it's lunacy. He made Mike promise that he would never try it."

"You are all wrapped up in cotton wool, aren't you," said Kat.

"What is the use," thought Jinny, "of even trying to talk to her."

"Bet Paul could have done it when he was younger. Bet I could do it now. You could ride out, climb it and ride back. Let's go and have a look at it," and although Kat suggested it, her voice was a twanging wire of nervous tension, as if the last thing she wanted to do was to go near the Chimney.

Jinny hesitated. Twice before she had ridden out to the Chimney, once with Mike on Bramble and once with Sue, and she remembered vividly the menace of the black rocks.

"Scared are you?"

"I was checking that the tide was far enough out."

"Couldn't be much further out. Come on," and Kat urged Lightning towards the Chimney.

Still Jinny hesitated. She knew how quickly the tide could turn, how the sea could seem far out one minute and, in no time at all, waves would be pounding up over the sands, the whole bay swallowed up.

Kat turned, shouting at Jinny. Jinny couldn't hear what she said but could see her face mocking, caught her jeering laughter.

"I'll show her," thought Jinny, and cantered Shantih after her. The Arab's hooves splashed fetlock deep, spray rising above her knees. "We mustn't wait," thought Jinny. When she had ridden out with Mike, they had been riding over gleaming sands on their way to the cliffs.

The Chimney was on the far side of Finmory Bay, in the opposite direction from Mr. MacKenzie's farm. It could only be reached from the sands, there was no way of reaching it from above.

"That's it," said Jinny, when they had reached the right place in the black cliffs.

"How do you know? All these cliffs look the same to me."

"Because I do. You go right in there, look up and that's it."

"Here, hold Lightning," and, before Jinny realised what she was intending to do, Kat had jumped down from her horse and handed her reins to Jinny as if she was parking a car.

"In here?" Kat called, splashing her way to the narrow opening in the cliff face.

"Yes, but don't be long. We can't wait."

Kat scrambled over the rocks in front of the cave and ran into darkness. Again Jinny shuddered. There had been no need for her father to make her promise never to try to climb the Chimney. Left to herself, Jinny would never have gone near it.

She looked out to sea, away from the black terror of the cliffs. The tide was coming steadily in. The waves slapped against the cliffs with a changed intention, sending up spumes of volatile lace, brilliant against the ebony backdrop of the rock. Suddenly the far horizon seemed to tip up, threatening to unload tons of ocean on top of Jinny and Shantih.

"Kat! Come on! Hurry up!" Jinny screamed, unable to keep the panic out of her voice.

The minutes that it took Kat to reappear seemed endless to Jinny.

"Come on!" she yelled again. "Hurry up or we're going to be trapped."

Waiting, Jinny thought how it must have been for the man who was drowned here. Had he tried to swim round the cliffs to the bay and been swept out to sea by the current, or had he climbed down from the Chimney to find the waves crashing in on him? Her nightmare stirred in the depths of Jinny's consciousness. She was not thinking about it but it reached her as a rising panic, a nameless fear that made her desperate for action.

"Come on," she screamed as Kat came into sight.

"Calm down," said Kat, deliberately walking slowly towards Jinny, stopping to straighten her jacket before she took Lightning's reins from her. "You're perfectly safe."

Jinny didn't even wait to see Kat mounted. She swung Shantih round and galloped full speed back to the bay.

"The water's not even up to their knees," Kat said as she caught up with Jinny. "Didn't you want to have a look inside? I could climb it without any trouble. Expect I shall if Paul decides to buy Finmory."

Jinny closed her ears to Kat's voice. Even the taunt of Finmory being sold couldn't reach her just now. They had to reach the headland where the cliffs opened into the bay, had to reach it without wasting another second.

"Glory!" exclaimed Kat as they turned into the bay and saw its expanse of sand already shrunk to half the size it had been when they had seen it last. "The tide does come in fast."

"As I did mention," said Jinny, but she was limp with relief. They were safe. For moments before they had reached the end of the cliffs, the swell had been breaking over Shantih's chest. Jinny had felt the grabbing drag of the tide. Five minutes, ten minutes more and they would have had to swim their horses to get round the headland.

"Paul would really be interested in that cave," said Kat, as they walked their horses back through the crimping shallows to the sand. "He would really be impressed if I climbed it."

"What does it matter what Paul thinks? You're always going on about what Paul will think. Do what you want to do."

"You're not allowed to do what you want to do. You're always saying that your father won't let you do things."

"Am not."

"Dare say he won't let you enter for the cross-country in case you hurt yourself."

"He'll say it is up to me."

"Does that mean you're entering?"

"Of course it does," snapped Jinny, caught off her guard.

"I can tell Miss Tuke?"

"Yes."

"You against me?"

"Yes," said Jinny again.

She hadn't in the least meant to get involved with Kat. The last thing she had wanted was a challenge between them. She knew that Miss Tuke thought the course at Brandoch was a stiff one, but it didn't matter. Jinny was sick of listening to Kat's conceit; sick of her boasting, when underneath it all she was so nervous. She would show Kat what Shantih could do. Even if Lightning had cost six thousand pounds that didn't mean to say that, with Kat riding her, she could beat Shantih and Jinny.

"See you at the party," Kat shouted, as she left Jinny to ride back to Hawksmoor.

"Suppose so," said Jinny, wanting to say, "Not if I see you first," and she rode on to the empty field.

CHAPTER EIGHT

Jinny, wearing one of Petra's outgrown dresses, sat on a settee in Nell's room and glowered about her. The party filled Nell's flat with music, laughter and human voices loud in their enjoyment of food, drink and company. It was one in the morning, and the main room of Nell's flat was crammed with dancing couples. Jinny wanted to go home.

"Hate it," thought Jinny. "Hate the smoke and the drinking and the noise; hate Nell going away; hate Easter having to be shot; hate their stupid laughing when there's nothing to laugh about." She wanted to be home in bed with another day safely over when nothing had been said about leaving Finmory.

Ben, the man Nell was to marry, was small with thick, badger-grey hair and an intense, hawk expression.

"Ah, Jinny Manders," he'd said, kissing Jinny, when Nell had introduced them. "I bought one of your drawings, a pencil drawing of an Arab horse. Hangs in my study."

And that had been the high spot of Jinny's evening. The rest had been spent watching her parents' eyes glaze with boredom as Paul and Helen established themselves, one on either side of her father and mother, and proceeded to boom and twitter without pause. Petra had been tracked down by the only young man at the party who was wearing a suit, and Kat was being charmingly sophisticated and so false it made Jinny sick. Mike had stayed at home, and although Ken had come with them he was nowhere to be seen.

"At least try to look pleasant," Petra had said. "You cast such a gloom just sitting there."

"What would you like me to do? Just stand on my head?"

"Oh well, if that's the mood you're in . . ." Petra had said and, abandoning her sister, had gone on dancing with her pinstripe suit.

Even when Nell and Ben had come to sit beside Jinny, inviting her to stay with them next Easter, Jinny had only said she didn't suppose she would and that next spring was too far away to be sure of anything.

"Then think about it later," Ben had said. "Come and dance with me just now."

Jinny had said no, she couldn't, because if she moved about too much in Petra's dress it would probably split.

"In Petra's dress?" asked Nell.

"The one I'm wearing."

"Jinny," said Nell. "Don't."

"Can't help it," said Jinny. "It's the way I feel."

And even when Nell said it had been great knowing her and she would be looking forward to coming to Jinny's first exhibition, Jinny had only been able to make a kind of grunting noise and gone on staring at her feet until they left her alone.

"Nearly two o'clock in the morning," thought Jinny furiously. "Why can't we go home?" And she got up and dragged her way through to the room where the food had been laid out. Only the remains of the feast were left. The cheese straws that Jinny had been hoping for were finished. She stood looking down at the nearly empty plates, wondering if she could eat another chocolate cake.

A door that opened from this room into Nell's studio stood ajar.

"My interview is on Saturday. It's ninety-five per cent certain, but I can't discuss anything definite until then," said her father's voice.

"Don't waste too much time," said Paul Dalton.

"I can't possibly make any decisions until I know I've got the Stopton position."

"Remember, I have my eye on one or two other properties. I want Finmory but . . ."

Jinny fled back to her settee.

"We're going home," said a girl about an hour later.

Jinny stared at the stranger, not knowing what she meant.

"You've been asleep, haven't you? I told Mum it would all be too much for you," and Jinny knew her sister.

But she hadn't been asleep. She had been sitting, cold and alone, in a desolate, waste world where her own father was planning to sell everything Jinny loved; to take away her home, her own room with the mural of the Red Horse; the sea and the open land; all to be sold without telling Jinny.

She looked up blankly at Petra and wondered if she knew.

"Have you been crying?" Petra asked suspiciously.

Jinny wasn't sure. She shook her head numbly and followed Petra to the room where they had left their jackets. She said good-bye to Nell.

"You will come to see us? Promise?"

Jinny shook her head. It would never happen. Nell had chosen to go and that was that.

Squashed between Ken and Petra, Jinny stared at the back of her father's head as they drove home.

"How could he do it?" she thought. "Knowing how I hated living in Stopton; knowing how I love living here. To have it all fixed up and never to have said a word.

Going for an interview next Saturday and never to have told me. I bet they all know except me."

When they got out of the car, an icy wind was blowing in from the sea.

"Back to winter," gasped Mrs. Manders.

"The ice age cometh," said Ken, as they were blown like dead leaves into the house. "The wolves are running."

Kelly was jubilant at their return, leaping to welcome them back.

"Did you have a good time?" asked Mike.

"Don't tell me you're still up," said his mother.

"Fell asleep in the chair," admitted Mike sheepishly.

"To bed," said Mr. Manders, bolting the front door now that they were all safely home.

Normally it was the moment that Jinny loved — to be home, to know that all her people were securely about her, to be going up to her own room. But tonight there was no security, it was all false. Next weekend, if her father got the job in Stopton, Finmory would be sold.

"Everyone to bed," said Mr. Manders, and began to go upstairs. Mike, yawning, made to follow him. Mrs. Manders was going into the kitchen.

Jinny stood without moving, staring about her, seeing it all with the over-bright garishness of a badly tuned T.V. Suddenly she could bear it no longer.

"No!" she screamed. "No!"

She saw her family swing huge dandelion-clock faces against her. Was sure that they all knew what she was going to say.

"We've got to talk. You've got to tell me, because I know. I saw the letter on Dad's desk about the job, and I heard him talking to Mr. Dalton about it tonight. You can't sell Finmory. You can't. I don't want to go back to Stopton. Why didn't you ask me? Tell me!"

"What's up now?" said Mike. "Who's going back to Stopton?"

"They haven't told you either?" said Jinny. "Next Saturday Dad's going for an interview in Stopton. Mr. Wright's fixed it so that he'll get the job. Then he's selling Finmory to Paul Dalton and he'll turn it into a holiday home."

"Not really?" said Mike incredulously.

"Couldn't it wait till tomorrow morning?" asked Mr. Manders.

"So we could all go on pretending it's not going to happen?" said Jinny.

"I want to know now," said Mike.

Mrs. Manders made coffee, they opened up the Aga and sat round the kitchen table.

"We didn't want to upset you," Mrs. Manders said. "You were so worried about Easter. And when you would insist on seeing the whole thing through yourself, it seemed so unfair to burden you with this as well."

"But how could you think it would help me, not telling me?"

"It may not happen," said Mr. Manders.

"Then you would never have told me," said Jinny bitterly. "It would always have been there in your minds. Something that Jinny hadn't been told, so that we could never have spoken straight to each other again."

"But what *is* happening?" demanded Mike. "You never told me either."

"Ken knew and I knew," said Petra. "Mum and Dad knew I'd be sensible about it. Not start and make a scene."

"We just have not got enough money to go on living here," said Mr. Manders. "Without the income from my writing we cannot afford to live here. I know I should have looked around for other markets for my pottery and not just been satisfied with selling to Nell, and odd batches here and there, but I didn't and there's no use going on about it. And now Nell's gone it's even more impossible."

"But . . ." interrupted Jinny.

"And that is fact," went on Mr. Manders, ignoring Jinny. "To begin with there was still some money left in your grandmother's estate. That's nearly all finished now. When the publisher sent back my book, wanting alterations made in it, I knew I had to do something in case they didn't take it. I wrote to Bill Wright asking if there were any vacancies."

"You couldn't stand Stopton," stormed Jinny. "You utterly hated it. You can't have forgotten how awful it all was. What do you want to go back to that for?"

"Making a scene," said Petra smugly.

"These days you go where there's a chance of a job. They know me in Stopton. Wouldn't have a chance anywhere else. Not at my age. Bill wrote back sending me an application form. They're looking for a liaison officer between the schools and the juvenile courts. Jon Brady would still be my boss. I got on well with him. Wouldn't mind working for him again, so I'm going for an interview on Saturday."

"'The interview should be no trouble,'" quoted Jinny. "I saw the letter from Mr. Wright. I couldn't help reading it. It was on top of your desk."

"So you mean Jin's right. We really might be going back to Stopton?"

"If I get the post, they want me to start as soon as possible. Beginning of September."

"Not go back to school here? But I'm in the football team. I can't leave Finmory."

"And what about Shantih?"

"We won't be going back to live in the city," explained Mrs. Manders. "We'll get a house on the outskirts. Branchford or Wearby. They're both very nice. We'll find somewhere near stables, and you can keep Shantih there. There'll be other children for you to ride with, and you'll be able to join the Pony Club."

Jinny stared blankly at her mother. Here they were, calmly proposing to erupt her whole life, and her mother was holding out the Pony Club as a carrot.

"I never want to leave Finmory," said Jinny. "Never, never. I want to go on living here, keeping Shantih here in her own stable, her own field. I want to have Bramble back again in September, not be going to Stopton. Branchford's all bungalows and Wearby's plastic. I don't want to go and live there."

"Neither do I," stated Mike. "I'm on Jinny's side. And I think you should have discussed it with us before it was all settled."

"But it's not settled," said Mr. Manders.

"Mr. Dalton is going to pay a fantastic price for Finmory," said Petra. "And we can all have a present out of the money. A proper present. I'm to have a new piano, and Jinny can have riding lessons or oil paints or whatever she wants."

"I want to stay here," stated Jinny, not bothering to wipe away the tears that were beginning to trickle down her face, for it seemed as if the whole thing was settled, as if they were already back in Stopton; Finmory no more than a memory, photographs to be shown to people they had known in their Stopton past.

"Wait until Saturday's over," said Mr. Manders. "See if I get the job. Then we'll have a real discussion, thrash the whole thing out."

"Be too late then," said Jinny. "If you get the job, it will have happened."

"Fact," said Ken, speaking from silence, challenging Mr. Manders. "You are fed up living here and, because you want to move, all your family have to go too."

" Not at all. We just cannot afford to stay."

"Rot," said Ken. "And you know it. You have everything here. Put down roots. Grow. Stop being so afraid," and Ken got up, walked long legged to the door, Kelly shadowing his steps, and went out.

"He's right," pleaded Jinny.

"Bed for everyone," said Mrs. Manders. "Half-past three in the morning is no time for discussions."

Jinny went upstairs, sat on her bed with her knees clutched beneath her chin, too desperate even to cry. She could not believe that they really might be leaving Finmory, that her father could possibly think of selling Finmory. She loved it all so much. Knew it as she knew her own being. It was where she belonged. She could never leave it. Yet Jinny knew that if her father decided to go, she would have to go with him. No place for her. She must go where her father chose to go.

She hugged her knees tighter, her shuddering desperation gripped her and shook her. There was no Jinny Manders left, no Shantih, no Finmory. They were all taken by the tempest of the night wind and blown helplessly about the edges of the world.

Then Jinny heard her name called; called without sound from somewhere inside herself and yet, also, from the mural of the Red Horse. Obeying the summons, Jinny crossed her room, went under the arch, drawn to the presence of the Horse. She stood in front of it, seeing it clearly although the room was dark — its powerful being, its unmoving strength, the yellow eyes drawing her to it.

Last summer when Jinny's dreams had been haunted by the presence of the Red Horse, she had experienced it as terror, now she was without fear. She felt the Horse as a source of power, a strength on which she could draw to give her courage. Courage to face what was coming, for the Red Horse offered no easy way out. It did not assure Jinny that they would stay at Finmory; that was in the future. The Horse was NOW and, knowing it, Jinny was drawn out of past, present or future; out of the illusion of time.

Shivering with cold, Jinny came back to herself. The Horse, hardly visible now, was no more than a crude painting. Yet when she lay curled under the bedclothes, on the brink of sleep, Jinny was comforted, her hopeless desperation gone.

CHAPTER NINE

Shantih's neck, with its winnowing mane, arched in front of Jinny as she rode schooling circles at a slow sitting trot. She was concentrating on her riding, forcing Shantih with seat and hands to pay attention to her rider; driving her forward on to her bit; making her use her quarters.

Jinny had woken early, lain thinking about how things were, and at last decided that there was nothing she could do to change them. Easter was dead. Nell's life was her own, Jinny could not tell her what to do. If her father decided to go back to Stopton he would go, and all the family would have to go with him. In a few years' time she would be free to do what she wanted, but now she could only wait to hear the result of his interview on Saturday. It wasn't certain. Someone else might get the job, and then he would come back to Finmory, settle down, forget it had happened. Yet Jinny knew that no matter what the result of the interview was, it had happened. Paul Dalton had offered to buy Finmory, and as long as her father wanted to leave, the threat would be there, and nothing Jinny could do about it.

But there was one thing she could do — she could beat Kat Dalton on Saturday. She would show her that Shantih was better than Lightning; that Shantih could gallop faster, leap higher than Lightning. Even if Kat's horse had cost thousands of pounds and was perfectly schooled, it didn't mean that she was better than Shantih. The desire to beat Kat grew in Jinny's mind until it seemed the most important thing in her life. All the other things were beyond her control, but she could beat Kat on Saturday.

Kat had phoned Jinny that morning, saying in her high-pitched, supercilious voice that Paul, Helen and herself had so much enjoyed Nell's party, and what had been wrong with Jinny that she had sulked all night? They were to go over to Miss Tuke's as usual that evening, and Miss Tuke wanted them to give their horses two hours' road work in the morning, and would they ride together? Jinny had said no, she would see Kat that evening, and hung up.

Jinny knew that Shantih didn't need road work. Shantih was hard and fit, could gallop and leap round the Brandoch course without noticing it. What Shantih needed was schooling. Once she had thought about it, Jinny knew that Miss Tuke had been right. It was months since she had done any serious schooling with Shantih. Now and again she had trotted circles on the sands, but only for a few minutes. Then Shantih would toss her head, kick up her heels saying how bored, bored, bored she was and how about a gallop? Jinny would agree, and off they would go, sea wind blowing against them, the screams of gulls applauding their speed.

Jinny touched Shantih into a canter, felt the moment when she would have leapt into a gallop but was ready for it, caught her in time and steadied her to a collected canter, no faster than a trot. She circled Shantih at the canter, sent her on at an extended canter, brought her back to a collected canter. Then a circle at a sitting trot, then into canter again. She worked for nearly an hour, varying the spells of faster work with figure eights and diagonals at a free and extended walk. Jinny forced Shantih to listen to her, to pay attention, to concentrate.

"You remember it all fine," Jinny told her horse, as she rode a little of the road to Glenbost to comply with Miss

Tuke's instructions about a road ride. "Remember to listen to me on Saturday and we'll win okay."

Miss Tuke spent most of their evening lesson schooling over smallish jumps. It wasn't until the end of the lesson that she set up four sizeable jumps made from an assortment of poles and cans.

"Ride the four as a course," Miss Tuke said. "The third's a spread. Let them go on at that. The last's an upright, so you want them back under control before you jump that. Plenty of impulsion. Kat, you go first."

"Thinks we'll smash them up," Jinny whispered to Shantih. "But we'll show her."

"Right, Kat. You'll need to wake her up a bit if you're to clear these."

Lightning had been jumping in her usual calm, fluid arcs. Kat sat in precisely the correct place, bending from the waist as Lightning jumped, her hands sliding forward on either side of her horse's neck. But Jinny couldn't help thinking that there was something wrong about her riding — it was riding by numbers not by the seat of her jodhs. There was no joy in it.

Lightning cleared the first two jumps, and Kat turned her to face the spread.

"Not going nearly fast enough," Jinny thought, as Lightning cantered to the spread with Kat sitting perfectly but doing nothing to encourage her horse.

"Ride her! Ride her!" bawled Miss Tuke, as Lightning put on her brakes, shooting Kat up her neck.

"You must wake her up," warned Miss Tuke, as a white-faced Kat struggled back into the saddle. "Now take her round, and this time let her know that you're intending to jump. Ride her at it."

Kat turned Lightning and rode her clumsily, almost blindly at the spread. The black mare, shaken out of her usual composure, trotted at the jump with a high-kneed, hackney action, her head in the air.

"Canter on. Don't hold her back."

But Kat was clinging on to her reins, shortening them desperately as she approached the jump, all her previous style forgotten.

Lightning cat-jumped, bouncing skywards in a vertical take-off, screwed in mid-air to clear the spread and pitched forward on landing to toss Kat over her shoulder.

"There," exclaimed Miss Tuke catching Lightning. "Told you that would happen. That's what you did up the hill. Hanging on to her back teeth. Up you get and try again."

Kat lay where she had fallen, face into the grass. Miss Tuke crouched down beside her.

"Winded," she said. "That's the way. Lie still for a moment. Get your breath back."

It was long minutes before Kat sat up.

"That's the spirit," encouraged Miss Tuke, helping Kat to her feet. "Up you get again."

"No!" cried Kat, but with a skilled hoist that had reunited many a fallen trekker with her pony, Miss Tuke had Kat back in the saddle.

"Canter round once or twice, then, in your own time, jump the spread and the first two jumps again."

Kat nodded, her face tight, closed in.

"And remember, let her go on at it. She'll take you over if you don't try to stop her."

"She really is scared," decided Jinny, watching as Kat rode round, turned Lightning and, white faced, clutching Lightning's mane, crouched over her withers as the mare stretched to clear the spread. Before Kat could regain control, Lightning rose like a bird over the upright. Letting go of the mane, Kat circled her and she hopped sweetly over the first two fences.

"No problem," said Miss Tuke. "Let her go on over the cross-country on Saturday and she'll take you round it. But leave her mouth alone!"

"Oh, I will," said Kat, loud with relief. "I expect she'll be one of the fastest horses there. I should think if we were competing we would be bound to win."

"Glory!" thought Jinny. "She can't possibly have forgotten that seconds ago she was scared to get on again."

Shantih jumped a clear round. Jinny just managed to catch her when she landed from the spread and stop her doing her uncontrolled tear away over the last jump.

"Could it be," queried Miss Tuke, "that some of us have been doing a little schooling?"

As they walked back to the horsebox, Miss Tuke asked Kat where she had learned to ride.

"We all go to riding lessons from school. Last term Paul discovered that Mark Lawrence's equitation centre was close to school, so I went there to ride. It is absolutely the best place, you know."

"I have heard of it," said Miss Tuke.

"But of course, who hasn't?"

Jinny hadn't but she didn't feel she needed to mention the fact.

"It was Mark who found Lightning for us. Paul wanted to buy me a really good horse so I could compete in top cross-country events, and Mark said Lightning was *the* horse for me. I expect he knew I wouldn't be bothered fighting with crazy squibs that would never be any use anyway."

"She means Shantih," thought Jinny furiously. "There

she is, having flipping well fallen off and been scared to get on and now she's being rude to me again."

"What made you want to take up cross-country?" asked Miss Tuke, before Jinny had time to say anything.

"It was Paul's idea. And mine too. Naturally I've always wanted to ride over cross-country fences."

"Plenty survive without it," said Miss Tuke. "Not like breathing."

"Oh, but I want to," said Kat, almost shouting, her voice saying one thing, her words another.

On Thursday evening they both rode round Miss Tuke's cross-country course.

"Not bad at all," praised Miss Tuke, when Kat had been taken round by Lightning with only one refusal at the spread of railway sleepers, and Jinny had gone clear and in control.

"Well done. The fences at Brandoch won't be any stiffer than those. You will both do very, very well. I shall be proud of you!"

"That will be right," said Jinny, and Miss Tuke said she meant it. It was her new policy of positive thinking.

"No more jumping. Give them a hack tomorrow morning, and you two, plus nags, are coming over here to spend the night. Sam will take the box back to his farm and collect us at seven, at the latest, on Saturday. That means you'll be up at six."

Jinny shivered at the thought of Saturday, not tomorrow but the next day; not only the cross-country but . . .

Mr. Manders was going to Stopton on Friday to stay with the Wrights. His interview was on Saturday morning. While Jinny was at Brandoch, Mr. Manders would be answering questions, trying to persuade people that they should employ him, allow him to come back to Stopton. Immediately after his interview he was phoning Finmory to let them know how he had got on. When Jinny came home from the cross-country it would all be settled. If her father had got the job, Jinny knew there was no hope. They would leave Finmory.

Jinny had asked her mother what she felt about leaving Finmory, and Mrs. Manders had replied that it would break her heart but it would be rather nice to live near a supermarket again. Mr. MacKenzie had heard that Paul Dalton had offered to buy Finmory. When Jinny had told him that they might be going back to Stopton, he had spat disgustedly and said the English were "like fleas on a deid dog, aye jumping off." So that Jinny knew he would miss them.

"But it may not happen. It's not definite."

"We'll pick you up at the usual time tomorrow," Kat said, when Jinny had unboxed Shantih and was standing by the Finmory stables waiting for Sam Marshall to drive the box away. "Can't wait to see what you're going to wear for this cross-country."

Mrs. Manders had patched and let out Jinny's original jodhpurs and done her best to clean up Jinny's hacking jacket — letting down the cuffs and moving the buttons. That was what Jinny was going to wear.

"Will it be your jeans?" mocked Kat.

"To tell you the truth," Jinny heard her own voice saying," I'm wearing my new riding clothes. I didn't want to muck them up messing around here but I'll have them on on Saturday."

The box drove away, leaving Jinny transfixed with the awfulness of what she had said.

"How could I? How could I have said that when I know I've no chance of getting new clothes. Jinny Manders, you are an idiot."

"Are you?" said Ken, passing.

"Talking to myself."

"Sign of sanity," said Ken.

"I went and told Kat I had new riding clothes for Saturday. I just went and said it! I'll need to tell her they've been stolen," and Jinny took Shantih into her box.

Ken watched while Jinny watered Shantih and tipped her feed into her trough. The Arab ate slowly, pausing between mouthfuls to gaze into space, savouring the last oat before she took another mouthful.

"Would you like new fancy dress to ride in?" Ken asked.

"Jodhs made from that thick white material," said Jinny longingly. "Black boots, a yellow polo-necked sweater, string gloves with patches between the fingers, and a proper crash cap with an orange silk to tie over it. And, although I wouldn't actually need it for Saturday, I'd love a black jacket," and Jinny twirled around at the thought.

"Light in the darkness?" asked Ken.

"Well . . . Light would be having Easter back, fit and well, Nell staying, and Dad seeing how absolutely no one with any sense would dream of leaving here. Oh, but I would love a black jacket."

"I'll buy them for you," said Ken, his slow smile lighting his eyes.

"Don't be daft. You couldn't afford them. Anyway, even if you had that much money I could never let you spend it on riding clothes for me."

"Enough of that," said Ken. "Or I won't. Inverburgh tomorrow morning. Mr. MacKenzie's going in about ten."

"But they would cost hundreds of pounds."

"What do you think I do with the cheque my dear parents send me every month? Tom won't take anything.

Even now, when he has this illusion that he is about to be bankrupt, I can't make him take anything. I spend a bit on plants, food for myself, but apart from that I am your supersonic, cheque-book-carrying millionaire."

Jinny laughed aloud at the thought of Ken having a cheque book. "But I couldn't," she said.

"Say that again and you won't get the chance. Do you or do you not want to be all posh-pawed up for Saturday?"

"Oh yes," said Jinny.

"Well then," said Ken.

The thought of boots and a black jacket took Jinny's mind off the sounds of her father packing; helped her to ignore Petra's long messages to be given to Susan Wright by Mr. Manders, which seemed to Jinny to consist of nothing but how great it would be when Petra was living in Stopton again and they would be able to see more of each other.

"How can he want to go back to Stopton?" demanded Mike, punching the cushions of the settee. "I'm not going. I'm staying here. I'll stay with Mr. MacKenzie."

"If Dad goes, we all go," said Jinny. Not long ago she would have been the same as Mike, been making desperate plans to live with Shantih in the stables. But that sort of thing was for books. It didn't happen. For real was Finmory being sold to Paul Dalton. "But it's not certain," Jinny said to Mike, offering him the only hope she had.

"I'm driving in in the morning," Mr. Manders said when he heard that Jinny and Ken were going into Inverburgh. "You can get a lift with me."

"We're going with Mr. MacKenzie," Jinny said, turning her back on her father. "Ken's arranged it."

Ken and Jinny went to the bank first, since Ken felt that shopkeepers might have doubts about accepting his cheques and that cash would save any fuss. It was an old building with a marble floor and marble pillars. Ken danced his way to the counter, a weird, maniac figure surrounded by the respectable citizens of Inverburgh who looked lifeless as sleep-walking zombies compared to Ken's lightness. They were of earth, Ken of air.

"Looks an awful lot," said Jinny, eyeing Ken's wad of notes when they emerged from the bank.

"Give it a passage, set it free," said Ken, and he tore a five pound note into tiny shreds and scattered it, confetti-like, down the wind. "We once burnt a hundred pounds. Great. Like a new element. It set you free."

Jinny, remembering Ken's Stopton friends with their strange eyes, long hair and bright, dangerous clothes, wondered who 'we' had been.

"Morrisons?" asked Ken, naming the exclusive shop that sold everything to do with horses, from pink coats to hoofpicks to made-to-measure dressage saddles.

"There's Bells and Jones," said Jinny. Bells and Jones was a huge store that had a department selling ready-made riding clothes. "It's much cheaper."

"Morrisons it is. The best. That's what money's for. To give us little treats. God takes care of all the rest."

Morrisons' heavy plate-glass door opened on to a paradise of black jackets, breeches, misty-hued tweed jackets, jodhpurs, hard hats stacked on top of each other, rows of boots, and glass counters containing stocks, cravats, ties, gloves, shirts and sweaters. In a side room were saddles and bridles, bits and stirrups and all manner of tack.

A staidly disapproving gentleman took them over to the girls' department and left them with a bright squirrel lady.

"Jinny will tell you what she wants," said Ken and sat astride an old-fashioned, wooden rocking horse to wait.

Half an hour later Jinny emerged from the fitting room.

"Okay?" she asked.

"Pow!" exclaimed Ken. "Boom! Boom! Tremendous."

Jinny was wearing a brown tweed hacking jacket, yellow polo-necked sweater, a crash cap with an orange silk tied over it, cream-coloured jodhpurs, string gloves and black rubber riding boots. She felt stiff and unreal but fantastic. Looking at her reflection in the fitting-room mirror, she had hardly known herself.

"Black jacket?" queried Ken.

"I put the temptation behind me. I need a tweed one."

"Your account, sir," said the squirrel lady discreetly, passing Ken a slip of paper.

Ken took his wad of notes out of his pocket and handed most of it to her.

Jinny wanted to say, "Are you really sure?" but she didn't. She grinned at Ken, lifting up her shoulders, laughing with pleasure. They were super clothes.

"Thanks," she said. "Thanks, thanks, thanks."

When they came out of Morrisons, Jinny clutching her parcels in both arms, there was a man walking along the pavement opposite them. His beard and the hair that ruffed his bald patch were newly shorn. He was carrying his travelling bag over one shoulder, in his other hand was a battered briefcase which Jinny hadn't seen since she'd left Stopton. He was walking smartly, eyes straight ahead. It was Mr. Manders. As they watched, he squared his shoulders and, where Jinny would have flicked back her hair, her father pushed his splayed fingers through his.

"He doesn't want to go!" exclaimed Jinny, knowing the

gesture in her bones, as Mr. Manders walked on without seeing them. "He's forcing himself to go. He doesn't want to go back to Stopton!"

"Let's hope," said Ken, "he finds it out for himself before it's too late."

CHAPTER TEN

The wind began to rise in the early evening, and by the time Jinny and Kat went up to their camp beds in one of the trekkers' bedrooms, the gale was sweeping over the moors, roaring through the pines and raging about the house.

"Don't let it rain," prayed Jinny, waking in the middle of the night, thinking of her new clothes and take-offs churned to mud. Outside, the wind howled like a banshee as it rattled windows, clawed the roof for loose slates and tested the chimney stacks. "Please," murmured Jinny and was asleep again. Next morning it buffeted the high sides of the horsebox as Sam drove them to Brandoch.

"Get that under their tails and we'll see some fun," said Miss Tuke.

"Obvious that she's not riding," thought Jinny. "Or she wouldn't be so cheerful about it."

In the box behind them Shantih and Lightning shifted uneasily. Both horses were excited by the wind. Shantih had refused to box until Miss Tuke attached a long rope to her leather head collar, threaded the rope through a fixed ring at the front of the box and pulled relentlessly, leaving Shantih no alternative but to allow herself to be drawn into the box. Lightning's eyes rolled white-rimmed and her ears zigzagged in frantic semaphore. Between her loosebox and the horsebox she had plunged and shied, flinging herself this way and that in terror at the wind.

"Up to you to give her confidence," Miss Tuke had said, taking the halter rope from Kat and loading Lightning herself. "Day like this you've got to have your wits about you. Seems to be her thing. She can't stand the wind. Still, can't expect her to be totally knitted all the time. Not with her breeding."

"Oh, I love the wind. It makes everything so much more exciting," enthused Kat. "I can't wait to be galloping over the course with the wind blowing all about me."

Kat's hands flickered in wind-blown arabesques to express her words. She smiled at Miss Tuke, her yellow eyes wide, her pink lips laughing, and her make-up as perfect as ever. But her smile was a mask covering up Kat's fear.

Sam had done Lightning for Kat, so that she was as glistening as a show horse, her tack immaculate. Jinny had scrubbed at Shantih's stained knees and hocks, sweated to groom Shantih, her jeans covering her new jodhpurs, her anorak over her yellow polo neck.

It was ten by the time they turned up the drive to Brandoch Country Club. The original stone house was surrounded by snow-cemmed extensions. To the left was a golf course, to the right paddocks hem-stitched with white posts and rails.

Sam followed signs directing horseboxes until they came to an open yard already filling up with trailers and horseboxes. From the cabin window Jinny could see the beginning of the cross-country course — red and white flags horizontal in the wind; a fallen tree trunk that was the first jump; a bulk of telegraph poles stacked solid with straw bales; then steps of two banks to a low pole perched on the edge of the world — over it and you would drop into space.

"Not fair," thought Jinny. "Too soon for a drop like that." You would still be in full view of the watchers at the start. Shantih would hardly have had time to find herself. They would still be horse and rider; separate, not yet fused into one being.

Yet Jinny shivered with anticipation. To ride the course was something positive, something real that she could do, tackle for herself, instead of the interminable waiting — waiting for the results of her father's interview, waiting to be told that they were leaving Finmory for ever.

Jinny looked round at Kat, ready to make some remark about the monstrocity of the telegraph poles, the calculated test of the banks and drop. Kat too had seen the jumps. She was staring out of the window with an expression of numbed horror on her face.

"Coffee?" offered Miss Tuke, producing flasks from a voluminous canvas bag.

"Last thing," said Jinny, and Kat shook her head.

"Green at the gills?" suggested Miss Tuke. "Hours before you have to ride, and we've to walk the course before then. Come on, have a cup. You'll need it."

Jinny wrapped her hands round the hot plastic beaker. Where was her father now? She tried to remember the details of the Stopton Town Hall that she had known so well, but could only picture red-brick walls lichened with soot, pavements pulsing with conveyor-belt crowds and the throb of traffic.

"No! No!" thought Jinny. "Don't let it happen." The idea of leaving Finmory was so impossible that in a way she couldn't really think about it. It was out of thought, pressed down where her nightmare raged. Unthinkable.

"We'll leave the nags in the box," organised Miss Tuke. "You'll keep an eye on them, won't you Sam?"

"Aye, I'll be here."

"And we'll march out and view the enemy."

Before they left the comfort of the cabin, Jinny went into the back of the box to check the horses. They were both electric to the noise of the gale against the sides of the box; rolling eyes glistered white, ears were pinned back. Lightning crashed a peevish hoof against the side of the box and strained her neck against the halter rope. Jinny held Shantih's head between her hands, smooched her face against the soft muzzle. "Win," she whispered. "We're going to beat Kat. We are."

"Bedding down for the day?" called Miss Tuke.

"They're okay," said Jinny, returning. "But I'll need plenty of time to ride Shantih in."

"Come on then," said Miss Tuke.

They jumped down from the cabin into a raging world. The wind bannered out Jinny's hair, ballooned Miss Tuke's unzipped nylon jacket, and blew Kat's silk headscarf over her face as they made their way to where the secretary was installed in a trailer.

Horses and ponies were already being ridden in. All were high with the wind. Their riders' voices, shouting against them, were cultivated with long-drawn-out vowel sounds, but all, or so it seemed to Jinny, held a note of nervous tension. When they had entered for the cross-country they had imagined a calm summer day, not this fury of the wind spirits.

Miss Tuke knew the secretary.

"Sophie!" she cried, beaming on the hook-nosed, scarlet-cheeked woman. "What a day you've picked."

"Chaos, utter chaos. Waiting to hear that some of the fences are on the move, but at least it's not raining."

"Do appreciate you fitting these two in. Both frightfully keen to have a jolly round."

"In Class Two, Junior Twelve to Sixteen Years of Age?" asked the secretary, shuffling papers.

There were three classes. Junior Under Twelve Years of Age, which was over a different course and had already started; Junior Twelve to Sixteen Years of Age, which was over a modified section of the permanent cross-country course; and Senior, over the full course.

"We've had a last-minute cancellation," said the secretary. "Would one of you take his place? It will be Number Ten. Normally we stick hors concours people — the ones who're not competing — on at the end, but it would help us keep things straight if one of you slotted in there."

"Certainly," said Miss Tuke. "Kat?"

"Oh no," said Kat swiftly. "Paul and Helen are coming to watch. I don't want to ride before they get here."

Jinny took the Number Ten tabard. Kat, the last to ride, was Number Sixteen.

They stopped outside to study the plan of the course pinned to the trailer's side, but the carefully inked tracks meant nothing to Jinny. On the plan, the banks and drop, so huge in reality, were inoffensive lines, held no relation to the solid obstacles that Jinny could see if she turned her head.

Kat asked questions about take-offs and angles of approach, tracing out the course with a well-manicured finger, putting off actually seeing the fences.

"Let's get weaving," said Miss Tuke. "I can explain things as we go round."

"Now, in our class we don't jump the whole course, do we?" questioned Kat. "Is that the bit we miss out?"

"That's it," said Miss Tuke impatiently. "It'll be clearly marked. Come on," and she strode out to the start, her green wellies marching her on as if she were a wound-up clockwork toy.

"It is such a wind," Kat said to Jinny. "Wouldn't you think they'd cancel it on a day like this? No horse could jump at its best on a day like this."

"If it was the second flood," said Jinny, "they'd fit it in before the water got too deep."

"I'm really lucky getting a chance like this. I was saying to Paul last night what a piece of luck it was fitting this in while we're staying at Hawksmoor."

"Straight forward," said Miss Tuke, clapping the fallen tree trunk that was the first obstacle.

"We'll clear that okay," squeaked Kat, her voice strained and high. "Lightning won't even know it's there."

"Fair spread over the telegraph poles. The straw bales make it quite a jump. You'll need to have them going on from the start. Not out of control, Miss Manders, but a good going canter. Try holding Lightning back and you've had it Kat."

"I shan't hold her back. Time counts, doesn't it? Why would I want to hold her back?"

Jinny thought Miss Tuke was going to tell her why, but she checked herself and stood, hands on hips, viewing the third jump.

"It's a bouncer," said Miss Tuke. "Up, up, over and drop. Too long a stride and they'll try to take both steps in one, and then you're in trouble for the drop. Steady control. Ride straight at it and they'll take you over."

"Thank goodness there's a decent jump that can be seen from the start," said Kat. "Paul should get some idea of how good Lightning is when he sees me take her over those two."

"Puke and double puke," thought Jinny.

On the far side of the drop, the land dipped then rose again to give a level run-in to a low white gate. Once over the gate, they had left the field behind them and were into woodland. The track wound through trees, the going treacherous with roots and slippery with fallen leaves.

"Take a breather here. I don't mean have a picnic, but let them settle into their canter. You're not here to win. You're only aim is to get round."

"I'm here to win," thought Jinny. "To beat Kat."

"Oh, but Paul expects me to win. He always . . ."

Jinny stopped listening; she was thinking about her father, knowing that his interview might be over. Already he might have phoned home. Her mother, Petra and Mike might know if he had got the job. The pit of leaving Finmory opened at her feet.

She plodded on, vaguely aware of impossibly high jumps — poles into a dew pond, barrels to be jumped downhill, wattles lashed solidly to a wire fence standing black against the skyline, and a strange 'W' fence that Jinny only thought about after they had passed it. She could see no way of jumping it. She opened her mouth to ask Miss Tuke, but the barrier of Kat's high, nervous, conceited chatter made her close it again without speaking. By the time they reached the fence they would be going so fast that, even if she did know where she intended to take off, it would make little difference to Shantih.

Jinny wondered what Ken would do if they went to Stopton. She didn't think he would stay with them. Go his own way? She had been too afraid of his answer to risk asking him.

"Did you see that, Jinny?" shouted Miss Tuke.

"Yes," said Jinny, not even knowing what she meant.

"Nearly home," encouraged Miss Tuke, as they walked along a lovely stretch of galloping turf then turned sharply to the left across a corner of woodland, over a turfed wall and out again into the fields around the Country Club.

There was another jump of poles and straw, sloped railway sleepers over a ditch, and a last jump of heavy timber posts and rails.

"Well within the scope of both your nags. A walk-over for Lightning."

"She'll wonder why she's being asked to jump such tiny things," said Kat, laughing, but somehow her laughter got stuck, stayed too long on a high note of hysteria.

"If you lose your bearings – red flags on the right, white flags on the left. RED RIGHT. And remember, it is all fun," said Miss Tuke. "Now, who's for the loo before we unbox the horses?"

As they passed their horsebox, Sam leaned from the cabin window, shouting against the wind to tell them that Mr. and Mrs. Dalton had arrived and would see them at the Club.

Paul and Helen were sitting in a corner of the clubhouse, Paul swelling out over a window seat, while Helen perched on a stool opposite him. The table between them was half filled with empty glasses.

"Have a drink," Paul called to Miss Tuke. "Come and sit down. Take the weight off the wellies."

Kat and Jinny had changed in the cloakroom. Jinny had her sweater on, her number over her sweater, her new jodhpurs and boots. All were satisfactorily correct.

"Quick nip," said Miss Tuke, accepting a whisky. "Then we've got to get the gees out."

Paul turned to Kat. Behind his thick lenses his pale blue

eyes were liquid, undefined. With his loose face and blubber lips he appeared a Dr. Who creation.

"Well, did you manage to view the jumps without fainting?"

"It is some course," said Kat. "I can't wait to be riding round it."

"That's my little Olympic gold medallist. You'll show them," mocked Paul, and Jinny saw Helen pick up her glass, tip the clear liquid down her open mouth as if she were swallowing medicine, while Miss Tuke looked up at Paul in sharp surprise.

"You'll let them see how to do it. You're not scared of a few jumps, are you?"

Bright patches burnt on Kat's cheeks.

"Of course I'm not scared," she said coolly and tried to laugh, but the sound was embarrassingly closer to crying than laughing. "Why should I be scared when you bought me such a super horse? Lightning will be the best horse here today."

"Don't need to tell me that. Where do you think the money came from to buy her? Out of the nowhere? Kat, sweetie, grow up. Paul paid for her."

"Who's for drinkie poos?" chirruped Helen, but Paul was not to be diverted.

"I bought her for you because I know you're a winner," Paul continued. "You knew that too, didn't you Miss Tuke? Minute you saw Kat sitting on that horse, you knew she was a future gold medallist? Eh?"

"Oh, Paul, don't," twitched Helen.

"Took her to Mark Lawrence's place. Paid top prices to get her some decent tuition. Oh, beautiful place, everything the best. None of your pony-trekking rubbish there."

Miss Tuke fixed him with a calculating eye, and Jinny could see her doubling her charges for organising Kat's first cross-country ride.

" They brought out a horse for her, magnificent beast. And what happened, Kat? You wouldn't get on it would you? Not your kind of horse. So they bring out this white carthorse, sit her up on it and. . ."

Paul threw back his head, mocking laughter sludging out from between beer-speckled lips.

"You couldn't make it move, could you Kat. Talk about a pea having hysterics on a mountain! Laugh? I nearly ruptured myself."

"Come along, Kat," said Miss Tuke. "You'll show them today," and she stood up.

"Just a minute," insisted Paul. "Let me tell you about her climbing. Sent her on a course to the best climbing instructor I could find. And after three days, back she comes — expelled. With a letter in her pocket asking me to pay for the helicopter they'd had to hire to get her off the rock face. Stuck there screaming, weren't you Kat?"

"Well, that's nothing to be ashamed off," said Jinny loudly. "I wouldn't go climbing for anything. I'm terrified of heights."

"Too much," said Miss Tuke. "Come along, or they'll be calling Jinny's number while we're still pigging it in here."

"See you at the start, darling," called Helen. "What time?"

"About an hour," answered Miss Tuke, hurrying Kat and Jinny out. "Must pop into the loo again," she said. "Sam will help you unload. Be with you in a jiff," and Jinny was left alone with Kat.

There was an awkward silence. Jinny couldn't think what to say when she had just been forced to listen to Kat being humiliated like that.

"He's quite a character, isn't he?" Kat said. "I told you, he is so keen for me to win. Pity your parents couldn't be here today, but then I suppose they'll have other things on their minds. Your dad's to let Paul know tomorrow, hasn't he?"

Jinny hadn't known. Finmory sold. Final decisions to be made when her father came home tomorrow. The clock at the Club doorway said twelve-thirty. If it was correct, Mr. Manders' interview would be over. He would have phoned home. Jinny closed her mind against the thought. She shut out Kat and Paul and everything except the cross-country course and Shantih.

CHAPTER ELEVEN

"Number Ten," called a steward. "You're next," and Jinny rode Shantih towards the start.

The chestnut was tight as a closed spring. Under the saddle, Jinny could feel Shantih's back, hard and resisting, so that she couldn't sit down, was perched where Shantih chose to carry her. Even wearing her martingale, Shantih's neck seemed far too close to Jinny's face. Her new crash cap dug into her ears, and her new boots felt clumsy moon-walkers.

"Steady Shantih, steady," Jinny pleaded, as a force of wind hit them out of the storm, making Shantih surge forward, fighting, mouth braced against the bit for freedom.

Already Jinny's arms and shoulders ached with trying to hold Shantih back. There had been no point in trying to ride her in. Shantih's blood raged wild as the storm. Her clarion whinny rang across the field and, from where Miss Tuke was lungeing Kat, Lightning answered.

"It's only the wind," Miss Tuke had told Kat, as Lightning reared straight up, goggle eyes rolling, nostrils red pitted, mane heraldic, all her schooling forgotten. "Let's get her settled." And Miss Tuke had led Kat away to lunge her in a corner of the field.

Thumb on her stopwatch, the starter looked round for the next competitor.

"For real," thought Jinny. "My first real cross-country. Red on my right," she thought. "Red on my right." For, once past the obstacles she could see, Jinny had no idea of the course.

"Ready? You go on my whistle."

Shantih's forefeet were lances. The power her quarters drove through her body was held in the muscles of her chest, her dancing, violent forelegs and Jinny's hands.

"Three, two, one," counted down the starter. Her whistle was shrill above the wind.

Jinny didn't feel Shantih clear the log, hardly felt her rise over the telegraph poles. Not until they dropped over the pole and came sounding up to the white gate was she really aware of anything. Shantih took off, strides before the gate, and they sailed out into the trees.

"Too fast, too fast," Jinny shouted at her, standing in her stirrups, riding low as a jockey over Shantih's withers, her knuckles braced against Shantih's neck. "Steady. Whoa." At this speed they would only need to touch one of the fixed fences and Shantih would go tail over head, Jinny sprawling into space before she whammed into the ground.

Jinny dug her heels down hard, knees locked to the saddle she fought to establish some control. Furiously Shantih shook her head to free herself from the irritation of the bit; reaching her neck, demanded more rein. In the wood the wind was a chained Titan, tearing the trees down to free itself.

"You'll kill us," muttered Jinny through clenched teeth, knowing that once they were out of the woodland they would be jumping again. Despite her gloves, Jinny felt the reins beginning to slide through her fingers. "Shantih," she cried, and the sound of her own voice burst the bubble of rising fear. She had sounded like Kat.

Jinny grinned, relaxed, began to enjoy herself. She

forgot Miss Tuke's warnings. Shantih's speed was, as it had always been, delight and joy, setting Jinny free.

At the edge of the woodland, the ground sloped down to a stream with a pole beyond it. Shantih cleared both with a reaching leap.

"Red right, red right," chanted Jinny. She was completely lost. Only the visible track, the wind-strained red flags seen out of the corner of her right eye, and the sprinkling of spectators, gave her any idea of where to go.

They were galloping over moorland grass now, over a jump of tyres where Shantih spooked and soared, fearing their crouching, animal shape, then over the wattles lashed to the wire fence. The dew pond rose in spray about them as Shantih flipped over the poles in front of it. The mud caught at her feet. Jinny felt her peck, regain her balance and fight to free herself before she breasted on to firm ground again.

Rising up the next slope, Shantih was still full of galloping but her first fury was dying down. Three strides over the lip of the hill was a row of barrels. Caught off balance, Jinny let the reins slip through her fingers, leaned back in the saddle, her legs stuck forward. She landed on the other side minus a stirrup with her arms wrapped round Shantih's neck, and stayed there until she reached level ground.

Once on the flat she found her stirrup, gathered up loops of rein just in time to see the 'W' jump bearing down on her.

"Jump it! Jump it!" she yelled, driving Shantih at it without the slightest idea of how Shantih could take it. Shantih skidded to a halt, and Jinny saw the two outer bars of the 'W' as a double. "Of course," she shouted. "Stupid girl," and was aware, for the first time, of the jump stewards at the sides of the fences.

Jinny turned Shantih. Keeping her straight between hands and knees, she cantered her at the 'W' again. This time Shantih took off exactly where Jinny wanted her to, so that they bounced neatly, together, through the in and out.

"One refusal," thought Jinny and urged Shantih on. She must have no time faults.

Jinny's eye caught sight of a brush jump to her right, red and white poles crossed in front of it.

"Nearly missed that one," she thought as, just in time, she checked Shantih and swung her round to face the jump. Shantih took one stride and cat jumped. As she galloped on, Jinny half heard someone shouting behind her but it was no concern of hers.

The next fence appeared to be a row of thatched cottages. The front of the jump was painted with windows and doors, the top thatched.

"Don't even remember those," thought Jinny in disgust, as Shantih shot skywards and Jinny clutched mane to stay with her.

At a steady pace, Shantih galloped on through an open gateway and along a broad track between rows of beeches. As far as Jinny could see, there were no spectators. She might have been out for a ride by herself. The beat of Shantih's hoofs, the moan of the wind in the beeches, rose in joy through Jinny's being. The post and rails that barred their way seemed hardly higher than one of her own jumps in Mr. MacKenzie's field. Yet Shantih, of her own accord , steadied herself before she took off, and again Jinny had to clutch at handfuls of mane to stay with her.

The track curved left. Lost in their speed, Jinny vaguely

remembered a stretch of turf she had walked along with Miss Tuke and Kat. She thought she should have reached it by now.

A massive great pile of timber — tree trunks roped together — loomed up in front of them.

"Surely we aren't meant to jump that," thought Jinny. It was the height of a double-decker bus, the height of a house. Monstrous it rushed at them. "Glory. No!" And almost Jinny checked Shantih but stopped herself in time.

She felt Shantih sink down on her quarters, jump from her hocks. Salmon leaping up a weir, Shantih sought upwards. She banked on air to twist herself over the bulk of the timber and poured downward. Crouching over her withers, mane in both hands, feet jammed in the stirrups, Jinny endured. She felt Shantih peck on landing, stagger, so that Jinny thought she must come down, then save herself and gallop on.

Jinny threw her arms round Shantih's neck, shouting her praise. Yet, strangely, there was no one at the timber jump to record her triumph. But it didn't matter, Shantih had cleared it, was Horse.

Checking on her flags, red on her right, Jinny cantered Shantih out of the trees, hopped over a turfed wall and was back into the fields surrounding the Club. The last three jumps seemed nothing compared to the timber pile — more telegraph poles, sloped railway sleepers over a ditch, and a last jump of post and rails flowed beneath them and they were cantering through the finish.

Jinny threw herself from Shantih's back, ran at her side on lally legs that would hardly hold her. As Shantih slowed to a walk, Miss Tuke was beside her.

"Well?" she asked.

Jinny's face shone with sweat and glory. "It was super,"

she said. "Absolutely terrific. Shantih was super. Super. She only stopped once."

"Very good," praised Miss Tuke. "Didn't want to say too much in front of Kat but it wasn't the easiest course. Better get back to her. Almost her turn."

"She'd better watch out for the timber fence," warned Jinny, but Miss Tuke had gone.

"Oh, horse," said Jinny, as Shantih butted her head against her arm. "You were the utter MOST. Dear Shantih. Dear splendiferous horse."

She loosened Shantih's girths, lifted her saddle and began to walk her back to the box to sponge her down as Miss Tuke had told her to do, when she heard Paul Dalton's voice.

"Being led about are we? Feel safer that way, do we? Could have bought you a donkey if you'd let me know sooner."

Paul, with Helen clinging to his arm, was standing close to the start. His voice was carried by the wind as he jeered at Kat.

"We'll wait just a minute," Jinny told Shantih, and walked closer to where Miss Tuke's hand on Lightning's rein prevented her from rearing. "Just to see her start."

Kat, Number Sixteen, was the last to ride.

"Sixteen," called the steward. "Ready to go?"

"Good luck," shouted Jinny. The ecstasy of her ride had wiped her mind clear of anything as petty as beating Kat. "Let her gallop on and you'll easily make it."

Kat turned her head at the sound of Jinny's voice. Her mouth was a hard, set line, her nostrils tight, her flesh drawn in against her bones, her terror visible for all to see.

Miss Tuke released her hold on Lightning's bit ring, and the black horse, wind crazed, reared upright.

"She's coming over," thought Jinny in a clench of panic, as Lightning touched down again and Kat rode her to the start.

"Now let's see you blooming win something," yelled Paul. "Don't be nervous, helicopters are standing by, ready to air-lift you over the jumps."

"Three, two, one," shouted the starter, as spectators turned to stare at Paul, drawing away from his disturbance.

Jinny heard the whistle, saw Kat clutch up her reins as Lightning plunged forward. Hardly breaking her stride, Lightning cleared the tree trunk, came at the telegraph poles as if she were a steeplechaser, checked, soared, and landed far out beyond the jump. Kat was a helpless passenger as the black horse thundered to the banks, propped to a halt, then leapt both banks from a standstill. Rag-doll limp, Kat sprawled on air and fell in front of the pole on top of the banks. Lightning refused the drop and rearing round, leapt down and back to the start. Miss Tuke caught her, while spectators and officials crowded round Kat, and Paul's laughter blurted out over them all.

A tweedy mother brought Kat back to Miss Tuke.

"Nasty toss," she said. "But no bones broken. Rather nervous? Not to worry. 'Next time,' I always tell mine. 'There'll always be a next time.'"

Still snorting with laughter, Paul staggered across to them.

"Brilliant! Brilliant! Congratulations," he sneered. "That's the way to do it. This cross-country business is going to be your thing, I can see that. A natural. That's what you are, my dear, a natural disaster," and Paul tipped Kat's chin back, forcing her to look at him as she shrank away.

A bruise was spreading over her left cheekbone, and her

expensive clothes were muddied from her fall. If she had been afraid of riding Lightning, her face, without its usual mask, showed she was equally afraid of Paul as he stepped closer to her, forcing her to retreat. "As usual," said Paul, "you have managed to be outstanding or outfalling. Falling out? Falling off? As always. Oh, most impressive with your big talk before the event, and then this."

"Not here, dear," Helen twittered, plucking at Paul's arm. "Let's go back to the Club. We can see Kat later."

"Sometimes I think you do it on purpose," raged Paul, shaking himself free from Helen. "You do it to show me up. I spend thousands on you, and then this. You enjoy it, don't you? Don't you?"

Jinny stared at Kat and Paul, longing to escape from this involvement that had nothing to do with her, and yet, despite herself, drawn to it. She stood mesmerised.

"'Oh, Paul,'" sneered Paul, mimicking Kat. "'I do want to ride at Badminton. I do, I do. I know I could win.'"

Still Kat cowered in front of him, allowing him to beat her down with his words.

"As if it's a play," Jinny thought. "They both have parts and they've got to stick to them."

"What's the next thing going to be? Back to climbing? Going to tackle the Chimney next, eh? Isn't that what you were telling me last night. 'Oh Paul, I know I could climb the rocks at Finmory. I could. I could. I know I could.'"

Jinny saw Kat's face change, the naked fear that had cried from her was covered up. Her features re-formed, her nostrils relaxed, her lips thickened, her yellow eyes that had been staring at Paul lost their glazed terror and flirted up at him. She lifted off her crash cap and shook out her straight fall of hair.

"Goodness," she said, her voice following Paul's mockery was so similar that, for a second, Jinny hardly realised that it was Kat speaking. "Of course I could climb the Chimney. I know exactly how I would do it. When Lightning's so fast there'd be no danger in it at all. I'd gallop out when the tide was low enough, climb the Chimney and gallop back long before there was any danger of the tide coming back in and trapping me. Of course I could do it."

Kat's words broke the spell that had bound Jinny to Kat and Paul. She jerked back to herself, was aware of Shantih's reins looped over her arm while Shantih grazed about her; of other people staring at Paul, and Miss Tuke still holding Lightning.

"And that is enough of that sort of nonsense," declared Miss Tuke, pulling herself together as Jinny had done. "Let's get Jinny's nag seen to. And you, my lady, are riding Lightning back to the box."

"Of course," said Kat and smiled, gracious, plastic, at Miss Tuke.

"As if nothing had happened," thought Jinny as she led Shantih over to the box.

Jinny and Miss Tuke took off Shantih's saddle and bridle, sponged her down, covered her with Miss Tuke's sweat rug.

"Lead her around for a bit," said Miss Tuke, handing Shantih's rope to Jinny. "She must be fit all right. Don't suppose you dawdled round the course, and she's not much bothered."

"It's because she's an Arab," said Jinny, unable to resist the chance.

Jinny led Shantih through the parked boxes to an empty part of the field, where she walked her up and down.

"That's her," Jinny heard two official-looking ladies say, and then they came cantering across to her.

"Do you know what you did?"

"Did?" demanded Jinny.

"You jumped part of the senior course."

"Those tree trunks?" said Jinny.

"And the cottages and a post and rails."

"They did seem," said Jinny, thinking about it, "a bit higher than the rest of the jumps."

"Afraid you'd be disqualified if you'd been competing, but a pretty good show. Wouldn't mind having that combination in my Pony Club team. Where do you live?"

"Finmory," said Jinny, and realised as she said it, it might no longer be true. "I'm here with Miss Tuke."

"Oh yes. Bit far for rallies. Come back next year, jump the correct course and you'll be the winner."

"There won't be a next year," thought Jinny, drowning in the certainty that her father had got the job, that they were all going back to Stopton.

"No point in hanging about," Miss Tuke said, when Shantih had dried off. "Got to get back. Fix my beadies on the new bunch of trekkers."

Seeing the full haynet, Shantih went willingly into the box to join Lightning.

In the cabin they ate rolls, biscuits and coffee, all provided by Miss Tuke. Then Sam, light foot inside his heavy farmer's boots, shuddered life through the inert mass of the box and drove it away from Brandoch.

Every turn of the box's wheels took Jinny closer to Finmory; closer to the moment when she would walk into the kitchen and know, before her mother spoke, whether they were going to go back to Stopton or not.

Kat's high-pitched descriptions of Paul's discos filled the cabin. Miss Tuke folded her arms, settled her chins and slept. Jinny stared out of the window, filled with the icy knowledge that she was being driven closer and closer to where she would have to listen to the words she dreaded. "He's got the job." Sitting in the cabin, Jinny's feet felt the ground at Finmory's back door, the handle turned in her fingers and she heard her mother's voice.

They dropped Miss Tuke first.

"I doubt if I'll have time for any more lessons," Kat said, "but I do want to thank you for all your trouble. Paul has settled with you, for Jinny and myself?"

"Look here, my lass," said Miss Tuke. "Take my advice. Sell that horse. She's far too good for you. Buy yourself a reliable pony and give up all notion of eventing. It is not for you."

"Goodness," exclaimed Kat. "Because I came off today? Oh, once I get Lightning back to Mark, he'll soon sort things out, and you saw for yourself how keen Paul is for me to do really well. How disappointed he is if I don't."

Miss Tuke put her hand on Kat's shoulder in a clumsy gesture of affection. "Oh well," she said, and shouting good-bye she bustled away.

"I don't suppose we'll see each other again," Kat said, when Jinny was standing outside Finmory stables holding Shantih. "Life will be rather hectic for you, won't it? Packing up and going back to Stopton."

"Thank you for the lessons," said Jinny, because she had never thanked Paul. "And the entry money for today."

"Such a pity Miss Tuke couldn't do more to improve you both. Shantih is such a tearaway."

As Sam craned up the ramp, it blocked out Lightning's sleek face, her twitching ears, sweet muzzle. It was too late for Jinny to say any of the things she had been saving up to say to Kat on their last meeting; to tell her what she thought of her. And anyway, she didn't really feel them now. No longer knew what she felt about Kat.

"Bye," Kat shouted, waving from the cabin window. "Bye. I'll look after Finmory for you. Bye."

"The end," thought Jinny. "Even after today! If I'd let Shantih down the way she let down Lightning I'd have been in the depths for weeks."

But it was all over. Didn't matter any more. She led Shantih into her box, watered her, groomed her, praised her and left her with a feed and a haynet.

"When I come back I'll know."

Slowly Jinny walked left foot, right foot through the garden, across the yard. In minutes it might all be taken from her. The Daltons would live here. Finmory would be theirs.

Jinny opened the kitchen door. Her mother looked up from her ironing and Jinny knew.

"He's got the job," said Mrs. Manders.

CHAPTER TWELVE

Jinny lay flat on her bed, her face buried into the fold of her arm to muffle the sound of her crying. She sobbed her heart out, gulping sobs that rose from the core of her being and shook her whole body with their intensity. She couldn't leave Finmory. Couldn't ever. She loved it too much. She had lived too long in this freedom ever to go back to Stopton. But this was what they were going to do to her, take her back to Stopton. She had grown so used to the open skies, the sweep of the moors and this freedom of sea and sand. All her living was here. Riding Shantih, Jinny had made moorland and bay her own, more so than anyone else in her family. Only Ken in his far walking had shared this kingdom with her. How could she take Shantih to live in a riding school field, to trot along suburban streets, to think a ten minute gallop the most wonderful ride?

"They can't," she wept. "Can't take me away. Can't!" but Jinny knew they would.

Her mother had brought coffee and sandwiches up to her and, sitting on the end of Jinny's bed, had tried to comfort her, promising a family discussion when Mr. Manders came home. Jinny hadn't been able to look at her. She knew her mother's words were false, were only a way of telling Jinny not to make a fuss.

"Please," Jinny had muttered. "Leave me alone. I just want to be by myself. Don't come back tonight. I'm okay. I just don't want to see anyone."

When her mother had gone, Jinny had stood in front of the Red Horse, tears pouring from eyes and nose, her face mottled with crying. But the Red Horse was only a crude painting, without power.

"They'll paint over the Horse," thought Jinny and flung herself back on to her bed, engulfed in hopelessness.

Jinny had no idea how long she had been crying in her room before she remembered that Shantih was still in her box. Jumping guiltily to her feet, Jinny scrubbed at her face with the sodden remains of a box of paper handkerchiefs, changed out of her new jodhs into jeans and sandshoes, pushed her hair back behind her ears and went out to Shantih. No one saw her go through the kitchen or across the garden and down to the stables.

The warm summer evening was toning to grey, the wind that had died down in the late afternoon was rising again. It blew in from the water, whipping back Jinny's hair, lifting white crests on the far line of the sea.

"Late," screamed Shantih, crashing her box door with furious forefeet. "Far too late. Where have you been?"

"Forgot about you," admitted Jinny, reaching for a halter. "Dad's got the job. We're going. Going back to Stopton."

Shantih tossed her head. Her white face was luminous in the gloom, her mane dark flames. She pushed her head impatiently into the halter, charged past Jinny, trying to push first through the box door.

"Ride her down to the bay," said the thought in Jinny's head that was against all the advice that Jinny had ever read on how to treat a cross-country horse after an event. It was the thing that you must never do. But this was Shantih. The time a time of desperation.

Jinny fetched her saddle and bridle, still sticky with sweat, tacked Shantih up and led her out. She sprang into the saddle, sent her cantering along the track to the sea.

Jinny rode through a world that was no longer hers. So

often she had ridden to the bay to lose herself in its immensity of sea and sky, alone on Shantih; felt her human isolation fade away, known herself to be part of the weaving of sea and sky, of gulls and living ocean.

Shantih's hoofs clattered over the bulwark of stones, her ears sharp, her dish face poking eagerly forward. She adventured on.

The tide was far out but coming in fast, and Jinny rode over the sand to the far, iridescent line of the sea. From beyond the sea's horizon the wind drummed up grey cloud kings that rose in ponderous gravity, bowing towards Jinny, arching over her.

This would be the Daltons' bay now. They would be where Jinny was, this view their view, Jinny's kingdom theirs. Tears dried on Jinny's cheeks as they fell.

Suddenly Shantih stiffened, her head shot up, eyes bursting from their sockets she stared out to sea. Her thunderous whinny shook her whole body. Beyond the cliffs to Jinny's left a horse answered, and from behind the rocks came Lightning — reins and halter rope dangling about her knees, her stirrups flying from her saddle. She came charging towards them, through cascades of foam sent up by her plunging hoofs. She came straight up to Shantih, blown nostrils scarlet as she snorted, high-stepping around them, then galloped on. Dark crescents flowed from her hoofs as she high-tailed it over the sand to the boulders and on in the direction of Mr. MacKenzie's farm.

It happened so quickly, was so close to Jinny's dream world that, but for the palpable hoofprints, Jinny might have believed that she had dreamt it all. But the hoofprints were there.

For Lightning to have come galloping from beyond the cliffs could mean only one thing — Kat had ridden her there, ridden her out to the Chimney intending to climb it and ride Lightning back; that somehow Lightning had escaped. Already the tide was too far in for Kat to walk safely back to the bay. She would have to be rescued. Mr. MacKenzie had a boat but he kept it in one of his outhouses, hardly ever used it. Even if he was at home, it would take too long to launch it and row out to Kat. By that time she might have tried to swim back, and Jinny knew that even for a strong swimmer that was impossible, the current at the headland would carry them relentlessly out to sea. If she rode home and tried to phone for help, it would take hours to reach Kat. Jinny had no idea how soon the incoming tide would fill the Chimney, how soon Kat, clinging to the rock, would be swept off and drowned.

There was one chance. It might still be possible to ride Shantih out to the Chimney and rescue Kat. Once she had thought of it, Jinny knew that she would have to do it. If she didn't and Kat was drowned she could never be her true self again. That she might have saved Kat and had chosen not to try would lay death fingers on the rest of her life; would come between her and the paper when she tried to draw; between her and Shantih when she tried to ride.

But fear held Jinny paralysed. The terror of the black rock shivered her spine. Fear of the moment when she could hold on no longer and the sea would suck her down. Fear that through her actions Shantih would be harmed.

"You've got to do it," said the voice in Jinny's head. "Got to. You've no choice. It's Kat's life. Do it now." But she could not force herself to move.

Shantih plunged, wanting to follow Lightning. Released, Jinny turned her to the sea, sent her on towards the cliffs.

Shouting her bannering words of power — "Shantih! Finmory! Keziah!" — into the wind, Jinny galloped through the waves, forcing her horse on, knowing that every moment was vital.

"Maybe I'm wrong," thought Jinny. "Maybe Kat isn't here at all."

As she rounded the headland the water was over Shantih's knees, breaking over her chest. Jinny felt the sucking drag of the undertow. It was far deeper than when she had ridden back from the Chimney with Kat.

"Go on! Go on!" Jinny yelled, forcing her horse on towards the cliffs, and there, standing on the rocks in front of the Chimney, waves crashing about her, was Kat.

"Jinny!"she screamed. " Jinny! How did you know I was here? I thought I'd drown. I thought no one would ever hear me. I thought . . ." and Kat grabbed frantically at Jinny's arm.

Jinny tried to pull Kat up to sit behind her, but Kat's clinging terror tightened on her, dragging her down.

"Spring!" Jinny yelled. "Don't pull at me. Spring up."

Shantih plunged away and Kat fell back.

"This time spring when I pull. Now!" Jinny fought to keep a grip on Kat's arm, to stay strong in the saddle, to brace herself against Kat. Sprawling, digging with elbows and toes, Kat squirmed up to cling behind Jinny.

"Saw Lightning," Jinny told her as she swung Shantih round, through the deepening water, to gallop back.

Hauling Kat up had taken longer than Jinny dared to realise. They had almost reached the headland when Jinny felt Shantih lose her footing, surge forward, leaping, springing, thrusting through the water to find it again.

"It's too deep," Jinny yelled, warning Kat. "She'll have to swim. Hold on to me. Hold on!" And with a last, frantic eruption, Shantih was swimming.

Jinny had often swum Shantih in the bay. She knew the moment well, when her horse sank beneath her and the swell of the sea lifted her from the saddle; the moment when she threw her arms round Shantih's neck, twisted her hands into Shantih's mane and half swam, was half carried along, beside her. But that swimming had been in calm seas, under blue, summer skies. Then there had been no limpet Kat.

The shock of the water tore the breath from Jinny as she clung desperately to Shantih. They were no longer carried above the clawing hunger of the sea but had slipped down into it. The horizon was above them. The numbing, icy mass of the water was a living being that slapped and sucked and tore at them with thousands of clawing fingers. The rolling breakers that came riding in, sweeping Shantih off course, were a wolf pack pulling her down.

Shantih's face was close to Jinny's own. It was a face from a Stubbs anatomical drawing, as if some subtle covering had been removed, leaving Shantih's face a peeled death mask, a weird thing, held above the fury of the sea by the unseen mass of her body. Shantih's huge eyes blazed from it like lanterns, burned with silent terror.

Kat, knotted on to Jinny's back, began to scream with a high, piercing hysteria.

"Sing!" Jinny yelled, gulping burning sea water, and she shouted against the waves, "Mine eyes have seen the glory of the coming of the Lord."

She could only remember the one line but it was enough. She shouted it over and over again. It held her to her own centre, stopped Kat's screams from reaching her. For the screaming was part of the sea, part of the force that murmured of sleep, sought to spread them out into a myriad fragments, to lose their identity, to become part of wind and water. To scream was to lose her hold on Shantih and drown.

They rounded the headland to see Finmory Bay a distant curve of sand, the sea filling it. Far beyond them white-crested waves rode in to the shore.

Jinny's hope sank. She had been so certain that once they were in sight of the bay they would be safe, but now she saw the reaching expanse of sea still to be crossed. Shantih too saw the land and renewed her efforts to reach it, giving Jinny new hope.

"Nearly!" Jinny cried. "Nearly there, Shantih. On you go! On you go!" And she felt her horse straining to obey her.

The night was folding in on them, light coming now from the dancing, pulsing face of the water.. But soon, soon they must be on firm land again.

"Not long," Jinny cried to Kat. "We're nearly there!" But looking out to the bay, it didn't seem true. Almost it seemed that it was further away. Yet how could that be when Shantih was swimming so strongly towards it?

Forcing her numb body, Jinny looked round, searching for the cliffs of the headland that should be behind them now. When they had been swimming from the Chimney to the headland they had been close to the cliffs, but now the line of the cliffs to Jinny's right seemed to be as far away as the shore and, incredibly, ahead of them. Jinny couldn't think how this could be, for all the time Shantih had been swimming strongly towards land. They were past the headland. They must be closer to land.

And then, with a deadly certainty, she knew. The current that made it impossible for anyone to swim back from the Chimney was carrying them out to sea. Even Shantih wasn't strong enough to swim against it. At the same instant, Jinny felt Shantih tiring, as if her consciousness of their danger had flowed from her to her horse.

"Dead," thought Jinny. "We'll all be dead. All drowned," and Kat began to scream again.

"But it can't be," raged the voice in Jinny's head. "Not us. Not me. I've to go on living for years and years. I've still to paint and draw. Haven't even started. Not me. Not me."

Now that she had realised what was happening, Jinny could feel Shantih being carried further and further from the shore. Jinny's nightmare that had lain dormant for days enveloped her. Was real. Was now. Here was no place to stand. The sea was the evil force that would drag her down, tear her from all she loved. Easter was dead, Jinny had failed to save her; Nell had gone; Finmory taken from her; and Jinny was powerless. There was nothing she could do against it.

Weary now, Shantih was being carried more surely out to sea. The screaming burnt in Jinny's ears as it had in her dream. Its noise carried her away.

But it was not her screaming. She was not screaming. It was Kat that screamed.

"Shut up!" swore Jinny. "Shut your screaming mouth. Shut it!"

And there rose in Jinny a force that said she would not drown. Would not allow her beloved Shantih to drown because of Kat Dalton.

"Go on!" she shouted. "On you go, Shantih, on you go!" And, as if she rode at the timber jump, Jinny gathered herself together for the leap. "No!" she shouted against Kat's screaming. "No!" She would not allow Shantih, her horse of air, to die in an element so foreign to her. It was not right. Not fair.

"Not fair! Not fair!" Jinny shouted through frozen lips,

as if this fairness that she knew in her innermost self was the Law, could not be broken. It was the word of the Red Horse, and Jinny stood before the Horse, felt it come raging from the confines of the wall, burning through the dark, come molten-hoofed over the water.

Shantih raised her head, and the Horse was all about them.

"Not fair to let Shantih drown."

The power of the Horse charged through Shantih. She broke from the current that had drawn her seawards. Jinny felt the incoming tide lift them towards the land. Behind them the sea wolves snarled, fell back defeated.

Wearily, Shantih swam on towards the shore. Jinny's being was ice cold. She could not feel her arms that held her to Shantih; could not feel Kat clinging to her. Could hardly see.

Shantih felt the sea bed under her feet, stood, staggered, pitching forward on aching legs that would hardly hold her. Somehow, grappled on to mane and saddle, Jinny and Kat were dragged towards land. Somehow they reached the shallows and fell on to the sand. They lay where they had fallen, Kat still clutching on to Jinny.

"Home," Jinny thought, fighting off the desire to sleep. "Finmory. Home."

She pulled herself up by Shantih's leg and stirrup, dragging Kat with her. And staggering, falling, sleep walking, they made their way to Shantih's field, where Jinny fought the buckles of saddle and bridle to let the tack fall from her exhausted horse. She threw her arms round Shantih's neck, felt her horse warm, living, vital. By now they might all have been drowned, the living bulk of Shantih sea roiled. "Oh, horse, horse," Jinny sighed.

Arms round each other, Kat and Jinny made their slow way to Finmory. The house was in darkness.

"That you, Jinny?" called her mother's voice.

Jinny went into the hall, clung on to the bannister.

"Yes" she shouted. "I went down to see Shantih."

"Are you all right?"

"Yes. I'm going to have a cup of coffee and then I'm going to bed."

"Don't be long then. It's late," and Jinny heard the bed springs as her mother turned over.

She went upstairs, climbing slowly to her own room. Standing in front of the Red Horse, she felt its power like the sun's energy. She had intended to say some kind of thank you, some acknowledgement that the Horse had saved their lives. But it was not necessary. The power of the Red Horse was in Jinny herself; had always been there, waiting for Jinny to discover it.

Jinny collected bath towels and dry clothes and took them down to Kat. She opened up the Aga, and they changed and tried to warm themselves but couldn't stop chittering — teeth chattering; shaking, shuddering — both knowing they had nearly drowned, so close to being dead, so very close. They had been where there was nothing but flux and flow, no fixed hold, all motion. Had been there and survived.

"I know," Jinny said, and went through to find her father's brandy, poured out two glasses and took them back to Kat. They sipped it, the spirit firing their blood, bringing warmth and life back to sea-cold flesh.

Jinny made bread and butter and heated a tin of tomato soup. They sat over the Aga eating it, not speaking. Thoughts flashed through Jinny's mind and were gone — the moment when the Red Horse had infused Shantih with strength and brought them to the shore; the timber jump; Kat; her father taking the job in Stopton; leaving Finmory;

and even the thought of Finmory being sold flowed through Jinny's mind as the other thoughts had done.

Suddenly Kat began to talk.

"Helen's not my mother either," she said. "My own mother left when I was about five. I can just remember her. We came in from shopping. She put down her basket, it was a wicker basket, on the table and bent over to kiss me, and went. I can remember the smell of her hair. I guess my father was stuck with me. When I was eight, Helen came. She lived with us, looked after me. It was all right. Then my father got tired of her, went off with someone else. This time it was Helen who was stuck with me. We hate each other, but she can't help feeling responsible for me. When she hooked up with Paul, she tagged me along too. I was even their bridesmaid. Suited Paul. He likes his victims to be good looking."

And Kat's voice took Jinny into a world that she hadn't known existed before. A world as terrifying as the maelstrom of sea and wind. Where the rage was the torturous emotions of human beings. Kat told of lying in bed listening to the adults in her life fighting with each other, using her as a weapon against each other; of the extremes of love and hate that had come to seem normal to her; how each day with Helen and Paul was a tight-rope walk of evasion and fear, yet had an addictive compulsion that made ordinary living seem tasteless, no longer enough for Kat.

"I never know when he's going to attack me."

"Not hit you?"

"Might be easier if he did. You heard him today. In a way he made me climb the Chimney. When he finds out that we nearly drowned, he'll enjoy that."

"He won't find out."

"I'll tell him," said Kat, knowing herself. Her wet hair

clamped to her head, her thin face without its make-up had no sophistication, was naked and vulnerable. "I want to please him."

"Can't you leave them?" demanded Jinny, sure that she would.

"Where could I go? It's okay when I'm at school. These holidays have been a downer because of Lightning."

"But she's such a super horse. Just ride her, enjoy her. You don't need to jump cross-country jumps. And she is super!"

"I know and so does Paul. He wants to see me getting fond of her. But I won't. He can do what he likes with her. I don't care if he sells her."

Jinny remembered how she had never seen Kat speaking to Lightning, never seen her with her arms round Lightning; only heard her talking about winning to please Paul.

"She's your horse. He couldn't sell her."

"He bought me a dog last summer. I had her all through the holidays. I came back at half term and she'd gone. He said he'd sold her to a laboratory. He was laughing when he told me, so I don't know, do I? Might only have been one of his jokes, but I'll never know."

Jinny had no reply, could not believe such things could happen.

"Paul's the same with people. If he thinks I like them he mucks it all up. So I don't."

"You were so stuck up," said Jinny. "So unfriendly."

"You weren't exactly best friend material yourself. Sitting on Shantih without a nerve in your body, despising us all. And me, scared stiff at the thought of having to jump. Had to cover up somehow."

They grinned at each other. "Might never have known,"

thought Jinny. "So blind I couldn't see the real Kat at all."

"You'll have Finmory," she said, still hardly able to believe it.

"Not a chance. Paul will do it up. Rent it, make money from it. Why does your father want to sell it?"

Jinny shook her head. Suddenly she was too tired to go on talking. Her whole body ached. Against her will, her eyelids dropped leaden over her eyes.

"I called my dog Penny," said Kat, but Jinny was asleep.

When the phone woke her it was morning. Kat's chair was empty. Her wet clothes had gone. The clothes Jinny had lent her lay in their place. Cramped and stiff with sleeping in the chair, Jinny answered the phone.

"It's Kat. I went to look for Lightning. We forgot about her. I found her close to Finmory and thought I might as well ride back here. Less fuss."

"Right," said Jinny.

"Thank Shantih for rescuing me."

"Yes," said Jinny, still dazed.

"And you. Bye."

"Bye."

"And don't worry too much about me. I do enjoy Paul's money, you know," and Kat's laughter mocked in Jinny's ears.

She went back to the kitchen, heard her mother coming downstairs.

"Whatever's happened?" demanded Mrs. Manders, taking in bath towels, dirty dishes, the open Aga and sodden clothes.

"Will tell you," said Jinny, and the outside door opened. Her father came in.

"Caught the night train," he said.

Jinny backed away. It was too sudden. She couldn't face her father just now. Couldn't start to come to terms with the fact of leaving Finmory. Not when she had to sleep. She stared at him suspiciously, warily. That he should have done such a thing.

"Big success?" asked Mrs. Manders.

"We're not going. We're staying here."

"What?" cried Mrs. Manders. "But you said you'd got the job."

"Not going?" yelled Jinny. "Not going?"

"I got the job. All dead keen to have me back. I was all safe again, knowing I was doing the sensible thing. Hemstitching up my coffin. It was all settled."

Jinny held her breath. She could not believe that her father meant what he said. She had come so close to giving up Finmory that she could not allow herself to believe him.

"I was walking back through some of my old haunts when I saw Paula Hay. She started all this business. It was when they wouldn't listen to me and sent her to prison that I knew I had to get out. When she saw me, she recognised me. She'd a baby in a pram, an infant hanging on to her skirt. She looked straight at me, and I knew she associated me with one thing — sending her to prison. Didn't remember all I'd tried to do for her. Only one thing. I was the bloke who had sent her to prison. She didn't speak; pushed the pram straight past me. But that was it — I can't go back. You'll all need to starve, for I'm not going back to Stopton."

"But no one wanted you to go back!" cried Jinny.

"It'll not be that when you're needing things," said her father ruefully.

"It's you we need. You and Finmory. Things that don't change. Just to be there so we have something to hold on to when we need it. So that the ground doesn't move. So that we know who we are."

"What are you going to do now?" asked Mrs. Manders, smiling at her husband.

"Make pots," said Mr. Manders. "Chat with Ken. Write about the things I know — you and Petra and Jinny and Mike. Be part of the answer, not part of the mess. Be with you."

"And I was so looking forward to the supermarket."

"We won't even be able to afford Mrs. Simpson's shop," said Mr. Manders grimly. "Things will be really tight for a bit. Basic basics, and that will be all. First thing I'll start to look around for new markets for my pots. That should bring in some cash."

Jinny left them together. She went out into a world re-created, given back to her.

"We're not going," she told Shantih, still hardly able to believe it herself. "Not going. Staying here," and Jinny stared about her at moor and mountains, open sky and sea, all her own again.

And for a moment of insight, Easter cantered free, renewed, made whole again, a red rose on her forehead. She came to the wise woman, Keziah, who laid her hands on either side of Easter's head and kissed the rose.

Ecstasy sang through Jinny. She soared eagle-winged through sky-freedom of joy; was without limit or bounds.

When Mr. MacKenzie heard how nearly Jinny had drowned he shook his head at her, told her she had the luck of the tinkers to have found her way out of the current.

"I could be taking you out in the boat and showing you the exact spot where you can break free from the current. Three souls I've known taken off that headland and not one of them found the place, although they all had the knowledge of it."

The Daltons went away when Paul heard that Finmory was not for sale. Jinny didn't see Kat again. But two weeks later, when Jinny had had a postcard from Sue saying that they were going to manage a fortnight's camping at Finmory after Greece, and Mr. Manders had found an Inverburgh store with branches throughout Scotland that liked his pottery and thought they could sell as much as he could give them, there was a parcel for Jinny through the post. It was Jinny's watercolour of Shantih in a silver frame. The note with it said, "Yours — Kat."

Hardly able to believe her eyes, Jinny lifted the picture from its wrappings and stared at it with delight that was almost pain. The painting was part of herself; part of Shantih.

"'Her face is a lamp uplifted to guide the faithful to the place of Allah'," she quoted aloud. "Oh, Shantih. Shantih. Shantih."

The Jinny Series

PATRICIA LEITCH

1	For Love of a Horse	£1.95	☐
2	A Devil to Ride	£1.95	☐
3	The Summer Riders	£1.95	☐
4	Night of the Red Horse	£1.95	☐
5	Gallop to the Hills	£1.95	☐
6	Horse in a Million	£1.95	☐
7	The Magic Pony	£1.95	☐
8	Ride Like the Wind	£1.95	☐
9	Chesnut Gold	£1.95	☐
10	Jump for the Moon	£1.95	☐
11	Horse of Fire	£1.95	☐
12	Running Wild	£1.95	☐

When Jinny Manders rescues Shantih, a chestnut Arab, from a cruel circus, her dreams of owning a horse of her own seem to come true. But Shantih is wild and unrideable.

This is an exciting and moving series of books about a very special relationship between a girl and a magnificent horse.

ARMADA

Other titles by
Enid Blyton
in Armada

Mystery Stories	£2.25	☐
Adventure Stories	£2.25	☐
The Mystery That Never Was	£2.25	☐
The Treasure Hunters	£2.25	☐
Six Cousins at Mistletoe Farm	£2.25	☐
Six Cousins Again	£2.25	☐
The Children at Green Meadows	£2.25	☐
Adventures on Willow Farm	£2.25	☐
The Boy Next Door	£2.25	☐
Shadow the Sheepdog	£2.25	☐

All these books are available at your local bookshop or newsagent, or can be ordered from the publisher. To order direct from the publishers just tick the title you want and fill in the form below:

Name ____

Address ____

____

Send to: Collins Childrens Cash Sales
PO Box 11
Falmouth
Cornwall
TR10 9EN

Please enclose a cheque or postal order or debit my Visa/ Access –

Credit card no:

Expiry date:

Signature:

– to the value of the cover price plus:

UK: 60p for the first book, 25p for the second book, plus 15p per copy for each additional book ordered to a maximum charge of £1.90.

BFPO: 60p for the first book, 25p for the second book plus 15p per copy for the next 7 books, thereafter 9p per book.

Overseas and Eire: £1.25 for the first book, 75p for the second book. Thereafter 28p per book.

Armada reserve the right to show new retail prices on covers which may differ from those previously advertised in the text or elswhere.